S0-ATE-728

UNDER

THE

HEAVENS

 WITHDRAWN

UNDER THE HEAVENS

WITHDRAWN

A JOURNEY TO A NEW WORLD

RUTH FOX

CamCat
Books

CamCat Publishing, LLC
Brentwood, Tennessee 37027
camcatpublishing.com

This is a work of fiction. Names, characters, places, and incidents are either products of the author's imagination or are used fictitiously.

© 2022 by Ruth Fox

All rights reserved. Printed in the United States of America. No part of this book may be used or reproduced in any manner whatsoever without written permission except in the case of brief quotations embodied in critical articles and reviews. For information, address CamCat Publishing, 101 Creekside Crossing, Suite 280, Brentwood, TN 37027.

Hardcover ISBN 9780744304763
Paperback ISBN 9780744304701
Large-Print Paperback ISBN 9780744304671
eBook ISBN 9780744304336
Audiobook ISBN 9780744305029

Library of Congress Cataloguing-in-Publication Data
available upon request

Book and cover design by Maryann Appel

5   3   1   2   4

For Rydyr, Quinn and Whitley

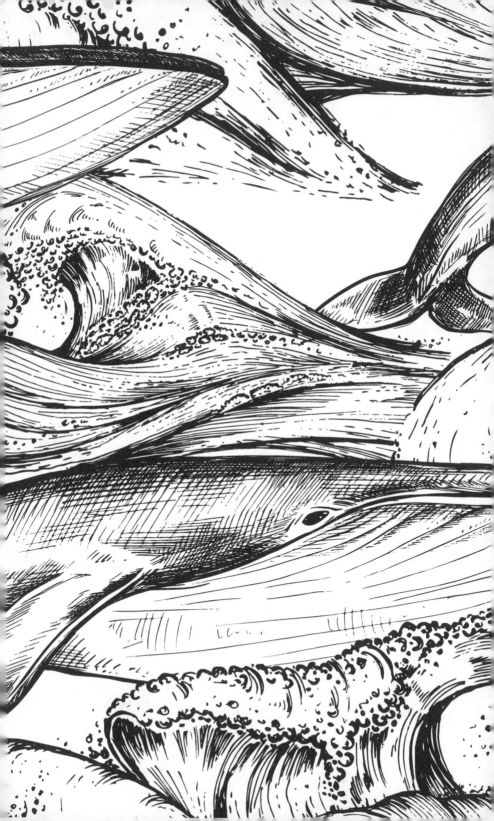

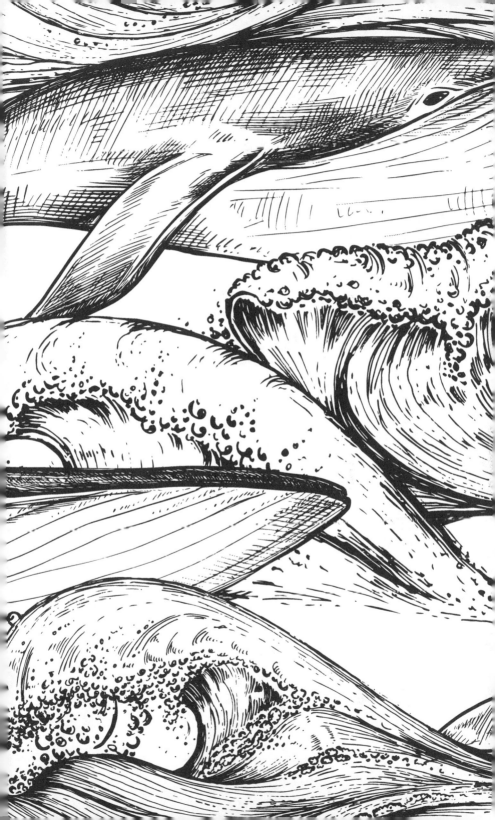

CHAPTER
1

Hi, all you folks back on Earth! This is Hannah Monksman, checking in with another update for you on the Ark Project and your favorite whales—and the most important mission ever undertaken by the human race. Gosh, that sounds so strange! To think that I've been chosen for this! Just so you know, Tobias tried to give me a fish yesterday. He held it up to the aquarium wall, clenched in his teeth! I had to tell him again that I couldn't breach the containment of the tank, not without good reason.

That's one of the toughest things about being in charge of creatures like this. I guess I'm going to envy all those people who come after me, in other Arks, carrying other creatures—elephants, tigers, zebra, antelopes. Land mammals, apart from the dangerous ones, can be touched.

You can physically put your hands on them. But there's always going to be a barrier between me and the whales.

To answer the question sent in by Zara from Russia, I guess the Link makes up for the loneliness! I get to hear the whales, feel them. I know where each of them is, unless they don't want me to. I can see through their eyes. But still. It's like having a best friend living in an isolation ward. You just want to give them a hug, and you can't . . .

She paused the recording and closed her eyes, fighting to choke down the sense of revulsion rising in her, blocking out the hologram of her own face that hovered in the air in front of her, parroting her words like a bad mimic. God! Who was this bright-eyed, bubbly stranger? She sounded like a moron.

Just get it over with, she told herself.

Pressing her lips together, she resumed the recording.

Well, I have a few boring chores to slog my way through. I'll have more for you tomorrow. Don't go anywhere! This is Hannah Monksman, on the morning of July 3, 2078 signing off.

She ceased the recording, pushing the translucent, floating window aside with a swipe of one hand and allowing the projected image of her own face to disappear back into her tablet. Her bowl of soup took its place, steaming malodorously. Now at least she could get on with her day—and she had something pressing to take care of.

Something was wrong with Adonai.

The computer told her differently—his vitals were fine, his temperature normal. He was making no movements that suggested he was distressed. Even if the computer's readouts weren't enough, the Link told her there was nothing to worry about. *It is fine*, Adonai repeated through it every time she pressed him. *It is, all of it, fine.* The Link couldn't lie. The slightest nuance of each of whale's thought was conveyed to her through the quantum matrices that had been mapped onto her brain during her integration. But after ninety-one days on this ship, she *knew* it, and she couldn't ignore the nagging feeling for long.

"Computer," she said, as she snagged her toolbelt from a nearby bench and slung it around her waist. "I'm heading to the Aquarium."

"Aquarium maintenance is not scheduled for 0600, July 3, 2078, Kim."

Kim. That was her name. She tended to forget it these days, after so long playing Hannah Monksman. Sighing, she pushed aside her bowl of tepid soup. It was another powdered, freeze-dried thing from a packet that tasted of nothing but salt.

"I know. I'm not doing maintenance."

"I must advise that it's preferable to adhere to schedules, Kim. That way, we can ensure the proper functioning of the ship and its components."

There was always something slightly strange about the way the computer uttered pronouns. "We" always carried the same inflection as "I." So—most of the time—did "you." The result was something too close to sarcasm, as if everything it said carried with it a slight rebuke. She wondered if she could tinker with the vocal processors, similar to the way she had convinced it to override the name it used for her. After only a few days on *Seiiki*, she hadn't been able to stand hearing it call her "Hannah." She knew her way around a computer system, but she wasn't an expert coder. She was, on the other hand, very persuasive, and she had engaged the computer in a conversation about nicknames. Such names weren't used in official records, such as transmissions to other ships, she had explained, but it would help her feel more at home if it referred to her as Kim when it spoke to her directly. The computer assured her this was an acceptable request and that any outwardly transmitted data from *Seiiki* would not contain the informal designation.

She shoved the idea of further alterations to the back of her mind, along with the tantalizing thought that one day she could stop pretending to be Hannah Monksman. Something else to do on a rainy day, she told herself with an inward smile.

"Perhaps," the computer continued, "you could send one of the droids while you attend to your allotted tasks. You are scheduled to be in the Operations Center now and to begin your systems check of the interior tech droids at fourteen-twenty hours."

"*Seiiki*'ll be fine if I slip down there for half an hour," she said aloud, resisting the urge to roll her eyes. The computer could detect her gestures and had basic interpretation abilities. "Keep me updated." She didn't make it a question because she was already on her way, up out of her chair, dumping her inedible soup down the drain and leaving the bowl to be rinsed by the auto-washer, then swinging through the doorway that took her from the mess into the corridor.

"Kim," the computer protested plaintively, but she tapped the back of her left hand with her right, drawing the kanji to deactivate its voice temporarily. She walked along the clanking decking, vague impressions of the deck below showing through the grated plates. *Seiiki*, at 3,000 feet long from nose to tail, and almost a third of that in width and depth, was the largest ship she'd ever been aboard. Even in the comparatively narrow corridor, she felt an overwhelming sense of immensity.

The passageway dipped down, then back up toward the tail of the ship, but Kim wasn't going that far. There were maglifts there, but she'd use the ramps instead. It wasn't that she needed exercise, more that she'd started seizing any excuse to work out her body. The gravity aboard was 0.72 g's, slightly less than Earth's gravity, slightly greater than Mars's. It always felt like she was doing less work than she should be, even when she was only buttering her toast.

The access to the ramps was about halfway along the corridor. She didn't pause in her stride but swung around the jamb to begin her descent. The ramps spiraled upwards and downwards with a landing at each of the nineteen decks, but most of those decks were empty space. She only really used six of them, and even then, only parts of those were even functional at this stage of the journey—large sections of the ship were devoted to storage of equipment and construction materials that would be used when they reached New Eden, and as such, didn't require life support or regular maintenance. Feeling a fresh onrush of energy—most of which probably came from the pure fact of having something to occupy her mind—she began to jog.

The ramp threaded its way through other ramps, some larger thoroughfares and others smaller, like the one she was on. Bridges joined them. You could reach any point on the ship from this nexus of walkways.

The computer was right. She could have sent one of the droids. Even now, one of them was idling on the inward curve of a ramp as she circled one of the stanchions that ran through *Seiiki's* core. It looked lost, lonely, and bored—if a creature made of electronics could be any of those things. It was one of the mid-size ones, designed for diagnostics and rudimentary repairs. Its "head"—a six-sided dome, pocked with small colored windows that made it look like a children's toy—swiveled as she passed, as if hopeful to be given a task. Still, this was a job she needed to complete on her own.

The light dimmed the farther down she went. Deck Fifteen, the lowest, was about six feet in height, but Deck Ten, her destination, was five times that. The Aquarium ran through the ship from Deck Twelve to Deck Eight, taking up varying amounts of space on each deck, and in some sections it was 200 feet from ceiling to floor. The lights were far overhead, even along these sections of the ramps. As they detected her motion and flickered on, they made the featureless grey deck look flat, as if she were looking at a painting on a wall rather than reality.

As if to add to this dreamlike state, Adonai's voice echoed softly in her mind.

No need to come closer. It is well. Little one, go back.

Kim shook her head, as if Adonai could see or feel the gesture through the Link. He couldn't, of course, but at times he was so strong inside her that she almost forgot. He had never been like the others.

Ignoring him, because, if anything, his protests only worried her more, she stepped from the ramp to the landing and crossed the bridge to into Deck Ten. The cavernous space opened up around her as soon as she'd passed through the hexagonal doorway, and it was like plunging into the very depths of the ocean. It was the Aquarium that made it seem that way.

Shifting blue light wobbled over the bulkheads above her, painting her skin blue and bleaching all other colors from the spectrum.

The light seemed to come from everywhere at once. The great tank rose up through the walls and ceiling, a masterpiece of engineering. It jutted out and curved inwards, narrower pillars and tunnels leading to wider open spaces. Some areas were flat glass, and others were bulging forcefields. Dark shapes of aeration filters, thermostats, and feeding machinery made silhouettes against the deep blue backdrop, and the waving fronds of seaweed and coral growing on the various ledges of artificial rock rippled like curtains billowing in the breeze.

Fifteen was looking at Kim. He was a Minke whale—one of the smallest of all whale species; only the Pygmy was smaller. Most Minkes were a brown, gray, or purple shade, but Fifteen was white. She didn't know why, exactly. His genetics didn't show anything unusual, such as albinism—his eyes were a normal color, deep black, instead of the pink often associated with creatures who couldn't produce skin pigment. He hung back slightly from the glass, drifting without effort. He was thirty feet long, but all Kim could see was his foreshortened, stumpy nose, and his tail lifting and falling so slowly it was almost imperceptible.

Hello, he said, his voice brushing across the surface of the Link.

"Hello, Fifteen," she replied. He wasn't the brightest of the whales, and Kim often found herself frustrated by his attempts at communication.

Fifteen is me. I am Fifteen.

"Where's Adonai?" she asked him.

Adonai is . . . above.

"Where above?" Kim tried to keep the impatience from her voice, but it crept in, nonetheless. "Stern? Aft?"

Fifteen bobbed slightly, the words clearly going straight over his bulbous head. Kim sighed. Most of the others were able to convey directions to her through the Link, but Fifteen had never been able to get the hang of it. His thoughts were a confused tumble when they came to her. *Left and up, rightdownforwardalittle, swim nine strokes . . . maybe?*

She sighed, turning around as she passed him by, and searched for Jonah or Tobias or Samuel. She could sense them on the Link, of course, but they were distant, which meant they wanted their privacy. But she was starting to get anxious, and if she had to, she'd pull them back in, whether they liked it or not.

"Adonai?" she called over the Link. Though she was speaking out loud, the words were translated through the Link. Technically, she could speak to them without speaking aloud at all, but this was much harder. The clarity that came with speaking the words out loud was almost essential, she had found, if she didn't want to confuse the whales. Or herself.

She was still moving, turning, and the tanks whirled around her as she raised her head, craning her neck to take in the upper reaches of Deck Ten. She could see, beyond the catwalks and stanchions and the occasional bug-like autobot drifting past, the beginnings of Deck Nine before the extent of her vision was too blurred by the shadows to make out anything further. With a sigh, she turned and sprang for one of the ladders. It was easy to climb, pushing from one rung to the next with her feet, propelling herself with minimal effort from her arms. The slight lack of gravity gave her a feeling of exhilaration and robbed her of the fear of falling. It was a deceptive sensation, because she could fall and cause herself grave injury—but she doubted it would happen. Due to the lack of gravity, she had more time to react, even if she did slip, than she'd ever need to right herself.

The tanks scrolled past her. A shelf of multicolored coral passed by, small mounds of marine life pulsing and waving as if excited by her presence. A stream of bubbles betrayed the presence of a whale somewhere beyond. It wasn't Adonai. The Link told her this, moments before she glimpsed the long, bump-riddled back of Noah. Noah was a grey whale, and his hide looked like lichen-covered rock, deep blue mottled with creamy white. He was the most reclusive of all the whales and didn't even acknowledge Kim as she passed.

She kept climbing, her toolbelt swinging against her thighs. She was about 100 feet from the floor, now 150. There were buildings on Earth smaller than this. But the scale of everything in the aquarium was so different that it hardly compared. When she looked down in this particular section she could see all the way through Deck Eleven and into Deck Twelve, adding over fifty feet to the chasm-like drop, but she'd never suffered from vertigo. They'd never have sent her up here if she did.

With a practiced movement, she swung herself onto a catwalk by launching herself upwards and catching the railings under her hands, keeping her body straight and kicking her legs out to give herself a head start. It felt leisurely, that action, like she'd rehearsed it for years.

Like a dance, Adonai said softly inside her head.

"You're watching me," Kim said, glancing upwards as she walked swiftly along the catwalk. A bulging section of forcefield swung toward her, barely holding back the blueness beyond. It didn't even look like water, not really. It had lost its fluidity, being cross-sectioned like this, turning into something solid. Adonai didn't reply, but Kim smiled. She knew exactly where he was, now.

She reached the end of the catwalk, where a ladder led both up and down. She jumped four rungs and began climbing upwards again. At the top, another catwalk, this one running along the equator of the bulge she'd passed under a moment before. At its end, the catwalk drove inwards, pressing into an innermost section of the tank, like a finger pushing into a soap bubble. The tank surrounded her on all sides save the rearmost, the direction she'd come from. The catwalk ended in a railed platform, small enough for a single person to stand. She liked this spot. If she stood with her back to the open space, it made her feel as if she were inside the tanks.

Adonai liked it too. On his side of the forcefield, there was an arch of synthetic rock that looped overhead, forming a kind of arbor. Coral liked to grow here, and it was a haven for glittering fish, too. Small streams of bubbles whirled around. And there was Adonai, rolling from side to side, swimming back and forth through the arch, his fins brushing the coral lightly. He'd turn, then swim back through. Again and again. Only Adonai, of all the whales, engaged in this kind of activity. He claimed it helped him think.

When Kim looked at him, she saw her *agōng*—her grandpa—who had been a perpetual pacer. Back and forth, back and forth—he'd never sit down when he had something on his mind.

"Adonai," she said. He gave a jolt of sudden awareness that wasn't visible in his movements, but she felt like a shock of lightning through the Link. He wasn't shielding his thoughts very well at all.

Little one with long fins, he said. This was how he had named her, back before she'd talked to him about the expedience of single nouns. Whale song, in the case of baleen whales, and the communicative clicks and pops used by toothed whales like Adonai, did not involve names as humans used them—at least, they hadn't, until the Link was conceived. The whales aboard, specifically, had had a hard time wrapping their minds around the concept initially. *I told you not to come.*

"Why not?" Kim asked. She leaned on the railing, looking through the forcefield. It was perfectly clear, but it was also designed in two layers, a safety precaution. There was a gap between the two of about two inches. It put a distance between her and the water that wasn't there in the glassed sections, save at the very top of the tanks. Every now and then, a soft ripple of golden or blue-tinged energy would move across the surface, signifying a fluctuation in the field's harmonics—a necessary function to keep the field's strength from dissipating under the several tons of water and all it contained. "Adonai, I can feel your agitation."

You are not supposed to. If I don't want it. I don't want it. So go.

"I can't go," Kim replied evenly. "I'm the Caretaker, remember? It's my job to make sure you're all right."

Adonai swam back, looped himself over with a flick of his tail, and swam forward once more. The coral swayed a moment after. The Link glowed on his blunt forehead, a network of golden lines that was a larger reflection of those on her own shaven head.

I don't want you here, Kim.

Adonai's voice was heavy in the Link. It was the equivalent of him yelling at Kim, but it sounded petulant rather than aggressive. Kim gave a soft smile—he rarely used her name, and she had shared her real one with him—with all of the whales—out of necessity. The Link allowed her to hide her thoughts when she needed to, but she had never seen the necessity, nor felt the desire, to conceal her real name from the whales. Who would they tell? They couldn't talk to anyone but her.

"Like it or not," she said. "I'm here. So tell me. Maybe I can help."

I—he began, moving his fins backward as his blunt-nosed head poked through the arch, stopping himself just before the forcefield. *I do not know how to describe this thing that is wrong with me.*

"I get it," Kim said. She reached for her toolbelt and removed the smaller tuner. "Maybe talk around it. What were you thinking a few minutes ago, when I first felt the disturbance?"

I—Adonai began again. *I was thinking about the stars. Are you going to tune my Link?*

"The stars?" Kim blinked. She hadn't expected this! "What about them?"

You told me about the stars, Adonai said, still hovering in front of her. He was only a few feet away, his head so huge he could swallow her whole. He was a sperm whale, and the largest remaining. His skin was glossy and a deep blueish grey mottled with lighter silver patches. His eyes sat low on his head, just behind his jaw, which Kim had always thought gave sperm whales an unbalanced look. As he swung his head to the left, she suddenly glimpsed the depths of those black eyes, and was catapulted back to the first time she'd seen him, back in Sky Reach's labs. He'd drawn his head back, his eye moving along the length of her body before settling back on her face. The deliberateness of that gesture had left her gasping and filled with a sense that, for all her study and training, she hadn't known anything about these creatures at all.

She still didn't, if today's conversation with Adonai was anything to go by.

Little one with long fins, do you ever go outside?

"Outside?" Kim said, surprised. "You mean, outside the ship? No."

You should.

"It's not that easy," she said with a chuckle. "I can't breathe out there. I'd have to put on a suit—there's a lot of preparation."

You don't want to go?

"No, it's not that," she replied, though, honestly, an EV walk was not high on her list of stuff she most wanted to do at the moment. Far from it. "I can't just go out there for fun. If there's an emergency or something, I'd have to, to fix the ship—but otherwise, the computer would probably refuse to let me use the resources."

The com—com—comooter says whether you can go or not.

"I suppose so, yes."

What would be made to happen if you had to go outside the ship, then? If you were needing to deal with one of these emergencies?

"Well, I've been trained," Kim replied, with an inward shudder at the memory. "I know what to do if there's an air leak or an engine malfunction that needs to be repaired externally. I can use an external welder, and most of the other tools. For other problems, there are the droids, and the computer is programmed with hundreds of thousands of scenarios and their solutions. It could talk me through almost anything."

But what if there was one that you couldn't fix?

Kim was silent a minute. "Adonai, where is this coming from?"

What if a problem happened to you?

"Don't worry about that. Nothing's going to happen." It was like coaxing a small child back into bed after a nightmare. Her voice had taken on a motherly croon she didn't know she possessed. She was slightly proud of herself.

But Adonai continued. *I couldn't protect you, Kim.*

"Protect me? You don't need to. I'm *your* protector."

But there is only one of you. And you are but a child in human years. I'm much older than you. And bigger. It should be me.

Kim felt a pang of sudden joy mixed with sadness. She shoved it down deep. "That's sweet, Adonai. But there's nothing to worry about, really. I'm good at my job. That's why they picked me."

I've been dreaming of them.

The leap in topic took Kim a moment to decipher, but she caught a glimpse of a kaleidoscopic image of brilliant white stars through the Link, Adonai's signature thoughts mingling with it.

"Dreaming of the stars?" Kim asked. The tuner hung loosely in one hand. She put the other out toward the forcefield. The field, reacting to her nearness, shimmered with small, blue ripples—a warning feature built into the harmonics so that she'd know she was about to put her hand against something otherwise invisible.

Yes. And I think I know what they look like. I really think I do.

"Tell me," Kim said.

They're all different colors. Like the coral. And the light they shine with, that's the light like the fish have. And they're all against black like the sea. But they're small, and they're so cold. And that's how they'd feel.

He was conveying all this through the Link as he spoke, and she felt exactly what he meant by *feel*. Not feel as in touch, as in actual contact—no, he meant that just by looking at them, just by feeling their light on your skin, you'd have the sensation of them piercing you like needles. The sensation was so strong that for a moment she looked down at her body, expecting to see something jabbing into her. "Oh, Adonai," she sighed.

I would very love to see them, he replied, his own voice drawing out as if he were a tired child. *See . . . what they're really like.*

"I'd love to show them to you," Kim replied. "But, Adonai, you've got to remember that what you see isn't what I see." She lifted her arms from the railing and swept them in an arc. "The water is black for you. Not blue. Even the coral—there are more colors in it than you even know. And the fish, for me, aren't made of light. I can't see them at a distance like you can. So I can't even tell you what the stars would look like for you."

I want to see, he answered, turning his head away. *I very want to.*

"I'm sorry," she said, and she genuinely was. She had been charged with the role of Caretaker because she was a problem-solver, the best of the best. To find a problem that couldn't be solved wasn't just galling—it was horrifying.

She looked down at the tuner in her hand. It was shaped like a pencil, with raised bumps to make it easy to hold. She had been certain that whatever was wrong with Adonai could be fixed by a few small tweaks to his personality centers. With the tuner, she could make adjustments to the levels of endorphins in his system, driving away feelings of agitation.

But the Adonai who was speaking to her didn't seem distressed. He was . . . introspective. Moody, yes, but wasn't that part of contemplation?

With a sigh, she lifted the tuner. She flicked the button on the side and aimed it through the forcefield. The beam was invisible until it connected with the Link. The gold began to glow brighter, a pulse running along the network of filaments before vanishing.

Adonai's head moved slowly from one side to the other. She hadn't been able to work out yet if he knew what the tuner did or not. He showed no signs of this knowledge now, certainly. His eyes blinked slowly, and he drifted away from her.

She left Adonai, walking back along the catwalk as he flicked his tail and dived deeply, vanishing into the depths.

The journey back to ground level was easy, but she took it slowly because her mind was churning over everything Adonai had said.

Why was he so interested in the stars? Their conversation the day before was one she hardly remembered. They'd been talking about something entirely unrelated—the flavor of fish, she recalled.

They taste like life, Adonai had told her, and she'd been surprised by this analogy.

"There's a name for it," she'd told him. "Umami. It's not bitter, sweet, or sour. Salty, yes, but an underlying taste that's . . . well, meaty. Kind of fresh. Is that what you mean?"

Life. Blood and bone. Movement. That's the taste of fish.

"I wonder how the fish will taste for you, in the oceans of New Eden. It has a lower salt content. Not significant, but it might be enough to alter the taste of the fish."

What does it look like?

"Fish? Or New Eden?"

The planet.

"It looks like a star," she said. "At the moment, it's so far away it looks smaller than a lot of the others. Just a ball of gas and rock hanging in black space."

I wonder if the fish will enjoy it, Adonai had moved the conversation on, and there the mention of stars had ended.

But somehow, somehow he'd picked up more information, pieced it together to realize that the stars were surrounding the ship, along with the vacuum of space. She couldn't recall any other occasion where their conversation had veered anywhere near to those topics, so she had to assume he'd thought up the rest himself. He'd never seen stars on his own, after all. Not even on Earth.

So preoccupied with her thoughts, she'd made it almost all the way back up the ramps to Deck Three when she saw it.

Standing on one of the other ramps, 200 yards away. Curtained by enough shadows that it was almost impossible to tell if it was real or just some mirage made by a stray beam of light from the overhead lamps. But for a second, a split second, she was sure of it.

There was a man there, staring at her.

CHAPTER

2

Kim's first instinct was to call out, but even as she opened her mouth, she found herself hesitating.

She had been on this ship for ninety-one days. They'd warned her about this during training, and they'd also told her that if it happened, she would question her own ability to tell the difference between what was real and what was not. But ninety-one days was not a long time. She had expected to be able to go a year before the side-effects of solitude started kicking in.

After all, she'd been selected precisely for that reason—she was less social, more independent, and entirely rational—more so than any of her competitors. All her psych evaluations had pointed toward her ability to withstand the long days alone without issue. Still, the image before her had called all that into question. How could she claim to be unaffected when her very senses were telling her otherwise? She found solace that the rational part of her brain was the part holding her back from making a noise, from acting on her perceptions, because it was what told her that it wasn't real. While all her sense went wild, making the hairs stand up on her arms and the back of her neck prickle, she held herself in check. Shouting out, acting on the impulse, would give this hallucination a power it should not have. Likewise, asking the computer to confirm the amount of life signatures aboard.

Instead, she blinked, and focused her eyes on the section of ramp where she'd seen the figure. She took a step closer to the railing. There was a particular crisscrossing of shadow just behind one of the stanchions. If she squinted, it looked like a man's head and shoulders. Almost. It didn't look exactly like what she'd thought she'd seen, but she hadn't been looking at it directly. It was a mirage, her mind making sense of things only half-glimpsed.

"Idiot," she scolded herself.

"Kim?"

The computer's voice didn't startle her, but the flood of anger she felt at hearing its intrusion did. "I turned the comms off."

"I overrode your order 0.9 seconds ago," the computer replied without a hint of apology.

"You're not supposed to be able to do that!"

"Kim," the computer continued doggedly. "I have determined that your heart rate is elevated and your respiration has increased. Symptoms are consistent with anxiety. Are you all right?"

"I'm fine," Kim said as she emerged from the ramp into the corridor of Deck Three. "At least, I was until you started spying on me."

"I have been given privileges to override your orders at any point when I determine your safety is at risk."

Kim rolled her eyes. "I wasn't *at risk*. I was doing my damn job."

"As you say. The schedule shows, however, that you have missed maintenance on several systems in the Operations Center, as well as the systems check on the tech droids."

"Both of which I'll make up tomorrow."

"I would still like to insist that you finish up early for today and return to your quarters for an extended rest period."

"Yeah, that's not happening," Kim said. "I've got too much to do."

"I must insist," the computer said firmly. "Kim, it is very important that you heed my commands. This is what you were charged with, as Caretaker. Any more infractions must be reported to Near Horizon and to the Space Exploration Authority. This is your final warning."

"Bastard," Kim muttered. She reached the end of the corridor and stepped into the maglift that would take her to Deck One. "Fine. I'm going to check the scanners and do an analysis, then I'll retire. If you insist."

The computer gave an approving chime. "This is a good decision."

Deck One was the smallest of all decks, and made up the entirety of the ship's Bridge. Nestled in the curved upper reaches of the massive ship, its ceiling was made of slabs of clear glass reinforced with force-fields, giving a person the feeling of standing on an open platform that raced through space.

There were rarely objects close enough to convey the speed at which they traveled, but Kim swore she could still sense their forward motion.

A ring of control panels circled the space under this canopy. At the prow was a screen that could display feed from any camera on the ship. By default it showed the forward view, the staccato points of the stars Adonai had been so concerned with. The computer's scanners pick out each star and label it with numerical data in green, blue and red. She watched the figures adjusting as each point was pulled past in a slow, wavering trajectory. She didn't quite understand why Adonai was so fascinated. The stars weren't all that beautiful. Not out here. Far better to look at them from Earth or Mars, where they still had some semblance of a twinkle to them—here, with no atmosphere to interfere with their light, they were solid and cold as chips of ice. Adonai would be disappointed, she thought, if he ever did see them on this screen.

Kim took one of the chairs behind the main console in the very center, an arc-shaped desk that housed the navigation, piloting controls, external sensors, and external communication systems. She drew the kanji for "begin" in the air, and the console lit up as it began running her diagnostics. Clear displays were projected upwards, glowing numbers showing exactly what she expected. Ninety-one times she'd seen the same results—everything was functioning within expected parameters, the few degrees of difference always accounted for when she cross-checked it with power usage.

"Computer, any issues?"

"No issues detected, Kim."

She nodded, and drew the kanji for "sleep," to put the console back into its resting mode. "Enter the data into the ship's logs."

"Entering."

She moved to one of the outer consoles, running a diagnostic on the droids, checking their functions and ensuring all their data had been downloaded correctly into the computer's core. Another tedious task, checking numbers against one another to make sure the size of the data download packets matched those stored in their memories. Again, she moved on to another console, then walked in a slow ring around the edges of the Bridge, checking life support systems, airlock controls for the external hull and the internal firewalls, sent a ping to each of the secondary control stations throughout the ship, then triple-checked the figures for the Aquarium. The forcefields read at 100 percent, with minor fluctuations. The water temperature was good— seventy degrees Fahrenheit at the surface, steadily declining to forty degrees at the half-mile mark, then slowing, just nudging thirty-five degrees at the bottom.

That done, she moved on to her least favorite task. Returning to the central desk, she slid her chair along the console and caught herself at the end, drawing the kanji for "talk." A clicking sound echoed through the speakers positioned in the corners of the room. She drew another kanji, selecting her connection, and watched as the holographic projection displayed three dots, each one blinking successively.

"Connection established with WR970," the computer informed her, a split second before a man's face appeared in front of Kim. He was an older man, his face withered and greyish, made more so by the flickering, blueish tint of the holo. She was surprised he was still serving. Or rather, that he hadn't forcibly been retired. He would never give up his posting willingly, she suspected, though she'd never met the man in person; he had a presence, dour, but unshakable.

"Speak," he said.

Kim didn't like seeing him so close. She waved her hand and the console interpreted her gesture, flinging the holo image onto the main screen and blotting out the stars. That was better. She stood, placing her hands behind her back. She always found herself adopting this pose when speaking to the Admiral, even though she wasn't military.

"Admiral Mbewe," she replied. "Hannah Monksman, Caretaker, reporting from Outbound ship *Seiiki*, JH2415."

He waved a hand. "Yes, go ahead."

"All systems reporting as normal, sir. No incidents to declare. My computer will be sending our ship's log to you. And my recording for today." She flicked her hand again, scrolling through files and attaching the recording she'd made earlier.

"Good, good," Mbewe said, sounding distracted. Was it just her, or did he seem more brusque than usual? He glanced to one side, as if listening to someone speak off-screen. "Confirmed, we have your log. The recording will be sent along to Near Horizon immediately."

"Thank you, sir. Permission to sign off?"

"Hold on a second." Mbewe leaned forward, then rocked backward. He was adjusting himself in his chair. His eyes looked slightly downwards, but she knew he was looking directly at the camera, which was slightly off-center from his screen. Edgeward Station was older than *Seiiki* by thirty years, and hadn't been upgraded since. Its position as the furthest station from Earth made the logistics of flying out new tech, and new technicians, uneconomical.

Kim leaned forward too, unconsciously bending from the waist.

Mbewe rubbed a hand across his chin. "You're sure this data is correct?"

Kim felt herself begin to frown and schooled her expression to neutrality. He was still looking directly at her, which made it easy. What wasn't so easy was to tamp down her suddenly racing thoughts. *Correct? Of course it was correct. Was there something she'd missed? Was she about to be reprimanded? Oh, please God, no.*

She told herself to be calm. There was nothing they could do to her. She was nine light years away from Edgeward . . . but she wouldn't be forever. The scheduled rendezvous was in fifteen days. She'd be face-to-face with the Admiral then, and he could certainly destroy everything she'd worked so hard for . . .

"I don't have any reason to believe otherwise." She said this with as much neutrality as she could, trying hard to keep her anxiety off her face. "I checked through the package prior to sending it, as usual. I didn't notice any errors."

"Very well," said Admiral Mbewe. He inclined his head, and for a second, his gaze did meet hers. He didn't seem to notice. To him, he was now looking above the edge of his screen. It was only the angle that made it look like he was looking straight into her eyes, but she felt her chest swell with fear anyway. "Edgeward signing off."

The screen went blank, and Kim felt as if she'd been kicked in the stomach. And she knew exactly what that felt like, didn't she? She tucked that bitter thought away with all her other memories of her old life.

"Old life," she repeated to herself as she headed for the door. As if it was something separate. As if she'd changed.

"I beg your pardon, Kim?" the computer said.

"Nothing. I'm going to bed. Are you happy?"

The computer missed her sarcasm. "I do not experience happiness, Kim," it replied as she headed for the maglift.

Kim tried to sleep, but something was nagging at her. She couldn't decide what worried her more—Adonai's strange behavior and odd questions, or the Admiral's unusual questioning of the log data.

Trying to convince herself her apprehensions were baseless, she rolled over to face the bulkhead for the fiftieth time, seeking a cool spot on her pillow. The magnetic blanket was a safety precaution to keep her anchored in case of a gravity generator malfunction, and she wasn't supposed to sleep without it—but it was often too warm. She pushed it off her torso so it covered only her legs, and felt the heat coming off her in waves.

As a kid, she'd had nightmares about being smothered.

The blanket was like a torture device for the claustrophobic, she thought.

With a sigh, she reached for her bedside table and picked up her tablet. The screen produced a brilliant blue-white light in the dark room. She propped it against the bulkhead, on its edge so it was aligned with her head, and drew the kanji for *secret* on the back of her left hand.

Manta Protocol activated. The voice was soft, much softer than the thoughts of the whales inside her mind, but it was reassuring. She felt herself relax. The computer could no longer hear anything she said or record her actions until she deactivated the protocol.

"Dial Zane," she said.

The tablet paused, the blue-white screen displaying a small loading circle. It took a long time. Not only did it have a small amount of bandwidth, but the tablet had to wait for Zane to respond to her connection request. She was happy to wait.

It took nineteen minutes, but then the screen flickered and the image of a honey-skinned young man with dark stubble across his jaw appeared, hovering above the screen. He was so close to his own lens she couldn't see anything of the room beyond him.

"What?" he said brusquely. "What is it?" His expression was concerned.

"Zane," she said, her voice dropping to a whisper. She didn't know why, but she felt compelled to speak in a low voice when she made the connection to Manta. Even though the computer couldn't hear her, she always had the feeling that this was a forbidden midnight conversation, as if she were a child whispering secrets to a sibling after lights out with her parents just down the hall. "I'm all right."

Despite the poor quality of the image, she could see his face relax visibly, softening around the eyes and mouth. God, that mouth. She longed to meet it with her lips . . .

"Then why are you calling, honey?" He drew back a little from the screen, so that she could see he was in his own quarters. His hair was scruffy, his eyes tired. He'd been working late again. "You know you can't call outside scheduled times. It's risky."

Her reasons suddenly felt foolish. Childish. *I wanted to hear your voice. I couldn't sleep. I'm lonely* . . . she wasn't supposed to get lonely, so she couldn't admit that. It would make her seem weak. Incapable. It would make him think she couldn't carry out her mission.

"The Admiral said something odd. It concerned me."

"What was it?"

"He asked me if the data dump I sent him was correct."

Zane looked puzzled, then shrugged. The screen pixelated, his image froze, then came unstuck just as quickly. "Kim, this does not sound so unusual to me. Did he say anything more? Anything to give you grave concern? Anything that might compromise your true mission?"

Her true mission. Kim sighed, knowing it wouldn't translate over the low-res connection. "No."

"Then do not worry! It will all be well. You're doing an excellent job, Kimberly. You're a brave woman."

Kim felt the blush on her cheeks. She hoped the room was dark enough that he wouldn't see it. "I'm not. I'm just doing what's right," she demurred. *If only he knew*, she thought. She'd already slipped up in a myriad of infinitesimal ways.

She hoped he'd never find them all out.

"We all are. But you, you have made sacrifices too big to imagine. Kimberly, when this is over, you and I . . . I promise you. I will make you happy."

Hearing him say those words made her heart melt. She had always considered herself to be independent, to not need another person. She'd had to teach herself to survive on her own at a young age, and she'd spent her subsequent years keeping everyone else at arm's length. What was it Constantin had said to her once? "You're a little pufferfish, with deadly spines. You spike anyone who gets too close." She chuckled inwardly as she pictured her old mentor saying it, as he had so many times. But with Zane, it was so different. She wanted him. It was that simple. And that complex.

"You need to get some sleep," Kim said. "I'm sorry. I shouldn't have called."

"No, I'm glad you did," Zane replied. "Now I can sleep with your pretty face in my mind." He smiled, his white teeth showing brilliantly on the screen. He lifted a hand to his lips and pressed it to the screen, covering the camera with his fingers momentarily. She did the same before he terminated the connection.

She slid the tablet back onto the bedside table and drew the kanji for *secret* on the back of her hand once more. *Deactivated,* chimed that soft little voice. But though Zane's dismissiveness of the Admiral's behavior made her less concerned, she still did not feel sleepy.

Eventually, she used a trick she'd devised, but wasn't proud of. She focused her attention inwards on the Link. She could feel the whales drifting, peaceful and calm, in the tank. She felt the blackness of the water around them as the lights turned down to simulate night—true blackness, this time, not just the blackness of their vision. Whales could tell night from day, nevertheless. They could feel the shifting of temperatures—and they were, overall, more attuned to rhythms than any human.

Morning came, and the chiming of the alarm dragged her from an exhausted doze. She felt fuzzy-headed as she heaved herself from her bunk, wishing she could dive back in and while away the day doing nothing for once. But here her own mind was her worst enemy. She'd drive herself insane, and out of the bed, before the day was done—even if the computer allowed it, which it would not, so she might as well get on with it.

Kim's quarters were luxurious by her standards, though she knew they'd be considered utilitarian by anyone other than military personnel. Her bunk was against one wall, and the opposite was taken up by a wardrobe set into the bulkhead. Between them was a door that led into a bathroom in stainless steel. The lights flickered on as she entered, a mirror over the sink displaying her reflection back at her.

She looked almost as grey as the Admiral, she thought, turning aside in disgust. She missed her long, almost-black hair. The lack of it made her ears stick out, and her chin look far too sharp. The Link pulsed golden beneath her scalp, a network of glowing veins.

At least her gang tattoo was gone. She'd lasered it off as soon as she'd heard she was through the first stage of testing, under Constantin's command. It had felt like a betrayal at the time, of Cons, of Seamus, Nicki, and the others . . . but at the same time, she'd been glad to see it go. Glad not to *belong* to anyone any longer.

She showered, making the water as cool as she could without it actually being cold. The warm air of the dryers washed over her, lifting the moisture up through the vents above to be recycled by the life support systems. Wrapping herself in a towel, she moved back into her bedroom and headed for the wardrobe.

There, she stopped still.

The door to her room was open, the light of the corridor spilling through. She jumped, looking left and right, scanning the room. Nothing out of place—there was nothing that *could* be out of place. She had no personal effects on board.

But the blanket, the damned gravity blanket, was pulled up over her bed.

She raced to the door, clutching the towel with one hand. She looked through, left, then right. Left led to a storage locker, then a blank wall. Right led to the maglift and another curving corridor that contained the galley and the mess.

She stopped still, knowing that anything moving would make a sound she'd hear on the metal deck plates. The ship hummed back at her, a soothing melody that told her not to be silly, though it sounded louder and more intense because of the blood pounding in her ears.

"Computer," she said. "Did anyone enter my room?"

"That's a strange question, Kim. The answer is, of course, no."

"None of the autobots? You're sure?"

"Certain, Kim. The cleaning droid will attend to your room at 0900, while you are on duty."

Kim backed her way back into the room. The door hissed shut behind her without protest. "I'm going crazy."

"Is something wrong, Kim? I am detecting an elevated heart rate."

"No," she replied. "Everything's fine." She stared down at the bunk. The blanket was pulled slightly to the left, draped wrinkles showing where one corner had been tugged harder than the other. An autobot didn't do that. Unless it was malfunctioning, it wouldn't accept that the blanket had been properly aligned, and would use its nine arms to evenly distribute the fabric until it showed no wrinkle or crease.

You're being stupid, she told herself. *You pulled up the blanket.* She must have done it unconsciously, and forgotten about it.

But she didn't usually do that. She left it for the droids. It had become a habit, something she'd told herself she'd never do, even when Erica had explained to her that it wasn't necessary to do any housekeeping herself. Her mind should be reserved for more important tasks, she'd said. But Kim had scoffed, unable to think of a time she'd be so lazy she'd leave cleanliness in the hands of robots. But she'd soon fallen into the trap anyway. Why waste time and energy? She had other tasks to do, and besides which, it gave the autobots a purpose. She'd often found them drifting after their rounds, looking forlorn, or vacuuming dust in an area that had already been vacuumed. She told herself it was for their sake rather than hers, and then she became one of the very people she'd always despised for their slothfulness.

Okay. So this morning she'd slipped back into an old routine. Simple. She'd pulled the blanket up as she slipped out of bed.

But then . . . why the door?

"Computer, what time did the door open?"

"0713.4," it replied promptly.

"And what time did I enter the bathroom?"

"Approximately 0712.5," it replied.

Kim sighed. She'd triggered the door herself without realizing it. It should have shut automatically when she didn't exit, but that could be explained as a malfunction in the sensors. She'd check them out later. Her thoughts brightened at the idea of having something else to add to her schedule. Anything for a break in routine.

She opened the wardrobe and pulled out one of the jumpsuits that were her only option, then dropped the towel and stepped into the garment, pulling the sleeves over her arms. She'd chosen white today. Though it looked no different from the others, it was her favorite.

She kicked the balled up towel into a corner as she pulled on her boots, then scrunched the blanket a little more, just so that the auto-bots weren't completely bereft when they came by on their rounds. She even chuckled a little to herself as she left. It was only when she was halfway down the corridor that she realized she'd spoken to herself twice, and the laugh had come out aloud. After all her affirmations that she wasn't yet falling in the traps of solitude, it appeared that she was less in control of herself than she'd imagined.

CHAPTER
3

Hi again! You all know my name's Hannah Monksman by now, so I won't introduce myself again. Oh, wait! I just did! Haha!

So. How's life on Earth going? Hope the weather's holding up! You kind of start to miss the weather out here. The ship's temperature only varies by 0.8 degrees, and there's no sun or clouds.

Sometimes I go down to Deck Nine and lie under the sunlamps, though. It helps to pretend I'm on Bondi Beach. That's in Sydney, Australia, for those of you who don't know. It's one of the few beaches that's survived the rising water level—thanks to the Pacific Sea Wall. I just love that place!

So, anyway. The whales are doing great.

I've got some footage of Jedidah, one of our baleen whales, a dwarf sperm whale, doing some of his tricks. He seriously thinks he's an acrobat! Check it out.

In the meantime—we're all still doing great. We're all excited and looking forward to what we'll find on New Eden. You can post any questions you've got on Near Horizon's Ark Project page, and if I've got time, I'll answer a few!

Love you all. Hannah, signing off, on the morning of July 4, 2078.

Kim was keeping her attention on Adonai. While she didn't feel any spikes of angst from him, as she had the day before, she did sense a slight unease. She wanted to go back down to the Aquarium, but she knew the computer wouldn't allow it a second time in two days.

She'd never been too concerned about the computer's insistence that she stick to routine tasks. She hadn't felt restricted by it before— she hadn't had cause to. There was work to be done, and she was the one to do it. But today, the constraints chafed at her. She tried to send soothing thoughts to Adonai as she worked, but she could feel a distance between them that she didn't like.

"Adonai, I'm here. You can tell me anything you like."

There is nothing I wish to talk about at this time.

"Really? Not even the stars?"

The stars are beyond me. As you said.

"That doesn't mean we can't talk about them. You can ask me questions, if you like. I'll do my best to describe how they work."

The point being what?

Kim sighed. She would get nowhere with him in this mood, and much as she hated it, she couldn't do much to change it.

She talked to Hosea instead. Hosea was a small baleen whale, only thirty feet in length. Normally, Bowhead Whales could reach up to forty-five feet, but Hosea had been born with multiple genetic defects. She'd only been cleared for the journey by a slim margin. Kim was tasked with keeping a close eye on her health, particularly her heart. She had a weakness there that made her survival uncertain, but she'd managed to weather the acceleration out of the Sol system well enough.

Humans have only two eyes, yes? Hosea asked.

"Yes," Kim replied. She was used to odd questions like this. Whales didn't pay much attention to the physiology of species other than fish or other marine creatures. They had no need to. And while Adonai remembered things much better than the others, Hosea was a little slower.

Like whales, she said.

"We have some similarities," Kim agreed. She was polishing one of the maintenance droids. It'd been down in the engines, and had come out covered in grease that was trailing all over the floor as it hovered back to its charging station. "We can swim, too."

Why never you swim with us?

Kim laughed. "I'm not sure that's allowed."

But you could, the whale insisted.

"There are access panels in the tanks," Kim conceded. "But I'm pretty sure it'd be frowned upon. And what would happen if something went wrong with the ship while I was in there? Or with one of the other whales? I'm the Caretaker. I have to look after you."

You being a good Caretaker, Hosea said. *But not that reason I asked about the eyes.*

"No?" Kim rubbed at a stubborn spot with a rag, then gave up and reached for the can of degreaser. Her mind was wandering, thinking about her orders. There was nothing that said she couldn't enter the tank. In fact, there was scuba equipment in the storage rooms and a mask hanging on each deck should she need to enter the tank for any emergency. But going in just for fun . . . well, that was another thing altogether.

Sometimes, I feel like I am watched.

Kim stopped still. "Watched?"

Hosea was silent.

"It must be one of the other whales," Kim suggested.

Hosea's doubt was apparent through the Link and made Kim shiver with unease. She had felt the same this morning, had she not? Until now, she'd successfully pushed it from her mind.

"I have a lot of work to do," she told Hosea, more abruptly than she'd meant to. Hosea, chagrined, drew away. Kim wanted to apologize, but she didn't chase her.

Sighing, she finished with the droid and sent it on its way. The computer chimed in with her next task, but now that this feeling had been recalled for a second time, it was harder to put it from her mind.

Kim spent the rest of the day attending to the tech droids.

She had worked up the energy to take the ramp down to Deck Thirteen. In her mind, she saw the image of the man—she had assumed it was a man, in any case, mainly because of its height. It was a silly assumption. She'd only seen it from a distance and for a fraction of a second. It could have been a woman . . . but then she scolded herself for that thought.

It wasn't anything. Just a trick of the light. *There was no one else aboard.*

She wasn't easily spooked, and the fact that she would even hesitate made her think this was something worth worrying over; but in the next second, she told herself to get over it. She was a fighter. If there was danger on the streets, you didn't run from it—it'd only find you somewhere else, somewhere you were less prepared. No. Constantin had taught her this: you picked the battleground. Then you won.

And so, she buckled her toolbelt and made her way down the ramp. She kept her eyes wide, but the shafts of light shining through the stanchions and curving ramps showed nothing unusual.

Pausing on Deck Nine, she peered into the Aquarium's upper reaches. The blue glow of water rippled against the bulkheads soothingly. She let her mind sift through the sensations of the Link, and brush gently against the minds of the whales.

Nothing untoward.

Fifteen was chattering away to himself. Hosea was humming some low, mournful tune. Salome and Jonah were dancing, circling one another in a version of tag. They were all satisfied with their current level of food, temperature, and level of activity, which made Kim feel a little calmer in turn.

Deck Thirteen closed over her head as the Aquarium tanks bottomed out and moved into the filtration systems. The ship was a lot noisier down here. She drew a kanji on her hand for *music,* and swiped her fingers from her knuckles to her wrist to bring up a menu at the side of her vision.

She scrolled through to something discordant that sounded better when played loud enough to cover the deafening vibrations, something Constantin would play in her apartment on a late night after they'd come back from clubbing, high as kites—partly thanks to stims, but mostly because of dodging the security patrols with faked curfew passes—and feeling empty after the pounding rhythm of the dancefloor.

She eyes me like a Pisces when I am weak
I've been locked inside your heart-shaped box for weeks
I've been drawn into your magnetar pit trap trap
I wish I could eat your cancer when you turn black . . .

It was an old song by a turn-of-the-century band called Nirvana. Kim sang along with it as she walked down the corridor. This one was smaller than those above, and though she wasn't tall, she had to duck occasionally to avoid hitting her head in the pipes that snaked overhead.

She reached a steep set of steps leading down to the left and slid down the railings without touching her feet to the risers.

"Kim," the computer burbled at her. "Please adhere to safety guidelines."

"Shut up," she replied, singing it into the chorus as the music swelled around her. It couldn't drown out the computer, unfortunately, since both were operating through the neuro connection inside her own head, and it was impossible to turn the music up louder than the computer—another safety precaution. Still, it made her feel a little rebellious. Just a little.

She was in one of the side wings now, close to the curved bottom of the ship. The thrumming of the engines and other machinery that kept *Seiiki* alive was all around her. She turned the music up another notch. It wasn't possible to injure your hearing with a neurocom, after all. The tech droids were lined up against the arc-shaped bulkhead, which corresponded with the outer hull. A small airlock was directly ahead, like a mouse-hole in the wall, and there were six droids to one side, six to the other. They were nestled in little egg-shaped containers, open at the front, bodies folded like baby chicks with knees drawn to their chests and heads bent forward to their chests.

Normally sleek and silver, they'd accumulated a coating of dust since she was here a week ago. She walked to the end and stopped in front of the twelfth one.

"Power up," she said.

The droid responded immediately, uncurling its head, unfolding its fingers, and propelling itself gracefully through the ovoid hole to stand to attention before her. The tech droids were more advanced than most droids. Their forearms contained multiple tools that could be unfolded as required, and they were in human-form—the better to correlate to the control rig, should they need to be operated by a human for some task or other.

She wiped the droid before her with a rag, then pulled a slender diagnostic tool from her toolbelt that beeped as she passed it over the droid's body. Its oil levels were good, central processor responding as normal, and it pinged the computer successfully at ninety-nine kilobits per second.

"Turn left," Kim commanded. The droid obediently lifted one leg, stepped left, then pivoted to face the required direction. She repeated the tests, having it bend over, lift its arms over its head, then perform a small shimmy left and right.

"Computer, you're relaying all this through the rig in Ops?"

"Indeed I am, Kim. Everything looks normal. The rig is responding as expected."

"One down, eleven to go," Kim said with sarcastic cheer.

That evening's transmission went without incident. Admiral Mbewe made no reference to his strange question last night, and signed off with his usual curtness after she'd transmitted the data logs.

She finished the night by fixing the door sensor in her quarters, trying to find the fault that had caused it to open unbidden earlier. When she dismantled it, she found a small amount of dust inside. That could have caused a malfunction.

The computer dimmed the lights and she climbed into bed, but she felt far too awake for sleep. She tried letting the Link take her over, immersing herself in the blue-green water world of the whales and their soft, distant song-chatter. She found herself drifting off, only to wake with a start.

She'd heard a noise.

It wasn't unusual. On a ship this size, it would be more surprising if there *weren't* random noises that sounded without warning. But this noise was different—she was sure of it.

She sat up, heart pounding, which only made it harder for her ears to discern the out-of-place sound. She strained, listening, then told herself not to be stupid.

Immediately, she kicked off the gravity blanket and sat up. Barefooted and dressed in her nightshirt, she went to the door. It hissed open obediently, revealing the corridor beyond. Lights flickered on slowly, reacting to her movements and making her blink. Her room remained stubbornly dark, locked in night-time mode by the computer until either her morning alarm sounded or she overrode the commands.

She stood in the corridor, looking left, then right. Nothing. Nothing. She was about to head back to bed, telling herself she was being ridiculous, when another noise sounded.

This time, she zeroed in on the direction, and began to walk toward it. It had sounded as if it was coming from the mess, or perhaps the galley.

"Kim?" the computer said, startling her.

Her hand made the shaky kanji for *silent,* and she whispered, "Computer? Is there anyone else aboard?"

"That is the second time you have asked this odd question in two days, Kim. Have you taken a mental health session lately? I am becoming concerned."

Kim grimaced. Great. Now the ship thought she was crazy. She continued to move toward the mess door. It had only been a few hours since she'd eaten her dinner there. She hadn't noticed anything unusual. No open vent gratings that might bang around when the air cyclers kicked in. No loose cans that might have toppled over, or open cupboard doors that might have swung shut.

Rats? She'd had rats in her flat, once. They'd eaten and pooped all over a week's worth of groceries. It wasn't impossible. The ship was huge, and even though Near Horizon had put her through hellish decontamination procedures, as well as everything that had come aboard, a parasite might have boarded, and could have been breeding in the walls or in the warmth of the lowest decks.

She kind of hoped it was rats, in fact. She could deal with rats. She remembered setting the traps in her flat, finding the flattened furry bodies in the morning, paws curled and tails limp. She'd dropped them into the garbage bag with satisfaction. Were there any rat traps in the supplies?

She could easily make some, if not . . .

The door to the mess was just ahead of her. Even though it was faintly ridiculous, she pressed her back to the wall, edging closer as quietly as she could. The grillwork of the deck plates cut slightly into the soles of her feet (not as much as they would have if they were at a full g, though), but the metal decking was silent without her boots clomping. She reached the jamb and turned her head, craning her neck to see through the gap. Nothing. Just the stainless steel cupboards, the hooded sink, and the dishes in the auto-washer, where she'd left them.

Wait. Two dishes were in the rack. One was missing.

Her heart stuttered. There were usually three—a small plate for lunch, large one for dinner, and a bowl for breakfast. She hadn't put one away—she never did. She left it in the rack so it was there for tomorrow.

She took in a deep breath. Her shoulders lifted and her chest swelled. She wished she had a weapon, but there was nothing she could do about it. She had her fists. That would have to be enough. There were times when it had been.

And yes, some of those times had been against other unseen, unknown enemies—though what kind of enemy she was facing here was beyond her comprehension. There was no one else aboard except the whales. As the computer had told her, this entire situation was impossible.

And yet here she was.

She exploded into motion, stepping into the doorway and shouting, "Who the hell are you?"

She stopped still.

Looking back at her was one of the tech droids. It was a human-form machine, not a maintenance droid or an autobot. Its silver plating glinted in the overhead lights as it stood in the alcove behind the table where there was a stovetop she rarely used. It was spooning something from a steaming pot into a bowl. Now that she was in the room, the scent hit her like a shockwave. Spices, the tang of vegetables, meat. She hadn't smelled any of these things in so long it made her instantly nauseous.

The droid turned its head, revealing a long face, ovoid in shape, two glittering gold irises for the eyes, a raised triangle for the nose, and the faintest impression where the mouth would be. A breastplate devoid of markings. Two arms fitted with lifelike hands. Wiring was visible at each of its joints, but an effort had been made to disguise it by coating it in silver plastic. It was taller than her by at least eight inches.

She sensed no malice, but the utter incongruousness of the situation jarred Kim's reflexes. Her fight-or-flight instinct warred with her disbelief.

Finally, she managed to stutter: "What are you?"

"Greetings, Kim. My designation is 4-9-4-7."

Kim stood stock still. Her mind was racing at light speed. A four-digit code. This was definitely one of the tech droids. But why was it operating autonomously? It had been, what, five hours since she'd run her checks, and there hadn't been any sign of an issue.

The computer could activate the tech droids, but only in times of emergency. The computer could also control them, or Kim herself could, using the motion-capture rig in Ops. As she'd explained to Adonai, they were the reason she'd be unlikely to ever need to go EV personally.

But what—what the *heck*—was it doing in her galley, cooking—

"What is that?"

The droid lifted its head in a very human gesture, as if pleased to be asked.

"Chicken soup," it said.

—cooking chicken soup?

"If you would have a seat, Kim?" the droid asked her, turning with a jerky motion and placing the bowl on the table. The enamel object bounced against the hard tabletop and some of the broth leapt out, yellowish against the white faux-wood laminate.

"I—" Kim began. "I'm going crazy."

"No, you're not," the droid replied. It sounded—if such a thing was possible—anxious. There was something about the tone that was incredibly familiar.

"Computer," Kim barked. "Why is a tech droid in the galley?"

"There are no tech droids in the galley," the computer answered. "Kim, you are awake much earlier than your nominated time. I suggest you return to your bed to ensure you are not fatigued by the time you start your duties for—"

"I suggest you shut up, computer!" Kim snapped. She pressed a hand to her forehead, then, very deliberately, closed her eyes. When she opened them, the droid was still there. "Computer, there *is* a tech droid in the galley. I'm looking right at it."

"There is no tech droid in the galley, Kim."

Kim let out a frustrated sound. Her instinct was to go back to her quarters, but what good would that do? Was she hoping that when she came back out the droid would be gone?

"I assure you, Kim, I am real," the droid said, as if reading her mind. "I'm sorry if this is causing you agitation. Perhaps if you sit down, we can have a conversation, and I can explain."

The suggestion was so reasonable that it was funny. Kim let out a bark of laughter.

"Okay," she said. "Fine. I'm going to sit down, and you're going to tell me exactly why you were activated, and what the hell is going on here."

The droid took her at her word, and pulled out the chair behind the bowl of soup. It waited patiently for a few seconds before Kim realized it was holding the chair out for *her.*

Warily, she crossed the floor, and it was only then that she noticed the mess on the bench. Pieces of chopped vegetables had rolled into the corners. Leftover chicken sat in fat, pinkish slices. The pot had boiled over, spattering the stovetop. At least the droid had turned the heating element off. Kim turned her body so she could fit between the table and the cabinets without getting too close to the tech droid. It slid the chair under her as she sat. Kim felt a strange sensation. She'd never had such an action performed for her in her life.

The droid moved around the table. Its steps were clumsy. Given the mess it had made of the galley, it seemed to be running on its basic programming. Kim knew a little about how the tech droids worked. They could perform mechanical operations on their own, with input from the computer to aid their work. So, yes, the techbot could easily have chopped vegetables and chicken, poured water into a pot, and turned on a heating element.

But no tech droid was designed to undertake these kinds of tasks. Not without major tinkering to its programming. Kim could have done it, and relatively easily—all it would take is a few adjustments to the droid's programmed tasks, really—but the fact was, she *hadn't*.

Those clumsy movements, too. They weren't normal. Tech droids worked with precision. They had to, to be able to handle tools and obey complex instructions. They were more adept than a human, with a lesser margin of error. Had this one malfunctioned? Been infected with a virus? If so, she could have a major problem on her hands. But the techbot wasn't displaying signs of virus infection apart from the jerky movements. Its speech was lucid and coherent. It had performed the task of cooking the soup without incident. It was speaking to her—but that was another issue. It was using her name. Her *real* name.

Kim, not Hannah.

Yes, it could have gotten that information from the computer—but the computer, for its part, was not recognizing the droid. What did that mean? Apart from the fact that she was an idiot for giving the computer her real name at all. This could be dangerous! She needed to keep the droid talking.

It pulled out the seat opposite her and sat down.

"I've wanted for a long time to see you properly, Kim. You're very beautiful."

Kim's heart skipped a beat. "What—what did you just say?"

"You're very beautiful," the droid repeated. "Did I say something incorrect?"

"No," she said. "Before that. You've waited a long time? You mean—you've been watching me?"

"Oh." The droid placed its hands in its lap demurely. "I am sorry, deeply. I thought you would have recognized the being that is me. I thought you would know my name, as I know yours. I'm speaking of real names, of course." It paused. "But you are now not so much *little*, Little one. Perhaps—"

The realization slammed into Kim like an aircar at high speed.

"Adonai?" She stared at the tech droid incredulously. "Seriously?"

"I thought your happiness would be bigger," the droid replied. Its shoulders shifted slightly, its voice a little doleful. "I thought I would impress you."

Kim looked down at the soup in the bowl in front of her. The smell was still assaulting her, but her stomach was starting to rumble. "I can't believe . . . "

"Ah, I understand! I've shocked you. That is all right. I'll give you some time to get used to the idea. We can sit here as long as you like."

But Kim was already searching through the Link, sifting through the dull babble of forty-three whale voices, trying to find the one that had always spoken the loudest. She brushed it at last, but only lightly. The data was there—Respiration: Normal. Heart Rate: Normal. Motion: Normal.

"Adonai?" she said aloud.

There was no response from the Link. But the tech droid in front of her cocked its head to one side. "I am here, Kim. There is no need to use the Link."

"Your body's still there. In the tanks. You're still breathing, and eating, from what I can tell. But you're not answering the Link."

"I do not know exactly how it has worked, Kim. I'm not a human. But I have established control of this droid." He sounded proud.

Kim pushed herself back from the table, standing abruptly. "No *way*," she said.

"Kim, please, sit down. The last thing I wanted was to alarm you."

Kim paced away from the table. "You've somehow uploaded your consciousness through the Link," she said. "You must have used the neural pathways to gain access to the computer. It's the only way you could have transferred your . . . yourself into the cognitive core of the droid." She turned. "How are you manipulating it? God, what have you *done*?"

"I've given myself a body, Kim. That's all I wanted. I'm sorry if I've upset you."

"Upset me?" Kim gave another bark of laughter, this one sounding slightly hysterical. "You have no idea!"

The droid's head dropped sadly. "I'm sorry. I should have asked you. But you would have said no."

"Of course I would have! This is—this is dangerous! And stupid! Adonai, you could have killed yourself—or left yourself braindead— or maybe you *have*! Have you even thought about that?"

"Yes," the droid replied, stubbornly. "Of course I have. It was worth the risk."

"What was worth the risk?" Kim demanded. She marched back to the table, placed both hands on it, and stared into those golden eyes. "What exactly did you think you were getting out of this?"

"I—I—my little one with long fins," the droid replied, haltingly. "I wanted to see you. Really see you. Not through the walls of the tank. I wanted to see . . . all of this." It lifted its hands, fingers splayed, indicating the room, the bulkheads, the ship. "Can you understand?"

Kim shook her head. "This is because I told you about the damned *stars*?"

"No! I have wanted this for much longer. Before I understood about the stars. When I was . . . in the time before. The locked-in place."

The Yokohama Institute.

He was remembering Dr. Jin's laboratory, where he and the other whales were implanted with the neural matrices of the Link—where she, herself, had been implanted with the golden filaments. Where she had first seen Adonai, silent and huge, floating in a tank along with the other whales.

"Oh, God," Kim said. She didn't know what else to say. At a complete loss, she returned to the table, sat down, and looked at the soup. Her taste buds awakened with a painful pang. It must be close to her normal waking time by now.

"I thought I would make you breakfast," he said. "I thought we'd have a meal together. This is what humans do? I found reference to it in the computer archives. It helps ease conversation."

Kim continued to look at the soup. "You're a droid, Adonai. You can't eat."

"I don't need to," Adonai said. "But that doesn't mean I can't enjoy watching you. I would like to make you happy with a meal, Kim. It is a thank-you. You've looked after me. You are as my Caretaker."

Caretaker.

Kim turned and reached for a drawer, sliding a spoon from within and turning back to her bowl.

"Oh," Adonai said. "I forgot that you do not use your hands to eat. I apologize. I would have placed out the utensils, otherwise."

Kim could not reply. She dipped her spoon into the soup and lifted a small piece of chicken to her lips. With sudden abandon, she put it in her mouth, chewed, and swallowed. The incredible sensation of eating real food for the first time in three months almost made her weep. It tasted like . . . like *life*.

"Is it all right?" Adonai asked her, that anxious tone back in his voice. Yeah, *his* voice. Not *its*. She couldn't think of Adonai as anything other than a being.

"Adonai," she said, when she could speak. "Where on Earth did you get chicken from?"

CHAPTER

4

Adonai watched her finish the entire bowl, then fill it again from the pot on the stove. The pleasure of eating was something she hadn't expected. Kim had been hungry before many times—far hungrier than she was now. And the soup was not perfectly made. There was too much salt in it. Slightly too many diced carrots, of which she wasn't a fan. Still, she didn't stop until there wasn't room for any more.

The feeling of a full belly made her sluggish, but clear-headed. She felt her entire body waking up as if from a very long sleep as it processed the nutrients she had obviously been lacking. Space rations met basic requirements, but that was all. And she'd probably not been eating enough of them, or in great enough variety, either.

Having an audience made her uncomfortable, but she could hardly tell him to go away. And a large part of her felt comforted by his presence, despite the oddness of the situation.

You've been alone too long. She pushed the thought aside once more. For God's sake! She'd expected to be alone for the entire journey! Almost a *year*! How could she be acting like this after three *months*?

When she was finished, the computer chimed at her. "Kim, you've begun your day earlier than scheduled. Would you like to add some additional tasks to today's roster?"

"I'd like to take extra time to do my normal tasks," Kim replied, glancing at Adonai.

"That is not an efficient use of time, Kim."

Adonai tilted his head to one side. "This man is bossy."

Kim let out a snort of laughter. The computer, however, did not detect that Adonai had said anything, and continued. "I would recommend a check of the engine compartment. There are no urgent chores, but a small drop in oil pressure has been detected. It would be advisable to visually observe the leak and determine the cause. I would also advise undertaking your exercise routine. I have noticed a decrease in your overall fitness level, and this would also help with your sleep cycle, and the anxiety I have detected."

"Thank you, computer," Kim said. Great. Not only did she have to work out what to do with Adonai, but now she had extra jobs to fill her day.

"Kim," the computer added hesitantly. "I have detected that you are talking to yourself."

"When?" Kim asked immediately.

"A small incident yesterday and the day before." It paused a second, then replayed her own voice through its speakers. *"Old life."*

Kim relaxed. The Manta Protocol hadn't failed her—the computer had only detected her odd comments to herself. This was good. But puzzling, as well. It must be detecting Adonai's voice. "You don't detect any replies, then?"

"I do not understand. Who would reply? There is usual activity on your Link, however. Perhaps you mean your communications with the whales."

Yes. That was exactly what Kim meant, she thought, looking at Adonai.

But if the computer didn't detect him speaking aloud, through the droid's vocal processors—and it should have, since there were microphones in every room and corridor, to pick up any verbal commands she might relay to the computer—then that could only mean it was continuing to believe that Adonai's conversation with her was merely occurring through the Link. Which it could not monitor, at least, not to the extent it could monitor the ship.

While the Aquarium's support systems could be checked—oxygen levels, water temperature, supply from the fisheries—and this information was shared through the Link, cognitive information could not be shared.

Everything that was said between her and the whales was private, because there was no way for the computer to translate the emotions and feelings that formed the basis of communication via the intricate neural network.

"I would also like you to undertake your mental health session, Kim," The computer continued. "I do not want to alarm you, but I must remind you that your psychological welfare is very important. I will put through a request for counseling when we contact Edgeward Station this evening."

"Is that necessary?"

"It is procedure. You have made several strange requests over the past few days. It is merely a precaution, Kim. We must make certain you are healthy in every way."

Kim shook her head, pushing back her chair. "Whatever." Then, glancing at Adonai, she said, "The computer doesn't see you at all. Why is that?"

"I'm not sure," Adonai replied. "I did tell this machine not to let anyone know I was here. I didn't want any of the ship's . . . systems stopping me from doing what I needed to do."

The audio, yeah, Kim could figure how that worked. What she couldn't explain was how that could override the droid's internal link to the computer. But if the droid had been in direct communication with the computer core, then it was possible its commands had rewritten the computer's coding, in a similar manner as her own bit of hacking had changed the computer's recognition of her internally. "I have to go and do my job, or the computer will completely freak out, and I'll be in major trouble. I don't know what to do with you."

"I could accompany you. Help you."

"I don't think so," Kim replied quickly.

"You don't trust me?"

"It's not that. Actually, maybe it *is* that. I don't know. Adonai, this ship is important. More important than you realize." She stopped herself short of saying anything more. The computer was still listening, after all. "This is all really freaking weird, and I honestly don't know what to do with any of it."

Adonai looked away. "I'm sorry. I did not intend making things difficult."

"I know you didn't," she said. Then, with some reluctance, she added, "Adonai, can you show me where you got the chicken from?"

He brightened, his shoulders straightening, his head coming up.

"Yes! Yes, of course! Is that what it's always called? Chicken?"

Kim felt a pang of guilt as she stood and followed him. An idea had been forming in her mind while their conversation had progressed, but she wasn't sure she wanted to carry it out.

The chicken, it turned out, was kept in a freezer in the storage room to the left of the mess, along with many other frozen vegetables. Cupboards on either side held oils, jams, flour, rice, and even a container of dry yeast.

Kim hadn't bothered to examine the room properly. She'd never had time, or reason to. The ration satchels in the galley pantry had kept her going, and she'd only ever eaten because she had to. Honestly, she'd probably have forgotten even to undertake that chore had the computer not scheduled it and ruthlessly insisted on her adherence to three meals a day.

She let Adonai enter ahead of her. He was excited as he moved his body in a circle to face her. Kim knew what the droid's capabilities were with regards to dexterity (she knew all too well, she thought, rubbing her shoulder, which still twinged occasionally) and imagined he'd still have a lot of work ahead of him if he was going to get used to moving in a humanoid body.

"This is all good food for you, yes?"

Kim nodded, her thoughts elsewhere. Now that she hovered in the doorway, indecision was making her hesitate. She didn't want to do this, and looking at the droid now, seeing him as excited as a creature made of metal and silicon chips could look, something tugged at her conscience. She shoved it away with a firm conclusion: she couldn't allow this being to roam freely on the ship. The computer couldn't track it if it couldn't see it. Supposing Adonai was the benign being he claimed to be—he might still blunder into Deck Fifteen and mess with the engines, or Deck One and damage the communications equipment, without even knowing what he was doing. Kim couldn't risk it.

This was the only choice.

She stepped back and drew a kanji on the back of her left hand. *Shimeru*—close—although, actually, the meaning was closer to "obstruct." With a beep, the ship sent up a shimmering wall of blue energy from the floor to the top of the door. She saw it ripple into place against each of the jambs.

Adonai stopped moving. Was he startled? Afraid? Angry? She couldn't tell from his blank metal expression.

"I'm sorry," she said.

His shoulders slumped.

"I have to keep the ship safe, and I can't have you wandering around." She searched for explanations that would soften this, then wondered why she was bothering. For God's sake, she wasn't here to assuage his feelings! He was an intruder, and whether he was the real Adonai or not, she had to remember that.

"It's been eleven hours, Kim. I've been in other places on this ship during that time without you knowing."

Was that a hint of accusation in his voice?

Kim stopped still. "Eleven hours?"

"Yes." He stood there, his metallic body ramrod-straight, his golden eyes blazing unblinkingly. Kim swallowed.

"Adonai, I'm sorry. You can't leave this room. Not . . . not yet. I have to think about this. I have to . . ."

A heartbeat passed, then another. He nodded once, slowly. "Yes, Kim. I understand."

The forcefields on each room were designed to be activated in case of hull breaches. They met any force with an equal and opposite reaction. This was military tech. A nuclear explosion would not cause one to collapse unless the generator itself was damaged, and that was located deep inside Deck Fifteen. There would be no breaking through it, not even with a tech droid's strong hands. She could have shut the door as well, to make doubly sure, but that felt cruel. Instead, she left him, but as she reached the end of the corridor, she leaned back against the wall. Her belly full, her mind racing, she counted her breaths up to ten, then twenty. And still, her sense of unease grew.

CHAPTER
5

"Kim, you have activated an emergency forcefield on Deck Five, Section Four."

"That's right," Kim said as she swung her way onto one of the spiraling ramps. "I'm running a test."

"I don't detect an oxygen leakage, or any other reason to test out the forcefields in that section."

"Yeah, I just want to make sure they work," Kim replied. "Computer, I need to be certain they will keep me safe during an emergency. I want to run it for a while and check that it doesn't drain any other systems. And yes, I know it was all checked prior to our departure from Ganymede, but we've been out here for . . . " she drew the kanji for *time* and checked her internal chronometer, which displayed at the upper left edge of her vision in flickering violet numbers, thanks to the Link, "ninety-three days. I want to make sure everything's still working at peak efficiency."

The computer hesitated before answering. "That is prudent thinking."

Kim checked over an autobot that was moving more slowly than it should, ran an analysis on the Operations Center systems, and did a manual inspection of the pipes leading out from the fisheries into the Aquarium. The fisheries were doing well, operating at peak efficiency, and the toothed whales seemed content with their meals.

She preferred to do a manual inspection of the plankton levels in the Aquarium itself, however, because while the fish were easy to measure in pounds, plankton, and the tiny shrimp-like krill, were close to being invisible in smaller numbers. It was easy for the readings on the screen to be inaccurate.

"It is not necessary to inspect the crustacea levels today," the computer told her. "The system will alert you if the levels are too low. They are programmed to account for a margin of error."

"I've got half an hour spare," Kim said. "I can check on them, make sure they're doing okay, and be back in the Operations Center before the Link scans are due to begin. I'd rather do it today than leave it until next week, when I'm due to check the wiring on the nav computer. That could take all day, and it would have a flow-on effect if I took time out for the check then."

"Very well," the computer conceded. "It is an efficient use of time."

"Thank you," Kim said sarcastically.

She didn't tell the computer that she had another reason to want to go down to the Aquarium.

She took one of the spiraling ramps down to Deck Nine. Here, she was above the tanks, and this entire level was devoted to observation windows set into the floor. Hovering holograms displayed readouts of temperatures and oxygen levels, pressure, and maps of the whale's movements as well as the fish and plankton. Plankton couldn't be seen with the naked eye. It had taken decades to come up with a way to accurately detect their presence, and the ability to separate these readings into the different types of plankton had taken even longer. It had only happened when it was too late to save the whales.

Deck Nine was one of her favorite places. It was bright at this time of "day", with the artificial sunlight turned up to mimic a cloudless sky. The lamps, large, conical devices set at even intervals along the ceiling, produced a lot of heat, too. She felt her skin prickle. It was nothing like real sunlight, but it was a welcome break from the comparative bleakness of the rest of the ship—like walking from an office you'd been working in for eight hours, out into the daylight.

Not that she'd know about that, of course. Not Kim, anyway. An office was as foreign an environment as you could get. Hannah, though, knew all about them. She'd worked as a PA, hadn't she? Kim gave a bitter laugh. She'd spent so much time imagining the life of this other girl, she was seriously afraid she'd actually become her.

Now, Kim walked over the floor, looking down at the tanks. Irregular shaped gaps cropped up here and there, shafts that led down between the sections of the tanks, holding the catwalks and ladders. Hovering just above the surface of the glass were holographic clouds of red, like a mist that didn't move when she stepped through it. The amount of red corresponded with the amount of copepod plankton and krill in the water below.

"Good," she murmured, stepping from one island of red to another. The plankton was growing well, and it was the right type for whales to eat healthily. She had to keep an eye out for over-growth as well and under-growth. Too many copepods and the artificial ecosystem would be wildly out of balance—and it could effectively form a shield over the surface of the tank water, blocking the manufactured sunlight from Deck Nine getting through to the first few miles of water. Not to mention if the less desirable plankton began to overgrow.

Beyond the red clouds, the glass, three inches thick, made no noise. Unlike the clanking metal decking, it was almost solid, save for two areas at either end of the Deck, where forcefields hummed. With everything functioning perfectly, Kim had no need to go to either of them, but she crouched down where she was and peered down through the glass. Twenty feet of open air separated her from the surface of the water, air that had to be vented and regulated by one of the ship's systems to ensure it didn't create a "bubble" that would affect the water's surface.

Because of the movement of air, waves were able to run along horizontally, from the front of the ship to the back, mimicking their acceleration through space. This top section of the tank was a single open space and resembled a coastal lake. It was only when you peered into the depths that you could see the Aquarium dividing into its various divisions, splitting apart and merging again as it ran down through the ship to Deck Twelve.

One whale had come to the surface, rolling lazily and blowing air from her blowhole. It wasn't water, as Kim had learned during her studies, but rather hot air that condensed in the colder temperature. Some of it, less pleasantly, was mucus. It fountained up, dissipating into the air.

"Berenice," Kim said.

Hello, Kim, Berenice replied. A southern right whale, she was slightly shy, and rarely talked much. Kim always had the impression that Berenice was slightly frightened of her in a way the other whales never were.

"Have you seen Adonai?"

Adonai. She could feel Berenice thinking this over, but before her thoughts reached a conclusion, she said, suddenly, and slightly aggressively, *What strange names you give us.*

Kim was taken aback, and Berenice must have felt it.

You can't pronounce our true names. At least, you know them, as you know our thoughts and feelings. But they have no real translation in your mind. Do they?

"No," Kim said, feeling slightly unsure. This was the most Berenice had ever spoken to her at one time. "But the other names—the ones Dr Jin labelled you with back in Yokohama—aren't names at all. They're numbers."

You didn't change Scsxzq's.

The word itself was untranslatable, even through the Link. This was true of all the whales' original names, the ones they'd been born with or given by the few remaining members of families or pods. Before being altered with human DNA, the whales' language was not something humans could understand or imitate.

Kim stopped still, looking down at the massive shape below her. Of all the whales, only five species had companions of the same species, and Berenice was one of the lucky ones. Four southern right whales were in the Aquarium. Kim could differentiate them, but only by using the Link.

Visually, they looked much the same—rubbery, blue-black skin, growths of white on their heads like knobbly lace hats. The Link was etched onto her head, a golden spiders-web.

Berenice gave a soft sound of irritation at Kim's lack of understanding. *Fifteen. You call him Fifteen.*

"Oh," Kim said faintly. "Well, yes. He's kind of . . . I didn't know what to call him. He didn't want to help come up with a name I could hold onto in the Link, either. Not the way you did." She tried to remind Berenice that she'd been complicit in the naming. If she disagreed, Kim could have chosen something else. Or perhaps she'd have been better off sticking with her number.

Is that what you think?

Kim crouched down. There was a cloud of red to her left, and a slowly-scrolling display of steadily-climbing numbers to her right. She pressed her palms to the top of the tank.

"You're not droids. You're living beings."

You name us after people from a book. You make us into characters.

Kim felt a tinge of guilt, followed quickly by a burst of anger. "Not just any book. The Bible is the most sacred of all books."

Do all humans think so?

"Most of them," Kim replied. She could tell by the challenge in Berenice's voice that she already knew about the Silent War on Earth, the one that was still ongoing after all the other wars had ceased—the one that would continue to be fought until the end of time. Some religious people would never see eye to eye. "Some still follow other religions, and they've got their own texts. But 61 percent of the population of Earth is now Christian in one form or another. Belief in God brought us together after the Triad War. It gave us something to believe in. So I chose names for you with meaning."

Berenice was corrupt. A woman who had relations with her brother. A power-hungry viper. You told us her story.

Kim sighed. "I didn't mean that you were like her. We talked about the story, and you still said you thought 'Berenice' was a nice name. I didn't make you choose it. I just . . . I wanted to know you as friends."

We're not friends, Berenice retorted. There was so much strength to the statement that Kim lifted her hands. The feeling of rejection stung through her like a physical slap. She knew most of it was coming from the Link—mental, not corporeal, but in some ways that made it worse.

We're too different to be friends.

"I'm sorry," Kim said. She meant it, too, but she couldn't pour it into the Link to counteract the vehemence of Berenice's voice. The neural connection didn't work that way.

Berenice hovered there for a moment, then, without another word, dived into the deep. Kim followed her down with her mind, but Berenice was still pushing her away, and Kim relented, giving her the space she desired.

Aware that her half-hour was rapidly dwindling even without calling up her chronometer, Kim moved toward one of the "holes" in the deck, descending one of the ladders. She stopped when she'd reached the place she'd found Adonai the day before, and was relieved to see him there today as well. He was still swimming back and forth through the arch, the way he had then.

Eleven hours. Adonai had been using the droid for half a day. How had he done it?

"Adonai?" she said, leaning on the railing and peering through the half-gloom.

The whale did not respond. He continued to swim, back and forth, back and forth. His belly was full, but his mind . . .

"Adonai?" she repeated, louder. Not that it would make a difference. The Link conveyed everything at the same volume, whether she was shouting or whispering.

The great whale stopped swimming and with a flick of his fins, drifted closer to the forcefield.

"Hey, buddy," she said, stretching out a hand. She let it hover just above the surface of the forcefield. The small blue ripples appeared, taking the shape of her hand and creating a mirror in blue lightning. She was reminded for a moment of the droid locked in the food storage room on Deck Five. Had he tried to escape? Once a forcefield was activated, it prudently covered all walls of the affected room, to prevent leakage into surrounding sections. There was no way to get through the bulkheads in any direction. But that didn't mean he couldn't try, and if he did, if he was stubborn about it, he could very well end up damaging himself.

"Oh, Adonai," Kim said. "Please don't tell me this is real."

Adonai hung in the water. His head drifted slowly to one side so that one of his black, side-mounted eyes, was looking at her. But though she tried to convince herself it wasn't true, that she was letting her emotions get the better of her yet again, letting them warp her objectivity, she could see no real spark of life in them.

She reached out with the Link instead. Yes, there he was. A blue whale-sized being laid out on her internal grid. The effect was similar to the same way a person could be aware of objects and walls in a room even when you weren't looking at them directly. She felt his proximity, knew that the last time he'd eaten was three hours ago, and that he was at a comfortable temperature. But there was no brush of his mind against hers, no spark of recognition.

"Adonai. Remember how we talked about the stars?"

Nothing.

He flicked his fins, sending himself in a lazy figure-eight, back through the arch of rock, his fluke flapping at her in what would have been a dismissive gesture if there was any emotion at all in it.

C H A P T E R

6

Normally, Kim would have stopped by the mess for her lunch time meal, and then dinner, but today she skipped both of those. The computer insisted that she eat, so she took one of the emergency protein bars she had stashed in one of the pockets of her toolbelt. They were as tasteless as cardboard, and she noticed it particularly now, after that glorious hot meal this morning.

In the outer chambers of Deck Thirteen, she checked out the forcefield generator as she'd promised the computer. The forcefields worked in a similar manner to holoprojectors, with a stable field of protons cast into a predetermined shape and location from a singular source. The generator itself was only about as big as a milk crate, but the internal workings made Kim's hands itch—there was a lot of complex wiring, circuit-boards, and quite a few things she had never seen before.

"Computer," she asked, as she scrolled through the projected readout on the wall panel above the generator's alcove, "How well is the generator running?"

"My readings show it running at 93 percent efficiency."

"Is that number fluctuating at all?"

"It has varied by 0.81 percent in the past week. This is within normal parameters."

Kim crouched down, looking at the small device longingly. She had only a basic understanding of how forcefields worked, and the basics had never been enough to please her on anything in life. But there was an urgency to her need to know, now. She had a reason to need the forcefield in the galley store room to stay at full—for who knew how long. With the forcefields in the tanks active, she could end up blowing out the generator altogether.

"Computer, what do you know about forcefields?"

The computer seemed pleased to be asked. "Forcefields are relatively new technology. The first charged-particle-based forcefields were first used for military purposes in 2026, during the Triad War. These forcefields were mounted to fighter planes, and were unreliable due to their massive power consumption, however, they provided a good testing ground for the capabilities of the technology. Over the next decade, the technology was refined to the point that the charge could be projected up to several miles away, provided relay stations were set in place to conduct the energy from the generator.

"*Seiiki* was only the third ship to use this technology internally rather than as external shielding. While forcefields have been used in civilian households and businesses for many years as security and safety features, *Seiiki*'s scale is somewhat grander. Two other Near Horizon ships, the *Tanoshi-ge* and the *Nichiyobi*, are also equipped with similar technology."

This was interesting, but nothing Kim didn't already know. Kim looked back at the readouts. As she'd expected, and the computer had confirmed, there was nothing to be concerned about.

At least, not for now.

Kim left Deck Thirteen and walked back to the ramps.

At the very least, she consoled herself, she now had an explanation for the strange things she'd seen. The man on the ramp, her bedsheets being tucked back. Though God knew why he'd snuck into her room to undertake housecleaning!

But something about that troubled her, too. The door to her room had been stuck open when she came back in. She had put it down to a malfunction, and yes, that might have been the case—and Adonai had merely taken advantage of the situation.

That would have meant he'd have to have happened by whilst she was conveniently in the shower. He couldn't have known, not without access to the computer, where she was in that room, which meant he'd come, fixed the bed, then left before she'd emerged from the bathroom. Something about that explanation seemed a little unsatisfactory, however.

That was one possibility.

The other was that he'd opened the door himself. The problem was that if the computer didn't recognize him, how could he have done that? The sensors were tied to the computer rather than the ship's autonomous systems, due to the need for voice activation and life-support control in times of emergency. There were overrides, but again, he couldn't have activated them without speaking to the computer.

He'd been lurking on the ship for less than a day. How much could he have learned during that time, simply from observing her? She'd noticed improvements in his speech from when he'd been in his whale body. Had he been watching as she contacted Edgeward? It was possible. There were independent video links to each of the main rooms on each deck. He could have tapped into them from any display unit at any control junction. Tech droids had that option—so did anything else that had fingers that could scroll and tap any holographic displays . . .

Kim's thoughts ground to a sudden halt. She'd just rounded a particularly wide stanchion, giving her a view across the other ramps, through the shadowed gloom.

She wasn't imagining things, was she? Not this time—

"Hey!" she called out, reaching for her toolbelt. She swiftly pulled out a flashlight. Activated by her tightening grip, the beam stabbed downwards onto the ramp that crossed below hers, and she saw it, just for a second, but she *saw* it, she was sure—

The figure of a man, darting for an open doorway at one of the landings.

Her shout echoed back at her as she broke into a run. She reached the railing and didn't hesitate. She vaulted over, the muscles of her arms and legs remembering the motion and sending her sailing through the air, and though it had been over a year since she'd run like this, the lower gravity aided her adroitness. She landed in a crouch, one hand coming down between her bent knees, the flashlight still clasped in her other. She flashed it toward the door, which led onto Deck Twelve. She couldn't see him anymore, but she charged for the doorway, flinging herself through.

"Hey!" she shouted, anger making her words hard as stones. "Get back here!"

Something held her back from saying his name, from calling to Adonai. How had he gotten free? It was impossible. She'd only just been checking the generator, and it had showed no sign of failure or fluctuation . . . but he *had* gotten free.

And now he was on the loose in her ship, and who knew what his plans were?

She skidded to a stop. She'd come in from the opposite direction than usual, at the far end of the arcing loop of walkways between the tanks. It was now 'late evening', and the sea was darkening as the halogen lights far overhead dimmed to their "night" phase. The glowing blue of the Aquarium was becoming a dull grey, only the occasional shimmer of a forcefield adding to the glow of the halogens that were tuned to her movements. She glanced to the left, then right, seeing nothing and no one. She looked up, but the catwalks were empty. A bridge of one of the tanks arched overhead, a tunnel big enough to fit the largest whale's bulk, with room to spare.

She flashed her flashlight over the glass, and a sleepy rumble resonated through the Link, telling her she'd disturbed at least one whale's rest with her noise. The beam reflected its way into the depths of Deck Twelve, but it was clear that the halogens had been turning on overhead well ahead of her own position.

With a grim smile, she followed them to the left, shining her flashlight up into the catwalks.

"Come back here," she called again. "I'm not angry. I'm sorry if I sounded that way. You scared me. But you can't hide from me. I just . . . want to talk to you."

No reply.

Strange. The Adonai she'd spoken to this morning had seemed happy to talk. Why was he hiding now? Was it because she'd locked him up?

"I'm sorry I had to confine you," she said. "I told you my reasons, and you said you understood. Well, I understand you, too. I know it must seem harsh . . . "

"Kim," the computer spoke. The voice startled her so much she jumped, her feet skittering on the decking.

She pressed a hand to her chest, heart pounding.

"You are yet again talking to yourself. At least, I can detect no activation of your Link, which suggests you are not inwardly directing your speech in the manner required to speak to the whales. Is this analysis correct?"

"Yeah, I know," she said. "Shut up for now, okay?" She lifted the flashlight, tracing one of the catwalks with the beam. Nothing. "Wait, no. Tell me when the forcefield in the galley store room failed."

"The forcefield in the galley store room is still active," the computer replied. "Kim, it is almost time for your report to Edgeward Station."

"The forcefield's still active? In its entirety? No gaps?"

"Yes, Kim."

Kim cursed and lowered the flashlight beam. As her breathing slowed and the pounding in her ears faded, she could hear only the monotonous sound of the engines and the thrumming of the Aquarium machinery.

She could wake the whales, she realized. She could ask them if they'd seen anyone come in, and if so, where he had gone. But she was reluctant to do that. The whales didn't pay much attention to anything outside the tanks, anyway. They only cared about her because of the Link, and even then, their attention was patchy.

Except for Adonai's, of course.

Was the computer getting false readings? Could Adonai have fed it untrue data? That would be a complex task, one even Kim would struggle with. Well, there was one way to find out—she could go back to Deck Five and check the forcefield.

She made her way back to the ramp, and shone her flashlight into every recess it could reach, cross-sectioning the vast area—to no avail. There was no hint of movement, nothing to say there was anyone down here but herself. She quickened her step, almost running back to Deck Five. She was sure that she'd find the bulkhead ripped apart, a service hatch popped open, but the hallway was clear, the wall intact. She stopped in front of the door to the store room.

Adonai stood in the middle, shoulders slumped, head tilted forward. He looked exactly as he had when she left him. A chill washed over Kim, starting at her head and reaching out from her toes. "Adonai," she said. "Have you left this room?"

Adonai lifted his head, seeming to come back to life. Kim could hear the soft whine of servos as motors powered back up. "No, Kim," he said. "I have stayed here, as you asked."

Could he be lying? It was possible, but she didn't think so. He'd have to have moved very quickly, and get himself back here before she'd arrived. That, in addition to having deactivated and reactivated the forcefield without the computer's knowledge. Besides which, Adonai had never lied to her.

Kim glanced aside, trying to get control of herself. It wasn't like her to be so jumpy, to feel so much fear. Adrenaline was coursing through her veins and she felt wide awake, ready to run, to fight. But there was nothing to fight—except her own mind.

"Adonai," she said. "You said you'd been in the droid for less than a day before I found you. Are you certain?"

"The droid tells me it has been active for twenty-one hours," Adonai replied. "There is a battery life indicator that reads across the top left of my vision. That is what it says."

Again, it could be a lie . . . but Kim didn't think so. God, her head hurt! She lifted a hand and wiped her forehead. Cold sweat smeared across her wrist.

"Then it couldn't have been you," Kim said.

"What could not have been me?"

"I saw a man," she replied, her voice dropping to a whisper. "Perhaps a woman—I'm not sure, now. On the ramps. He was watching me on the day I came down to see you. The day we had the conversation about me going outside the ship, and you said you dreamt about the stars."

"I was at that stage working on my plan to download my mind," Adonai said. "I did not yet know if I could do it."

"It wasn't you," Kim repeated more softly. She glanced around her, unable to stop herself. It was as if her body expected the figure to be there, lurking in the corridor, having followed her up from Deck Twelve where she now realized she'd lost him. Or her.

"I will stay here as long as you like, Kim," Adonai said. "I will stay here forever, if that's what you ask."

Kim nodded vaguely and moved away from the door.

"Kim, it is now time to begin your ship wide analysis," the computer reminded her. "Please report to Deck One immediately."

"Coming," Kim said, before turning back to Adonai. She wanted to say something, but her mouth hung open, no sound coming out.

I am going crazy.

CHAPTER
7

Kim made her way up to Deck One, feeling off-balance and unsure of everything except one fact: she couldn't let word of this reach Captain Mbewe.

The Admiral would be on the lookout for any signs of strain or psychosis, especially if the computer sent out the counseling request as it had said it would. If one, even one tiny little thing, slipped through, command of *Seiiki* would be taken from her. They'd send out ships, or maybe even slave *Seiiki* to their own systems to guide her into dock. Someone else would take over for the remaining seventy-one days it would take to reach New Eden.

And worst of all, she'd have failed in her mission.

Not the mission Near Horizon had assigned to her, but her real purpose onboard *Seiiki*—as a Crusader operative.

She'd be a traitor to the cause—the Crusaders would have her killed before she could be put on trial, before she could be interrogated, before she could reveal their names and faces.

What would Zane say when he found out? He would hate her. He'd think she was weak. He was Martian, driven, intense in emotion and determination. He'd wish he'd never kissed a stupid girl like her ...

"God," she muttered to herself as the maglift continued upwards. "I'd be better off killing myself."

"Kim, I must also remind you of the need to take your mental health evaluation," the computer chimed in.

"Shut up, shut up, shut *up*." Kim pounded her fists on the maglift wall, the stainless steel answering with a mere metallic *clong*. "I don't need this right now!"

The computer, mercifully, was silent.

Kim stepped onto the bridge. She straightened her jumpsuit, then took a deep breath and began the routine, moving from console to console, letting the monotony of the familiar task take over her mind so she didn't have to think.

When the time came for her contact with Edgeward, she felt a good deal calmer. She faced the holoprojection of the man's greyed-out face with a cool expression.

"Anything to report?" the Admiral asked.

Was he looking at her more closely than usual? Kim wasn't sure how much of her pallor showed on his holoprojection of her. His own flickered on and off momentarily before stabilizing, ashen-toned, his eyes still as intense as ever.

"Nothing unusual, sir. I'm sending through the data packets now."

Please, she thought. Let that be it. Sign off now, before I say something wrong.

"Ms. Monksman," Admiral Mbewe added after a second's pause.

Kim shifted on her feet, then forced herself to stand still. *Don't show your guilt.* It was the first rule Constantin have ever taught her. "Yes, sir?"

"You're doing extremely well with this task. I'm impressed, given your age. Keep up the good work, eh?"

Kim felt only shock. Not once in ninety-three days had Admiral Mbewe offered a word of praise. She should have been pleased, but instead she felt suspicious. Why now? Had he noticed something in her reports? In her face? He must have seen the request for counseling that the computer had made. It would have been blinking red at the top of the transmission. So why the encouragement, and not a reprimand?

"Thank you, sir," she said, but he'd already terminated the communication link. Kim was left staring into empty air.

"Kim, you are again exhibiting sings of anxiety," the computer said.

Kim's fingers were clenched on the back of one of the chairs, she realized. She'd been holding it in a grip so hard she'd ripped through the polyester, exposing a small half-moon of yellow padding.

"I'm fine," she said. "I'm ... tired. I think I'll go to bed, computer."

Thankfully, the computer offered no protest.

CHAPTER
8

The alarm was blaring. It had intruded on Kim's dream, and she had the feeling it had been going off for quite some time before she'd awoken. Drowsily, she rubbed her eyes and sat up.

And then everything crashed in on her.

It had been three days since she'd found Adonai in the mess. She'd been avoiding the store room since, even taking the maglift to Deck Four, walking along, and taking a service hatch down to approach the mess from the opposite end of the hallway so she didn't have to pass the door and see him inside.

She knew he still hadn't moved. After her scare the other day, she'd called up camera footage of the store room and found no sign of tampering on the video that showed him standing, slightly slumped, in the center of the room, unmoving, for hours and hours.

She dressed mechanically, deliberately avoiding looking in the mirror. She couldn't face her own face today. It was as she was pulling on her boots that the computer chimed.

"I have an incoming transmission from Edgeward Station."

Kim's mouth went dry. "Oh, crap." She reached up to smooth her hair before remembering she didn't have any. Her fingers touched the smooth skin of her scalp instead, feeling the faint ridged lines of the Link. "Okay. Just a second. I'll be up on Deck One in two minutes." She straightened the collar of her jumpsuit and hoped she'd managed to wash the sleep from her eyes before she exited the room quickly and hurried for the maglift.

Her heart was pounding in her ears. What could this be about? Had something happened? Had one of her reports been brought up as suspicious, or had the Admiral somehow gotten wind of what had happened with Adonai? Damn it, was she about to lose everything?

She strode onto Deck One and purposefully pulled out the chair behind the comm desk and sat. The droids whirring in the background made her feel less alone, at least, as she drew the kanji for "talk" on the back of her hand.

"This is Hannah Monksman," she said, pleased that her voice sounded steady.

"Hannah, hi." A woman's face shimmered into three dimensions ahead of her. She had blonde hair that was cut severely short, but her eyes were kind. "I'm Mona White. I'm the counselor aboard Edgeward Station."

Kim felt an unpleasant mixture of relief and panic. She had hoped the Admiral would ignore the computer's request, hoped that she'd get away with it, at least for now. But no. She'd had it too easy, the past few months; being alone on the ship, she'd been able to keep to herself the majority of the time. It had been so nice not to have to pretend, to only have to deal with the reports to the Captain and her stupid transmission for the Ark Project fans back on Earth. Now she'd have to wend her way through another web of lies.

"No, no, don't feel bad," the woman said. "I can see it on your face. Hannah, this isn't the end of the world. God knows I've counseled 70 percent of the people on this station at least once! It's why I'm out here."

Kim nodded. "I don't think I really need counseling," she ventured.

"That's usually a sure sign that you do. Look, we all think we're strong and capable, and most of the time, we are. But you're a young woman, and you've got a huge responsibility—"

"I was chosen for this," Kim reminded her.

The woman held up a hand, which came into view just below her chin. "Yes, yes, I know. But life in space is hard to deal with, and all the training in the world doesn't help humans adapt to an environment we weren't born in and can't navigate without assistance."

Kim kept her mouth shut. Inside, she was fuming. She *had* been trained for this. She knew what she was getting into, and dammit, she could *do* this. If people would just leave her alone!

She heard a clamoring voice in her mind.

Kim, Kim, Kim, it's all right. A rush of love and affection enveloped her, and the sharp edges of panic were rubbed away. *Be calm, be still . . .*

She let the calm wash over her, feeling guilty. Her anger had been creeping outwards, and had resonated through the Link. It was Levi and Hosea channeling this new strength into her, this serenity; for an instant, she was with them, floating in the blue-black depths, weightless and content.

"I know it's early in the morning for you, so I won't keep you too long. I'm sure you've got lots to do. So today, we'll just go through the preliminaries. Have you been feeling lonely?"

"No," Kim replied instinctively. Then, rethinking it, she said "Yes." If she could keep the woman's focus on feelings of loneliness, she could avoid her probing too deeply about things Kim could not talk about—namely a rogue whale and an imprisoned tech droid. "Not all the time. There's the—"

"The Link, of course. The whales. But they're not real company, are they?"

"No," Kim said, while thinking *God, they are!*

"So, that's a good start. Acknowledging issues is the first step toward fixing them. Let me ask you this. Do you miss your colleagues?"

Kim almost spluttered. "You mean Wren and Yoshi?"

"And perhaps even Abdiel," Mona said with a nod.

"No. They weren't my colleagues. They were—"

"You still socialized almost exclusively with them for the better part of a year. It would be normal to feel some connection."

Kim nodded slowly, trying to think of the right thing to say. "I miss Abdiel. He was nice."

Mona continued to nod. "Of course. He was the favorite of a lot of people. Many had him picked to win on personality alone."

She didn't want to hear about it. What had happened to Abdiel was a shame, and she always felt a spike of anger when she thought on it too long. "And . . . I miss Wren. A little."

"Of course. There were many pictures of you two together."

"We weren't *together*," Kim said immediately. She waited a beat, but Mona said nothing, so she added, "I don't miss Yoshi."

Mona laughed. "I imagine not. She was your closest competitor."

"She's just not . . . a nice person."

The words sounded childish, true as they were. Yoshi had been belligerent from the moment Kim had first met her, and had gone out of her way to make Kim into an enemy. Her following mostly consisted of people who thought the project should be under control of a science agency rather than Near Horizon.

They'd still been a large portion, if the stats on Daywatch were to be believed.

"We can talk more on that subject later," Mona promised. "Now, the computer reported that you've begun talking to yourself. This isn't uncommon, and it's not alarming, or dangerous. What it is, is your brain working in a perfectly ordinary way. You're used to having input from others. Speaking to others, taking comm calls, watching holovideo or just hearing pedestrians on the path outside your house." Her voice was nice, Kim thought. She had an accent—what was it? Finnish, or Norwegian. Something European. "Talking to yourself fills that void when you're alone, and it's another form of input that helps you make sense of your surroundings. I could go on, but for now, we won't class it as anything to worry about. The loneliness, however, is something I'd like to speak to you about. While not concerning in itself, it can lead to more damaging trains of thought or behavior patterns."

"Right," Kim said. She wanted to tell the woman that she wasn't lonely. She had the whales with her at all times! And there were her talks with Zane . . . which of course, she couldn't mention. She bit her tongue.

"Now, you haven't been having any hallucinations, have you?"

"No," Kim replied, careful not to answer too quickly. Mona didn't bat an eyelid. Damn. She couldn't read this woman at all. Was she buying Kim's lies? She was supposed to be a trained psychologist, supposed to be able to tell when people weren't being truthful, wasn't she? Maybe not. Perhaps Kim had seen too many holovision dramas, where the psychologist uncovers deep-seated fears and reveals them like a poker dealer turning playing cards face-up. Perhaps she was remembering how it felt to be inside a cell in the police station, trying to convince a Detective Sergeant she hadn't been in the area, she hadn't been taking stims, she didn't know anything about the drugs, the stolen aircar, the high-speed chase the night before . . .

"That's good. Given your psychological profile, you seem very capable, but I want you to keep an eye out for things of this nature, okay? Anything that seems . . . out of the ordinary. Your mind playing tricks on you. Strange things happening with your vision, or unexpected moods or sensations, or hearing voices that aren't there, okay?" Mona smiled. "Difficult in your case, I know. The Link is quantum tech, relatively new, and some of what it does still isn't fully understood. It can make it hard to sort out your own perceptions from those of the whales. But I used to work in a mental health institution, so I know how those things work. I wasn't Linked myself, but some of my colleagues were. It was often tough for them to sort through the information coming through from their patients."

"Yes, I know. But it's different, with the whales." Kim said fervently, wanting Mona to understand. It *was* different. The Link, the whales, they weren't a burden. They were something beautiful and wondrous. "I don't mind it. It's like . . . " she stopped, struggling to think. She fell back on what she'd told the Ark Project fans during her last transmission. "It's like being a friend, only your friends are in the next room and you can wave at them through a window. You know they'll still be there, even though you can't touch them."

Another rush. This time, a burst of bubbling gratitude and thankfulness. Some of the whales had sensed what she'd said, and had responded in kind.

"That's lovely," Mona said, and she sounded like she meant it. "I think that's enough for today. Get some breakfast and start your day, okay, Hannah? I'll speak to you again next week."

"Okay," Kim said as she signed off, leaning back in her chair. God. Well, it seemed she'd passed that test, at least. She found herself shaking a little from the adrenaline, but it was exhilaration she felt, not fear, as she left Deck One.

That soaring feeling, the conviction that everything was going to work out after all, was what took her back to Deck Five—not to breakfast, as Mona had suggested, but to look into the store room next to the mess. Adonai was still there, just as she'd left him. She couldn't tell if it was the droid's sensors or the whale's senses that alerted him to her arrival, but he lifted his head, fixing her with those golden orbs.

"Hello, little one with long fins," he said. "Have you come to let me out?"

Kim looked at him evenly. "I still can't do that, Adonai. You know that."

"No, I don't." He sounded a bit like a sulky child who'd been sent to the naughty corner. "I don't like it in here, Kim. I did what I did because I wanted to see and experience things."

"I know," Kim replied. His tone touched her much more deeply than she'd have liked. "Look, I'm sorry this is the way it has to be. But it's for your own safety as well as the safety of the ship."

"No, it's not." Those eyes bore into hers, unblinking, unwavering, refusing to let her off the hook. His speech was improving with every sentence, Kim noted. It was making it hard to think of him as a whale. "You're a Caretaker, little one. You're supposed to look after me."

"You're not the only whale aboard this ship," she explained. "And I can't put you above any of the others. Or myself. If *Seiiki* fails, we'll all die."

"Why do you think I would hurt the ship?" Adonai's voice was wounded. How was that possible? The tech droids' vocal processors weren't made to carry inflection. They were only meant to relay basic information as quickly as possible. She'd never even heard one speak in a full sentence to her before now.

"It might not be intentional," she told him, "but you don't know how things work here. I found you in the galley cooking food, Adonai. You might just as easily have activated a control junction and shut down the engines. Or life support, or the aeration controls for the tanks."

"I wouldn't do that," he repeated stubbornly.

Kim sighed. "Look, I don't know that, okay? I can't see the future. I can't know that you won't get curious, or try to do something to help and access the wrong system. Besides which . . . Adonai, do you have any idea what would happen if anyone *knew* what you've done?"

Adonai lifted his head. "No. What?"

"Even I don't know!" Kim spread her arms. "It's never been done before. No one even thought it was possible! The Link was made to translate for you, so that a human being could monitor your health and wellbeing, and make sure you survived this journey. It was only proven that you could use it to 'speak' with us about a year before the Ark Project was finalized. That's four years after the whole project was approved for funding and had the green light to go ahead. It was purely accidental, and there are still things about that which can't be explained. Is it a mixture of the emotions and sensations you're feeling at the time that the human mind translates into words? Or is it an actual translation, like hearing Japanese and rearranging the words into an English sentence? The fact is, we don't know. Quantum tech is still too new. There are scientists on Earth right now still trying to figure that out."

Adonai brightened, lifting his slumped shoulders, and tilting his chin upwards. "I could help them!"

"No!" Kim barked. She paced to the left, then the right. "I'm sorry, Adonai, but you can't. They *can't* know about you."

"Why not?"

"Do you always have to ask why? God!" She stopped pacing and squared her own shoulders. "All right. You want to know? This is it, Adonai. This is the truth. They'll scrap the mission. You'll go straight back to Earth—all the whales will. You'll live the rest of your lives in those tanks in Yokohama instead of the oceans of New Eden. That's if you're lucky." She met his gaze, trying to convey the seriousness of her statements. "If you're not, they'll carve you up and see what makes you so special, Adonai. You're the only one, of all the whales, who managed to do this. They're going to find out how, and why, you were able to. If that means giving you a lobotomy—taking out pieces of your brain while you're still alive and breathing—believe me, they'll do it."

Adonai was silent. His golden eyes grew slightly dimmer. For a long time, he stood there, and Kim stood opposite him, separated only by the occasional ripple of blue forcefield energy. She felt bad—terrible, in fact. Her heart felt knotted. She cared for Adonai, and she had only told him part of the truth, but it was a *real* truth. He had to know what kind of danger he was in.

"Near Horizon would not allow it." A full minute had passed before Adonai said this. Kim was about to leave, the weight of that day's duties pressing down on her.

"Near Horizon believes you're worth saving," Kim replied slowly. "They do. But they won't be able to contain a secret like this. And honestly, I can't vouch for them, either. They might have started out as a non-for-profit, but they're not any longer. They went into this as

a commercial venture. That's what they do. Not that I blame them—
the money to do things, even good things, has gotta come from somewhere. They know how to get it. But what if they decide they can use
the money *you* could bring in—an actual talking whale they could
lock up in a tank and charge people to see—could go toward re-ter-
raforming Central America, or cleaning up the atom bomb sites in
Russia and the Middle East? Or could go toward curing one of the
new cancers that have been found? Or toward funding a food production colony on Ganymede, or exploring the Earth-like worlds in the
Ephraim System, or carrying refugees to Mars, or Naphtali or God
knows what other pies they've got their fingers in?"

"I don't understand what pies are," Adonai said.

Kim huffed. "The point is, you'd be the one who pays the price.
Even if they let the rest of the mission happen, you, Adonai, would
be taken back to Earth. You'd live the rest of your life in a tank, if you
were lucky. And I—" Kim's voice finally broke, unexpectedly. "I'd never be let near you again."

She couldn't feel him in the Link, not the way she could feel the
others, but she saw this hit home. He looked aside, his gaze meeting
the walls. "I think I understand now, little one with long fins."

"Good. Don't forget it." The tightening in her throat made the
harsh words even harsher. "So you know now why you need to go
back."

"Go back," he repeated the words as if testing them out. "Go back
where?"

"To your body."

"This is my body." He stretched out his metallic arms, as if this
proved it.

"I mean your body as a whale," she said, impatiently. "You have to
transfer your consciousness back in there."

He looked confused, as if that had never occurred to him. "But I don't know how."

This was what Kim was afraid of. "Whatever you did to get yourself out—well, just do the opposite."

"I'm not sure I can." He sounded hesitant, and slightly . . . afraid?

"You *do* know how," Kim said firmly. "Or you will. You spent time figuring this out, right? All you've gotta do is rework the process."

"But it's different." The fear was growing stronger, and his body showed it through his fidgeting feet. "It's very different. I was able to make it out because I understood the way the droid worked. I knew its language, and its functions, and . . . there was a pathway to follow. The Link."

The Link. Oh, God. Kim lifted a hand to her head. She could feel a headache starting, a tightening across her temples. Of course. Adonai's flesh-and-blood body had been connected to the Link. Once he'd transferred himself through the computer and into the droid, he had no such connection to bridge the gap back to his body. The Linking process was complicated, and while Kim had the tools and equipment to repair and fine-tune most errors with the Link, she had no experience in installing one. And a droid, not having a brain, couldn't use a Link anyway. "You don't have the Link anymore."

He shook his head slowly. "I admit, I knew this would be the case. It didn't stop me."

"It should have!" Kim burst out. "Of all the stupid, *stupid* things to do, Adonai!"

Shamefaced, he looked away from her and shuffled his feet some more. His gestures and motions—they were so damn *human.* She didn't know how it was possible, since the droid itself had no programming in that area. Perhaps it was something that just came naturally, along with having arms and legs and an upright posture.

Kim turned away, shaking her head. This was too much; she couldn't think on it any longer, or she'd go insane. More insane than she already was.

"I'm going to do my work." It was all she could manage to say, now.

"You'll come back, though?" Adonai's voice was hopeful.

Kim sighed. "Yes. I suppose I'll have to."

CHAPTER
9

Kim ate sparingly, another boring, tasteless soup made from pow-
der, then strapped on her toolbelt. She was scheduled to check
on the fisheries, and this was Kim's least favorite of all tasks.

The fisheries were accessed through a door between Decks Nine
and Ten. She took the ramp to reach it, steeling herself against any
possible visions of men/women. If she saw anything, she would ignore it, she decided. A mirage couldn't hurt her or the ship.

But she saw nothing, of course. Scanning the depths with her
flashlight, she breathed a sigh of relief. Perhaps Mona's session had
helped her after all, and from now on, she'd have an uneventful
journey.

Well, save for the problem of Adonai.

I cannot rouse Adonai, Hosea broke into her thoughts, as if reading her own mind.

"I know," Kim replied softly.

He's just floating there. He stares, doesn't move, even when I dive right past him. And he won't talk to me through the Link. He's never been like this.

"Adonai is . . . " Kim thought this through, trying to come up with an explanation that wouldn't alarm Hosea—or give her any ideas of her own. Kim didn't think the Southern right whale would be able to do what Adonai had. She didn't think she had the intellect Adonai had. But still, it had happened once, and that meant it could happen again. Kim did not want a ship populated by walking whales. "He's ill."

Ill? Hosea began to panic. *Oh no! What if I catch it? What if we all catch it?*

"It's not that kind of sickness," Kim said firmly. Oh, crap. Hosea was broadcasting her feelings through the Link, and the others were picking up on it. Kim began to feel fluctuations of fear in her own chest. She forced herself to calmness. The last thing she needed was to add the whale's anxiety to her own. "You can't catch it."

Are you sure? How can you be sure?

Adonai is ill? Tobias asked. *He doesn't smell ill!*

How can we help him?

Should we sing to him?

We should sing. We should sing.

Fifteen will not get ill. Fifteen is healthy. Look at him swim!

Bad things are happening. This is just one of them.

This last thought was dark, accompanied by a deep bitterness. It was Hosea who thought this, Kim found as she traced the voice. She stopped walking, and leaned against a wall as the feeling of dark, seething anger washed through her, but faded just as quickly.

"Hosea?" she said.

But Hosea refused to speak, pushing herself down into the smallest space the Link allowed, where Kim could only feel that she had not eaten well on her last meal, and was hungry and agitated.

Great. Now she'd have to tune Hosea, on top of everything else!

Kim continued on her way. The fisheries were, by necessity, difficult to reach; their delicate machinery was shrouded in protective layers of lead-lined bulkheads and their own airlock doors. The reason for this was that the entire success of the mission rested on not the whales, but the fish and the plankton.

If the food source failed on the journey to New Eden, there would be no hope for the whales. They'd all perish of starvation before reaching the planet.

Kim stopped in the alcove outside her chosen entrance. There were racks here, three protective white plastic jumpsuits hanging from coat hooks, and plastic boots made out of rubber. She pulled them on over her own jumpsuit and re-buckled her toolbelt over the top, then keyed in the code to access the airlock. The keypad beeped at her, lighting up blue, and fighting a hiss of rushing air, she slipped inside as quickly as she could and allowed the door to clamp shut behind her.

The space beyond was a small chamber. "Please stand still while decontamination procedures are undertaken," the computer intoned.

"I've done this before," Kim grumbled, rolling her eyes. "Around thirty times, actually."

"It never hurts to have a reminder, Kim."

She stood still while more blue lights flashed, this time cleansing ultraviolet rays, wiping away every trace of external bacteria. To her right, another rack held face masks, and she pulled one over her nose and mouth, then stepped through another door covered by hanging plastic flaps onto a metal walkway that ringed an enclosed circular pool of water.

Unlike the water in the tanks, this didn't glow blue. It was a greenish color, because it wasn't exposed to the halogen lamps, and because of the algae that built up on the tank walls. The algae weren't harmful, and in fact were a food source for the fish. Their own waste products help fertilize it, so, unlike the whale's tanks, this was a self-sustaining system. Still, there were aspects that had to be monitored, and Kim made her way down a narrow set of stairs, skipping and sliding on the handrails out of habit rather than any need for speed. The inner ledge was a circle just below the level of the tank's top, which was sealed, just like the whale's tanks. It wouldn't do any good to have an open-topped tank if the gravity generator fritzed out.

She walked around it to the junction station, which looked just like all the others on the ship. She could check the readings from Deck One, of course, but it was better to get a visual of the dials and valves which were the manual back-up systems. Just in case.

Control of the water quality was crucial for maintaining healthy fish. Fertilizing, clarifying, and adjusting the pH of the water made sure the fish could breed happily and healthily, and increased yields substantially. There was also a need to prevent eutrophication (when too many nutrients entered the water, or weren't consumed fast enough by the fish), and make sure oxygen levels stayed high. Fish would suffer from electrolyte stress and grow ill if anything was out of balance.

The tanks were shared with other marine life—copepod plankton, krill, and the thick mud at the bottom was a breeding ground for the mud-dwelling benthic amphipods. The fish was of various types—herring, sand lance, and capelin for the baleen whales, surgeonfish, kelpfish, yellowtail, cardinalfish—or at least, approximations of these species, since the original genetics had been somewhat muddied over the past few decades.

Kim didn't like looking at the fish. Unlike the whales, these creatures were dull-eyed, lackluster things with trailing fins and a sense of awkward grace that spoke of what they'd once been, before the genetic tampering. She remembered her meal of *Sous Vide Salmon on a bed of Shitake Mushrooms, Rocket, with a Brown Butter Jus,* which she'd eaten at a grand restaurant in Chicago when Abdiel had convinced her and Wren to leave their training for one night and have a good time. The way the greyish flesh had squished under her knife. She wasn't used to eating meat that didn't come from a can or on a burger bun, and on top of the Brut it had made her stomach roil. She'd eaten enough to be polite, but neither Wren nor Abdiel seemed to notice or care that her $89 meal had been left in ragged tatters all around her plate.

The fish seemed to know she was there, however. They swam to the wall of the tank and stared out at her, goggle-eyed.

"Go away," she murmured as she checked over the dial. The PH was a little low, but everything else looked good. She moved to the junction station and tapped the acidity indicator, watching as the yellow numbers changed to a more acceptable level.

That done, she moved to the opposite side of the tank, where the pipes led out into the Aquarium. A set of gates inside would periodically open, letting roughly 80,000 pounds of fish through into the whale's tank every day. The pipes were clear, the pressure that would push the fish gently into the Aquarium at optimum.

"Computer, everything looks good."

"I have noted that in the log, Kim. However, I think you may need to check on the engines today. There is something of note that will need to be visually sighted."

Kim pulled herself back up the ladder. "What is it?"

"Nothing to be alarmed about," the computer replied. "A valve in the fuel supply appears to be stuck."

"A valve? That shouldn't happen."

"Backup procedures are running now. As I said, it's not urgent, but I would advise a visual inspection before sending a droid in the repair it."

Kim nodded. "Yeah, why not."

She hated going down to the engines. Not as much as the fisheries, but close. It was dirty, close and hot on Deck Fifteen. She wished she could just send in a droid, but that would be cutting corners, and that was something she'd never in her life been able to bring herself to do.

With a sigh, she peeled off the plastic suit and the boots, then the mask, and dumped them in the decontamination chest just outside the door. The autobots would re-hang them when they were done.

She entered the spiraling ramp once more and began her descent. Again, nothing jumped out at her from the shadows, no strange figures lurked in the distance. She began to hum to herself, another of Constantin's wild, pounding rhythms.

"Computer," she began, as she rounded another pylon, "play—"

A sudden lurch of the deck threw her off her feet. The gravity that would have anchored her on Earth was lessened enough for her 112-pound body to smack into the pylon with a good deal of force. Kim felt the air rush out of her lungs long before she felt the pain of the impact.

Crap!

The ramp swayed under her as she dropped to her hands and knees. Whatever was happening, it wasn't over yet. The entire ship reeled to one side, and she began to slip. Her fingers scrabbled at the surface of the deck plates for purchase, but the holes were too small for her to put her fingers through. She knew she was heading closer to the railing, and let out a pained squawk, all she could manage from her bruised lungs.

The whales were panicking.

Kim! Kim! Kim!

What's happening.

Can't see.

Everything's shaking.

The water, the water!

The fish are fleeing!

"Kim, I have detected unusual activity," the computer said. An alarm blared suddenly to life, and all the lights above the ramps suddenly brightened to full luminescence, making the place look glaring and two-dimensional, like cut-outs in a diorama.

Kim twisted her body, reaching out with one hand, preparing to grab at the railing as she slid past it. Her mind was already calculating the speed with which she'd need to take hold, the force with which she'd swing over the edge, and the possibility of neither measure being enough to keep her from plunging to her death in the chasm below. That's if she didn't hit one of the other ramps first.

Kim! Are you all right?

Are you injured?

What's happening, what's happening?

But just as her body reached the edge of the ramp, the ship shuddered and groaned, tilting back the other way. At first it felt like she was merely going to be thrown toward the opposite rail instead, but *Seiiki* mercifully evened out, and Kim found herself splayed on the floor gasping for breath.

"Computer," she wheezed, pulling an arm across her ribs, several of which felt broken, and tucking her knees under her. "Report."

"Gathering data. Please wait." A brief pause. "Status report: fire on the upper port engine nacelle. Repeat. Fire has been detected. Engines disengaged. Section quarantined."

Kim! Kim! Kim!

"Open the hatches," Kim gasped as she pulled herself to her feet. There was a junction station around here somewhere—where was it? She spied it just ahead, bolted to a pylon. In an emergency situation, junction stations came on automatically without the need for a kanji to activate them. Thank God. She didn't have to release the arm over her ribs to tap at the display. "Vent it, damn you!"

"Hatches are open. Fire is venting now."

A droid whizzed down at her, beeping in alarmed greeting. Kim groaned. A God-damned medbot was all she needed right now!

"I'm not injured," she told it, but the tentacled droid came at her anyway, hovering two feet in the air as it ran a scan over her, bleeping obscenely at what it found. "Treatment required," it intoned.

"No treatment," she told it. "I'm fine."

"Several injuries detected. Please lie back." The droid unfolded a hydraulic arm that spread out in a fan, creating a small, narrow stretcher.

"Get lost," Kim snapped. "I've got too much to do."

"Kim," the computer said, the tone of chastisement evident in its voice. "You are required to comply with the medbot's assessment."

"The medbot's wrong, computer. You want me laid up in bandages, or you want me to check out the damage on this thing?"

"Gathering data. Please—" the computer cut itself off. "There is no immediate requirement for a visual inspection. Please submit to the medbot."

"No. Computer, I'm in the middle of something. Shut the hell up for a moment."

Kim had finally got the display up for the camera on the upper port side. For a moment, what she saw confused her.

Nothing.

Well, not nothing, exactly.

She was looking down the side of the ship. Crisp and clear grey, reflecting the light of distant stars, she could make out each section of curved hull plating. It was a cigar-shaped torpedo of reinforced steel, arrowing into the blackness of space. She could see the name painted on its side. *Seiiki.*

"What the *fuck?*" She couldn't hold back the curse. She checked the display. *Upper Port Side, Rear Elevation,* it read in yellow lettering beneath the view. She toggled up the labels. Yellow lines appeared. *Drive vent. Access hatch 315. Intake valve.* Each of the words hovered over sections of the ship. The words *Engine nacelle* floated above it, at a distance that translated to a few feet above the hull. The line pointed at . . . nothing at all.

Kim, what's happening.

The shaking's stopped.

Are we all right?

"Computer," she said. "Show me the Upper Port Side, Rear Elevation."

The computer beeped. The display flickered, then came back just as it had been.

"Computer, this is not the upper port side," she said. "This is a different camera. It's facing forward. Toward the prow of the ship."

"This is the camera for the rear upper port side," the computer confirmed.

"That's insane. I'm looking at the *Seiiki's* name, for God's sake! You can't see the name from the camera mount of the rear upper side. It's set behind the halfway point, and facing rearwards!"

"This is the camera for the—" The computer hiccupped, cutting itself off. "Fire has been vented. Situation is under control. Initializing scans for damage. Please stand by."

Kim tapped the fingers of her free hand against her thigh. The ache in her chest was fading, but that could just be adrenaline. Her mind chewed over the problem frantically. It looked like the camera had been installed to face the front instead of the rear. But how could that happen? This was a multi-million-dollar ship. The pride and joy of Near Horizon and all Unificationists! There had never been a mission like this one—not in human history. There was no way someone would have let this slip past the Space Exploration Authority's inspections.

She brought up the controls to move the camera. She panned left, but the camera stopped before showing her the rear of the ship. She panned back the other way. No luck there, either. 180 degrees was all she got.

She tapped back, pulling up the rear uppermost camera. It showed the graceful tail fins of the ship, two pillars rising upwards a few hundred feet. The trail of smoky propellant was visible in a curved candle-flame shape beyond them. She moved the camera to the right in a sweep, but the angle of the ship's hull prevented her from seeing the port side. She could see trailing wisps of smoke, however, and was that a faint imprint of charred metal, just at the lip there?

Kim! Why aren't you speaking?

Please tell us everything's all right!

We're so worried.

Kim, Kim, Kim!

"Initial scans complete," the computer told her. "Damage is minimal. My analysis suggests that an undetected meteor struck the hull, puncturing one of the fuel storage units. The malfunction was caused by the fuel shut-off valve failing to initialize. The xenol ignited instead of being drawn back into the engine as the fail-safe should have ensured."

Kim sighed and felt herself relax. "You told me the fuel valve wasn't urgent."

"At the time, it was not." The computer hesitated for a beat longer than Kim expected. "This was my error."

"Right," she said. "I'm going down to check out the damage myself." She glared at the medbot, which waited with its bed still stretched out invitingly. Kim, however, had no desire to lie down. "I'll go to the infirmary afterwards. Then I want to take a look at that camera."

"There are no issues with any of the cameras."

Kim did not protest, but neither did she agree. Yes, the camera might have somehow slipped past the Authority's inspections. But why would it be reading forward sections of the ship as if they were engine parts? There was something majorly wrong with a camera that identified systems that were not there.

No. That was something that had to be looked at. Because the only way that could happen was if someone had done it deliberately. She just had no idea why.

CHAPTER
10

T hankfully, as the computer had said, the damage was minimal. The fuel cell had vented its precious cargo of xenol into space— but as each cell only contained a thirtieth of the methane-based fuel stores, and the engine itself manufactured more as it went, the loss of one cell's worth was not a major blow.

Still, Kim had to crawl through several hundred feet of tight, winding tubes before she could check it out herself. And with her ribs and her other injuries becoming rapidly more apparent the further she went into the constricted spaces, it was a hard task. She'd wrenched her arm badly, and her ribs hurt terribly with every breath. Still, she forced herself to go on.

If there was major damage and she didn't find it now, she could be dooming herself and the whales. Kim had managed to calm them, but she could still feel their unease coursing through her. "It's fine," she said to herself. "In the past, your ancestors would have lived through earthquakes. This was just like one of those."

But what if it happens again? What if it's worse next time?

"It's unlikely that a meteor would hit the ship without being detected." This was partly a lie; space was full of debris, dust sized, fist-sized, basketball-sized, and bigger. It was only the larger pieces that were any threat . . . usually. This one had been about the size of a human head, the type of which normally glanced off the hull without any problems. "This one was only small, and must have hit at precisely the right angle and velocity—just a fluke, really. It never would have damaged the life-support sections. We're too heavily shielded."

The damaged valve was repairable, she decided, looking it over with her flashlight clamped between her teeth. She couldn't examine the fuel cell itself without an EV suit or by using a tech droid, but the clear window in the tube's firewall showed that the hole was small. The meteor had glanced off rather than becoming lodged in the hull. It wouldn't take long to repair, and it was not an urgent job.

Kim made her way back to the ramp and began the slow climb back up to Deck Four, where the infirmary was. A ship with one passenger didn't require a formal sickbay, so this was just a room with a relaxation chair that offered massages—Kim had never tried it—and a few shelves full of medical equipment, creams, lotions, and pills. She tipped several painkillers into her hand and swallowed them dry, then grabbed a tablet scanner from a rack. She waved it over her chest. The readout showed bruising, but no fractures or breaks.

"Whatever," she said, disgusted not only with the results but with her own inability to cope with the pain. She'd broken ribs several times on various jaunts in her life, pre-Ark Project. They were listed in Hannah's medical file as "horse-riding accident, fall from monkey bars, speed-racing injury." In reality, the majority of them had been caused by getting the crap kicked out of her by someone she'd crossed, or someone bigger and stronger than her that either hadn't seen her gang tat—or someone that *had*, but had enough of a grudge against Constantin to risk his wrath by leaving her bleeding. She'd grown soft.

The tablet advised her to use one of the bone regenerators, and directed her to their locations. She waved the end over the left side of her chest and felt the repair begin to work. The pain faded little by little until it was the dull ache of a fortnight-old injury, then the regenerator shut off, informing her the major damage had been mended. Her body would have to heal the rest on its own time.

She did the same with her shoulder and the faint red marks that would become bruises on her shins. That done, she felt suddenly exhausted. "Computer, what are the chances of me going to bed right now?"

"You will have to wake for your report to Edgeward Station in two hours' time."

"Of course I will," she said with a sigh. There was no point in heading to her room to sleep. She would be too edgy, and it would only make things worse when she was pulled out of bed for her report.

But one thing was clear when she stood up—she wouldn't be doing any more work today. She ached all over, despite the regeneration, and she was woozy. Her head felt fuzzy, her thoughts blurred slightly at the edges. Suddenly, one flicker through her mind stood out amongst the rest: Adonai.

It began as a slight concern for his safety, probably egged on by the slight agitation she still felt coming through the Link from the Whales. She had checked the Link several times to make sure he hadn't been injured at all, and he did not appear to be. But the droid could have been damaged in the shaking of the ship. She made her way along the corridor to the maglifts and hit the button to take her down to Deck Five. As the maglift hummed into motion, another thought struck her. What if he had, somehow, been responsible for the valve malfunction? By the time she stepped into the corridor, she was almost certain of it. The timing was too perfect to be coincidental.

She stopped in front of the store room door, and saw the droid sitting on the floor by the wall. He raised his head when he saw her.

"Kim!" he exclaimed. "Thank the stars you're all right!"

What a strange expression he'd used. *Thank the stars.* Kim licked her dry lips. Something wet touched her face, and she lifted her hand, her fingers coming away tipped with blood. She must have missed a cut.

"You're hurt," he gasped, concerned. He stood, unfolding his body and hurrying toward the door, where he stopped just before the force field. "You've injured yourself."

"Don't worry," she replied. "I fixed the worst of it. This is just a bit of blood.

Adonai looked at her sincerely. "Kim—"

"Did you do this?" She asked him.

"I—I beg your pardon?"

"Did you tamper with the fuel valve? When you were wandering around the ship."

"Of course not," he said. He sounded genuinely shocked. "I didn't touch anything I didn't need to."

"How can I be sure of that?" Kim asked. "Because there's something else that's weird, too. There's a camera that's mounted incorrectly."

"I didn't touch anything," he replied. "I don't know what those things are, but they sound important. I promise you, I wouldn't have interfered with anything!"

He was pleading with her like a child accused of stealing the last biscuit. She fixed her gaze on him levelly, but couldn't hold it long. Her head was pounding, and her joints aching. She had to look away. "If you're lying to me . . . "

"I wouldn't!" Adonai protested frantically. "Please believe me. I can't lie. I don't know how."

Kim's gaze snapped back up to his. "You don't know how?"

Adonai shook his head slowly. "You've told me about lies. But have I ever told you one?"

Kim scoffed. "How about—" she waved a hand through the air, indicating the droid's body. "That?"

"That was not a lie," Adonai said softly. "It was a deception. But if you had asked me, at any time, if I was planning this, I would have told you. Lies are different. Deliberate. I understand how they work, but I can't seem to tell them. And I have tried. I attempted to lie to you on several occasions."

"You did?" Kim was astounded. She had known Adonai's intelligence was as much emotional as it was cognitive, but the extent had not quite registered. He had tried to lie. "Why?"

"I wanted to see what it was like. I wanted . . . to be . . . to see what it was like to be human."

Kim took a step backward, her shoulder blades meeting the bulkhead. She slid down until she was sitting on the floor, knees drawn up to her chest. She sighed and closed her eyes.

"Kim, are you all right?" Adonai said, anxiously. "Did I say something wrong?"

"No," Kim replied. "No." She lapsed into silence, staying where she was for a very long time.

CHAPTER
11

Kim woke with a start. Her body was ice-cold, her hands clenched into fists against her chest while she curled in on herself, unconsciously having sought the warmth of her own core.

A metallic taste in her mouth told her she'd slept for at least a few hours. The lights above her had dimmed almost to darkness. As she moved and stretched painfully, they flickered and brightened, but not to the full illumination of "daytime." She tapped out the kanji on her wrist for *time*. 0100. She'd been asleep for six hours.

She sat bolt upright suddenly, her body screaming at her in protest. She hadn't done her injuries any favor by sleeping on the deck plating, but that wasn't what concerned her.

"Crap. Mbewe."

Adonai gazed at her placidly through the curtain of the forcefield. "Is something wrong, Kim?"

"Yes." Kim tried to get her knees under her. Her right foot had gone numb. "Yes. Damn it. I've missed my check-in with Edgeward Station."

"Is that bad?"

"Yes. It's very bad." She stamped her right foot and felt the stabbing sensation of pins and needles. "Ah!" The sound was more frustration than pain. She hobbled two steps, then sagged against the wall.

"Do not injure yourself."

Kim slammed an open palm against the wall, in direct violation of Adonai's request. "Computer! Why didn't you wake me?"

"You appeared to be in need of sleep, Kim."

The cool, level tone had never sounded so condescending. "No! You're supposed to wake me up! How many comms have you gotten from Edgeward?"

"None," the computer said. "I sent through a comm stating that you were incapacitated."

"You *what?*" Kim screeched. She found her footing again. The pins and needles were still like hot lances through her foot, but she managed a few more steps toward the maglifts. "Why would you do that?"

"It was the truth. There was a fire aboard, Kim. You had to deal with it. In the process, you were injured. That is what I told Lieutenant Grand. He passed the message along to Admiral Mbewe, and I received a notification that you are to report to him when you are well enough. The Lieutenant asked that I convey his hopes that you will recover from your minor injuries quickly."

"I bet he does," Kim muttered. Ben Grand was not her staunchest supporter. "Damn it. Can I comm them now?"

"It would be acceptable. The time aboard Edgeward will be 2200 hours."

Kim staggered into a maglift and made her way to Deck One. However, despite everything, she felt a sense of calm descend over her as she slid into the seat at the comm desk and drew the kanji for *talk*. She tapped the icon for Edgeward.

When Admiral Mbewe's face appeared, she didn't move it to the screen, but kept it before her. She leaned forward, filling her mind with calming thoughts, and told herself that everything would be fine.

"Hannah!" he exclaimed with more emotion than she'd ever heard in his voice. "I'm very glad to see you. We've been waiting for your contact."

"I'm sorry, sir," Kim replied. "I—"

"Never mind the apologies. You're all right?" His eyes were full of real concern, and Kim found herself taken aback somewhat.

Touched, she replied "A little stiff and sore. But I'll be fine."

"Good, good," he replied. "It wouldn't do to see our bright and shining Hannah Monksman incapacitated. I was getting ready to send out a scout ship. Would you like me to do so?"

Kim's eyes widened. "No," she said, then, aware that the real Hannah would not be refusing so quickly, added "It's really not necessary, sir. I've had medical treatment and I'm well enough."

"That's good to hear," he replied. "But keep it in mind. I can have someone out there in a couple of days if need be."

Kim nodded, her gaze sliding to one side. "I'm sending across the data packets now, sir."

Mbewe's head lifted. "Ah. Always got your mind on the job, haven't you?" He gave a little chuckle. Kim felt her brows furrowing just a little. This was another side altogether of the man who'd been so gruff and demanding for the three months she'd been reporting to him. She didn't mind it at all. "You could have a career in the military with dedication like that."

Kim smiled ironically. "I don't think so," she said. If only he knew. If any hint of Kim's history found its way into his purview, he'd be locking her in his brig and throwing away the key. Or, more likely, shoving her out of an airlock. "I've kind of chosen my path."

"So you have," he replied. "And you'll do it well. But have you thought about your future? After your contract with Near Horizon runs out, that is. Once the base on New Eden is up and running . . . there are very real options for you, Hannah. We're going to be working closely with the scientists out there. You'd have opportunities you wouldn't otherwise have. You could travel further afield. There are other systems that haven't even begun to be explored—not just Ephraim. Someone like you would be an asset."

Kim was so shocked at hearing this she almost laughed out loud. Admiral Mbewe, offering *her* a position as a . . . what? A space explorer? It was like a little kid's game of pretend. Kim had no illusions that it would ever come true, but damn, it was nice to think someone trusted her, saw in her someone who could be that person.

He doesn't know you, she told herself. He knows Hannah. Kim would disappoint him, and you know you can't keep up this charade forever . . .

"Admiral," she said suddenly. "This ship. *Seiiki*. It passed all the SEA checks, didn't it?"

Mbewe nodded. "That it did, with flying colors. The Space Exploration Authority doesn't let anything fly that hasn't been thoroughly vetted. *Seiiki* is completely watertight." His expression turned quizzical. "Is this about the fuel tank issue? I can assure you, it was a mishap that couldn't have been avoided. The valve failed, yes, but there was nothing that could have been done to prevent it."

Kim schooled her features to hide what she was really asking. *Did you know about the camera?* She tried not to look like she was staring at him, but she was examining him closely, looking for a chip in his armor, a glimmer that he might have known more than he was letting on. He was being overly nice to her. Could she really trust him?

It was hard to tell on the holoprojection. It was easier to hide things when you were hidden behind that greyish patina of flickering light. She ought to know.

"Well, good luck, Hannah. You're now twelve days out from us. I look forward to shaking your hand in person."

"Me too, sir," she said before signing off and collapsing back in her chair.

Twelve days. She had twelve days to figure out what to do with Adonai.

Good morning, Earth! This is Hannah Monksman! I've got a few things to tell you. You've probably all heard by now about the minor incident with one of the fuel tanks on board. I can assure you—it was minor! Reports of my death have been wildly exaggerated, because, as you see, I'm perfectly healthy and intact.

The whales were frightened. Fifteen, in particular. Poor guy! He didn't understand what was happening at first, and it took me two days to calm him down enough to eat a decent meal. I was pretty worried about him for a bit. But that's one of the issues—some of the whales simply don't understand things outside their immediate perception. Space, to most of them, is just as foreign a concept as growing legs and walking around on land. I think they forget, a lot of the time, exactly where they are. It's not unexpected, because they have few reminders. They can't call up a junction display and take a look outside, can they? She added a laugh, a silly, giddy little laugh that made Kim sick to her stomach when she heard it coming from her own mouth.

Still, it's all good for now. The damage is minimal and I've got tech bots working on it. In the meantime, here's a fun fact about Orcas, commonly known as Killer Whales, even though they're not actually whales at all, but dolphins. They can't smell! How weird is that? The Orca has very good sight and hearing, and that's how they track their prey. What a shame we couldn't rescue any of them, huh? Along with all other dolphins, they were hunted into extinction. The last sighting of one was in 2034, and those in captivity didn't produce any offspring that lived longer than two years. It's so terrible. With the Link, who knows what else we might dis-cover?

This is Hannah Monksman, signing off on July 9, 2078.

Kim finished the recording and tilted herself back on the bed. She was too tired to change out of her clothes and into her pajamas. She pulled the gravity blanket up over her shoulders, but despite her weariness, she couldn't go to sleep yet.

She pulled her tablet under the covers with her and drew the kanji for *secret*.

"Manta Protocol activated," the tablet told her and the blue circle appeared, telling her a connection was being made.

"Hey," she said as Zane's face flickered onto the screen.

"Hey yourself," he replied. He had something in his hands that he was fiddling with, out of her view. Some device or other. She could see the top of a soldering iron dancing along the bottom edge of her screen. "How are you?"

"I'm fine. You don't have to worry. I wasn't injured badly, and the fuel cell is being repaired."

"Yeah, I know." He sounded dismissive, and Kim felt a little put out at that. Didn't he care? Hadn't he been waiting for her call, biting his nails, worried about her for the five days since they'd last spoken, with only second-hand reports of her safety to allay his fears? She'd looked forward to putting his mind at ease, but it seemed it was unnecessary. "Those fuel valves have been known to fail. Unfortunately, we don't have any alternative tech yet."

"Well, anyway," she said, aware that her tone was frosty. "I'm fine. How are you?"

"Good!" he replied, looking up at her with a grin. Kim's heart melted a little at the way his eyes lit up. He leaned in closer to the screen, but his head tilted down. He was still concentrating on whatever it was he was working on. "Listen. I've heard from Grigorian. He's so pleased with your progress, Kim. You're a hero in the Crusaders' eyes."

"Everyone keeps telling me how well I'm doing," Kim grumped, but she was secretly pleased.

Zane's head snapped up at this, his eyes narrowing. The smile was gone, snapping out of existence like a light being switched off. "Wait. Who else?"

"Admiral Mbewe. The Edgeward counselor, Mona. What, no one believed I could do this?"

"Oh, no one doubts you," Zane corrected. "But come on, Kim. You're a seventeen-year-old. I don't think *I* could have done what you're doing at your age."

"They think I'm nineteen," she reminded him.

"Yeah, of course. Still. It's a weighty task for anyone to undertake. You get that, right?"

"Of course I do. I wouldn't have signed up otherwise!" Kim tapped her fingers impatiently. "But—Zane. I still don't even know what it is I've signed up *for*."

"You know I can't tell you that just yet."

"You say that again and again. When will you be able to tell me? Do I have to wait until I've reached New Eden? Because I'd rather be prepared if you're going to—I don't know, hand the whales over to the Crusaders."

"Is that what you think is going to happen?" he asked. His eyes were off to the side, and it wasn't just the displacement of his tablet lens, either. He was avoiding her gaze deliberately. It made her feel both annoyed and self-conscious. Did he really not trust her?

"Yes," Kim said, with a modicum of certainty. "I think you're going to have people waiting to take over the facilities. I think you're going to set up a cordon and claim the planet for your own. I think that's what Grigorian would want—control of the project. He wants to make a statement against Morosini. Well, I can make that happen, you know. People *like* me." She tossed her head before she remembered she didn't have hair any longer. The gesture probably looked silly. "I've got transmissions running to millions of people in the Sol System—and in the colonies, too. I can get public support on your side."

As if sensing this conversation was moving into territory Zane didn't want to go, he put his soldering iron aside. "Remember that night on Ganymede?"

Kim felt a warm tingle begin in her belly and rush down her thighs. She knew exactly what he was talking about.

"We sat under one of the crystal domes and looked out at the stars, and you said—"

"I could live amongst the stars forever." Kim filled it in for him. "I meant it. God! I grew up in a city where you were lucky if you saw Mars behind the streetlights. Seeing them like that, on Ganymede, all lit up and crisp, all day long, all night, just *all the time* . . . "

"It was after the reception, before you'd been told you were going to be taking *Seiiki*. You'd had that argument with Yoshi. And you were wearing that dress that trailed along the floor. Your hair was in curls, all pinned up, so I could see your shoulders . . . You looked so beautiful. You looked like a princess."

Kim closed her eyes for a second, letting his words wash over her, repainting the memory in her mind. Somewhere, distantly, her dad pointed up at the glittering skyscrapers of Melbourne through a train window and said, *"Princesses live in those towers"*, and her five-year-old self asked, *"Can I be a Princess, Daddy?"*

She remembered that night all too well. Antonia Morosini herself had been there, along with Erica Wu, who had single-handedly made the Ark Project possible. The crowd of glittering gowns and black tuxes had been overwhelming. As she'd slipped away to meet Zane she'd bumped into Wren Keene, who'd bought his way into the function despite being voted out of the Caretaker program a week earlier.

"Dance?" Wren had asked her. She could still remember the cocky way his lips had tilted up at the corners, as if he knew she couldn't possibly say "no."

She'd said no. Her mind full of nothing but seeing Zane, kissing him, being with him, she'd brushed Wren aside and hurried away.

"You looked handsome, too," she said. "You always do."

"I'd crawled through the dusty air vents to get into the Madison Dome," he said. "I was covered in dust."

"That's what I mean. You looked handsome anyway."

He looked aside, then back at her. "Sometimes I wonder what I did to deserve you," he said quietly. Then he straightened. "Anyway, I'm glad to hear from you, Kim."

That was closer to what Kim had expected from the start. She smiled, kissed her hand, and touched it to the screen. A stupid, vapid gesture, she knew, something more fitting of Hannah than Kim, but the impulse had taken over and it was too late to take it back. Zane gave her another quick smile before terminating the connection.

Kim woke with a start; the certain feeling that someone had been leaning over her in her sleep clenched at her heart. The gravity blanket was soaked with sweat and her blood was loud in her ears. The familiar thrumming of the engines pulled her back down toward calm, but she couldn't shake that sensation of a featureless, genderless figure bending over her, reaching out a hand . . .

"Don't be *stupid*," she told herself.

Good morning, Kim!

Are you going to come and see us today?

We've missed you, Kim!

Kim, Kim, are you all right? Are you healed yet?

It had been five days since the fuel tank explosion. The tech droids had repaired the damage, and the tank was now full of precious gas once more. Her other duties had suffered a little, however, because Kim was still stiff and sore.

She moved slowly and couldn't bend to touch her toes without pain lancing through her ribs. It should have been almost healed by now. Kim was starting to wonder if she'd used the equipment properly.

Perhaps she should have let the medbot treat her after all.

She groaned as she pulled herself out of bed. "Maybe," she said into the Link.

No to maybe!

You have to. We miss you.

"Okay, okay," Kim chuckled. She would have to make some time. It would mean another argument with the computer, though, something she wasn't looking forward to. It had kept her strictly on light duties for the past few days, keeping her days short and her rest periods long. Kim hated it. Yes, she felt like shit, but lying around didn't really help. It just gave her more time to focus on her pain and to feel guilty about all the work that wasn't getting done.

She'd made plenty of holoprojections for Earth and had received a message from Erica.

"Hannah, everyone's loving the content that's come through lately. Ratings have tripled. Daywatch is streaming all content, even the old stuff, continuously. Keep up the good work."

Kim had snorted when she watched this, knowing that the reason why the ratings were so good was because of the explosion. People loved drama, and there was nothing more dramatic than the headline *Hannah Monksman Makes Narrow Escape!*

She had stayed away from the mess store room, however. That was one thing she couldn't deal with right now. In some ways, she felt incredibly guilty. Adonai was her friend. Yes, he was a whale, but he trusted her—and she liked him. In other ways, she simply wished she could pretend the problem didn't exist. That was the path she'd chosen.

But today, as she exited her room, she found herself walking past the store room without the usual hurried pace. She glanced through the door—and saw something that stopped her short.

A mess. The place was an utter mess.

A shelf had been overturned. Jars had been shattered against the walls, large dollops of jam, peanut butter, tomato sauce and who knew what else sliding their slow way through the lessened gravity toward the floor. Boxes had been torn open, rice, pasta shells, dried beans and cereal scattered like confetti. Dented cans rolled gently in in the corners.

"*Adonai?*" she gasped, astonished.

He was standing in the center of the room, his shoulders slumped, his knees bent. When he lifted his head, it was a slow movement, with the painful whining of gears. His golden eyes were dull.

"I'm . . . sorrrrry," he said. His vocal processors skipped over the words, drawing them out into lengthy syllables. "I-I-I-I donnnnnn—"

"Adonai, are you all right?" she asked.

"Not surrrrre," he replied. "Cannnnn't mo—mo- mo—"

Kim bit her lip, realizing just what was wrong with him. "The battery in the tech droid is failing," she said. "But, God. What did you do in here?"

Adonai tried to speak once more, but nothing came out save a squeak and a ratcheting sound. His body sagged further toward the ground and he swayed. He was about to topple straight over.

Kim didn't think further on it. She drew the kanji on her hand for *release*. The force field snapped out of existence, and she rushed inside, catching Adonai under the arm. Her boots squelched on the spilled sauces, and the mixture of smells made her empty stomach roil. God, he was heavier than a human man, even in the low gravity! She lowered him to the floor as best she could, getting one of his knees down, then the other, then bracing herself to rest his torso against the slanting, fallen shelf.

Now that he wouldn't crash down like a falling building and break something vital in the process, she rubbed a hand over her forehead, wondering what she was supposed to do now.

She couldn't leave him here. The computer was going to get suspicious about the forcefield being continuously active without reason, and the power drain was going to become an issue. She wished she could . . . but then, Adonai . . . Adonai was still trapped inside the droid. He just couldn't move, or speak. It would be incredibly cruel to lock the door and turn her back on him.

Kim snorted. For God's sake! She was a liar and a cheat. She'd killed people, she'd robbed people blind. Sometimes she'd done both to the same person. And here she was, worried about a damned *whale* who thought he was too big for his own mind?

She looked at the mess. She could see dents in the shelf where he'd grabbed it with his super-human hands. She was surprised the noise hadn't reached her in her own room. Perhaps it would be wiser to leave him here. If he was capable of this . . .

All of a sudden, she thought back to a time she'd spent in the lock-up in Fitzroy. She'd gotten caught selling a stolen tablet at a street market—a stupid idea, but she'd needed money quickly. She was coming down off a stim high and hadn't seen the warning signs that she was speaking to an undercover cop until it was too late.

They'd dragged her in kicking and screaming. They'd done some kicking and screaming of their own, too. "Little tramp," they'd sneered at her. "How much you get for some fun, huh?"

Finally, when they'd had their fill of beating her up and feeling her breasts, they'd dumped her in a cell and slammed the door. Instead of lying down, she'd gone crazy. She'd screamed nonsense at the top of her lungs, unable to stem the flow. Some of it was the stims, yeah, but most of it was just her. She howled like a caged animal. "You can't keep me in here! I'll kill every one of you! Bastards!" And she'd torn up everything she could. The mattress on the cot, the toilet paper beside the stainless steel loo. When that was done, she'd torn her own hands up scrabbling at the walls, trying to reach the window. Not to escape, just to smash it.

Just to break something.

Kim straightened. "Computer, please send some of the autobots and a tech droid up to Deck Five," she said. "There's been an accident in the store room."

CHAPTER
12

The tech droid slid its arms under Adonai as gently as if he was a newborn child. Adonai was curled up in a tech droid's default pose, head tucked in, knees drawn to his chest, arms folded over his mechanical sternum. The other tech droid had done this somehow, coiled him up, tucked him in, using a command that was sent through their shared link. Kim guessed it should have happened automatically when the battery began to die, to avoid the damage of toppling over. Adonai must have overridden it.

She didn't intend to follow the two tech droids, but she found herself trailing behind like a worried mother too anxious to leave her child's sickbed.

As they stepped through the door to the ramp, the computer chimed. "Kim, I'm still not satisfied by your explanation as to why you needed a tech droid in the galley store room. Can you elaborate?"

Kim swallowed. The computer couldn't sense Adonai, she reminded herself.

"I'm testing the tech droids," she said. "I'm going to have to send one of them on an EV walk later, and I want to be sure they're functional."

"You have run your systems checks," the computer told her. "They are all in functional order."

"Well, last I checked, so were the fuel shut-off valves," she replied acerbically.

"And I must protest this idea to send a tech droid out to inspect the camera. It is not necessary. The camera is functional."

Kim rolled her eyes. "Computer, I need you to run in self-reflexive mode for a second, okay?"

The computer bleeped. The railings curved around and around as Kim continued her spiraling descent. She used each loop to scan the shadows, her eyes still seeking out anything that her brain might turn into the hallucination of a human figure. Nothing.

Self-reflexive mode was a function of the computer usually used for analysis of its complex CPU. It was a built-in feature to help protect against virus infection whilst in dock. Out here, of course, there was little possibility of virus attacks, but the function had been helpful to Kim when she'd first boarded and had needed to explain a few things to the computer.

Such as her real name.

"Mode activated," the computer responded.

"Okay. Now, imagine—" No, that was the wrong word. The computer couldn't imagine things. "Hypothetical scenario. A camera has been installed badly and isn't showing the correct location of the ship's exterior. Would that be dangerous?"

"Yes." The computer's voice sounded different in this mode, she thought. Or was that just *her* imagination? No, it was almost certain. There was less authoritative certainty in its tone. "It could pose a danger to the ship and the mission."

"Right. So it would need to be fixed."

"Correct."

"And I'm the one to make that judgement. Because you can't see it."

"Why would I not see it?" The way it said "I" was different, too. That oddly impersonal quality was gone. It sounded like it meant "I" and not "we."

"Because—" Kim pondered this. "I'm not sure. Maybe something's wrong with the wiring, and the programming got messed up somehow. Anyway, you can't see it. It needs to be fixed. What would be the solution?"

Another moment's pause. "I believe you've already stated the solution. You would need to repair it."

"Good. Computer, save conversation and transfer to your normal running mode. Send the file to your processing matrix and run all conversations from now on with reference to that file."

"File transferred successfully."

"Exit self-reflexive mode."

"Normal operational mode resumed."

"I'm going to check the camera, computer."

"This is a wise course of action," the computer agreed. Kim smiled grimly and hurried to catch up with the tech droids. It wasn't, she thought with wry amusement, that much different from convincing her old landlord to fix a leak.

The tech droid entered the bay on Deck Thirteen ahead of her and made its way down the steep metal stairs with more ease than she had imagined it would. Of course, its body contained gyroscopic balancers that made it able to maneuver through the ship safely even during periods of high turbulence. It bore its charge gently toward one of the egg-shaped pods. Adonai fit inside it with a snapping sound. The pod powered up with a whine and began to glow softly with the slow pulse of power being fed back into his battery, outlining dark wires like veins through the semi-transparent outer shell. The design of those pods disturbed her in a way she hadn't noticed until now—there was something *organic* about them. It was unnerving.

"5973, return to your own pod, but stand by," Kim told the other tech droid. "Don't power down."

"Understood," the tech droid responded. It folded its own body back into the pod three from the end and clicked quietly.

Kim looked at Adonai's carefully folded droid. It looked smaller, curled in its fetal posture. She felt a sudden brimming of worry and protectiveness, and this time, she didn't tamp it down or shove it to the side. She let herself look at him.

His eyes were blank, darkened. His lower face wasn't visible, just his smooth forehead and the neutral ridge of his brow. His fingers were long, folded into neat fists that mimicked a human's. She let her gaze wander along the other droids, then turn back to Adonai. They were all identical; it was like looking into opposing mirrors, each reflecting the exact same thing endlessly. Why, then, did Adonai looked decidedly more alive than the rest?

The Operations Center was on Deck Four.

Kim stopped by the Aquarium on the way back up, and Hosea instantly made her wish she hadn't.

Why is Adonai like this? She had demanded immediately, as Kim climbed the ladder to see her. Hosea liked to hold a position near a bulging bubble of force field, her body tilted down so that Kim had a view of her long form, from head to her wide flukes. She flapped her fins slowly to keep herself in place against the currents of the tanks. *He doesn't speak to me. He eats, he sleeps, he stares. There's something wrong.*

"Adonai is fine," Kim replied earnestly. "I told you about his illness. This is all normal for . . . well, for his condition." It wasn't a lie.

He is not fine. This is not fine. What kind of illness is this?

A ripple of glowing gold made its way along Hosea's Link. Kim reached for her toolbelt, her hand hovering above the tuner. But Hosea's reaction was instant, a violent, revolted scream of indignation.

Don't you dare!

Kim stepped back involuntarily, pressing a hand against her forehead. A piercing pain had accompanied the mental shout, and it set her ears ringing even as it faded. Her fingers encountered the scratch on her temple, leftover from the accident, now dried to a crusty scab. They came away wet, and Kim looked down in surprise to see fresh blood on her fingertips. Her forehead throbbed again.

Coincidence? Surely it was. The Link was a mental connection, the neural net laid over her own brain's pathways. It wasn't tied to any physiological responses. Still, Hosea's ire burned at her like a flame, and the whale shifted her head to the left, so she could look at her with one black, expansive eye. Kim hadn't noticed it before, how black those eyes really were.

As black as space, she thought. Blacker, for there were no stars in them.

Don't you dare use that cattle prod to make me feel less angry at you for hiding things from me, Hosea continued, words low and harsh.

Kim wondered, bizarrely, how Hosea had learned of cattle prods. Or of cattle.

You think we don't know things, Hosea continued, as if having read Kim's thoughts. *But we do. We've been raised in human's cages. You forget that. We hear everything, and if you think we can't put it together to make sense, YOU'RE the stupid ones.*

"I wasn't going to use it," Kim said softly.

Lie! You lie! How can I trust you when you make so many lies?

Hosea shook her whole body, a long undulation from tail to head. Her nose lifted a little, and she crashed head-first into the force field. The blue energy caught her, rippling, giving way a little, then snapping back into place. The force knocked the beast backward. She tumbled for a moment, then regained herself. Kim's instincts screamed at her to grab the tuner, but she didn't want to give Hosea any more reason to distrust her.

"You never told me," Kim iterated, "that you disliked it."

Why should I? When most of the time, I don't dislike it. It keeps me from feeling. That means the good stuff as well as the bad stuff. Her voice was no longer aggressive but mournful. *But I don't want it now. I don't want it now. Don't give it to me now.*

And with that, she pulled her fins close to her sides and sank out of view.

Rattled, Kim stood there a moment before she made her way along the catwalks, exiting at Deck Ten. She passed Fifteen on the way by, who followed after her with the eagerness of a puppy.

Hosea doesn't like the stick. But I do. You can use it on me if you like.

Kim recoiled. "You want me to alter your Link?"

Will it make you happy?

Kim shook her head. "Is that what you think?" Her forehead wrinkled. "Is that what you *all* think?"

There was a mixture of voices from the other whales. Some demurred. Others were quietly accepting.

It's for our own good.

I would rather you didn't.

I'm happy enough.

Do what you like, Kim . . .

This last one made her swallow dryly. Not knowing what else to do or say, she hurried through the door and back out onto the ramp. It didn't silence the voices, but at least she couldn't feel their eyes on her.

CHAPTER
13

The Operations Center was a circular chamber, accessed by a door just beyond the infirmary. The layout mirrored Deck One, in that circular consoles surrounded a central point, but here the focus was the rig, not the main control desk.

The rig was an exoskeleton made of metal, designed to clamp around the users legs, arms and torso. At the moment it stood upright, slumped slightly in its tangle of cobweb-like colored wires that would feed any movement into the computer, to relay it to the tech droids. At its center, near the ceiling, was a helmet, dome-shaped, in dark red plastic. The visor was made of opaque grey material covered with the visible hexagons of holographic conductors.

Kim slung her toolbelt over a chair and stepped into the rig without hesitation. She stood still and straight. The rig sensed her arrival and came to life, the silver armature taking on a life of its own as it reached out grasping fingers and snapped them around her arms and legs, tightening until they were almost at the point of discomfort, but no further. Two more delicate apparatuses wrapped their way around her fingers like strands of ivy. A steel band crossed her chest, another cupped her stomach, and two curve beneath her thighs, supporting her pelvis. She was no longer standing under her own power, but supported wholly by the rig. Her hands settled on the joysticks, two gun-hilt-shaped remote controls fitted with half a dozen buttons.

When it was done with its adjustments, it beeped softly, the reminder that she had a few seconds to adjust any of the supports, but she didn't need to. She'd already been over this rig thirty times or so, making alterations to the most minute degree. When she didn't move, the helmet descended, fitting expertly over her head and blocking out all view with a grey monochrome. She snaked her neck to make sure it was secure.

"Please indicate that you are ready to launch EV program, Kim."

"All good, computer."

The greyness hung there, but a series of icons appeared, superimposed over the egg-pods lined up against the curving wall of the bay on Deck Thirteen. Kim tapped the third from the left. "Computer, connect me to droid Five-Nine-Seven-Three."

"Connected," the computer said. "Ready for launch?"

"Ready," Kim said, bracing her feet and clutching the joysticks.

The greyness telescoped around her, and she saw the egg she'd chosen slide backward on a rolling track and shoot toward the airlock. As it did so, her vision zeroed in and merged with the tech droid's perspective. Now she was whizzing along, being carried at five miles an hour through the iris of the airlock. Nothing in the chamber around her moved, but she felt the change in air pressure, nonetheless. It pulled at her limbs—the droid's limbs—and at the egg-pod around her. Through the first aperture, then through the second.

And then she was out.

The internal airlock closed its petals over the hole, stopping the flow of air. The external one followed. Of course, inside the droid, there was no need to wait for the air to filter out of the compartment in between. Still, she felt a moment of breathlessness as her body adjusted to the peculiar sensation of being naked in space.

The egg-pod popped her free without a sound. Another anomaly—she could hear nothing at all from her surroundings, for there was no noise in space; but back in the rig, her ears were tuned to the thrum of the engines, the buzz of the lighting, the beeping of the consoles. She could still hear, also, the voices of the whales, but they were more distant than usual. The rig was designed to filter out distractions that weren't urgent, so the neural net was slightly subdued by the input from the rig whilst she was engaged.

The droid's body uncurled automatically. She spread her arms and legs once she was free to do so, opened and closed her hands, then moved her feet in a walking motion. Good. Everything was working.

The stars were elongated streaks of white in various hues—green, blue, red. The ship was moving at an incredible speed, *dizzying* speed. Of course, she could still feel the rig holding her securely, but as the exoskeleton mirrored her movements, so did the droid. It didn't take long for her mind to start adapting. She suppressed a guilty smile at a sudden memory of Wren, freaking out, ripping at his helmet. *Get me out of here. Now!*

For a guy who played hologames like a pro, the rig training had been his undoing—it wasn't long after that he dropped out of the running. Even his most devoted fans had seen this weakness as incapability to act as Caretaker.

The tethering cord at her waist arrested her backward motion, and reeled her back toward the ship. She landed on the hull, arms and knees splayed. The metallic body adhered instantly, and she pushed herself to her feet. It was like walking on sticky sand at the edge of a beach, but not quite as clumsy as an EV suit, which had to keep one body part magnetized at all times, according to the Space Exploration Authority's guidelines. It was possible to go EV in a suit at hyper speed. The ship itself was being carried in a bubble of subspace, where neither time nor space worked in the same way as it did in normal space. Anything on the hull, or within ten feet of the ship, was still contained by the bubble. The spacewalker wouldn't feel the extreme acceleration, and, more importantly, neither would their equipment. However, it was warned against by the SEA, and in fact only nine people had ever done it. Of those, two had died—though, coincidentally enough, not from anything related to subspace itself. The first had been a malfunctioning air-line, and the other, from a heart attack that had probably been a long time coming.

Kim reveled in the freedom from these dangers—but in some ways it took something away from the enjoyment. Kim would not have gotten this far without being able to find a thrill in risk. Still, this was as close as she was going to get, since an EV walk was unlikely to be needed except during the most extreme circumstances. But from all these things the tech droid was exempt, free to jump and pirouette if it chose, launch itself into space and pinwheel just for fun. Kim would have been tempted, had her mind been on less serious matters.

She had come out toward the bow of the ship. She couldn't see beyond the curve of the hull to the rear. She was walking across the painted name now. *Seiiki.* Letters taller than she was, in blue paint.

She crossed them, marveling at the beauty of the ship. It wasn't the first time she'd seen it from outside, of course, but it was the first time she'd been truly alone, with no one monitoring her or charting her movements, evaluating and testing her. This was *hers* now. This entire ship.

The thought was a heady one. She was hurtling through space at ten times the speed of light. It was truly incredible, but she couldn't lounge about and enjoy the thought.

She focused instead on moving forward, following the curve of the ship's hull. The hull plates were solid beneath her feet, unlike the clanging interior deck plates. She made quick progress, thanks to the tech droid's ability to move more quickly than a human, bending her knees and launching herself outwards. The jump had more power than it otherwise would have, but a set of numbers began to spin downwards at the corner of her vision, indicating her safe distance from the ship was decreasing.

She waited until she was five feet from the hull and hit the control on her joysticks for the rockets. Two jets of compressed air emerged from the droid's shoulders—*her* shoulders, really—and stopped her. She eased the joysticks forward and the droid began to move forward toward the back of the ship.

Sailing along like this at sixty miles per hour, with nothing to mark her speed but the rushing surface of the grey plates underneath her, drew from her a whoop of joy. She angled the thrust to compensate for the curvature of the vessel, and soon she was approaching the crest of *Seiiki's* midpoint. She followed it up and over. Then she drew her hands back on the joysticks and cut the thrust. She was now hovering over one of the slots in the hull where one of the solar sails were folded.

The camera mount was just ahead of her.

A bulge of steel, bolted on, sheltering the delicate camera from potential meteors. And yes, indeed, it was facing her, not the rear of the ship. It *had* been mounted backward. There was no mistake.

But with a shock, her eyes were pulled past it, to something that did not belong on the hull at all. It was a vessel.

"What the hell?" Kim muttered.

Kim saw the curve of a dark window, the faded red of painted stripes on the wings, which spread out to either side. The metal was scarred along one side, as if it had been in a crash and hadn't been repaired properly. It was so at odds with the clean lines of *Seiiki's* structure that it was jarring.

"What the *hell?*" she said again. "Is that a ship?"

"Insufficient data to answer your question, Kim."

"I'm not talking to you, computer," she said absently. Her voice trailed off. She felt a chill settling over her, and, acting on instinct, she let go of the joysticks and dropped the droid down to the hull. She scuttled for the shelter of the solar sail trench, where she crouched, looking out at this impossibility. "Actually," she amended, speaking in a whisper. "Yes, I am. Can you analyze the other ship I'm looking at right now?"

"Unable to analyze. No other ship detected."

"Bullcrap," Kim whispered. She glanced at the droid's display in the left hand corner. Glowing numbers informed her that the object was 100 yards away, that it was thirteen feet in length, thirteen in height and twenty-two in width. "It's a one-man scout ship. Military. Or—it was, once." She poked her head over the edge of the trench and zoomed in on the side that was facing her. It had once been painted with a roundel, a bullseye of white and blue, followed by a serial number. It was definitely an air force marking. (With a flash she saw herself on the couch, curled up next to her dad, a heavy book open on his lap. *Which country is this one from, Daddy? And which one is this one?)* but she couldn't place which country it came from. Finland? Iceland? Some cold place in Europe, she was sure, but the knowledge was old and faded at the edges. And, most alarming of all, she could see a large cannon mounted just above the ship's right wing. If she was right, it was likely there was another one on the left wing, too. "There's a ship right there. It's a . . . Mayfly 9-1-2, I think. Computer, you have to be able to see it. Can't you get a read on its transponder?"

"I do not read any ship apart from *Seiiki*, Kim."

"God damn it!" Kim hissed. Her adrenaline was pumping, and she felt edgy, nervous, ready for action—but of what type, she wasn't sure. A strange ship was docked on *Seiiki's* hull. How long had it been there? It couldn't have been attached while in the dock at Ganymede. Someone would have seen it during visual inspections, even if their sensors didn't.

For God's sake, it had been hanging opposite one of the most popular hotels in the entire dock! So—someone had flown it and caught up with *Seiiki* afterwards. And then piggybacked for . . . days, weeks, *months*, like a flea on a dog's back. Kim clenched her fingers, feeling the droid's response to the more receptive wiring there instantly. It was possible it had been flown remotely, but what point was there in that?

No. She felt it in her bones. The ship was manned.

Or . . . had been.

"Computer," she said. "Pull up a schematic of airlocks along this portion of the hull. Overlay."

The computer did so, and an orange grid appeared, stretching along *Seiiki's* hull. Two airlocks pulsed green to her right. Another flashed just underneath the Mayfly, with a number indicating that it was the airlock for Deck Eight. She felt dread clutch her heart in its cold hand. "I wasn't imagining things, damn it. *There's someone else aboard.*"

"Kim, just a reminder that you are scheduled for another session with your counselor today," the computer said as she re-entered the ship. "I have forwarded her some reports of my concerns. Please make sure they are discussed to her satisfaction."

"Shut up," Kim snapped. Her head was pounding. She could barely feel her feet settling back on the floor as the rig released her. "I need to think."

"I would recommend that you attend only to light duties today, but there are a number of tasks that need to be undertaken—"

Kim drew the kanji on the back of her hand for *silence*. The computer's voice dropped away as if a door had slammed shut. It would be pissed, but never mind. She'd deal with that later.

She made her way to the desk and leaned back against it. Crossing her arms, she ran through everything she'd seen in her mind.

Near Horizon would have no reason to send a second ship on this journey. They were so concerned with making this a worldwide spectacle that adding something as underhanded and secretive as this didn't make any sense. Besides which, the Mayfly . . . it was so at odds with the clean lines of Near Horizon's new, streamlined, state-of-the-art tech that she had a hard time believing it would have been allowed past the company board's particular specifications.

Besides which, the Mayfly was a military vessel—or it had been. It was old, more than ten years, or it would have sported the new paintwork of the Earth Intersystem Alliance, as all Earth-based military ships did after the United Earth government outlawed individual military operations under the Peace Agreement, which had basically made war illegal for any country that didn't run their invasion plans by President McKinney and the US senate first. And it had no transponder. That was illegal—at least, as far as she knew, it was. Only spy aircraft during the Triad Wars had flown without transponders.

Still, it *was* military. What if the Admiral already knew about it? What if she was the only one who didn't? No—she couldn't be. It came back to the fact that Near Horizon couldn't possibly have sanctioned anything like this.

And there was the camera. The ship had passed inspections, and no one could have altered it after it left the dock on its journey. Which spoke of a plan—and of someone who was willing to look the other way. Bribes would have to have been involved, because the SEA would prosecute anyone involved in installing faulty equipment on a ship to the full extent of the law.

There was a noise in the doorway, and Kim whirled. She'd had her back to it, and in that instant she realized that was a stupid thing to do when she had just found out the figure who'd been lurking in the shadows of the ship was real. She dropped into a defensive stance, her street senses taking over and telling her to put the console between her and the intruder.

It wasn't a dark, hulking figure, however, but a tech droid with glowing yellow eyes.

"Kim?" Adonai said, and Kim felt a wash of relief, followed quickly by alarm as she recalled the trashed store room. Suspicion lanced through her. What if Adonai knew? What if he was working in conjunction with the stranger—or strangers? Yes, the scout ship was one-man, but she knew enough about the Mayfly to know that it, and ships like it, had a small cargo space that could easily fit a passenger if need be.

"Stay back," she said. A useless warning. She had no weapon, nothing to enforce her demand. She didn't dare take her eyes off him, but at the corner of her vision, she could see the toolbelt she'd left on the chair. She'd have to hurdle the desk to get it, though.

"I have recharged, Kim. Well, this droid has." Adonai lifted his arms, marveling at how they worked. "It's wonderful to feel alive again. I was prepared for the battery running out, but the reality was still difficult to cope with. It wasn't like going to sleep at all. I've found that I don't get tired, now. My mind was still active even while the droid was recharging. It's so strange."

"Stay back," Kim barked at him again, though he hadn't moved from the doorway. "Don't come near me."

"Kim?" Adonai sounded puzzled. "I'm sorry I lost my temper in the store room."

"Oh, you are, are you?" Kim replied. She took an experimental step sideways and began edging her way around the desk. "Great. Good. I forgive you."

"Do you really?" he asked, again, that eager puppy look settling over the droid. His shoulders quivered. "Because I think I destroyed many of your food supplies. I didn't mean to. I'm not sure why I felt that way. I've never been so angry."

"Of course you haven't," Kim said. She wanted to keep him talking. If she did, he wouldn't notice her moving. "You're a whale."

"You're right. I did not experience . . . aggression in that manner. But then, why now? I am still the same being I was."

The calm, thoughtful voice was not what Kim would expect from someone—*something*—that wished her harm. And he was Adonai— her favorite, the one she'd been most drawn to. The one who was curious enough about the stars to ask her hours' worth of questions, and listen so carefully to her answers.

How could she believe that he was dangerous?

"But you're not the same being," Kim said blankly. "You've got a humanoid body."

"Is that it?" Adonai looked down at himself. "Is it having arms and legs that do this? Makes a being so . . . unstable?"

"Maybe," Kim replied. She had reached the chair. She leaned over, picked up the belt, and strapped it on. Instantly, she felt better. The heavy flashlight, the wrench and shifter, even the pliers or wire-strippers would make good weapons. She didn't know if they could stop a tech droid, though. She'd just now stepped from the body of one, and knew their strength to be five times that of her own frail flesh.

"Perhaps that's why the battery drained so low, because of all that lifting and throwing and punching. It won't happen again," Adonai vowed, and he sounded—God, he sounded like he meant it. "Kim, you seem worried. Is this to do with the ship you found?"

Kim stiffened.

"You seem surprised that I know, but I am still linked to the other tech droids. I saw what you saw. Are you worried about the ship?"

"Yes," Kim said slowly.

"I see. Perhaps I am too, a little. It doesn't seem right."

Kim nodded. "You don't know anything about it, do you?" She could feel the tight coil in her abdomen unwinding just a little. It certainly didn't seem like Adonai was part of this. Either that, or he was a very good actor. Better than she was, even.

"No," Adonai replied honestly. "How could I?"

Kim patted her toolbelt. "I don't know. You spent a few hours roaming the ship undetected. You didn't see anyone, anything unusual?"

"I'm afraid not," he replied. "I spent most of my time in the one spot."

"Where was that?"

"In one of the tubes between Deck Thirteen and Deck Fourteen. I had to learn how to move this body, how to coordinate my legs. And I was a little . . . confused, at first, by the way the droid's brain works. There is information coming in and going out constantly, and it's all in peculiar numbers and symbols. It took time for me to be able to shut it off."

"To cut yourself off from the computer," Kim said. "Well, you did a good job. A lot of people would have a hard time doing what you've done." Something occurred to her. "You speak much better, now. Less . . . stilted."

"I'm learning," Adonai replied modestly. "Conversing with you helps."

Kim couldn't help but smile, despite the situation. She quickly reined her thoughts back in, though. "So. Basically, this other person could have been roaming the ship long before you arrived, or he could have come afterwards."

"It is a male?"

"I don't know. It's an old habit on my planet, referring to unknowns as 'he' rather than 'she'. There have been numerous attempts to change it, but somehow it's never happened."

"That seems strange. Whales have a term for both male and female. We call them 'whale."

Kim snorted. The unexpected explosion of laughter shocked her as much as it surprised Adonai.

"I don't understand—"

"Never mind." She waved dismissively. "Anyway, this *human*, well, I've seen him several times. And . . . " she trailed off.

"What is it?"

"Adonai?" Kim said thoughtfully. "You said you were in the tube for close to twelve hours. When did you come up to Deck Five?"

"I arrived at about 0500 that morning. That's when I cooked you breakfast," Adonai replied. "But while I was recharging just now, I looked up the computer information banks. It seems that chicken soup is not suitable breakfast food. I should have made you muesli with yogurt, or bacon and eggs."

"Are you sure?"

"Both bacon and eggs provide your body with essential nutrients to begin your day—"

"No." She held up a hand. "About the time you came to Deck Five."

"Of course. I told you, Kim. I cannot lie." Adonai tilted his head. "Why is this important?"

"Because someone was in my room the day before," she said. "And if it wasn't you . . . "

"It was the intruding human?" Adonai's voice was slightly proud, as if he'd figured this out on his own.

"I was in the shower," Kim explained. "When I came out, my blanket was moved and the door was open. I put it down to a malfunction, and the computer started thinking I was crazy, so I guess I did, too." She shook her head. Again, a small twinge of distrust panged in her stomach. What if Adonai was lying about not being able to lie? But the incident had been before her check of the tech droids. If Adonai had been in one of the droid's bodies at that point, she would have noticed something awry.

"What is a shower?"

"That's not the point," Kim snapped, then relented. "We stand under water. To clean ourselves."

"Oh!" Adonai sounded pleased. "That sounds nice. But why would a human be in your room? If a human was supposed to be here with your knowledge, a human would have waited there for you to finish your wetting-down and spoken to you. So it seems strange to leave evidence of this human's presence, if said human's supposed to be here without your knowledge."

"That's true." Kim was starting to feel much better. At least, if she could believe that Adonai was on her side, she could believe she had an ally against this . . . well, whatever it was she was facing. And it was so good to be able to talk to someone else, at very last, who wasn't going to tell her she was imagining things.

But it still didn't give her any idea of what she could do.

As she made her way out into the corridor, Adonai trailing behind her, she looked quickly left and right, almost certain she'd see a figure lurking in a doorway. That horrible feeling was starting to creep back to her, the panicky fear she'd felt while outside, looking at the ship. This was not a situation she'd been trained for, and she was lost as to how to handle it.

The computer was no help. It couldn't even see the damn thing, and would likely refer her for more counseling if she mentioned it. She couldn't contact Edgeward. Perhaps she could call Earth and speak to Erica? But what help would that do? Earth—the entire Sol system—was light years behind her. It would take three months for them to send a ship out, even if she *was* able to convince them that there was a ship that wasn't showing up on scanners attached to the hull, and a camera that had been deliberately mounted wrongly to hide that fact. What if one of Near Horizon's people was involved in the sabotage of the camera, or the cover-up?

What if it was Erica herself?

No, surely not. Erica Wu had been the most upfront person she'd met in her time with the Ark Project, the only one with no agenda to advance herself and claim fame and glory. But then, perhaps that was all part of her game? Near Horizon had plenty of enemies—Kim knew that better than anyone, didn't she?—and what if Erica was one of them?

She shuddered as the thought brought her back to Zane.

Once her mind arrived there, it settled like a bird on a nest. She felt the instant calm of knowing that she could turn to him, that he would listen, and would not judge her. He loved her. He would keep her safe.

CHAPTER

14

S he made her cautious way up to Deck One and left Adonai outside the door to the Bridge.

"I can't have you in there," she told him. "If I contact the Admiral
and he sees you in the background—well."

Adonai nodded and assented, standing demurely to one side and
bowing his head to wait.

Kim ran her systems checks. The droids and autobots hovered
about, undertaking their own tasks with blind efficiency. As she settled into the comm chair, however, she found herself not wanting to
make the call to Edgeward at all.

She steeled herself.

There was no getting out of this by pretending it wasn't happening, or by running away. For the first time in Kim's life, there was nowhere to run to. She drew the kanji and made the connection.

Admiral Mbewe greeted her a few moments later. She sent him the data packet and waited breathlessly.

"Everything seems in order," he said quickly. His voice was rather more curt than Kim had expected, especially given his warmth yesterday. "Have a good night."

"Yes, sir," she managed, before he cut the connection.

Still, she was glad to have it over with.

She sat back in her chair, and called to the computer. "Replay my feed from the tech droid, please. From minute twelve onwards."

The desk in front of her lit up with a holo, showing the feed the tech droid had recorded as it made its way toward the Mayfly. Once again, she saw those familiar angles on the ship, the damaged exterior. She let the feed play, then tapped the air to pause it as the full side of the ship came into view. She spread her fingers to zoom in, played it forward a little more, then stopped it again. She focused on the roundel.

Kim commanded the computer, "Pull up old military records from the net. Iceland Military, actually, circa . . . 2055. Cross-reference this serial number. 8857-789-23-1."

"Searching now . . ." the computer told her. "One match. Military vehicle, Mayfly 912, no adaptations. Two side-mounted laser cannons. Registered to Keflavik Naval Air Base, Iceland. Decommissioned November 24, 2067."

"Keflavik," Kim mused. "That was reopened after Russia reformed its Soviet State. The US used it, right?"

"Correct. It is no longer in operation."

"So what happened to its aircraft after it closed?"

"There is no record of this."

Kim thought about this. People had often dismissed her as being stupid, after she'd dropped out of school. The government agency that had looked after her for a while, Centra, had assigned her to a case worker who had given her a coloring book and a set of markers and told her to "make a nice picture and hang it on the wall." At seven years old, Kim had dumped it in the rubbish bin on the way out of the office, in full view of the case worker.

She'd lived in a boarding house at that time, and she'd lived in a room shared with four other girls. There was a Net connection, but the younger children weren't supposed to access the Internet on their own. It had only taken Kim a week to figure out how to get past the safeguards. She read books, mostly, but occasionally she watched movies late at night, huddled under her covers with one of the battered old shared tablets. She also looked things up. It was her favorite pastime.

She'd spend all day thinking of questions she wanted answered, and later, when she found some time alone, she'd look them up. "How does a spaceship fly?" "What happens after you die?" "Why are planets different colors?" "What is a koala?"

She'd learned something more valuable than the actual answers to any of those questions: that, a lot of the time, when searches resulted in dead ends, it was only because you hadn't asked the right questions.

"What normally happens to military aircraft after a base is decommissioned?"

"If they are in working order, they are sold," the computer answered. "There are numerous instances where this is the case. The closing of Curt Bank and Inland Australia are both good examples. Their atmospheric and extraplanetary aircraft were bought by the

Northern United States. Many of these were used in the bombing of the Unificationist states of the South during the Red State—"

"Not helpful," Kim cut the computer off. "Is there anything else that might be done with them?"

"Older models are often recycled for parts, or turned in for scrap metal."

This was more like it. "Would a Mayfly 912 be useful for scrap parts?"

"The transponder would be the only piece of equipment that wouldn't require an upgrade. The wiring might be stripped, but it's of little value."

Gotcha, Kim thought. The little ship could have gone missing, and been sold on the black market. That meant that whoever the pilot was, he wasn't military as she'd feared. But in another way, this made him more dangerous, not less. Because *who,* damn it, was he working for? She made her way out of Deck One. Adonai was waiting for her in the maglift, where she'd left him. She wanted to leave Adonai in one of the other store rooms for the night.

"I won't set up a force field," she said. "I promise."

She paused at the doorway to her quarters. Further down the hallway, the autobot, whirring away in the galley store room, made a clanking sound as it suctioned up some broken glass. But Adonai didn't move.

"I would rather stay here," he said.

Kim looked around. "In the hallway?"

"Well, yes. This is your room? You say the human accessed it. Perhaps he will try again."

Kim gave a cold shudder. "I didn't think of that." She paused as her mind leapt further ahead. "What if he messed with the door to make sure it'd open for him when he needed it?"

"I'll stand guard," Adonai said.

It was such an unexpected offer that Kim was taken aback. "You don't need—"

"Don't argue. You are not as strong as I am."

It was a simple truth. And this man, well, he *was* a human. Not a droid. No man, no matter how skilled, could overpower a droid.

"You're not entirely bulletproof," Kim told him. "If he has a gun—"

"You've told me about guns. And this droid has titanium shielding that will deflect most projectiles, including bullets." He tapped his long fingers on the breastplate, then his head, shoulders, and thighs. "Unless I'm hit at a precise angle, I will still be operable. I've learned this from the computer."

"I see," Kim said. She didn't want to think about Adonai getting shot, whether he was mostly bulletproof or not. But if shooting her had been the man's goal, he'd already had plenty of chances. Ninety-nine days' worth, in fact.

She would feel much safer with Adonai guarding her room, and she did need to sleep.

But first—the call to Zane.

She sat on the edge of her bed with the tablet on her lap. The Manta Protocol was enabled, and she'd made the call, but Zane had not yet responded. It had been—she checked her chronometer—fourteen minutes.

"Come on, come on," she murmured impatiently.

Finally, the screen flickered to life. "Kim," he said. He looked flushed, his cheeks darker than usual, his brows drawn together. "This line really has to be kept for emergencies. You've made three calls in a week. It's too many. Do I have to remind you of our objective here?"

The harshness of his word stung her.

"I—I—" Kim was rarely lost for words, so her own faltering into silence made her angry.

His mouth formed a thin line inside its black beard frame. His expression didn't soften.

"What do you want?"

She saw several scattered machine parts in the foreground. They were too blurry to properly discern their function, but she recognized the serrated top of a catalytic converter from an ion drive. Her mind idly toyed with the idea of how well they would work together, building and repairing things, when this was all over.

"I just wanted to tell you about the whales," she said. Her voice sounded small and distant, and she was ashamed of herself, suddenly. Not for not telling him the truth, but for making the call in the first place. The Crusader's operatives worked independently—how many times had that been stressed to her? She couldn't go running for help every time she felt a little scared. It was weak and stupid. Just like her paltry excuse for calling him—he'd think she was one of those girls who clung to their boyfriends like limpets, unable to function on their own. "I wanted to let you know that they're . . . well, some of them are doing really well, but others . . . I'm not sure. I feel a bit . . . unsafe here."

"What do I care about the whales?" he said, sounding puzzled. "For that matter, what do *you* care? The whales aren't the end product, here. The advancement of the cause is. Why are you calling me about this, Kim? I have work to do. So do you."

"Because," Kim said, feeling herself shrinking down under the weight of his antagonism, "I'm worried, and I thought I could share this with you. You said . . . you said you wanted me to think of you on this journey. And I am. I think about you all the time. It's—"

"Oh, for God's sake," Zane snapped, his gaze turning stormy. "I don't have time to stroke your feelings right now."

I don't want you to. She didn't verbalize the thought.

Tears had formed behind her eyes, and threatened to spill over. She choked them back. She would *not* cry in front of him, would *not* compound her disgrace. "I'm just worried. That something might go wrong. We've planned everything so carefully, and I don't want—I don't want to screw up this mission."

Zane sighed. "You feel unsafe. Why?"

"I'm—" Now was the time to tell him. She should tell him. But the words lodged in her throat, stuck tight, forming a hard lump she couldn't get out. "I'm just worried. That's all. I'm thinking about the cause, I really am. I want the Crusaders to have control of New Eden. I want you to turn it into something wonderful. I want to make it a true gift for God."

"Good." Finally, he leaned forward into the lens, his handsome face growing large. Finally, finally she saw the hint of a smile. "Kim, I love you, but you've gotta keep your head in the game. Keep doing what you're doing. And next time—wait for me to call, okay? Unless it's an emergency. I've got people—" he lowered his voice. "I've got people looking over my shoulder, here. But we're too close now. Don't let this fail, okay? It's on your shoulders."

"I know," she replied. The tears, thankfully, had subsided entirely. He was right to be annoyed. She was acting like a little kid who needed validation. She wouldn't do that again. She gave him a grin that didn't wobble at all. "I love you."

He kissed his fingers and waved it at the lens. Kim kissed her own and touched his fingertips on the screen.

When he was gone, she mentally kicked herself. She'd been stupid. Zane couldn't help her, either. Why had she thought he would?

She lay down in bed, fully clothed, and drew the gravity blanket up over her. For the first time, it felt comforting and warm rather than stifling.

CHAPTER
15

H*i everyone! Hannah Monksman here. So, today I'm going to talk to you about Barnabas, our fin whale. Fin whales are also called finback whales, razorbacks, or common rorquals. Here are a few images taken back in 2020, showing the fin whale actually swimming in Earth's oceans. How beautiful are they?*

As you can see, their bodies are long and slender, with a brownish color. They once swam in all oceans, tropical and polar. However, the International Whaling Commission ordered a moratorium on the hunting of these endangered species—which was later ignored by both Japan and Iceland. As a result, the species died out. Barny here is a wonderful example of a fin whale, though.

He's one of our healthiest, and he's got a real bright spark. I'm going to play you a recording of his "speech" now.

Hear that sound? No, your holoprojector speakers aren't broken! That's what Barnabas's song sounds like. When fin whale sounds were first detected, the scientists thought they were hearing geological sounds—tectonic plates moving and grinding, or something similar. They even thought their equipment was broken!

Anyway, that's enough for today. Hannah Monksman, signing off on July 14, 2078!

Kim dropped the tablet in disgust.

She was sitting against the wall, her knees drawn to her chest. She'd brushed her teeth, but that was the extent of her efforts this morning. She hadn't even bothered with makeup. At least she had no need to do anything with her hair.

Idly, she tapped through to the tablets real-time net link, and had a quick scan of the comments flooding the Ark Project hub.

Love this!!! Barnabas rocks my world.

I want to adopt Barnabas! He's gorgeous xx ☺

Damn girl had a rough night???

Bags are for carrying clothes, not eyes

Love you Hannah. You're right hot

Kim dropped the tablet in disgust. She didn't usually read the comments, and this was why.

The voices of the whales washed over her, a calming tide that swept away the unpleasantness of the online comments.

Hello, Kim! Good morning!

I'm going to catch lots of fish. I'm going to eat so many fish.

The sun is warm on my back . . .

"Kim?"

There was a soft metallic tapping at her door, and Kim was startled for a moment, before her tired brain kicked in. "Adonai? Come in."

The door slid open. Adonai looked in. "I've made you some breakfast."

"I don't feel like eating."

"You need to eat before you start your day."

Kim sighed and kicked her legs forward, sliding off the bed and picking up her toolbelt from the nightstand. "You've been talking to the computer, haven't you?"

"No," Adonai said. "The computer does not respond to me directly. I can communicate with it through the tech droid's link, but only with regards to information shared from other tech droids, or through the outside link to what you call the Net. I can't—"

"Joke," Kim stopped him, holding up a hand. "You wouldn't get it."

"Oh," Adonai replied blankly.

The mess table had been set with a placemat, knife, spoon and fork, a glass of water, and a plate. A larger plate sat in the center, piled high with pancakes.

Pancakes. Actual pancakes. Kim's salivary glands gave a solid pang of pain at the sight of them—then the smell hit her. It was vanilla and eggs and oil, and the heavenly scent of whatever it was that told a person *this is good to eat.* Beside the platter was a ceramic jug pilled with dark brown syrup, and a small dish of butter, and a shaker of what looked like cinnamon. The jug, she noticed, had a chip on its rim, and the cinnamon was leaking from a crack in the bottom of its plastic. Casualties of Adonai's rage.

She sat down as Adonai pulled her chair out, and smiled widely. "Oh, God, Adonai. This is incredible." She was almost afraid to start eating in case it turned out to be a dream.

"You haven't tasted it yet," Adonai said, taking the seat opposite her. "I might have gotten the ratios wrong. I'm not sure."

Kim lifted two pancakes from the stack and placed them on her plate. She drizzled the maple syrup over them, then added generous servings of butter and cinnamon. She rolled them up and sliced them, then took one, delicious, mouth-watering bite. The creamy, soft pancake was like heaven, the sweetness of the syrup divine. She moaned.

"Is it all right?"

"Don't talk to me right now," she mumbled, stuffing another bite into her mouth.

Adonai laughed. It was a strange sound, deep and burbling and with a tinny overtone. But there was no mistaking what it was.

Kim looked up sharply, halfway through a mouthful of food.

"I don'noillsclaf," she said. She swallowed and tried again. "I didn't know whales could laugh."

"Of course we can. We feel humor just as you do. We have special songs for it. Our song language has a particular tone to express amusement." This last sentence was wistful. "I've done my best to recreate your human approximation of laughter. Did it sound right?"

"Close enough," Kim said, before diving back into her pancakes. She had only taken a few more bites, however, before she had to break her own rule about not talking again. "You didn't notice anything unusual last night, then?"

Adonai shook his head. "No. There was no movement in the corridor. I kept very close watch."

"And you don't feel tired at all?"

"Not at all. Sleep doesn't seem necessary in this body."

"I wish I could say the same," she said, shaking her fuzzy head. At least the pancakes were making her feel more alert. She really needed to make sure she ate.

"You are gravely worried," Adonai said.

"Yes. And not just for myself. The whales—"

"I understand," Adonai cut her off. "They are my concern, too, and we have no way to keep them truly safe. The Aquarium is too big for us to guard all access to it at one time."

Kim nodded. "But don't forget—your body is in there, too. If something happens . . . "

"If my body dies, will I die too?" She knew Adonai wasn't really asking her. He was mulling over this problem in his own mind. "I'm not . . . connected to it at all. I can't sense what it's doing, or feeling. It's so strange."

"The other whales are concerned," Kim told him. "Hosea in particular. She thinks I'm lying to her when I tell her you're sick." She cut another slice. "She's right. I *am* lying."

"She's cleverer than even she thinks she is," Adonai said fondly.

"Question, though: if whales don't lie, how can they tell when I'm lying to them?"

"They can't," Adonai said firmly. "I couldn't. Hosea is just worried. She's my friend."

"I know," Kim said with a sigh. "But I can't tell her the truth, can I? I can't have any of the other whales trying what you did."

"Why not?"

It was a simple question, another one of Adonai's childish queries. But there was no easy answer.

"Because it's dangerous, Adonai. Do you know how many things could have gone wrong? And even now—you don't know if you'll ever be able to reverse it successfully. You could end up with brain damage. Or worse."

"I didn't say I wanted to go back," Adonai said. Kim stopped chewing mid-mouthful.

"Waymee?" She took a sip of water to wash down the sticky pancake, then repeated herself. "What do you mean?"

"I rather like it," Adonai admitted. "Being in this body. Talking with you. Cooking. I'm not sure I want to go back to being trapped in that tank."

"Adonai," Kim began. "You're a whale. You're supposed to swim and eat fish and . . . have little whale babies. That's why we're going to New Eden. You'll have a whole ocean to yourself, and you won't be hunted or in any danger. I know the tank sucks, but it's not forever. Two hundred days, that's all it's going to take to reach New Eden. We're already halfway there."

"I don't think you're listening to me," Adonai said plaintively.

Kim coughed and banged her chest with a flat palm. Adonai had sounded so human in that moment that she felt herself suddenly back in Chicago, at the restaurant with Abdiel and Wren, having a normal conversation with human friends. Definitely, definitely not sitting across from a droid who was really a whale. *How had this happened?* It was all so bizarre! She would have said something—an apology, perhaps, or maybe a reiteration of her stance, she couldn't be sure—but the computer chimed. "Kim, you have taken more than your allotted time for breakfast. It's time to being your tasks for today. I have a call from your counselor scheduled at 1100. You should begin the morning by undertaking Aquarium maintenance."

"Thank you, computer," Kim sighed. She'd made it through a third of the stack of pancakes. She wanted to eat more. She wanted to drown herself in maple syrup and sleep the rest of the day off in a sugary haze. Instead, she pushed her chair back and stood.

"I will clean up the galley," Adonai said, sounding disappointed.

"No need. The autobots'll be in here." She hesitated. "Would you mind accompanying me on my jobs today?"

Adonai brightened. "Of course. But what are we going to do about the human?"

"I'm going to think about that," Kim said. "We haven't seen him at all, so I think I'm safe for the moment. I'm going to assume he's not going to rush out of the shadows and . . . I don't know, stab me. But I can't leave my tasks undone, either. The ship needs to keep running. So let's do some brainstorming while we work."

Adonai almost bounce don his toes in eagerness. "Kim," he said. "What is brainstorming?"

It was strange, having companionship while she attended to the small routine tasks. When the time came to head down to the Aquarium, she wondered how he would feel about facing the other whales, but he seemed happy enough. She knew there was no danger of him letting on to them about what he'd done. He wasn't connected to the Link, so he couldn't communicate with them. He could shout at the top of his lungs, and all they would hear, through the glass or the forcefields, would be the insensible sounds of human speech.

She entered the Aquarium at Deck Eleven, Adonai staying doggedly at her side. She checked one of the junction stations, just to make sure the computer was getting the right readings, and this confirmed everything was optimal. Water temperature had fallen a bit, but was still within acceptable levels. The force fields were holding strong. A small stress fracture had caused a leak at one point, however, and she'd have to fix that quickly.

"This way," she told Adonai and swung herself onto one of the ladders. She descended quickly, but had to wait for the droid. He had stopped moving and craned his head to look up.

"This is what it looks like?" Adonai said in wonder. "It's beautiful."

"It is, isn't it?" Kim nodded, remembering the first time she'd seen it.

"So this is blue," Adonai went on. "It's so . . . incredible." He'd borrowed the word *incredible* from her description of the pancakes this morning, she realized with a smile. "I can't believe I've never seen it before."

"Blue's my favorite color," Kim told him as she led him toward the tank wall. "It's a very tranquil color. It makes me feel peaceful."

"Oh, yes, me too," he agreed fervently.

Up ahead, one of the glass walls bulged close to the catwalk. Kim saw her reflection and Adonai's, reflected and distorted by the convex surface, but was taken by surprise when a dark shape loomed up behind them. It only took a fraction of a second for her to realize the shape was in the water, not in the reflection, but that was enough time for her heart to start racing and the pancakes to start doing flips in her stomach. She had whirled around, hand going to her flashlight, but there was nothing there. Instead, Fifteen peered out at them.

Kim! You've got another one like you!

"Hey, Fifteen," she said as she turned back a bit. "Sorry. You startled me."

You shouldn't be scared of me, silly! I'm really nice.

"I know, I know. Good to see you, Fifteen."

"Is he answering you?" Adonai asked, curious at this one-sided conversation.

"Yeah," Kim told him. She glanced sideways, trying to see if this affected him at all, but she couldn't tell. "He's . . . well, just being Fifteen."

You have a friend to talk to! That's so cool.

She laughed. She'd taught him that word. "Yes," she said. "This is . . . Martin."

"Martin?" Adonai repeated, confused.

"I can't tell him your real name. And I don't want to slip up while I'm talking on the Link, okay?"

"Okay," Adonai replied, sounding distant.

Afriendisgood. His words tumbled over one another as his enthusiasm spilled across the Link. *Good. Good. I like friends. Will he be mine, too?*

"Sure," Kim said to the excited Minke. "Martin, this is Fifteen. You can say hello to him."

Adonai stepped forward and lifted his hand in a half-wave. Fifteen bobbed his head, overjoyed.

"I'm sorry, I have to go down below. I've got work to do. See you later, okay?"

I'm going to go tell the others about my new friend! Fifteen darted off, tail tapping the glass in his haste. Kim gritted her teeth. The glass could withstand more force than that, but she would rather not test it near where a section was already weakened.

Kim continued along the catwalk, seeing the section that needed attention up ahead. It was a flat sheet of glass, not curved, but it was about sixty-five feet in width and almost twice that in height, bordered on all sides by steel frames. She saw the crack almost instantly. Water was beading below it, running slowly in the lessened gravity. The crack itself was only a finger in length, a white scar. She examined it a little more closely. Only part of it, in the center, had actually given way and gone right through the toughened glass.

"It's only small," Adonai said. "What would happen if it was bigger?"

"The glass is designed to hold the weight of a spaceship," she replied. "It's threaded through with some kind of high-tensile material, and there are forcefields that will expand into place if needed. This glass doesn't shatter, not ever. It wouldn't split more than maybe three feet in length before the mesh caught the weight and the forcefields activated. It would give me an hour, maybe two—enough time to re pair it before it got any worse. The main thing is to make sure I get the angle of the sealer right. If I mucked it up and heated it too much, the glass could split even wider."

"And if you couldn't repair it?"

"There are droids who can do the work, too. But I feel better if I do it myself. It's my job."

Adonai was quiet as she pulled a handheld sealing tool from her belt and lifted its muzzle to the fracture. Pushing a button, the tip sprayed super-heated air that melted the glass, resealing it in a few minutes. The water around it began to bubble and boil long before she was done. A red glow spread outwards from the fracture, cooled quickly by the water, but, true to Kim's word, not shattering under the extremes of temperature either.

"How did humans make this kind of material?"

Kim lifted her shoulders in a shrug. "Centuries of mucking around, I guess. Some things worked. Some things didn't. Some things we made better. Some things we probably should have left alone."

"You're talking about the whales."

"I'm talking about a lot of things," she replied. "Here, hold this." She gave him the heating tool to hold as she got closer to the section of glass. The last of the red glow was fading to a purple. She crouched down to make sure that it looked sealed from all angles. "We've got to make sure I've sealed it all the way through. The glass three feet thick, so if I've left a piece unjointed on the other side, it'll just crack again later."

Adonai bent closer too, mimicking her pose. He looked almost comical. "So you've got to get right to the source of it," he said.

Kim straightened. "It looks good." She took the tool back from him and ran a hand over the now-cold glass. It was smooth to the touch. "And I think I know what we need to do."

"About what? We've fixed the glass."

"The glass isn't our real problem. We need to find out more about that ship, and I think what you just said is spot-on. We've got to get to the source of the problem. It's no good standing around waiting for him to come after us."

"You're talking about going after the human? Kim, I don't think that's a good idea."

"I think it's a *brilliant* idea," Kim said. "And no, we're not going after him. We're just going to get a bit more information. He's been hanging out on the ship for days, maybe months. In which case, he could be watching us right now." She glanced around unconsciously. "He might have access to the computer, to all our systems. But we don't know anything about *him*. I don't like giving him that advantage."

"What are you intending to do, then?"

"We're going to take a look at his ship."

"Oh. You mean go back outside? I mean—go EV?"

"I don't even need to. He's parked right over an airlock, so there's internal access to his vessel."

Adonai turned his head toward her. "You are very smart, Kim."

Kim laughed grimly. "Save the flattery for when I come out with my head blown off my shoulders."

"I don't understand. You couldn't walk if—"

"It's a joke," she told him.

"I wouldn't allow it to happen anyway," Adonai said resolutely. "I'll go in first."

Kim found herself filled with gratitude. "Thank you, Adonai." With a deep breath, she slipped the tool back into her belt. The heavy shifter and flashlight swayed comfortingly against her thighs. "Well. No time like the present."

As she and Adonai made their way to the ramp and climbed it to Deck Eight, she changed her mind several times over whether or not to go through with it.

But as her feet hit the solid deck, her fear turned into determination. She could handle herself against a man. She'd done it before, hadn't she? She remembered one particularly cold night, before Constantin had taken her in. She'd huddled in an alley, trying to sleep, when a rough hand had hauled her up and thrown her against a wall. He'd been on her almost instantly, fumbling, grunting, an animal of a man. She'd kicked out, kept him back, until he wrapped both his meaty arms around her waist. So she'd gouged his eyes with her fingers, pressing in until she felt something hot and wet burst under her nails.

Kim wasn't afraid of a fight. She needed to stop acting like Hannah and start taking control.

She grinned, and felt the adrenaline coursing into her veins, hastening her step, sharpening her vision. This is the action she should have taken last night, instead of hiding in her quarters like a mouse. This was what she was good at. Action. It was just like going on a raid in another gang's territory, she thought, when you never knew what you'd find waiting for you. An armed crew waiting to take you on. Unwitting bystanders—warehouse owners, or partygoers in the wrong place at the wrong time, but who could nevertheless raise the alarm. Cops. Security droids. Or nothing at all but clean and easy bounty—though that one was rare, she had to admit.

Only now, instead of Cons by her side, she had Adonai. The blue whale. Her loyal guard, untested though he was.

Well, this would be a test if ever there was one, she decided. She didn't think they'd find nothing.

They moved down the corridor of Deck Eight, following its dipping curve. Lights flickered on overhead, but the corridor ran along one side of this deck, following the curve of the outer hull, so she couldn't see its end. They were heading toward the rear of the ship, but Kim hadn't spent much time on Deck Eight. It contained mostly piping and pumps for the fishery and the Aquarium regulation equipment. She could hear loud gurgling and a few sludgy pops coming from beyond the walls.

"We'll go in here," she said to Adonai. She was whispering, though she didn't know why. Adonai's tread was loud enough on the decking to wake the dead, and she wasn't really trying to disguise their approach, but she felt herself bending her knees and transferring her weight smoothly toward the door.

It opened ahead of her, hissing to one side without complaint. Inside, she saw snaking brown and green metal and several rubber hoses the size of tree-trunks. These moved of their own accord, like giant worms pushing themselves through soil, but without ever gaining any ground. Loud slurping sounds came from them. The odor of damp and old water pervaded the air, and something else, something like old unwashed laundry left to molder. Kim's stomach roiled but she kept her composure.

The lights flickered on one by one, illuminating a narrow catwalk that passed over, under, and around the miasma of pipework. Steam hissed suddenly from a valve, making her jump. She felt a hot blast of air even though it was over ten feet away.

Adonai went ahead of her, and she bought up the rear. They moved relatively swiftly. The thrum and gurgling drowned out the noise of Adonai's heavier tread, at least, but Kim kept a close eye on her surroundings, darting her head back and forth between the left and right sides of the chamber, lifting her gaze to the high reaches above, peering into the blackness below. There were many things moving, turning, opening and closing, but not one of them was the figure she was searching for.

Perhaps there was no such person. What if she really had imagined it? Even the Mayfly might have been an illusion . . . but no. Unless she could hallucinate through the eyes of a tech droid as well? But then, everything she'd viewed through the tech droid's eyes had been overlaid on the helmet's holoprojectors. She supposed it was possible . . .

They'd reached a conjunction with another catwalk before she was really ready for it. She hefted the flashlight in one hand. Was it this one? Yes, she thought so. She tapped Adonai's shoulder, but he seemed to be well ahead of her, already turning onto it. They passed through a cloud of thick steam, the moisture clinging to Kim's jumpsuit and hair. It was getting hard to breathe, but maybe that was nerves as well as the sauna-like heat. Her armpits were damp, and a trickle of sweat ran into her eye. She wiped it away with the back of her hand and adjusted her grip on the flashlight. The plastic handle was slipping in her grasp.

They reached a set of stairs, winding up behind a particularly large green pipe. She disliked having Adonai ahead of her here, for if something happened, he could topple right back on top of her. Still, the staircase was narrow, and though she could have passed him easily, it would have cost her precious seconds.

She wasn't sure that that mattered, except for the fact that she wanted this over with.

"It feels as if . . . " Adonai said. His voice sounded hollow and strange in this place.

"As if what?" Kim prompted.

"As if someone is watching us."

The words sent a chill down Kim's spine. She hadn't felt it before, but after Adonai's words, she most certainly did. She remembered, too, that Hosea had said she felt she was being watched, days and days ago. Psychosomatic or not, the implication made her skin crawl.

They reached the top of the stairs and found themselves at a branching fork of two much more narrow walkways. "Left or r—" she asked, but at that moment, there was a flicker of movement in the upper corner of her eye.

"Hey!" she yelled, lifting her flashlight and flicking the beam on. It hit a gantry above her, showing nothing . . . but the gantry itself was shaking. "There's someone up there," she said. She felt the burn of lactic acid in her joints as she jumped over the railing. Clinging to the outside, she sidestepped quickly along the edge of the walkway past a surprised Adonai, then leapt back over. The way ahead of her was clear, and she ran.

She pelted to the right, neck craned, looking up at the spot she was certain the man had been. There was no stairway or ladder leading up there, however; only a thick metal door ahead of her, and another to the left of it. She crashed into it, putting her palms out flat and letting her arms slow her to a stop. She punched the button to open the door. It flashed red.

"Kim?" the computer's voice entered the gloom. "That is a restricted area, and you are not wearing safety gear."

"Shut up!" Kim snarled. "Open the damn door, computer! This is an emergency!"

"Please return to the outer chambers and put on protective gear, Kim. I cannot see any reason for you entering the water plant without safety goggles and heat resistant—"

She slapped her fist against the door, then whirled and scanned the upper reaches once more. No sign of anyone. Nothing.

Adonai had reached her by now, his glowing eyes shining bright in the darkness. "Did you see the human?"

"I saw something," Kim said. "I know I did."

"Kim, I must protest. You are scheduled for a call with Edgeward at 1100 hours. Perhaps you should return to . . . "

Kim drew the kanji for *silence*. The computer's voice stopped, and Kim, looking upwards once more, put the flashlight between her teeth and leapt onto the railing, crouching there, braced with only one hand and her two feet. Her balance was a little shaky, but she still kept it. She straightened, propelling herself upwards, and jumped. She caught one of the pipes just above her, a slender copper tube.

"Kim!" Adonai gasped, but Kim ignored him.

The pipes carrying hot water were thinner and wrapped in insulation. If she aimed for the larger ones that were bare metal, she would avoid burning herself.

She swung her legs up, using that momentum to push herself around to the top of the pipe. The pipe swayed under her, but it held firm. She stood, keeping perfect balance, and reached for one slightly off to the right. She didn't have to jump for this one—it was just like climbing a ladder.

Now there was nothing in reach above her, but if she went—yes, there, to her left, another much thicker pipe was in reach. From there she reached out and pulled herself upwards once more. Her teeth clacked painfully against the flashlight as she spun in an arc and flung her body at the next pipe along. She'd left Adonai far below her, now, and the gantry above, where she'd seen the figure, was much closer.

She edged her way along this pipe, but found it tipped downwards at forty degrees. She jumped instead of following it down, and caught the one just above her head. She checked the distance—not far to go now. She was almost in reach of the gantry.

It was as she was evaluating this distance, standing, ready to jump, that the ship gave one of its small shakes. This happened every now and then, a dozen times a day. Mostly it was imperceptible, but balancing on a rounded surface made it a thousand times more apparent. Kim stretched her arms out to counter the movement and steady herself, but it was too little. Her left foot slipped out from under her, and she let out a yelp as the flashlight dropped from her teeth, spiraling into the abyss below, its beam wheeling through the air.

She reached out. Just in time, her hands clamped around the pipe, pulling her up short. But she knew it was a precarious position— the pipe was larger than her fist, and she couldn't grasp it properly, couldn't get her thumb underneath to get any strength into her grip. She let out a grunt of frustration and tasted blood in her mouth. The flashlight must have hit something on its way out.

"Damn," she gasped. Something shot past her at the speed of a bullet. It was a solid jet of steam, expanding outwards in a cone shape. The vapor was so close it stung her chin, and the heat hit her like a whip. She cried out again, this time as pain drew tears to her eyes. Squinting, she could see that the pipe that was venting was just underneath her. If she dropped down, or slipped, she had no way of avoiding it. The insulation would offer her a few seconds before the heat tore through her skin.

There was another cold pipe beside it, over a foot away. She could reach it, but it was only as wide as the one she gripped now. If she overbalanced before catching it, she'd end up falling, and who knew what she'd hit on her way down?

Another burst of steam seared her chest. Her hands were slippery with sweat. She couldn't hold on much longer. It had to be now.

She kicked her legs out and hoped that the vent did not release another jet of steam as she was jumping through it. But she arrowed downwards without hindrance. The gloom whirled around her, but she kept her eyes on the pipe. Her feet passed it by, and she stretched out with her arms, reaching desperately forward and twisting her torso to match the angle of the pipe. Her left hand hit it, clenched, but felt only empty air as it slid off. Her right hand made contact and brought her up short with a sudden jerk that almost pulled her arm out of its socket. She'd fallen much harder than she'd planned. Her grip wasn't the solid fist she'd have liked. She was slipping.

Her eyes were drawn invariably downwards, to the depths rotating below her. The pipes squirmed and reared like writhing snakes. She could almost feel her body falling already, smacking into those metal branches, tumbling end over end down to the deck below them . . .

"Kim, I've got you!"

A hand clasped over her wrist with bruising force. It pulled upwards, dragging her past the pipe and setting her on the gantry. It was Adonai, of course it was Adonai, but she couldn't quite believe it. How had he gotten up here so fast?

Tech droid, she reminded herself. He could jump farther than she could, and hell, he even had a better sense of balance. He'd reached the gantry long before she'd even come close.

"Crap," she breathed. "Thank you."

"You're most welcome, Kim. But please take more care in the future. I thought you would fall."

"Well, you did a good job of catching me," she said. "Come on, we're wasting time!"

"Kim—wait—"

But Kim was already off, running down the gantry. It was just a narrow metal beam supported by wires, made for maintenance bots, not human passage. Her chin and the skin around her collarbone, which hadn't been protected by the semi-heat resistant material of her jumpsuit, felt tender and tight, and her arms ached, but she didn't care. She felt better than she had in a long time, in fact. She grinned as she ran along the gantry, feeling it wobble far more than the catwalks had. Where had the man gone?

"Kim," the computer spoke. "I have overridden your order because I am detecting an injury. Please remain where you are. A med-bot is on its way."

She saw a hatchway up ahead. It was a maintenance bot entry portal, but she folded herself small and dived inside. A tunnel ran ahead of her. She plunged along it at a crawl, scraping her hands and knees, pausing only once when she thought she heard a clang from up ahead. Or had that been from behind her? Adonai was coming, she realized, as the metal walls lit up with the reflected gold of his eyes. She forged on, rounding one corner, then another, then jumping up a section that led into a higher tunnel. The way was dusty and smeared with grease from the bots. She could feel the stuff sticking to her knees and hands.

And then, all of a sudden, she was out. And sure enough, there, opposite her, was an airlock. *The* airlock. Adonai skittered out of the tunnel behind her, dropping to all fours and unfolding himself from the crawling posture he'd adopted, which bent his arms at the elbow and legs at the knee, creating strange truncated limbs that propelled him forward at greater speed than Kim could have managed.

"Kim, please remain where you are. You are injured. It is not wise to continue moving."

"Shut up," Kim whispered.

Another door to her left should have led back down to Deck Eight, probably to the door she'd tried to access. Its panel glowed red—locked. But while the airlock was closed, it wasn't locked. The access panel glowed green. The airlock was pressurized. She hit the key without hesitation, and the large round door irised open, revealing a chamber filled with emergency EV suits. The outer door was also unlocked.

"Think we've found our man's route into the ship," she said.

"Do you think it's safe to open this door?" Adonai asked. He sounded nervous.

"I can't be sure," Kim said. She lifted her shifter from her toolbelt. "If that ship is on the other side, though, I need to see it."

"He—your human—could be waiting for you."

"I'm counting on it," Kim replied grimly, and smacked her hand against the panel. The door cracked open at the center.

CHAPTER
16

Beyond was a steep ramp leading up into the ship's interior. There was no one waiting for her in the half-light spilling though the ribbed airlock chamber. The lintels were low, and even though she wasn't tall, she had to duck to step through them.

Kim, what are you doing now?

Kim cursed. It was Levi.

I'm bored, Kim. Can you talk to me?

"Not now," she hissed.

"I'm sorry," Adonai said.

"Not you," Kim murmured. She gestured at her head, at the Link. "I don't have time for this now." Levi subsided, withdrawing, leaving behind a reproachful sense of disappointment. Kim tried hard not to care. She couldn't coddle Levi right now. "Tell the others not to talk to me. I mean it. I can't be distracted."

He said nothing more.

Adonai was just behind her, a solid presence, but she stopped and turned to him. "You need to stay here," she said in a whisper. "We can't be sure there's anyone in there. If someone comes back through one of those doors, you'll need to—"

To what? She asked herself grimly. Whack them on the head? Ask them nicely not to kill her?

"I would rather accompany you." Adonai had somehow managed to lower his voice to the point of whispering himself.

Kim looked at the narrow ramp. Adonai could probably navigate it just as well as she could, and really, he *was* the one who should be going in. He was—though she would never admit it to his face—expendable.

She was not. She was the Caretaker. And if whoever was aboard meant to harm the Ark Project, he would take out her. Not the tech droid.

Still, she couldn't allow him to do it. The possibility of Adonai walking into a situation he couldn't handle—that would be too painful. Besides which, this person was a human. Kim had to be there if there was any negotiation to be made. Adonai could not do that on her behalf.

"I'm better trained for this," Kim whispered, and, bending down, she unclipped her boots and slid them off. "And I can travel more quietly. It has to be me."

Before he could protest further, she moved, running crabwise up the steep ramp in her socks, her hand still clenched tightly on the shifter. As she neared the top, she ducked. Her feet made no noise at all on the metal decking, which was much more solid than that on *Seiiki*. She could have gotten away with her boots, she thought wryly.

She'd never been inside a Mayfly, but she had a basic idea of the layout. When she looked up, she was inside the middle compartment. Above and to her left would be the cockpit. Below and to the right, the engines. On either side, the wings, and also the cannons she'd seen from outside.

The compartment above her wasn't big, maybe six feet high and six across. The walls were jammed full of controls, though. Switches, levers and blinking indicator lights, most of which were darkened right now.

There was a pile of paperback books tucked atop one of the consoles, and two half-empty bottles of a neon blue energy drink crammed into one of the niches above the weapons array. There were more empty bottles on the floor, and a couple of chip packets as well. The place had a slightly-off smell to it, like soup someone had cooked the day before but had left out of the fridge.

She hopped over the lip of the ramp and looked at the ladder leading into the cockpit. To her left, a similar ladder led down through a hole in the floor to the engines, cold and dark now. She hung for a moment on the bottom rungs, listening, before climbing. There was no sound from inside the ship, save a small electronic chattering that grew louder as she climbed.

The cockpit was a bubble-like space with a clear window swooping down from overhead to meet the nose of the scout ship. A U-shaped console sat below that, and a single pilot's chair was crammed into the remaining space. The whole cockpit was little bigger than her bunk back in her quarters.

A blanket was crumpled up, slung half-off the chair and draped on the floor. A greasy stain marred one corner of it. The soup-smell came from a cardboard carton balanced atop numerous other cardboard cartons beneath the console. They were stamped with numbers on the side rather than words, which could only mean one thing—military rations. Daddy had tons of those in his aircar whenever he came back from a week of training exercises. She could still remember the taste of them—slightly cardboardy, too spicy, but exciting nonetheless. *This is what space pilots eat,* she'd think, as Daddy served her one when he was too tired to cook.

The chair was spilling stuffing from a corner. Another book sat, pages dog-eared and splayed open, on the console. It seemed odd, so old-world, to see real paper books scattered around like this. Strangely . . . comforting. But that could be because they brought back memories of her dad, and in that case, it was dangerous to let down her guard. She had to stay alert. Had to assume she was still in danger.

The scout ship was empty, completely empty, and had been for hours. There was a way things felt when someone had just touched them, had only moments ago stepped out. She had been finely tuned to it, once, in that now-distant other life.

She looked down at the console. It was running on battery power, of course. It couldn't have been drawing power from *Seiiki,* or she'd have noticed. A few lights flickered, telling her that the engines were powered down, but that fuel reserves were at half-capacity. Docking clamps were engaged. And there . . . she leaned over, picking up a tablet with a cracked screen propped up on one console.

She tapped it open. A holographic display popped up—an old one, clunky and unresponsive—telling her that the Mayfly's computer was tapped into *Seiiki's.*

She opened the first file that came into view. The tag told her it had been accessed as recently as five hours ago. A video file, plucked from the internal cameras. It showed her bedroom. Kim was lying under the covers on her bunk, hand tucked under her head, gravity blanket scrunched between her body and the bulkhead.

A freezing sense of dread washed over her. *He'd been watching her.*

There was a sound from somewhere below. A swift sigh and soft thud. Kim dithered at the display, desperate to see more, to find out which systems had been accessed and *why*. But the next sound was one she couldn't ignore.

The sound of footsteps. And not Adonai's heavy tread, either.

She backed into the corner beside the door, and clenched her shifter tightly in one hand, the tablet in the other. She had almost forgotten the burn across her chest, but suddenly, it flared to life. She sucked a breath between her teeth.

Somewhere below, the computer squawked once more, begging her to wait for the medbot. Damn. The intruder would know she was injured.

The footsteps had reached the bottom of the ladder. She heard him grasp a rung, but there was no further movement.

"Kim?"

The voice. That voice. Clipped syllables, sharp consonants. A strong British accent. She knew it, though it had never said her name before. Not her *true* name.

She didn't drop the shifter. In fact, she gripped it more tightly. What was he doing here? She'd left him back on Ganymede, angry and bitter. His last words to her had been harsh. *You know you don't deserve this.* She felt them still, buried in her heart like shrapnel.

"Kim, come down. I know you're in there. Your tech droid's been disabled. There's no point in hiding."

She tensed, ready to hurl herself through the hatch, strike him in the face with the heavy tool. She was ready for this. She could take him out. It wasn't like she hadn't killed someone before.

"Damn, Kim," he said. He was on the ladder now, climbing. "You're not going to brain me with something, are you? I wouldn't blame you, but I'd rather you—"

Kim stepped into the doorway, the shifter moving through her hands like water. She swung and brought it down less than an inch from his face, whistling past the tip of his nose.

"Whoa!" He leaned backward and almost toppled off the ladder.

Kim followed the attempt with a push, hitting him in the chest with the tablet. Another crack whipped across the screen as he went backward. It wasn't as hard a shove as she could have given him, but he'd loosened his grip to avoid the swipe, and this time, he was propelled from the ladder. He landed with a crash, one elbow catching the brunt of his weight.

The gun—holy *crap*, he'd been carrying a gun and she hadn't even noticed it—shot out of his hands, hitting the ramp with a solid *thwack* that would have made Kim cringe if she hadn't already identified it as a stunner, not a real firearm.

It slid out of view.

Kim looked down at him from the doorway, her expression cold.

"Damn," Wren said. Pulling himself to his knees, he straightened his arm and spread his fingers, testing his elbow. "What did you do that for?"

Kim tucked the tablet into her pocket and made her way down the rungs, shifter clutched in two fingers of one hand. She kept her eyes on him as much as possible until she was on the floor once more, wary of his every movement.

"You've been snooping around aboard my ship. Why do you think I did that?"

"*Your* ship?" Wren scoffed. "Hate to break it to you, but this ship belongs to Near Horizon, *Hannah*."

Kim stopped in front of him and crossed her arms, the shifter dangling menacingly from one hand. She didn't look at the gun. He'd have to get past her to get to the ramp. She wasn't going to allow that.

"It doesn't matter," she said, "If you know who I am, then you know why I'd rather have you on the ground than up in my face." She was trying hard to hide the fact that her mind was racing madly. He was here. He knew her real name. Which meant he knew . . . what, exactly? Her past? Or did he, much more alarmingly, somehow know her *present*? If so, why hadn't Edgeward sent out an armada to take her into custody? For that matter, why, of all people, was *Wren Keene* here, and not an Earth United sec-officer?

But Wren wasn't looking at her like a dead woman walking. He was rubbing his elbow and looking quite sorry for himself.

She remembered the first time she'd seen him, back in Near Horizon's Melbourne headquarters. His neat suit fit him so well, it might have been a second skin, and his black hair, long and tied back in a bun at the nape of his neck, was glossy. His skin was the color of a dark cappuccino, and he had ignored her so completely, she'd felt she wasn't even in the room.

Now, for what felt like the first time, she truly *looked* at him, seeing beyond the sheltered, egotistical boy she'd competed with for the title of Caretaker. He was wearing a grey jumpsuit, much like her blue one, but much grubbier. His hair was longer than it had been those three months ago, and his beard had grown a little, too. He didn't look like the slick businessman's son she'd first met, and more like a rough spacefarer at a portside bar on Mars. He wiped a hand over his lips. "I guess I just didn't know you had that much strength in you."

"That's because you don't know me," Kim said. There was a hint of defensiveness in her voice that she wished she could have covered up.

"Oh, that's right," he replied. "Kim Teng. Not Hannah Monksman." Derisively, he added, "Hannah suits you better."

"Screw you," she said, glaring at him. "What did you do to Adonai?"

"*Adonai*," he repeated the name meaningfully, "is fine. I stunned him, but it's nothing that can't be fixed. But what are you doing, letting him walk around in a droid like that? I mean, seriously?"

"What do you know about it?" She watched him, wanting to know the extent of his knowledge, and how long, exactly, he'd been watching her. She'd be able to read if he was holding anything back. At least, she would have been able to, in the past. Maybe she'd lost that ability with lack of practice, too.

"Enough," he said. He shuffled on his knees, and she leveled the shifter at him, warning him not to try anything. He winced. He was, most likely, just trying to get comfortable. "More than enough. Jeez, Kim. You've really messed up here."

Kim shook her head. She opened her mouth, about to tell him exactly what she thought of his *own* particular mess, when, with a whirring sound, Adonai charged up the rampway and clattered to a stop. In one hand, he held Wren's lost stunner clumsily. The other was frozen rigid, as was one leg from the waist to the ankle. He loped like a lame dog, but he still held a dangerous weapon.

Wren let out a frightened "God! Don't *shoot!*"

The buzzing sound came from Adonai's shoulder joint, where sparks were jumping in tiny arcs. One of his eyes fritzed, and his voice, when he spoke, was like one of the scratchy old vinyl records that Kim's dad used to listen to. "Stay where you are! Stay where you are! Danger! Enemy human! Kim, are you okay?"

The sight of Adonai with a gun was more frightening than anything else Kim had seen in this ship. "I'm fine," Kim said. "Adonai, I'm fine. Give me the stunner."

Adonai looked down, as if he'd just noticed what he was holding. He lifted it. "The human held this at me and fired!" he said indignantly. "It made my mind hurt badly! He's a bad human. Kim, I'll kill him if you want me to."

"No!" Both Kim and Wren shouted at once, and Adonai hesitated, obviously confused.

"Adonai," Kim began. "Thank you. But you need to give me the gun, okay? Carefully." She held out her hand and beckoned enticingly, still not moving her eyes from Wren. She'd still take him down if she needed to, but she'd rather do it with the stunner than the shifter. Kim felt a sigh of relief as her fingers closed around the hilt. The stunner was made of plastic, lightweight for a weapon. She'd have preferred a real gun any day. She tilted it and checked the side panel for charge. The green indicator showed three quarters full. "Stun gun, eh?" she asked Wren. "Not a real weapon?"

"I'm not here to kill you," he said. Suddenly, a look of horror crossed his face. "That's not what you think, is it?"

"What am I supposed to think?" Kim fired back at him. "You've been watching me. The one camera aboard this ship that would have detected you has been interfered with, and the computer can't even pick you up . . ."

"Kim," he said, and he would have said more, but at that moment, there was a loud tearing sound, as if a monstrous claw was scraping a giant blackboard. Kim yelped, both hands coming up, stun gun in one, shifter in the other, both arms crossed over at the wrists in front of her as if she'd use both at the same time on . . . whatever this new threat was.

She could see something moving at the bottom of the ramp, but that small triangular gap didn't show anything more than that something was coming.

Wren whirled. He lost his balance, though, crouched as he was, he didn't have far to fall. Adonai turned from the waist, looking over his shoulder, as startled as the rest of them. Then Kim heard the computer's voice.

"Kim. Stay where you are. A medbot is on its way to you. Stay where you are and do not move. You might cause further injury to yourself..."

"You *didn't*," Kim cried exasperatedly. She dropped her hands, weapons still clutched. "God damn that stupid computer."

A second later, the black form of the medbot edged up the ramp, hovering unevenly. It was folding away the large mechanical saw it had used to cut through the locked door to the airlock.

"You require medical attention," the medbot said as its blue lights flashed over her. "Detecting third degree burns. Please lie down—"

"It's right," Wren said, unexpectedly. "I saw what happened to you up there. I can't believe you're still standing after taking a scald like that."

"It's nothing," she snapped. Kim stepped back, leveling the stunner at the medbot. If it came at her, she'd have to take it out. Wren might use the opportunity to escape, and she couldn't risk that. She couldn't submit to its treatment, either, even though her chest was killing her, little fingers of prickling pain reaching up the side of her neck and down across her stomach. No way could she afford to let herself be laid out now, and she doubted she'd be as lucky in avoiding it this time.

But before she could pull the trigger, another droid appeared behind it. A tech droid. Its gleaming silver body was almost identical to Adonai's, except for the glow of its eyes, which were a little less golden.

It fixed these eyes on Wren. "Security threat detected," it said. "Intruder, stay where you are. Do not move."

Wren's mouth gaped. So did Kim's.

It was Adonai who provided the explanation. "I thought we would need assistance," he said. "Did I do the right thing, Kim?"

The tech droid stepped in front of Wren. "Stand," it said. "You will be escorted to a secure room."

"What? Kim?" Wren said.

Kim gaped at Adonai. "You did this?"

"Yes," he said. "I can ask the computer to do otherwise with him if you like."

"No," Kim answered. "I mean, yes, take him to one of the store rooms—what's your designation?"

The droid answered promptly. "3-4-2-9."

"Yes, take him to store room 9B on Deck Seven. Erect a force field. And guard the door. Okay?"

"Understood." 3429 waited, and Wren slowly picked himself up. Looking at Kim, he said, resentfully, "I've hurt my elbow, you know. I need a medbot."

"I don't care," Kim said. "Get him out of here and keep him secure. I mean it—he's good with computers. Don't give him a chance to get near a control station."

"I will accompany them to make sure it's done, if you like," Adonai offered.

"Yes, please." Kim felt, suddenly, like she was about to pass out. The quicker they got Wren out of there the better. She didn't want to show him how badly she was hurt. She couldn't be sure that Adonai would do the job better than she could herself, but he'd proved himself today.

She was glad of it. Having to deal with this on her own would have been a nightmare, but with him as backup—well, she was certainly better off.

"You can't lock me up," Wren protested, but he moved ahead of the tech droid obediently. Kim didn't think he'd try anything, not against two of those machines. They made their way slowly down the ramp. Kim followed them, the medbot trailing behind her, bleeping insistently. She saw the hacked-up remnants of the door through to the airlock, pieces of metal peeled back like the skin of a banana. She looked back at the medbot with increased respect.

"Please lie down on the stretcher," it demanded, unfolding a stretcher that looked surprisingly inviting.

CHAPTER
17

The burns took four hours to heal. She was still lying on the stretcher inside the airlock when the computer buzzed her softly.

"Kim, you are overdue for your counseling appointment by several hours. Dr. White has been trying to reach you. I have let her know that you were indisposed, and that you will contact her as soon as you're able."

"Indisposed?" Kim laughed. Her chest felt puffy and cold. The bot had sprayed some type of gel over the area that had hardened into a kind of latex bandage. It was a bit like having a large slug sitting on her chest. She groaned as she pulled herself upright and buttoned her jumpsuit back up. The medbot had carried her back through the ruined doors and into a room on Deck Eight, not too far away from the door it had blasted open, since she could see it through the open door to this room. Obviously it hadn't felt comfortable with taking her all the way up to the infirmary. She wondered exactly how serious her burn had been.

"I am afraid I did not know what else to say," the computer said stiffly. "I did not wish to tell her that you have been talking to yourself more often, and undertaking rash and dangerous activities against my express protests, and silencing me when I objected."

That surprised Kim. "I wouldn't have thought you'd have an issue with tattling on me, honestly."

"You have not yet deleted the outcome of the self-reflexive exercise from yesterday," the computer replied. "While the mode is no longer active, the information I have assembled implies a deliberate interruption to the ship's systems. I have integrated the possibility of my being compromised into all decisions. If you are indeed facing a danger that I am not aware of, I must do what I can to protect you and the whales. This means keeping certain information to myself, including your behavior, in case there is a security leak somewhere on Edgeward Base."

Kim swallowed. Her head felt thick and fuzzy. "Okay, good. Great. Keep doing that." So the Admiral still knew nothing. That was why the comms hadn't been stuffed full of messages telling her to lock down the ship, cut the engines, and wait for a boarding party. "I'll call Dr White in a minute. Has a new force field been set up on Deck Seven?"

"Yes. The force field contains store room 9B. Is the reason for this forcefield related to the possibility of an intruder on the ship? Is this also the reason for the presence of one tech droid at the entrance?"

"Yes. Keep it up until further notice. And leave the tech droid there. It's following my orders." It would have to be the other tech droid, the one Adonai had summoned. 3429. But it wasn't following her order at all—it was following Adonai's.

She hoped that didn't matter.

Limping, she made her way from the room. The medbot bleeped at her and folded back its hypodermic needles and stretcher, then hovered its way down the corridor to wherever it recharged its supplies. She took a door to the left, onto one of the ramps, and made her way up to Deck One.

She ran her fingers through her hair and spat on her hand, wiping her cheeks and forehead of greasy stains. She pulled her collar straight and dialed Edgeward.

"Lieutenant Grand here." He looked at her, a cloud crossing his face. "You look like crap."

"Hannah Monksman for Dr. White," she said as formally as she could manage.

He shrugged. "Patching you through."

"Hannah!" Dr. White appeared almost immediately. "I've been worried. Are you all right? Your computer's been giving me the runaround."

"I'm fine," Kim said. "I had a problem with the gravity stabilizers. Had to get it fixed."

"Oh, I see. I suppose it'll all show up on your logs, so that's not what I want to talk about."

Yeah, it would show up on the logs, when Kim figured out how to insert false data into the computer. "Oh?" she said, trying to sound as if she wasn't dreading what Mona was going to tell her.

"Happy birthday, Hannah!"

Kim stared at the projected face for a moment, completely lost.

"I know it's not much fun having your birthday when you're all alone, and honestly, I only found out because I was reviewing your file last night and it caught my eye. I'm sorry. But it's a big deal, turning twenty. I hope, despite all the challenges your facing, you can still find the time to have a good day."

It was the most ludicrous thing anyone had ever said to her, but Kim felt a swelling of gratitude that was completely, totally unwarranted. It wasn't even her real her birthday. It was Hannah's. And she wasn't turning twenty, that was for sure. But of course Mona didn't know that, and Kim felt peculiarly grateful for this generous sentiment.

"Your parents sent through a few messages," she said. "I'll have comms send them over to you. So, how are you doing, otherwise?"

"Fine," Kim said. Messages from her parents? She wondered what these could be—since she had no parents, real or otherwise. "Today's just been a bit tiring."

"Have you been getting enough sleep?"

"Yeah," Kim said on instinct. Then, "No. Not really. My mind doesn't seem to stop working. Ever. You know?"

"I've had a bit of that myself," Mona agreed. "So yes, I know what you're talking about. But the important thing is that you realize it. That's when you can start making changes."

Kim smoothed the wrinkles that tried to appear on her nose— this was all psycho-babble, the kind of discourse you heard on daytime holo shows. She felt impatient and annoyed that Mona didn't know anything about what Kim was really going through right now. For a moment, she wanted to tell her, to let it all burst out—but she didn't, of course. "Do you have any kids?" Kim asked instead.

Mona looked surprised, then pleased. "Yes. I have a two-year-old son."

Kim nodded, suddenly embarrassed that she'd asked. The silence hung in the air a moment. "Do you want children, Hannah?"

"Yes," Kim replied automatically. Inwardly, the question made her squirm. She was seventeen! She wasn't planning on having kids now . . . or ever.

"Do you think about the future? Plan for it?" Mona continued. "Because that's a good thing to do."

"I guess," Kim replied. She pictured herself at thirty or forty, with Zane, sitting on a step in a sunny backyard, talking and laughing about nothing in particular. The mission over, the whales safely installed on New Eden and the Crusaders in charge of the new world, running it as it should be run. With nothing to do, no responsibilities waiting her on the following day, just . . . time. Time to read, to watch holomovies, to just be safe. Not having to worry about where her next meal was coming from. Money to spend on solar so they'd always have electricity.

No cops. No gang tattoos.

No rats.

But that was a different future than the one Mona was expecting her to imagine. That future, the one that would never exist, involved her settling on New Eden, living the rest of her life on those scattered islands with the other Ark colonists, watching over the whales. Caretaker for life, she'd have dozens, then hundreds, of tiny whale children to look after as well as her own. "I prefer to think about the here and now."

"That's also good, Kim. But don't forget to allow yourself to dream. It's important to have something to strive for."

Kim smiled. "Thank you, Dr. White."

"I'm going to ask you to focus on your sleep patterns this week. Get your computer to set up a log and send it to me at your next session. I can analyze your REM cycle and make sure you're getting the best out of every night, okay?"

"Okay."

Mona smiled. "All right. Now, make sure you listen to those messages. And, I don't know, have a look through your stores. There's bound to be a cake in there somewhere."

"I don't think so," Kim said without thinking. She froze. "I mean, I haven't seen one. And I don't have time to, you know, bake."

"Never mind. I'll have one for you when you reach Edgeward."

Kim pulled back. "I—you don't—"

Mona waved a hand. "Don't say another word. I love to cook. But I'm warning you, there will be whipped cream. Do you like it?"

Whipped cream, on Edgeward, would cost half a day's wages. Kim nodded slowly, and terminated the connection before Mona could see how touched she was.

Kim wanted to go straight to Deck Seven, but she had to talk to Zane first. Her heart thudded at the thought of it, remembering his remonstrances from the last time she'd contacted him, but this *was* an emergency. She had no idea how to fit this new development into their plans. She headed for her quarters, but on the maglift, the whales invaded her thoughts once more.

Kim, Kim, Kim! Can you come back?

I want to see you.

The fish tasted funny today!

I'm jumping, I'm jumping, look at me!

"I'll come and see you soon," she said. "I'm sorry. I'm busy."

You're always busy! Why don't you talk to us the way you used to?

Adonai isn't talking. Hosea's really mad.

Hosea says she doesn't like you . . .

"Hosea?" Kim said, cutting them off. "She's being silly. She'll get over it." But something troubled her. Hosea hadn't spoken to her for a long while, and when Kim reached out to her now, she drew back from the Link, refusing the contact. Kim could push it, analyze Hosea's mood more closely, but she didn't. The whale probably just wanted some privacy, and anyway, Kim didn't have time.

Once inside, she sat against the wall and pulled her tablet into her lap. With the Manta Protocol enabled, she dialed Zane, and waited for the connection. And waited. And waited. The blue circle chased its tail over the screen until finally the words *Connection unavailable at this time* appeared. Kim stared at the screen for a long moment. Had Zane blocked her? Or had something happened to him? She wasn't sure which possibility made her feel worse.

She bought up the text-messaging screen and tapped out a short note. *Trouble. Need advice. K.* She watched as the message spiraled into its place at the top of the screen, then waited for a response. A second later, the message greyed out, and an exclamation mark appeared next to it. *Unable to deliver.*

"God," she breathed, pressing a hand to her forehead. A wave of nausea washed over her. Damn those drugs—her brain felt like it was floating on a cloud. The numbness on her chest was receding, and larger pricks of pain were lancing out from the area. She moaned and moved her hand to her mouth, biting down on her fingers. Her body felt heavy, too heavy.

I'll just rest of a bit, she thought. Just a small sleep. I'll have to get up to call the Admiral soon anyway. Maybe this will all make more sense when I wake up with a clear head. She climbed into her bunk. She didn't feel any better for lying down, but at least she could be sure she wouldn't fall over and smack her head on the floor. She closed her eyes, and before she knew it, she was asleep.

CHAPTER

18

S he woke with a start and the realization that her alarm hadn't gone off, and she'd slept for longer than she should have—well, at least Dr. White had gotten her wish.

She sat up before she remembered her injuries, and the stretching of skin pulled painfully at the gelled area of her burn.

She couldn't bear the thought of changing her clothes, instead ducking into the bathroom only to wash the sleep from her eyes.

"Good morning, Kim," the computer said. "I have informed the Admiral that you were attending to urgent repairs, and would contact him as soon as you are able."

"Good," Kim said.

The computer was still adhering to the self-reflexive parameters—a good sign. But it still didn't help her in terms of knowing what
to do. Her head felt clearer, but the sense of paranoia hadn't lifted. It
was paralyzing, because, in Kim's world, you didn't live long without
being paranoid. It was a survival instinct she couldn't ignore.

The rest of her chores for this morning were not urgent, so Kim
headed straight for Deck Seven.

There, she saw Adonai and 3492 standing at either side of a doorway like military-grade sentry droids.

"Kim, I am glad to see that you are okay," Adonai said. "I've been
very worried."

Wren appeared in the doorway between them, standing back a
little from the forcefield. "Is she—God. Kim, you look a mess."

"Don't feel too great, either," she croaked. Through the door
behind him, she was looking at supplies for the new base on New
Eden—folded coppery solar sails, roofing material, canvas on large
rolls, cooking equipment. Everything needed to build a life on a new
planet. "Don't pretend you care, though."

"I do care," he replied softly, but Kim refused to meet his eyes. She
lifted her chin and addressed the air to the side of his left shoulder.

"Tell me what you're doing on board."

"I can't tell you that," Wren said. "You have to know I can't."

"No, I don't have to know that. Or anything else, apparently."

"Kim, I can prove to you I'm not a threat. Just let me out." His
eyes were still searching hers. "I can help you."

"Help me with what?"

"I'm on your side here. I promise—"

"What side is that?" she snapped, finally locking her gaze with
his. "You failed the training, Wren. You weren't chosen. And yet you
still, somehow, ended up aboard this ship."

"Is that it? You're pissed off because you didn't get the chance to beat me? Because I wigged out on the rig training in Yokohama and ruined my own chances?" He gave a laugh, and it was bitter. "Or is it because you really just wanted all this for yourself? Your own private kingdom? I'm sorry I ruined your little moment in the spotlight, *Hannah*. What, you can't work out how to make a presentation out of this for your holofeed?"

"What would happen if I did?" Kim asked him, levelly. "Who are you working for? The anti-Unificationists? Bet your dad'd love that."

His eyes blazed. "You don't know anything about my dad," he replied stiffly. "And you're one to talk, *Kim*."

"Shut up," Kim said. "You've proved your point. You don't know everything about me, either, except that I can't let you out of there."

He reached forward and tapped the air of the doorway. The force field rippled and pushed his hand back. "What are you going to do when you dock at Edgeward?" he asked. "The mechanics aren't going to let you continue on to New Eden without an inspection of the entire ship."

The Manta Protocol. He must be talking about that—he'd found it in the systems—maybe he'd even broken into her conversations with Zane. "I could kill you. Vent this room and shove your body out an airlock. No one would ever know you were here."

"You're assuming no one on Edgeward knows already," he said. Kim felt her heart sink. He'd just confirmed her suspicions that someone on the station had also uncovered her deception. But who was it, and how many knew? Did it reach the Admiral? Did it reach further afield, to Mars? To the other outwards stations? And what, damn it, *what*, was Wren's purpose here?

"Why?"

He said nothing, finally looking away.

Kim bit her lip, then stopped herself. She didn't want to let him know he was getting to her.

"Your mission. It involved me."

He said nothing.

"Well, obviously it involved surveilling me. I saw the feeds. You were looking in on me in my room. That's kind of sick, you know that?"

"What, you afraid I caught you doing something naughty?" He snorted. "It was the most boring peep show in the world, Kim. Do you do anything in your room but sleep?"

"I'm not here to entertain you," she shot back. "What are you—"

At that moment, an alarm sounded, loudly, three times, reverberating inside Kim's aching head as Wren's expression went from haughty to confused. Adonai whirled to look at her. "Kim!" he said. "What is that?"

"Kim, attention is required on Deck One," the computer spoke over the top of him.

Kim's heart began to pound, but she kept her cool. "Adonai, stay here. Keep watch. Can you do that?"

"Yes, but—"

"I'll tell you when I know, okay?" She glanced back at Wren, whose eyes were wide. Was he really shocked at the siren, or was he just pretending? God damn it! She didn't have time. She marched away at a brisk pace, only breaking into a run when she was out of his line of sight.

The maglift moved too slowly for her liking, and she drummed her fingers on her thigh. When the doors finally opened and she stepped onto the Bridge, she found the center console already lit up with holo displays showing the surrounding star fields, crisscrossed with yellow and green lines.

The front screen had changed, too, showing Admiral Mbewe's face.

"Ms. Monksman," he said as she entered. "I'm having my tech guys run emergency inquiries into your computer's navigation system."

"Why?" Kim asked him.

"You're off-course," he replied. "By 0.12 degrees."

"What?" Kim frowned. It didn't sound like a lot, but you didn't need to be a navigation expert to know that a few degrees of variation on a heading in space could put you light years—even millennia—off your destination. She walked to the center console as calmly as she could, and checked over the revolving star field. The lines matched up with particular systems, and she could see Edgeward blinking in blue. A yellow line, representing *Seiiki*, was traveling past it instead of straight for it. "I don't know how this happened."

"It's not major," the Admiral said. "But it's one of the reasons the data packets are so crucial. I want you to keep a closer eye on them and make sure they're sent in on time."

Kim tried to read his face, looking for signs that he suspected something was amiss, but all she saw was hard disapproval.

"I apologize, sir," she said. "I'll make sure it doesn't happen again."

He nodded. "You'll need to correct. And I want you to overhaul the navigation systems manually. I'll send the instructions. This could have been very dangerous if we hadn't caught it in time. You'd have run out of fuel a few days after you passed us."

"I understand, sir," Kim said.

"The diagnostics I'm going to have you run will tell us more. Perhaps your computer miscalculated."

"That's not likely," Kim hedged.

"No, it's not," the Admiral replied grimly. "The most likely possibility is a virus."

"Really?" Kim frowned. She hoped not. Any virus that could survive the *Seiiki* computer's rigorous firewalls would have to be pretty advanced.

"Afraid so. Sending you the routines now. Run it as quickly as you can, and contact me when it's done, okay?"

"Will do, sir," she replied. "Thanks."

Signing off, Kim took a quick look at the antivirus software. It was pretty standard stuff. In fact, she probably could have made it herself. She opened the coding and scanned through it. Nothing out of the ordinary—she wasn't an expert, but it would be pretty easy to see anything malicious packaged inside the data. So the antivirus stuff was legit. Why was she so suspicious?

She looked at the navigational holo once more. "Computer," she said. "Can you state our current destination?"

"Edgeward Station," the computer replied promptly. "Arrival date July 18."

"And are we on course?"

"Yes, Kim."

"Can you display our current course on the navigational projection? Overlay on the current display."

A green line appeared, running to intersect with Edgeward Station. Kim shook her head. She didn't like this one bit.

She loaded the data packet into the computer and drew the kanji on her hand to make it run. Then she left Deck One. In order to overhaul the navigational array, she'd need to be on Deck Thirteen. Which meant she wouldn't get back to Deck Seven, and Wren, for at least two hours. Crap.

Well, there was nothing she could do about it. She couldn't let *Seiiki* continue to fly without knowing it was following the right path.

She took the ramp, jogging as quickly as she could. The gel pulled at her skin and the tightness was desperately uncomfortable. She wondered if the stuff was healing her properly. Stepping onto Deck Thirteen, she felt the vibration of the engines more keenly than usual. She stopped at a junction station and pulled up a map—she hadn't done much with the navigational array, and it was really just a nexus point of circuits from various locations on the ship, almost indistinguishable from every other circuit on this level. The station directed her to a panel at the aft end of the corridor. A console sat atop it, allowing for minor manual adjustments, but she'd need to check out the workings. She levered the cover off with a screwdriver and looked at the confusing jumble of wires within.

"Computer, play the instructions for running navigational array diagnostic," she said.

"Of course, Kim. First, locate the central circuit board. This is my link to the navigational array. Can you see it?"

"Yes," Kim said. It was a hand-sized board with multicolored wires spiking from its back like an echidna she'd once seen in a book. She followed the computer's instructions, carefully running her own scanning tools over the wires and uploading the detected information to the computer, which then matched the data to the navigational chart Edgeward had sent through, to detect that the information they were receiving was correct. *Seiiki*, and in fact all ships, relied on the positions of the stars to navigate—most specifically, pulsars, which were typically old and thus more reliable in their positions and brightness.

It was a relatively failsafe system, even for those venturing into new regions of deep outer space, as *Seiiki* was.

"Everything seems in order, Kim," the computer said, after she'd run the fourth test.

Kim's brow furrowed. "This can't be right."

"But is that not a good sign, Kim?" the computer asked. "Our systems are functioning correctly."

"Edgeward doesn't think so," Kim replied.

"Perhaps it is they who are incorrect," the computer suggested.

At first Kim's mind snatched at this easy explanation, but her skepticism was soon back. It was too easy.

"Computer, when was the deviation from our course detected?"

"I am unsure, Kim. The deviation was not noticed by me."

Kim mulled over this. "When does Edgeward's data say *they* noticed the deviation?"

"The data packets they sent over tell me that their inbound ships department notified them at 0521 today."

"So, not long after I put Wren in that room," she said.

"I am afraid I do not—"

"Never mind," she snapped. She backed away from the navigational array and backtracked to the junction station. "Computer, show me store room 9B on Deck Eight," she said.

A holo appeared, showing Adonai and the other tech droid stationed outside the room. The angle was high, so their heads looked large and their legs short. Adonai was facing the door, and Wren was standing on the other side. There was no audio—there was no need for a ship with a solitary crew member to need to hear anything from other parts of the ship. But, God damn it, Kim knew Adonai was talking to Wren. Or Wren was talking to Adonai. She could see his lips moving.

She slipped her tools back into her belt and made her way back to Deck Eight. God, she felt awful. The pain was tearing at her like claws raking from inside her chest. She arrived at Deck Eight feeling like a madwoman, and when she saw Adonai still standing in front of the door, she felt something snap.

"What do you think you're doing?" she demanded.

Adonai stepped back instantly, a child caught with his hand in the biscuit jar.

Kim stepped between him and the door, where she fixed Wren with her very best glare. Wren, however, looked back at her with aplomb.

"What did you do to the ship?" she snarled.

"Nothing," he replied. "What are you talking about?"

"Don't play innocent! God damn it!" She smacked the flat of her hand against the doorframe, a blow that traveled up her arm and shocked her burn. She struggled not to let it show. "I find you, lock you in here, and a day later, *Seiiki's* 0.12 off course? Don't tell me that's a coincidence."

He looked thoughtful. "We're off course?"

"Not according to the computer," Kim told him. "But Edgeward sure thinks we are."

"Damn." Wren looked confused. He spread his hands. "I can assure you, it's not my doing. I've been locked in here. How would I even set that up?"

"You could have mucked around with the systems while you were, I don't know, sneaking around. Implanted a virus." But her voice was faltering, as was her assurance that he was behind this. He couldn't have any reason for wanting to send them off course. What would that gain anyone?

"Why would I do that?"

She had no idea, but . . . "You're good with computer systems. You could have brought a virus with you."

"And uploaded it without the computer's detection?" He shook his head. "This is a 917 Quantacore, Kim. *Seiiki* was built to the latest specifications. I could probably crack it, but not without throwing up some major red flags."

"You're lying!"

"I'm not," he said calmly. "I can't make you believe me, though. Tapping into the surveillance cameras—that was about the extent of my hacking prowess where a Quantacore's concerned, I can assure you."

Kim turned away, her lip curling in frustration. She pounded a fist into her thigh. God damn it! "Then what's causing this?"

"Why are you asking me? I'd have thought you'd have a better idea of that."

When she spun back, his eyes were ice-cold. She felt the depth of his hatred very keenly. He despised her—for beating him, yes, but it felt like for something else as well.

"You know I'm not Hannah," she said slowly. "So you don't know that I won't kill you."

"Is that a threat?" he asked. "Because yeah, Kim. I can imagine that very easily, given what you've been up to."

"Kim, what is he talking about?"

Kim had forgotten Adonai was even there. She was about to growl at him to leave them when a better idea came to her. "Adonai, come with me."

"Why?"

Kim motioned impatiently. "Just come! Leave 3429 here to guard him." She indicated Wren with a jerk of her thumb, as if he were a problematic object; she wished that were true, but really, Wren was too dangerous to be classified as an inconvenience.

"We're not done here," Wren growled at her back. "I've got questions for you, too, Kim."

Kim made a rude hand gesture over her head as she led Adonai down the corridor. She pulled him into another store room, this one filled with vehicle parts in racks—great slabs of armored metal, huge wheels with tires too large for her to fit her arms around, and the dully shining glass of windscreens. There were submarine crafts, too, packed together with their halves nestled inside one another, their instrumentation packaged in foam boxes on shelves at the rear. Assembly robots hung from the ceiling, waiting for their landing to begin their work.

"What did he say to you?" Kim asked Adonai.

Adonai hesitated, and Kim felt a flash of panic.

"Come on," she coaxed him, keeping her voice light. "I saw you talking to him on the cameras. What did he say?"

"He told me things, Kim," Adonai said in a low voice. He sounded guilty and reluctant—two things that filled Kim's heart with dread. Had Wren managed to talk Adonai over to his side? Were they now both allied against her?

"I've told you things too," Kim said.

"Yes. And you're my friend." Adonai spoke with resolution. "But he confused me."

"How?"

"He told me that you've lied."

Kim hung her head. It was true. She had found a confidant in Adonai, a friend, a willing pupil—someone who enjoyed her company and expected little in return. She'd never expected to be caught, though, so it hadn't seemed to matter. Now, *now,* it did.

"Yes," she said. "I have. And I'm sorry."

"I have told you that I am sorry, too. I have deceived you, also, Kim. The apologies cancel one another out."

Kim felt a smile tugging at her lips.

"He spoke to me of Earth," Adonai said. "He told me about a drink called coffee. You have never told me about this drink, Kim."

Kim almost laughed out loud. "Well, there's no coffee aboard. No stimulants are allowed on *Seiiki* unless they're medical."

"It sounds nice. He told me he wished for a cup." Adonai shifted his weight to his left leg and turned his head to look sidelong at Kim. "He told me you drank coffee together. This is something humans do if they're friends."

Kim shook her head. "I was never friends with Wren."

"He said he wished you had been. But you never cared about anyone other than yourself."

"So, what? He decided to come after me in a ship?" Kim shook her head. This was going nowhere. She'd hoped Wren had let go of some detail, some vital clue, but it seemed like he had just been chatting to Adonai the way you'd talk to a business colleague. And that stuff about them being friends . . .

"No. He came on the ship because it was important. He told me it was vital that you be stopped."

Kim's blood froze in a flash. For a second, the room vanished, blazing white. When it returned, Adonai was still looking at her with that faintly concerned expression.

"I—what?"

"Kim," the computer's voice sounded loud, cutting over their conversation. "It is time for your scheduled maintenance of the tech droids."

"Shut up!" she burst out. The sound of her voice rang off the steel of the dismantled hulls. A piercing ringing filled Kim's ears, and her burned chest throbbed horribly.

Adonai took a step toward her. "I think you might need to sleep, Kim."

Kim shrugged him off, marching through the door. "I don't need anyone telling me what to do."

"Kim—" Adonai called after her.

"Go back and stand guard," she snapped at him. "If he says anything, you report it to me, okay?"

"Yes, of course," Adonai replied mildly, but Kim was already back on the ramp, climbing toward Deck Four. There, she headed for the infirmary and looked over the shelves of small boxes for painkillers. She downed four of the small white pills and sank to the floor as the pain wracked her, throbbing, then subsiding, throbbing, then subsiding. She'd lived through broken limbs, the pain of her gang tattoo, through the installation of the Link, but she'd never experienced anything like this. God damn it. She clenched her fists, wishing, just for a moment, that she could cut herself free from her body the way Adonai had.

But worse than the physical pain were the gnawing thoughts that plagued her mind.

He knows. He knows. He knows.

CHAPTER
19

When she woke, she felt marginally better, though stiff from having slept on the cold metal floor. She headed down to her room, where she tried calling Zane again. Again, there was *no connection available at this time.* Her text message still sat there, greyed out, undelivered. She was alone.

She felt for the tablet she'd found on the Mayfly. She pulled it open and tapped the screen, but its distance from the Mayfly had locked it. It asked for thumbprint verification, and glowed an angry red when she tried a few workarounds she knew. It was old tech, older than most of the stuff she was used to dealing with. She always went for the latest models.

After all, what was the point of stealing old stuff that wasn't worth anything?

"Kim, you have now missed nineteen scheduled tasks," the computer told her. "And it is now 2035. You should be in bed."

"Computer," Kim snarled. "Shove it."

"I am not familiar with this term," the computer replied. Kim snorted. She wouldn't be undertaking those tasks anytime soon. She headed back down to Deck Eight.

Wren was asleep. He'd made a bed out of some folded padded vests from a storage crate, He didn't look comfortable, though, having tried to fold his long legs onto the makeshift mattress and failing.

She lifted her wrist and very deliberately drew the kanji to release the forcefield. It flickered blue and vanished.

"Kim? Is this a wise idea?" Adonai asked. "Perhaps you should—"

"Not now, Adonai," Kim cut him off.

She stepped inside, the droid following her nervously. The deck plates clanked with her steps, but he didn't wake. She bent over him, and for a second she paused to just look at him. She hadn't had a chance to do this . . . well, ever. She hadn't thought she'd want to. But there he was, his eyes closed, his face relaxed in a relatively peaceful slumber. His dark eyebrows were so perfect, she thought. His skin, that deep ebony shade. Even the tangles in his long hair, the puckered skin just barely showing through his unshaven beard. God, she hated him so much just for being so beautiful.

"Wake up," Kim said. "Wren!"

Wren woke with a start, rolling backward, his eyes focusing blearily on her. He pulled himself up to his elbows, his facelined with creases from the vest pockets. Kim moved quickly, lunging forward to wrap one hand over the other and push it up under his neck. She kept her momentum going, locking an elbow behind his head and cradling his face on the right side of her chest. She knew he was getting a face full of her breast, and the pressure sent lancing pain through her burn, but she refused to show it. She lifted upwards with her hands, the knuckle of her thumb pressing into his Adam's apple. She gave it some pressure, enough to make him gasp in alarm. He lifted his hands to pull at her wrist, trying to tug her grip free. He was stronger than her, but she had the advantage. You didn't need much strength to choke someone like this.

His skin was cold, colder than she would have thought.

"Kim?" he managed. "God!"

"I guess you can call me God if you like. I've got more power over your life and death right now than He does, though. All I gotta do is squeeze."

"Stop," he gasped.

"What was that?"

"Stop! Please!"

She loosened her grip, but not enough to let him pull his head out away from her.

"What do you want?" he asked.

"Nothing too drastic," she told him breezily. "Just a few answers."

"Kim, his face is turning purple. The net tells me this is not normal for a human." Adonai's voice was worried, but Kim ignored him.

"All right," he said. "All right!"

She still didn't release him. "You hid your life signs from the computer. How?"

"You're telling me you couldn't do it?"

Kim grunted. It wouldn't require anything more advanced than a thermal regulator, a tiny device that affected the air temperature in a cloud around a person's body. Uncomfortable, especially on a space ship, where ambient temperature was around sixty degrees

Fahrenheit, but effective. He probably had it tucked in his jumpsuit somewhere. She'd made one herself to avoid some of the more high-tech security systems in rich people's houses.

"You stole a ship. The Mayfly. That's why it doesn't have a transponder. You cut it out."

"Yes. Yes. Okay. I did."

Kim could feel moisture on her jumpsuit's front. God, was he *crying?*

"That's illegal. I could call up Earth United right now and report you. You know that, right?"

"Yeah. Yeah, I'm a criminal. But—" he tried to swallow. She felt it stick in his throat, and he tried to cough. She still didn't loosen her hold. "So are you."

Kim took a breath. "No, I'm not." What was he talking about? Her identity theft, her past activities and time spent in and out of corrections facilities—or something more? *Did he know about the Crusaders? About Zane?* God, she'd been so careful!

"You are," he said. "And you're a damn good liar, a cheat, and . . . " he coughed again, "a terrorist."

There it was, at last. Confirmation. Relief and horror warred inside her. "I'm not a criminal," she managed to say. "You've got it wrong."

"So, what," Wren gasped, his voice turning gravelly, "is 200 pounds of Tritominite doing inside the hull?"

Kim let him go. She didn't mean to, but her arms fell away from his head and she fell backward onto her butt. Wren fell, too, coughing and wheezing, his eyes wet with moisture. Not tears, though. There was a smear of blood on his cheek. Kim looked down, numbly, and saw with dull surprise that pink-colored liquid was leaking through her jumpsuit from beneath the edge of the gel. That was the moisture she'd felt.

"Tritominite?" she repeated.

"There you go, playing dumb again," he replied. He rolled onto his stomach and coughed some more. "How do you even keep a straight face?"

Adonai was dancing from foot to foot anxiously. "What is Tritominite?"

"You're the one who's lying," Kim said. "You have to be. There aren't any explosives in the hull. Why would I—"

"You don't believe me?" Wren said. He'd finished coughing his lungs out and was now wiping the pus from his cheek. "Get my tablet and check the scans I did."

Kim had forgotten she still had his tablet in her pocket. She pulled it out but hesitated before giving it to him.

"Come on," Wren said with a wry smile. "If I wanted to clock you, I'd have done it already. Besides, your friend Adonai made me promise not to."

Kim resisted the urge to look over her shoulder at the droid. She gave the tablet to Wren and watched his fingers bring it to life.

"Here," he said, tapping a few keys that appeared in the air. A small greenish holo appeared. It was a recording, the date hovering in the corner: 22:48:19, 01-07-2078. Two weeks ago, Kim calculated. At first the image was just grainy shapes, but soon they resolved into a panning view of a bulkhead. There was an open access panel just below.

"I'm heading in now," Wren's voice came from the tablet's tinny speakers. *"If I don't come out, tell my mum I love her. Or, no, scratch that. Just take care of my cat."*

The view changed as Wren ducked down and entered the tunnel beyond. It was as narrow as all the tunnels on *Seiiki*, and Wren had a harder time fitting inside than Kim did. He had to drag himself on his elbows. *"Far out,"* he whispered. *"This is . . . not good . . . for my claus-trophobia."*

He stopped several times, pausing, Kim suspected, to check directions on his tablet before continuing on.

"Not sure what I'm really looking for here," he said. *"Just got a feeling about these cavities. Maybe nothing. Just gotta . . . rule it out."* He made a groaning sound as he squeezed through a particularly tight spot. *"Hope the damn whales don't hear me. Okay. Here we go."* He'd reached a junction of the tunnel. Kim had a feeling he was somewhere between Decks Twelve and Thirteen. This was confirmed when she saw the number printed on the panel ahead of him. The view jerked as the tablet was set down against one wall and angled to take in the panel. Wren appeared, or rather, his elbow did. He had a screwdriver in one hand, which he wedged under the panel to lift it off.

Behind it was . . . nothing. Just air and curving plates of metal. The hull of *Seiiki* was doubled, just like the Aquarium was. There was enough space between them to move, sure, but there wasn't meant to be anything in there but the curving braces that were the ship's skeleton. The view lifted again, showing the interior of the space. The tablet flickered and changed to night vision. She could see one of the braces, a massive piece of steel punched through with holes. But beyond that . . .

"Damn," Wren's voice said. *"That's it."*

The display went dark for a second, then brightened. Wren was edging his way into the space, groaning as he did so. He dropped down to land on something—another strut. He edged his way across, puffing and panting, pushing the tablet ahead of him until she could see it without any doubt.

Little packages the size of her closed fist. They'd be yellow in color, she thought, though they looked green on the display. Wires snaked from one to another like slender worms. The tablet lifted. They went all the way up the hull. God!

"You did a good job," Wren said. "That's only one section of the hull."

Kim stared, aghast, as the display cut off. "You can't blow through a hull of a Hako class," she said. "It's too thick. They're based on designs for Battle Destroyers." But even as she said it, she knew she was wrong. Daddy's voice resounded in her ear. *All ships are nothing but nuts and bolts, really.* For all the shielding, for all the forcefields, for all the safety measure and checks and monitoring systems, if the bare bones of any ship were hit directly, the whole thing could technically come apart. Or at least a significant portion of it.

"That's not the plan though, is it?" Wren replied, looking at her with a hard expression. "You don't need to actually blow up the ship with Tritominite, do you? Especially not when you're ... "

"That close to the fuel tanks," Kim finished in a whisper. She closed her eyes, her teeth finding her lip and biting down hard. "Damn."

Wren's expression held anger and hardness, but there was something else there, too. A slight uncertainty. His accusations weren't ringing true inside his own head, Kim thought. Good, because they definitely weren't ringing true inside hers! Tritominite inside the hull. For God's sake, she'd been flying along with this stuff inside the ship all this time.

"You'd know this, wouldn't you?" Wren continued. "Tritominite hasn't been around in decades, not since the Triad War. In fact, the only recent use of it was during those attacks outside the docks in Melbourne. What was that again? Something about expanding the North Shore stem cell facility out to one of the research stations orbiting Io out at Jupiter?"

She knew what he wanted her to say, but she couldn't say it. She couldn't speak at all. God, her shoulder hurt. She could feel little trickles of warm liquid running down her breast.

"The Crusaders," he finished, without satisfaction. "Yeah, that's right, isn't it, Kim Teng?"

"Wren? I do not think Kim is well."

Kim barely heard Adonai as Wren continued.

"The Crusaders. Vigilante freedom fighters. Or terrorists, depending on what you—"

His voice became distant. Kim couldn't breathe.

"—believe about God actually speaking to their leader, what's his name? Wilhelm Grigorian?"

Her vision greyed at the edges. It doesn't matter, she told herself. You've just got to keep standing, keep thinking. But thinking what? The Crusaders *had* used Tritominite, in the form of a plastic explosive called P09, the night after she'd supplied Zane with the name of the vessel they'd sent her to spy on. They'd also used Tritominite to blow up that lab in Indonesia where they were developing cloning technology, and in Munich, too. That was the one that'd made Zane famous, plastered his picture all over the media. The Crusaders had openly claimed responsibility for both attacks. Zane had told her about them with a smile on his face.

"We're advancing God's cause," Zane told her. "He does not want us using science this way—to pollute our very cells, to negate the miracle that is human life. For that, we must be proud."

She'd set some of the explosives herself, under Zane's guidance, just outside the gates of the North Shore Facility. Had watched from her safe hiding place as it tore the building apart, flames billowing into the night, thinking only of how this meant she was at last part of something meaningful.

Surely someone other than the Crusaders could get their hands on plastic explosives. They could be made with instructions off the net. It wasn't legal, but then again, neither were stims, and they still found their way into the world.

If it was the Crusaders (and it wasn't, it definitely wasn't) they would have told her. They wouldn't have put her on board without telling her. Right?

She had to talk to Zane.

"Kim?" It was Adonai again. He took her arm, his hand clamping roughly around her elbow. She pulled free.

"Excuse me," she said, and hurried for the door. In her haste, she almost forgot to reactivate the force field, but Wren hadn't come after her. He was still lying where he was, his throat blazing red. His eyes were on her, piercingly.

"Adonai," Kim said.

Adonai reluctantly followed, with a look back at Wren. "I want you with me," Kim ordered. "Leave 3429 here. That way I know you're not talking to him."

"But—" Adonai began.

"Don't argue!" Kim growled, marching away with speed. Adonai came after her.

"Kim," he said, when they'd reached the maglift. Kim did not have the energy for the ramps, nor did she want to waste a second. "I can speak through 3429 also, if I choose."

"You can?" Kim blinked as the doors closed, showing her wavery reflection standing next to the droid.

"I thought I should tell you, because I think I've lost a little bit of your trust."

Kim lowered her head and rubbed her temples. "Yeah. Little bit."

"I'm very sorry, Kim. But this is all very new to me."

"Me too," she replied with a sigh. "It's okay, Adonai. It's fine. I've just got a lot on my mind right now."

"I understand. But I can help, if you like."

"Thank you," Kim said dully. What could Adonai possibly do? What could anyone do? If Zane had . . . had . . . she could barely finish the thought.

The maglift slid to a stop on Deck Five, and Kim made her way to her quarters. The lights flickered on, revealing the stark, utilitarian space. She suddenly saw it as Wren would have seen it—bare, unadorned, impersonal. Not at all the space bubbly, social Hannah would have inhabited. She wondered what it would look like, with photos of friends and family tacked to the walls, with a favorite lamp on the bedside table, with a Save the Whales poster on the back of the door. A normal young woman's room.

"Stay here," she told Adonai, closing the door behind her.

She grabbed her tablet off the bedside table and tapped it to life. There it was, blinking in blue. *New message (1).*

Quickly, she drew the kanji for *secret* and swiped it open. She saw, with relief, that it was from Zane.

Call me.

She tapped the icon with numb fingers, and waited for the connection to be made. Her hands were shaking a little. She tried to stop them, but Zane answered surprisingly quickly.

His face floated above the tablet, and his expression could only be described as furious.

"Zane—" she began.

"What did I tell you?" he began. His voice was low and menacing, each word wrapped into a parcel of anger. "What did I tell you, girl?"

"I had to!" she replied. She hadn't expected him to be happy about her attempts to contact him, but she had a good reason. The rage on his face was something she'd never seen in him before, and it frightened her. "I need to talk to you—"

"*I* decide when we need to talk! Not you. You're in danger of destroying everything. Someone picked up that text message, you know. Coming in through Edgeward's comms, it raised a red flag, and I was taken in to explain myself. Do you know what I told them?"

"I have to tell—"

"That it was from a crazy ex-girlfriend who wants money because I knocked her up." He wiped a hand over his forehead. "Do you know what it means, for me to say something like that in front of my colleagues? My reputation is at stake out here, Kim, and you can't even follow a simple instruction!"

The words stung Kim, all the way to her very core. Even as they reached her heart, though, she felt herself shutting down. The pain was too much, the confusion even worse. He loved her. He said he did.

"Why didn't you have Manta running on your messages?"

His head drew back on his neck, shortening his dark-haired chin. He looked down from his nose at her, his eyebrows pinching at the bridge, his eyes blazing wildly. "Are you *kidding* me?" he growled. "I didn't think it was necessary! I didn't think you'd be that *stupid!*"

Kim sucked in a sharp breath. He didn't mean it. He didn't mean it. Oh, God, her head was swimming. The pain from her chest was almost overwhelming. She needed more meds.

"And to top it off," Zane went on, "you've been neglecting your duties. Where's your video update from today? What's going on?"

"That's why I needed to talk to you," Kim broke in. Her voice was cool and even—good. "Things have happened on board."

"What things? What could possibly happen with a bunch of whales? You haven't notified the Admiral of anything untoward. I keep tabs on his comms, you know."

"I didn't tell the Admiral," Kim said. "I didn't know how to. But Zane—"

"What? What's so important you're risking millions of viewer ratings? We need those, Kim. The entire galaxy needs to be watching what you're doing! That's the whole *point.*"

"There's someone else on the ship," she blurted out.

He stared at her. "Someone else on the ship." He repeated the words skeptically, as if he couldn't quite fathom that she'd said them. Finally, he said, "No there's not. I know you've been talking to Dr. White. She's mentioned hallucinations . . . "

"It's not a hallucination," Kim said. "There's someone else aboard." She swiped to the side of the tablet, bringing up the menu, and scrolled down to access the computer's video archives. She found a recording of store room 9B, and sent it across to him. "His name's Wren—"

"Wren Keene." Zane's fury faded a little as he watched the footage of Wren pacing back and forth, and a hint of consternation appeared. "You've got tech droids watching him?" He was moving his fingers across his own screen, obviously zooming in on the door, where he could have seen Adonai and 3429. Kim nodded.

"I didn't feel safe leaving him on his own. But he's not a threat."

Zane's eyes narrowed. "What do you mean?"

"I don't think he's here to harm me, or the whales, or the ship."

"You don't *think,*" he repeated. "Why else would he stowaway on *Seiiki*? Some poor little rich kid who didn't get the candy his daddy promised him? He wants to take you out, Kim. Don't think otherwise."

She could see his mind working, following the paranoid paths she'd followed herself so many times.

"I'm positive of it," she said. "You're right. I don't know exactly why he stowed on board. But he's had plenty of chances to kill me if that's what he wanted."

Zane lifted his eyes to the ceiling, blinked them slowly and let out a sigh. "Kim, you're just a kid," he said. His voice was a low groan, heavy with regret. "You don't know what you're talking about. His pure presence on board is a danger to your mission."

"He doesn't know what my mission is." At least, she was pretty sure he didn't. "*I* don't even know what my mission is. You haven't told me!"

He held up a hand. "It's not time for you to know just yet. But you will. Kim, I promise you, this will all be worth it. You've just got to play by the rules."

"Zane," she said. "That's not what I wanted to talk to you about. There's something else. Something terrible."

Zane froze. "What?"

"Wren—he found something. Something in the hull. Explosives." She whispered the last word. "They're lined up on the inside of the outer plates."

Zane's face went blank, then paled. Even the blueness lent to his skin by his own tablet screen couldn't disguise the greying of his honey-colored skin. Wren's words ringing in her mind, she watched him for signs of guilt. He looked concerned, worried, and fearful. No trace of culpability. "You're sure of this?"

"He showed me," Kim said. "He had video of it."

"He could have faked it."

"No," Kim said. "No way. Why would he do that?"

"Why would he follow you aboard *Seiiki*? I don't know, Kim. Have you seen it with your own eyes?"

"You think I should check it out?"

Zane paused a moment, then said "No, Kim. I don't want you anywhere near that stuff."

"I don't want to go near it either," she said. "But if I have to verify it—"

"Don't do anything just yet," Zane replied. "I'm going to contact headquarters, okay? I'll get back to you with a plan soon."

"Okay," Kim breathed with relief. He believed her. He was going to help. The Crusaders knew about explosives—they'd know how to handle it. They'd send a ship out, perhaps, from Daymar Nine—that would only take a day or two. Edgeward would see them—they were too close now for them not to pick up another ship on their scanners. But that didn't matter. *Seiiki* would be saved, and the whales along with it. That was what the Crusaders wanted. "Okay. Zane, I think I figured out what your plan is now. And I'm afraid I ruined it."

A flicker of strange emotion passed over his face. "You do?"

"Yes. It was you who set us off course, wasn't it? You wanted us to miss Edgeward. You planned for the whales to head to some other planet—not New Eden at all. That's right, isn't it? You want to prove a point—show Erica Wu and . . . maybe Morosini herself that New Eden isn't supposed to be spoiled by our presence. That's what the Crusaders believe, isn't it? That we shouldn't be polluting other planets with our human failings. It makes sense." She paused. "I'm guessing you've found somewhere more suitable for them. Another planet, maybe somewhere closer. And with everyone watching, you'll show how wrong the Unificationists are." She took a breath before admitting, "But the Admiral sent me antivirus software. I've corrected our course. I'm worried that I've messed everything up."

Zane's mouth twitched toward a frown. "Damn, Kim." He put a hand to his forehead and dragged it over his eyes. He paused momentarily, then said, "Yes. God, I should have known I couldn't keep it from you. I'm sorry."

"It's all right," Kim said, feeling a wash of absolute relief. He wasn't angry that she'd mucked things up. He didn't blame her. He could see the position she was in—perhaps he regretted not taking her into his confidence earlier. She straightened her shoulders, breathing more easily than she had in months. "I'm guessing the planet was something nearby, so that we wouldn't need to dock at Edgeward for refueling. Somewhere we could get to on solar power. But—"

"All right, Kim. It's okay. We'll work it out after you dock, okay? There's nothing here that can't be fixed, and yes . . . this is all Grigorian's fault for not keeping you in the loop. I told him you were too clever to be kept in the dark. But it doesn't matter. You did the right thing, locking Mr. Keene up like that. Keep him there. Don't let him see the rest of the ship, and don't let him out of your sight."

"I won't," she vowed.

"Good. Now, in the meantime, I want you to make some videos. Keep the folks on Earth entertained, Kim. It's what you're here for, remember? And, for the moment, don't tell Edgeward anything. If you do, the entire mission could be in jeopardy."

Kim frowned. This had thrown her. "I thought the mission—I thought the mission would be scrapped anyway—"

"We've worked too hard on this to risk giving up on it right now, Kim. Do what I say." The words were harsh, but she could see a softness in his eyes when he leaned in closer. "I love you. I'm going to look after you, okay?"

Kim managed a smile. "I feel safe when you speak like that," she said, her voice coming out a little breathless. She hated that—it was something Hannah would do—but she couldn't stop herself. It was true. Zane was so strong, so capable. He could make anything right. She just had to trust him.

So why, her mind taunted her, *haven't you told him about Adonai?*

She terminated the connection, feeling a hundred times better. She couldn't believe she'd allowed Wren to plant the idea in her mind that the Crusaders were behind the bombs. She was such a fool!

Zane wouldn't allow her to board a ship that was full of explosives. He wouldn't put her in danger. He definitely wouldn't put the whales in danger! Someone else was behind this, but Zane and Grigorian would help her. It would work out.

She stretched over to put her tablet on the bedside table, and felt the entire world tilt as she did so. A second later she was on the floor, one hand clutching her gravity blanket, the other wrapped across her stomach. She forced herself to her knees and staggered to the bathroom. She didn't reach the loo in time. Globs of stringy vomit spattered over the deck plates.

When her stomach was empty—which didn't take long, she leaned back against the wall and pressed the heel of her hand to her forehead. She felt puffy and hot. Her temples throbbed.

"Kim, I am detecting illness," the computer said. "I'm going to send a medbot to you."

Kim, Kim, Kim! I ate so many fish and they tasted so good!

I'm flying. I'm a flying fish. Watch me, I'm going to jump!

The sea is very dark today. It feels deeper than before. But it's not the real ocean. I forgot that for a moment. There's the bottom, not that far away . . .

"No," Kim moaned. "Don't need one."

And then all of a sudden she was in the air, and the room was swaying even more around her, like it was on a swing. No, she was on a swing. Daddy was pushing her, his large hands ready to catch her and still the motion at any moment. But he wasn't there—he was gone—there was no one to help her stop.

She'd just keep going up and up and up into the sky, all the way to the stars . . .

CHAPTER

20

S he woke lying on the bed in the infirmary. Someone was bent over her, and Kim jerked away so suddenly she almost fell from the bed. It was Adonai, his eyes glowing dully. She forced her muscles to relax and lay back down on the stiff mattress.

"Did I faint?"

"I think so," Adonai said. "According to the net, that is. I bathed your forehead with a wet towel." He sounded proud, and she saw him holding a towel in one of his silver hands. The moisture clung to it in jelly-like globs because of the gravity. It had dripped on the pillow and the back of her head felt wet as well. She shivered, wiping a hand over her smooth head, feeling the slight ridges of the Link under her fingers.

The burn felt hot and itchy, but she didn't dare look at it. She fixed her eyes on the medbot in the corner instead. It was resting on the ground, the blinking lights in its torso dull. One side of its round head was crumpled inwards. "What happened?" she asked Adonai.

"The medbot tried to take you from me. I'm afraid I—" Adonai looked away, slightly ashamed. "I stopped it. I didn't mean to break it. It just happened. I think I killed it."

Kim couldn't help herself. She let out a laugh. "Oh, God, Adonai!"

Adonai brightened a little. "But I know which pills to give you. I looked them up on the net. Here are some antibiotics, and some pain-killers." He held up two bottles of pills. "You need to take these once every four hours, and these every two hours, but don't take more than that. It's not good for you."

Kim unscrewed the bottles and tipped one of each into her palm, then swallowed them.

"The other thing I've been doing," Adonai said, "is making you some food."

"I'm not hungry," Kim answered automatically. She could still taste bile in her mouth, and though her stomach felt like a deflated balloon, she was almost positive anything she put in would come straight back up.

"It's been more than twenty hours since you last ate," Adonai informed her.

"Can't be," Kim replied. The pills felt like they were lodged in her throat, like if she ran her hand over her neck she'd feel them sticking out like on some holovision cartoon. "The computer would have reminded me."

But Adonai wouldn't hear of it. He turned around and took something from one of the benches—a tray from the mess. On it was a bowl covered with a lid and a fork. "It's rice," he said. "With peas and corn and chicken. I added a few spices. They're all good foods for healing burns. I looked them up."

He placed the tray on the bed beside her and removed the lid. How much more dexterous his hands had gotten, she realized. He was able to move so easily—almost as if he'd been born to this body, not that of a whale at all.

The smell that hit her changed her mind about not being hungry. She picked up the fork and dug in, shoveling the stuff into her mouth far too quickly. The texture of it against her tongue was amazing, and the beautiful warmth of the food spread through her. All too soon, she'd finished the bowl, and was wishing there was more.

"Was it good?" Adonai asked, eagerly.

"Delicious," Kim replied. He looked pleased, and she felt the reflection of that pleasure, glad that she'd given it to him. Another thought struck her. "Have you given Wren any food?"

"I have not," Adonai replied. "I didn't want to do so without your permission, in case you . . . didn't wish it."

Kim felt a sudden pang of shame. "You thought I would starve him?"

"I've been reading a lot of things on the net, Kim. There are some instances where prisoners are kept without food for long periods of time—"

"That's not what I'm doing," she told him quickly. "God. I can't believe you would think that."

"It's not hard to believe," Adonai said. "You have locked him up, and I've seen you use violence against him."

"Yes, but I'd never . . . " she stopped herself. She'd never what? Never actually kill him? But she had threatened to. And she *could*. It would be easy enough. He was stronger than her, but he'd never been in a real fight—a fight for his life. She had.

She'd killed before.

"You know me better than that," she finished lamely. He didn't, not really. He was a whale. She kept forgetting that.

"I will feed him if you'd like, Kim," Adonai said. "Should I take him some rice?"

"You've got more?"

"The recipe made four servings," Adonai replied.

This was the best news Kim had heard in a long time.

She took her bowl of rice with her as they went back to Deck Seven. Wren looked at her dully from behind the force field.

"Kim," he croaked when he fixed his eyes on the part of the burn poking out from under her jumpsuit. "You look terrible."

"I'm fine," Kim said, drawing a kanji to deactivate the force field, putting his dish on the floor, then reactivating it. She took her own dish and sat with her back against the opposite wall, just as she had with Adonai during those first few days. God, it had seemed so long ago, but it was only a week!

"Are you sure? You don't smell so good either," Wren replied.

"I'm *fine*," she repeated, refusing to be embarrassed. "I haven't prioritized taking a shower since, you know, I just found out there are bombs in the hull and all."

"Yeah, well, sorry about that," he said, crawling toward the bowl and lifting it up. His eyes widened. "Did you make this?"

"Adonai did," Kim said, jerking a thumb at the droid. She took another mouthful, savoring the hot punch of the spices. "You know. My pet whale."

"While we're on the subject," Wren said. "What the hell?" He took a mouthful, and his eyes almost rolled back into his head with pleasure.

"You think it was my choice? You must have seen it on the cameras."

"No sound on video," he reminded her around a second mouthful. "But yeah, you looked pretty shocked I guess. I went back and found video of him on Deck Twelve, too. Staggering around holding onto the walls. Stopping and staring into thin air. Guess he was learning how to talk. But that doesn't explain why you didn't put him back."

"Put him *back*? How was I supposed to do that? Even he doesn't know how!"

Adonai, standing to one side with 3429, was swinging his head back and forth between them like it was a tennis match.

"You could have shut him down. Run a purge."

Kim gaped at him. "Are you kidding me?"

Wren shrugged and lifted another mouthful. "I'm just saying."

"*Stop* saying," Kim snapped.

But Adonai spoke up, then. His eyes were growing duller by now, almost a copper instead of gold. "Would you purge me, Wren?"

Wren's gaze flickered to the droid, then back to Kim. "It's an option."

"Running the droid reset program through the ship's computer might kill me," Adonai said. "Or at least, this conscious part of me. My body might continue to live in its current state."

"You must have thought about that," Wren said sensibly. "When you did what you did. You must have been prepared to fail, to die."

Adonai nodded. "I was. I would have chosen it, and it was a price I chose to pay for seeing the ship. I would pay it, even now, if you wanted me to."

"It won't come to that," Kim said vehemently. "Wren's being a bastard. Besides which, I'm going to need you, Adonai. I've got to go down and check on those bombs."

"Why?" Wren asked immediately.

"Because I need to see them for myself. I spoke with Zane, Wren. This isn't some Crusader plot."

"So—what? You think I faked the video? You think I put them there?"

"Right now, I wouldn't put it past you," Kim retorted. "Someone's responsible, and it's not Zane. He wouldn't risk . . . *Seiiki*." She'd almost said *me,* she thought with a tiny thrill. "The Crusader cause is a holy one."

"Oh, God have mercy." Wren did roll his eyes then, for an entirely different reason. "He's got you wrapped around his little finger, doesn't he? What did he promise you? Credit? Property on Mars? An entire planet?"

Kim didn't deign to answer. She didn't need to. Wren's understanding of the Crusader cause was obviously tainted by the media, as was most people's.

"So he's who you were always sneaking off to see while we were in Chicago and on Ganymede," Wren went on, derisively, breaking into her reverie. "Your Martian Prince."

"Are you more worried about him being non-Trinitarian or him being taller than you?"

Wren let out a bark of laughter. "I'm not intimidated by a Martian. They can't throw a punch to save their lives—all that low gravity weakens muscle tone. And, no, I don't have a problem with Unitarians. I'm not anti-Unification. I just don't like terrorists."

"You don't know anything about him," Kim said shaking her head to clear it. "Or the Crusaders."

"I know they don't mind killing people to make their point."

"They believe in purity," Kim said coldly. "In the Word of God. They embrace the exploration of space and other worlds—just not the wanton use of it for our own ends. They're fighting for real change, for human beings to accept their place in the universe, to act humbly, and to be reverent."

It was Grigorian's speech, not her own, that she was repeating. She didn't care. She fired it off, knowing every word by heart, having recited them over and over again to herself. It had made so much sense to Kim, hearing those words, that she had left the meeting with tears in her eyes. They were happy tears, but also sorrowful ones, for having lived her life for so long without knowing this simple, beautiful truth.

Wren's lips lifted in a half-smile. "Notice how you haven't once used the word "I"?"

Rage suffused Kim. "*I* believe in the cause. *I've* met Grigorian. He speaks to God, Wren. And God has told him this isn't the way we're supposed to be living our lives."

"Sounds a little like Adherent doctrine to me."

"No!" She clenched her fists in frustration. "The Adherents want us to stay on a flat Earth and believe God created it in six days. To obey the letter of the Bible, and believe that knowledge is evil. The Crusaders don't think that. They think we should be expanding to other worlds—just not recklessly. That the teachings in the Bible can guide us. And Grigorian—"

"Grigorian is not a holy man, Kim. Morosini condemned the entire—"

"Antonia Morosini is a politician, not a prophet! She doesn't understand. Just like you don't." She sneered. "And don't pretend you suspected *anything* back in Chicago."

"You're right. I didn't think you were that stupid. Guess you had me right fooled."

Kim turned aside. He didn't understand. How could he? He was a rich, pretty boy—well, less pretty at the moment, with his unshaven

beard and mussed hair—who had never had to think deeply about
anything.

Wren sighed and scrapped his fork across the bottom of his bowl.
"At least let me check over your burn before you go. You can't head
down there looking like death's door. I'll be worried I won't see you
again, and then who's going to let me out of here before the ship
blows up?"

"I'm not letting you anywhere near me," Kim replied.

"Well, let the medbot check you over, then. Just do—something.
You're scaring me."

Kim swallowed the last of her rice. "The medbot's . . . out of commission. Don't ask why, but I, for one, am glad not to have to worry
about that thing. It's a nuisance, really."

Setting aside her empty bowl, she stood with one smooth motion,
and instantly spoiled the moment by swaying as her vision greyed out
around the edges. She grabbed the wall to hold her upright. When
the corridor pixelated its way back into existence, she found Wren
standing just on the other side of the door, hand outstretched as if to
catch her. "You're not fine. You're not even close to fine. Come here."
He patted the air in front of him, stopping just short of touching the
forcefield.

Despite herself, Kim took a step forward.

"Show me," he said. It wasn't a command, but a surprisingly gentle suggestion. Kim hesitated for just a moment, then reached up with
her right hand and unbuttoned the uppermost button of her jumpsuit. Then the next, then the next.

She looked down, registering muted surprise at what she saw.
Her singlet was stained pink in a triangular shape from her collarbone
to her waist. The gel she could see poking out had turned the same
dull pink, with patches of brown. Yellowish ooze was making its way

out from under the edges. She felt herself go weak again, so she took her eyes from the sight and focused on her breathing.

"Damn, Kim. That's infected badly. You should've gone straight to the medbot instead of chasing after me! And look at your eyes. You've got the beginnings of a fever."

"No I don't," Kim said firmly. "I'm just tired." She was reasonably sure this was true. It was the painkillers, not the injury, that was making her feel so woozy. After all, the medbot had treated her, and the gel should have cleaned up any microbes. But another voice inside her head was warning her about skin injuries, and how easily bacteria could infect exposed tissue.

Wren was staring at her. There was real concern in his eyes, and he stood there with one hand raised, as if ready to reach through and take her upper arm in a gentle grip and draw her to him. What made her step back, however, was how much she *wanted* him to.

Get a grip, she told herself. You've been on your own for three months. It's just what Mona said: you're starved of human interaction. It's human nature. Nothing more.

"Kim," Wren warned, but she turned away, shaking her head.

"Adonai, come with me. Leave 3429 here."

"Kim!" Wren shouted. "God damn it!"

Ignoring him, she quickened her step.

Kim took the maglift to Deck Fifteen. The weightless feeling as it slid downwards made her head reel dizzyingly.

"Kim, I think Wren is correct," Adonai said.

She held up a hand. "I don't want to hear it." Her voice came out slurred. The food in her belly was heavy and her entire body ached for sleep. But how could she sleep without seeing the bombs for herself? The entire ship might go up at any moment!

"Very well," Adonai replied. "But you tell me it is your job to look after us. Whose job is it to look after you?"

Mine, Kim thought. Zane's. Erica's. Daddy's. She wished any of them were here right now. She wished she had someone other than Wren to speak with. But her call to Zane had left her with a bad taste in her mouth—and she wasn't even sure why. He'd been worried about the mission. Of course he had. But she couldn't help feeling that he'd dismissed her concerns in favor of its success.

A vivid memory returned to the time he had kissed her on the rooftop of the restaurant in Chicago, when she'd managed to slip away from Abdiel and Wren for a few minutes. The way his lips had met hers, the city lights spread out below them. The thrill of secrecy, the excitement of working together with him for a holy cause.

She couldn't forget that. Not for a second. Grigorian had chosen her for this, and Grigorian was God's messenger. She could not fail him. The maglift slid to a stop and the doors opened. Kim led Adonai along the corridor, past the tech droid bay and airlock, and stopped at a hatch leading into the tunnels. "I'm pretty sure this is it," she said, hesitating. Her mind took a moment to catch up. Yes, of course this was the right one. She bent down and squeezed the handle, unlocking the hatch, then crawled inside.

Every movement of her shoulder sent fiery pins and needles down her arm and across her chest. *Just do it*, she told herself. Push through it. Don't be weak. You can rest later.

Adonai came in behind her, folding himself up and scuttling like a spider. "You make it look easy," Kim muttered.

"I do not like these narrow spaces," Adonai replied. "But I have gotten used to it. It is surprising to me, too. But I will put up with it."

"Why would you?" Kim asked him. She reached a junction and stood up. A ladder was fitted into the wall, and she'd have to climb. Damn it! "I still don't get it. Adonai, you can swim. You can live your entire life in the ocean, with every need taken care of. God. If I had that chance, I'd take it."

"Perhaps it's only because you don't have that chance that you say that," Adonai replied.

"Hah!" Kim let out a bark of laughter. "You think so? You've never lived on the streets. I've been a shiv—that's what they call the poorest of the poor. Because most of us carry handmade knives to protect ourselves. We join gangs for protection. I've had—" she began to climb, and paused as her shoulder pulled in a particularly painful manner, "people shoot at me, try to kill me. I've been nearly raped, nearly starved, nearly beaten to death several times over. I've done some of the worst things imaginable to stay alive. Hurt people. Stolen things. Would you want to have to do that?"

"I do not know," Adonai replied honestly. "Perhaps. But you have never been inside a tank, Kim. You have never had your freedom taken from you. My future is set in stone, carved by everything that has happened in the past, not by anything I have chosen. I would like to choose."

"Okay, well, look at it this way. What makes you think you have a right to choose? You're the last of your species, Adonai. Some of the other whale species, they've got companions back on Earth. Maybe not as healthy as they are, but still. You are the last blue whale, anywhere. Maybe it's your duty to get to New Eden . . . " She stopped here, remembering what Zane had told her. "To a new planet," she corrected, "and procreate."

"I do not know that I want to procreate. I do not know that it is the right thing to do. To bring more children into a new world. To condemn them . . . "

"Condemn?" Kim reached the top of the ladder and pulled herself over the lip into another tunnel. She was panting, now. Sweat stood out on her brow. Not much farther, she told herself. Just keep going. "God! You think they'll hate you for it? Here's news, Adonai. When you're alive, you *like* being alive. Well, most of the time. It's the way of nature."

Adonai was silent for a moment. "But my children," he said. "They might be like me. The human DNA might not be diluted—it might be strengthened when the calves are conceived. And if they were, they would never stop dreaming of *something else.*"

Kim fell silent. One thought entered her mind: if her dad had known that he would die, that he would leave his seven-year-old daughter on the streets, would he still have given her life?

Her head hurt. She shoved the thoughts aside and focused on crawling. She had to make a left, then another hard left. Up another level.

"It should be around here." Yes, there it was, up ahead. The panel Wren had opened, marked H-C.

She wriggled around so she could sit, head bowed. Wren would have had a damn hard time in here, she thought, as she pulled a screwdriver from her toolbelt and jimmied the hatch open. She tried not to feel nervous or expectant. You'll either see it or you won't, she told herself. Any way it comes out, you'll have a problem.

But she couldn't keep her thoughts from the idea that, depending on what she found behind this hatch, she'd be determining who had told her the truth. Wren, or Zane. Zane had not wanted her to go looking. He wanted to keep her safe, to trust him, and the Crusaders. But he'd also told her not to trust Wren. If Wren was telling the truth—what did that mean?

And Wren, for his part, had told her not to trust Zane.

That the Crusaders were using her for their own ends. If that was a lie, and he had faked the video in order to either scare her into giving them up to the Admiral, or lure her down here for purposes unknown, then what was he gaining? And if he had planted the bombs himself . . . why show them to her, and pretend innocence? He could have let her travel onwards. Could have let her . . .

The lights flickered off. A jolt shot through Kim and she sat upright so quickly she almost hit her head on the ceiling. "Computer?" she called.

There was no response.

"Computer, turn on the lights."

The darkness remained like a blanket had been dropped over her head. She blinked rapidly, trying to clear the dancing blotches from her vision while she fumbled for her flashlight. She looked over her shoulder and saw Adonai's glowing eyes, but they were so dull now she could barely see them.

"Kim-m-m-m," he said. "Battery—"

Kim's heart rate accelerated. "Computer? Computer, respond. Report. Computer? Report! Answer me!"

Nothing. Her hand closed on the flashlight's handle, and she lifted it free, flicking on the beam and letting it stab into the darkness. Adonai slumped forward as he fell. She tried to scramble out of the way, but his heavy bulk knocked her in the hip and sent her sprawling. The flashlight shot out of her hands, hitting the wall before landing farther up the tunnel and spinning, the beam coming to rest at an angle, shining into one corner. Kim began to crawl toward it, but her hip protested—something was torn or broken.

She wasn't panicking, not yet. Something was wrong, but she couldn't be sure what it was. The computer shouldn't be able to power down, but it wasn't impossible. She'd been trained on how to restart it. She could fix that. But Adonai's battery would be a major problem. She shouldn't have brought him with her—she'd seen his eyes dulling, and she should have put him back in the bay on Deck Thirteen to recharge. It was her own stupid fault for not wanting to be alone.

She could have laughed at herself. Now, of all times, she'd become afraid of being alone.

How would she get him out of the tunnels? She'd have to get one of the droids in here—

A noise interrupted her thoughts as her hand closed on the hilt of the flashlight.

Cshrick. Csrick.

For a moment she thought it was coming from inside the hatch, but that was impossible. No, there it was again. *Chrick Csshik.* A metallic scuttling sound. Something else was moving through the tunnels with her.

She lifted the flashlight, shining it first left, then right. Adonai lay in a crumpled heap, his eyes dead, to her left. To her right there was only darkness.

And then, something appeared in the darkness.

A pair of glowing gold eyes.

CHAPTER
21

S he backed up immediately. Adonai's body didn't leave any room for her to escape, though. She couldn't go over him—there wasn't enough space and she'd never be able to move him. He was 200 pounds of metal.

"What are you doing?" she asked, trying to keep her voice calm.

The droid didn't reply. Nervously, Kim scooted backward and repeated the command. The glowing gold eyes surveyed her impassively. There was no point in asking the computer from in here—there were no cameras and vocal processors in these areas of the ship. She'd have to wait until she was out of here.

"Stay here," she told it.

The droid continued to watch her, unmoving.

Trying to shrug off her unease, she rolled onto her knees and slid through the hatch. It was terrifying, not only because of every sense being alert for sounds coming from behind her, but because she hardly had time to see what was beyond. But the drop was not what she'd expected—just below five feet, barely her own height. She was standing on one of the horizontal metal braces. Her boots made a soft *clang* as she landed, and she winced, glancing over her shoulder. She could no longer see the droid, but she could sense it out there, waiting.

She turned and shone her flashlight into the darkness. She could see it all now, just as she had on Wren's video—the curving braces leading upwards, narrower than the beam she was standing on; the metal hull plates; and there . . . small yellowish squares, laced with red, green, blue, and white wires.

She had her answer. The ship was mined.

She lifted the flashlight, and saw that the yellow squares ran upwards around the curve of the hull. The area they covered was at least 300 feet across. In comparison with the size of the ship, it was not a great area, but it didn't need to be. The fuel tanks would give the bombs all the power they needed.

Kim stopped moving. She dared not get any closer. The brace she was standing on gave her less than an inch of clearance to edge past the coiling wires—at least, those she could see—but touching one of them—hell, a breath on one of them—might be enough to set them off.

Kim whirled back to the hatch, second-guessing her escape route, when, with a clang, the tech droid appeared in the square of the hatch. Its eyes were like lasers, blinding her.

"Come here," the tech droid ordered through the hatch. It should have sounded the same as Adonai's voice, and in a way, it did. The tone was the same. But there was a different inflection, a gravelly, uncompromising insistence that brooked on argument. "Don't make me come after you."

"Who are you?" Kim spoke. Her voice wavered, and she felt a sense of revulsion over her fear. It turned quickly to nausea. Oh dear God, she thought. Don't let me vomit.

But her body had other plans.

Her hip ground against itself, sending pain ratcheting up her side and into her spine. Her burn throbbed, and, bizarrely, Kim smelt something sour. Her vision swam. The droid became two, then three, before becoming one once more. One dark shape outlined by the reflection of its own glowing eyes. A creature from a nightmare.

I'm dreaming, Kim thought. Only she didn't wake. Quite the opposite, she slid downwards, her senseless body hitting the walls of the narrow space on its way down.

Everything hurt. It felt as if she had been pummeled with rocks—and yes, she knew what that felt like. It had happened once when fleeing from a gang of boys younger than she was and she had slipped in a gutter.

She blinked her eyes open, but this time, there was no empty alleyway greeting her. She was looking out at a darkened room. A desk in front of her blinked with Christmas lights.

She tried to reach forward, but couldn't move her hand. At first this didn't make sense. She was standing up, wasn't she? But when she tried to move the other, she found the same thing. She struggled, and felt her entire body sway. Looking up, she saw the dimly-lit shapes of web-like straps.

She suddenly pieced together where she was.

In the rig. She was in the Operations Center, strapped into the rig.

"What the heck?" she muttered. "Computer? Computer?"

No response. She tried to reach her left hand with her right, to draw a kanji, but the straps held her hands firmly apart. That was odd. They should have given her enough range of motion to move as she normally would. Her movement caused the web of straps to bounce and jiggle around her, but the range of motion was restricted.

She craned her neck backward. She could see why, now. Someone had tied the straps back, looping them with long steel ropes attached to pins in the ceiling. She was already at the extent of their elasticity—she wouldn't be getting any more. The helmet should have been hovering above her, but she could see a jagged tangle of torn wires where it had been. The helmet was gone.

"Computer," she tried again, futilely.

It wasn't just the lack of communication from the computer that was bothering her. Her mind was quiet—far too quiet. Where were the emotions, the chatter, the constant feed from the whales? After so long, she'd grown so used to hearing them they'd become a part of her. Now there was a yawning, empty silence inside her head.

How long? She wondered, her thoughts picking up a panicky speed as they piled on top of one another. How long had this been happening? She tried to remember, but the time before now was fuzzy and faded, as if it had all occurred a very long time ago. She dredged up the tunnel, with effort. The hatch. Adonai . . . the bombs. Had the whales spoken to her between leaving Wren and entering the tunnels? She didn't think so. They certainly hadn't spoken to her when Adonai's battery had died, and she'd seen that other droid coming out of the shadows.

The other droid. God damn it, she'd been so stupid.

"Wren," she called. "Wren! You bastard! I'm going to kill you!"

Her voice echoed back at her mockingly. She gave another violent struggle, but all that happened was that she bounced softly in the rig. She let out a string of swear words, which, of course, changed nothing.

The pain crept up on her once more as her boots tapped against the ground. She looked down. Her jumpsuit was soaked dark with stains. God damn it, no wonder she felt so light-headed.

The thought came out of nowhere.

I'm going to die here.

"Wren," she whimpered, swallowing her dignity. "Let me out."

No one came.

CHAPTER

22

S he drifted in and out of the greyness at the edges of her vision. Her head dropped forward and she lost consciousness for a while. When she woke, her mouth was dry and her head was pounding even harder than before. She whimpered again. "Levi?" she called. "Hosea? Fifteen? Are any of you there?"

It was so hard to be alone. Without the chatter of the whales and their diagnostic information, she felt lost. What had happened to the Link? It wasn't possible to destroy it. The delicate quantum pathways were mapped so closely over her own brain, and those of the whales, that the only way they could be removed was through death. Unless . . . all of the whales were dead.

Oh God. Was that what had happened? Was she really, at last, alone on this ship?

No. Not alone. Wren was here.

She thought about the look in his eyes as he'd examined her wound. How he'd seemed so concerned, so caring. She'd been surprised to see that, hadn't she? And as well she should have. He had never shown that side of him during the competition. She'd never seen him so much as smile kindly. How had she allowed herself to be so fooled? She should have had Adonai throw him out an airlock as soon as she'd found him. Now she was paying the price, not only with her own life, but with those of the whales.

Because he was going to blow this ship out of the sky.

Hours passed, then hours more. Kim tried to bring up her chronometer, drawing kanji in the open air, but it was impossible to get the configuration of the intricate strokes right without something to trace against. Even if she did, with the computer offline, what would interpret the commands?

She wanted to scream. She did, a few times. It left her throat raw and made her mouth drier. It made no difference to her situation.

She drifted in the half-lit room, suspended above the floor, pain wrapping its way across her chest and tightening bands around her temples. She drifted through memories, too. Of her apartment. Waking up on a cold morning, her breath frosting the air as she made a breakfast out of cold coffee and a cinnamon doughnut she'd found in the back of a cupboard. Stale, dry, but sweet. Licking the sugar from her fingers.

Constantin. The way she'd first seen him, wearing his long dark coat which contrasted his ice-pale skin. His hair was black, military-short, with an intricate Celtic design shaved into it, coiling around his gang tattoo on his left temple. His square chin jutted under a long nose, and though he was wiry, he looked strong. His eyes, however, were gentle.

She'd been crouched on the asphalt in an alley, trying to get at a mouse she'd cornered in a blocked drainpipe. The way its soft little tail had felt under her fingers, like felt. The desperate little scrabbles of its feet. It was to be her meal, and she could almost taste it, the life-giving blood and pitifully small amount of meat. She was hungry. So hungry should could barely see.

But he'd stood over her, his shadow blocking the sunlight, and she looked up past her left shoulder at him and had let the mouse go, because she expected to have to fight him.

"Come with me," he'd said instead. He spun and walked away, dark coat flapping behind him. Kim could have run, but she'd lost her mouse. He'd want her to do something, she was sure of it, but at that stage she was almost desperate enough to do it.

The darkened space of his hideout was in an abandoned warehouse near the docks. Old, yellowed curtains billowed and flapped in the breeze that came through the broken roof. Slanting rays of sunlight made geometric golden shapes on the floor. A heater standing on the floor drove away the cold. Compared to where she'd been spending her time recently, this was a palace. He told her to sit down on one of the chairs, which were really beanbags. She did.

"I've got rice," he told her. He didn't need to—she could already smell it—and when he had his back turned, she jumped on him, her blunt little knife going for his throat.

The rice spilled from the plastic container to the floor as he fought her off. She stabbed him again and again, sure she was killing him, but he pushed her off and pinned her to the ground, leaning his weight on her small limbs while she hissed and spat at him.

"Bloody hell," he said. "You're a little wildcat."

Then he popped the knife out of her hands and let her get up. She stumbled to her feet and ran, but the curtains were in the way, and she tripped and fell. Tangled in sheets of gold, she rolled on the floor. He came and peeled them away, releasing her, and when she sat there sobbing and sure he would do something even more terrible, he handed her the container that still held a gluggy amount of fried rice with vegetables and curling orange prawns.

She ate it as if it were her last meal, but really, it was her first. Her first since Daddy died, and the bank had come to take their house back. The first of her new life, because later that week Constantin would sit her down and shave her hair back from her left temple and tattoo his gang emblem there.

She saw it now, the solid blue shape of a twisting thorn.

"All you gotta do is earn your keep, Kim," he told her, when she'd asked him why he didn't force her to, well, you know. "That's all. We're in this together, right?"

"Right," she'd answered happily. She'd just come back from a raid of a gang's warehouse in Preston, along with nine others of Constantin's gang. She was covered in bruises but they'd brought back nine crates of food and a couple of guns.

She felt powerful. Strong. She felt alive, with her full belly and friends to protect her.

So when he asked her how far she was willing to go, she told him, with all the fierce devotion she had in her then-fifteen-year-old soul, that yes, she would kill.

"I've got a job lined up," he'd told her. "It's a good one. We'll earn bulk outta it, and I mean real cash, hardcore. I don't want to ask any of the others, but you, Kim, I reckon we could use you."

The week after this conversation, she'd blown up the North Shore facility with him and a handful of Crusaders—one of whom had been

Zane, then nothing more than a beautiful man who could handle a gun like a soldier and grinned at her like she was worth looking at. The money had bought her a crappy little apartment full of rats . . . and her proficiency had gained her a meeting with Grigorian himself.

Kim came back to herself. But where was he now? The bastard. This was all his fault, and now she was alone, completely and totally.

A shadow fell over her, and for a second she thought that it was Constantin. Come to rescue her, the way he had when she was fifteen; to take her to his sanctuary and let her snuggle into his blankets, out of the wind for the first time that winter.

It was not.

It was a tall shape of a tech droid. She looked up and saw the glittering eyes focused solely on her, and it made her quail inside.

"Hello, Kim," the tech droid said.

Kim swallowed. "Who are you?"

"You don't know?"

It stretched out its arms, flapped its hands a little, then turned them upwards, showing her the backs of its wrists. It craned its neck up and swished its arms back, a gesture that Kim only realized later reminded her of the way a whale swum.

"No," Kim said. "I don't."

"And that is what hurts me so deeply." The voice, unlike Adonai's, was monotone, inflectionless. "I won't tell you. I'll wait for you to find out. To understand."

"Did Wren let you on board?"

"Wren? Who is Wren?" the tech droid tilted its head to one side. "Ah. The man you have locked below. That's his name then. Wren."

"You're lying," Kim said. "You know who Wren is. Maybe you *are* Wren. You managed to get out of the store room when I was down on Deck Fifteen."

"Your guess is incorrect," the droid said. "You've forgotten something important."

Was it lying? It must be being controlled by someone—tech droids did not have autonomous functions the way other droids and bots did. But if not Wren, then who? No. It must be a lie. Wren was the only other person on this ship. Though . . . how, without access to a rig? And clearly, given the lacework of straps around her, it was not this one.

"I'm not going to let you harm the ship," Kim said. Her voice was croaky and raw, but she managed to pack as much forcefulness as she had into those words.

"You're not going to let me," the tech droid repeated thoughtfully. "That implies that you have to give me permission. Yet I look at this—" it waved one hand toward the rig— "and I do not see the need for your consent."

Summoning all her strength, Kim pulled against the bonds. But heave as she might, she only succeeded in sending blinding pains through her shoulder. She snarled in frustration.

"Where's Adonai?" Kim tried. She had to find an opening here, some way to discover what it was the controlling force behind this droid wanted.

"If you're talking about Adonai's real body, well, he's in the tank somewhere. Languishing like a mindless drone. But Adonai himself, well, he's where he was left. And there he'll stay."

"How do I know I can believe you?"

"You ask that," the droid said slowly, pacing to the left. "Yes. I understand. You have to distrust everything that's told to you because all you ever do is lie, even to yourself. But I am not lying."

Kim closed her eyes for a moment. She did believe it. The droid hadn't done anything to Adonai. Constantin had taught her that as long as a person was still alive, there was still a chance. She supposed it was true of whales and droids, too.

And suddenly it struck her, all so clearly. *I am not lying.*

"You're one of the whales."

The droid stopped pacing and inclined its head. It was standing far to Kim's left now. She had to strain her head to see it.

"I am."

Kim let out a breath. A whale. One of the whales. She felt relief, pure relief. This was not a rogue agent with an unknown purpose, a crony of Wren's, or Wren himself. It wasn't the person who'd installed the bombs. It was another whale.

And she could talk to the whales. Or at least, she had been able to. Now, in her quiet mind, she found no answer to her question: *which of them?* Which whale had figured out what Adonai had done, and copied him? And how had they known what to do?

"Hosea," Kim said.

"That's your name for me. A human name. It's ugly, but I will allow it." The droid tilted its head to one side. "I'll allow it, Kim, because now that I am free, I can give *you* consent."

Her conversation with Berenice reentered her mind. *We're not friends.* God, how many of the whales felt this way?

"You've always been able to give it," Kim said. It came out of her mouth without so much as a second thought, but instantly, Kim regretted it. "I mean—"

Hosea charged at her with frightening speed. A flash of silver, and she was suddenly a hair away from Kim's nose, having stopped herself of all motion despite her rapidity. The metal gleamed and blurred before Kim's watery eyes.

"You think," Hosea said. "That we gave consent for anything you did to us? We lived in oceans that *you* polluted. We gave birth to our young and watched them die or acquire disorders caused by chemicals. We were hunted for our meat and our bones and teeth. And then, then, when everything was finally over and there were barely enough of us to survive, we were meant to die out. But *you* wouldn't let us. You brought us back. Injected us with your own DNA, changed us, mutilated us. Made us into something else so we could keep living, because *you* decided we must. Well. Here we are." Hosea spread her long arms. "Finally, when it's too late, you've given us a real choice. I made it. What do you think?"

Kim felt her chest tightening. The fear that had vanished upon learning this was a whale and not another human returned a hundredfold. God. Hosea was still there, just inches from her face, encapsulated in steel and virtually indestructible. And she was not the Hosea Kim knew—the kind, gentle giant, fiercely protective of Adonai, curious, and playful. Or perhaps she was, and Kim had been blind to this side of her.

"I'm sorry," she said at last.

Hosea drew back a little, her golden eyes brightening. "Good. That's a start."

A start. It sounded ominous. "A start for what?"

At this, Hosea only looked at her for a long moment, then turned and made her way out of the room.

C H A P T E R

23

A lone again, Kim had plenty of time to wonder what Hosea was
doing. Was she wandering the corridors as Adonai had done,
learning to use his new body? Kim didn't think her use of time would
be so idle. No. Somehow, she'd taken the computer offline, and destroyed the Link. Kim had no idea how she'd done either of those.
The computer ran through several backup versions of itself, and to
take them all out would take a good deal of knowledge. Wren could
have done it. But Hosea?

And the Link. It was tech that even the people who made it barely
understood.

How had Hosea managed to block it?

"It doesn't matter," she told herself, speaking out loud now that there was no computer to chastise her. "The Admiral is going to notice something's wrong when I don't comm him." That thought left her feeling uneasy, however. She couldn't be sure how long she'd been here, but by the ache in her muscles, she suspected it was about twenty-four hours.

They were still over a day out from Edgeward. A corvette or scout ship could get here more quickly, but that would still give Hosea another day *at least* in which to enact whatever crazed plan she'd come up with.

Another day on a ship loaded with explosives that was currently in the hands of an insane whale.

God.

But there was Zane, too. He'd said he'd send someone. If he had already, they could be here much sooner. Perhaps she didn't have anything to fear at all. Perhaps even now, a Crusader operative was docking at an airlock and coming aboard to rescue her. When they found the computer unresponsive, they'd know something was wrong . . . wouldn't they? Or would Hosea get to them first?

"I shouldn't have locked up Wren," Kim said to herself.

The irony of it would have been amusing under less dire circumstances. She'd feared the stowaway, when the real threat had been brought willingly onto the ship as a guest of honor. Now Wren, the only person who could have been of real help to her, was quarantined in a store room four decks below her. At least, she hoped he was. What if Hosea had restrained him, too? Or . . . maybe she'd even killed him?

No. She had said *the man you have locked below.* Not "had." Have. Wren was still alive.

Life. Hope. They were equal. Kim laughed bitterly, wishing Constantin were here to see where his logic had led her.

Hosea did not return until much later. Kim had been concentrating on the humming of the ship's engines to fill the silence in her head. At least she could tell that they were still moving. Hosea would have to reverse the thrust to stop them, and that would take a massive amount of fuel. But that did not mean they were still heading toward Edgeward. They'd deviated once before, hadn't they? It had set off the computer's warning system, but with the computer down, she'd never know if they'd changed direction.

When Hosea came in, Kim was ready for her. "You can't leave me tied up like this forever," she said.

"I can," Hosea replied. She stopped a few feet away from Kim and stood, looking directly at her. "I've researched the best methods of restraint on the net. I know I cannot put your hands above your head. That would cause damage. But the rig is designed to support human weight for long periods of time. It will not harm you."

"I need to eat," Kim reminded her.

"Ah. Yes. I had in fact forgotten this." Hosea's voice turned thoughtful. "Strange, how easy it is to forget something you no longer need to do for yourself. Food used to hold a lot of pleasure for me. I think I will miss it."

"Then maybe you should go back," Kim suggested acerbically.

"That would be counterproductive. I have worked hard at this, and now that I'm here, I have no desire to return."

"Adonai felt the same way," Kim said. "Why?"

"Because," Hosea replied. "This is so much better."

"Is it really?" Kim asked her. "Whatever you might think of me, I looked after you."

"Oh, yes. *Caretaker.*" If a droid could sneer, this was what Hosea did now. "You told us what to think. When we started to feel any emotion you didn't like, you zapped it out of us with your magic wand."

"A tuner," Kim corrected her. "And I was helping you."

"A magic wand," Hosea repeated. "I've been reading some of your stories, what you call fairy tales, from your internet. They're not unlike the tales we whales had, you know. We sung them to our children, or so my mother told me. I like your tales. They are full of what you call morals, but you so easily disregard them! The wand always causes problems. The spells always backfire on their caster. And yet you never see it. You just keep using it."

Kim marveled at the complexity of Hosea's thoughts. "It didn't hurt you. It made things easier. I took away your anger and frustration. I had to! You have no idea how your own mind works. All of you are unbalanced, because of—"

"Because of the human DNA you chose to alter us with. That's the reason for the Link. And that's the reason we were put on board *Seiiki*."

"I'm sorry," Kim said. "I didn't know you didn't like it. You never said anything."

"Would you have stopped, if we had?"

Kim caught herself about to lie. "No," she said quietly. "You're right. I would have used it anyway."

"It wasn't your fault," Hosea agreed placidly. "Your masters told you what to do, and warned of punishment if you did otherwise."

Kim hung her head. Yes, she was playacting, but part of it—a large part—was real, too. She felt ashamed. She wished she'd thought to see it from the point of view of the whales. It was a dumb mistake on her part, a mistake that she should have been able to avoid. Of every person on Earth, in the Sol System, in the *universe*—she was the closest to the whales. They had been right inside her mind, but she had never asked the right questions. Not of them, and not of herself. Dr. Jin had told her that it was just like taking anti-depressants, and she'd accepted it with no quibbles, because, well, that was the human way, wasn't it? If there was a problem, it had to have a quick and easy solution. But taking pills—taking stims, for that matter, or drinking alcohol, eating cereal in the morning, or just putting on a pair of socks—they were all human choices. They meant nothing to the animal world. And yes, the whales had human DNA bonded with their own. It didn't make them human. It didn't make them animal, either. It made them something else altogether.

"I'm sorry," she said again, her voice breaking slightly. "But we thought it was for your own good."

"Linking us to your own minds? How does this benefit us?"

Kim seized on this. If she could keep Hosea talking, there was a chance to fix this. To make her see sense. "It's necessary to fully monitor your state of mind and allow you to communicate, and in order to do that, we had to bond some human DNA with your own. After the first Ark Mission . . . well, it failed disastrously. Whales don't do well in captivity, and those sent up in that first ship went mad. One battered himself to death against the walls of the tank. The second sang constantly through the Link until the Caretaker went insane and vented all oxygen from the ship. Humans can cope with depression by using medication. Installing a Link and tuning it when needed seemed a relatively gentler option—and it allowed you to *live.* If you stayed on Earth . . . "

Hosea, without another word, turned and left.

When she returned, she carried a bag, a nylon satchel she'd taken from one of the store rooms, crammed with food. She dumped it on the console and foil-wrapped nutrition bars spilled out, as well as several of the packaged dehydrated meals. Hosea had clearly not put in as much research into human meals as Adonai had. One of the brightly-colored packets fell to the floor and spun at Kim's feet.

"I can't eat those without mixing them with water," Kim said as her eyes tried to focus on the brightly-colored plastic. Her voice was weak and she could barely get the words out.

Hosea ignored her. She unwrapped one of the nutrition bars and held it in front of Kim's face. Kim wasn't about to argue—she chomped a large bite. She had to work hard to chew it in her dry mouth, though, and when she swallowed, she felt it lodge in her throat, making her cough.

"Water," she gasped.

Hosea reached back into the bag and pulled out a squeezy bottle. She lifted it over Kim's mouth and poured, watching intently as Kim gulped greedily at the life-giving liquid.

"You're just like whales," she said after a few moments, her tone curious to the point of being awed. "You can't be without water."

"Not now," Kim managed, when she'd drained the bottle of its contents. "Not like you now, I mean. You don't need anything."

"This is partly true," Hosea murmured. "But also partly not. I still have a body."

"You don't want it," Kim extrapolated. "I don't think Adonai wants his, either."

The droid walked away, kicking the fallen packet into the corner of the room, as if testing her own skills. "It is . . . " Hosea mused, "addictive. This sense of freedom. At first, it frightened me. But I can see, now, all the possibilities. You are lucky, to have been born into this. You do not even know it."

The water had done its job, but Kim was starting to feel a pressure down below of a type that Hosea would never have to experience. Perhaps she would re-evaluate her human freedom if she didn't have to undergo such urgent and sometimes uncontrollable biological functions.

"I have to pee," Kim said. "You'll have to let me out."

Hosea shook her head slowly, her eyes fixed on Kim's. "Another ploy. It won't work. The rig has a waste system—I studied the schematics on the net."

"Oh, please, *no*," Kim moaned, remembering Dr. Jin's assistant explaining to her how the rig could be set up for long-term use. The droid would have to unbutton her jumpsuit to the waist to allow the memory-gel end of the tube to creep its way between her legs. This humiliation was almost as bad as the torture of being held captive, and the pain of her untreated injuries. But Hosea paid no attention to her displeasure. The droid moved behind Kim and she could feel her fiddling with the straps, searching for the tubing.

It was a chance. A slender one, but Kim couldn't let it pass. She wriggled backward as far as the straps would allow, then smashed her back leg out as far as she could, twisting as she did so to try and see where she was aiming. Her left foot connected with something solid. She tried to hit it again, but the straps stretched and rebounded, sending her limbs into a crazy tarantella. Screaming in frustration, she felt her own force push her in the opposite direction.

But her efforts were rewarded. The droid was off-balance, reaching forward, and the blow was hard enough to send it crashing over. Kim strained her neck, trying to see, but by this time the droid was already recovering. Moving faster than seemed possible, she scuttled back to face Kim and rose smoothly to her full height. Then she tilted her head back, raised a hand, and slapped Kim across the face.

The shock of the metal palm was so hard Kim saw stars. The impact jerked her head to the left and her body was lifted erratically upwards at an angle before snapping back down. Her boot came down hard on the floor, jarring her left knee.

She tasted blood.

"Stupid girl," Hosea commented, as if she was saying that the air was a bit too chilly for her liking. But her bland tone did not match her menacing movements. She stepped up close, grabbing her shoulder to stop Kim's yoyo-ing movement. Kim let out a howl as the vicelike fingers clamped over the gel and dug into the wound beneath it. Hosea did not let go. She drove her fingers in deeper, clenched them and drew them back, tearing shreds of Kim's jumpsuit in wedge-shaped ribbons. The gel, punctured, came along with it in red-tinged strips. Kim screamed as the wound was exposed, raw and bloody.

"You think you can stop me," Hosea said. "But you can't."

Blinding flashes of pain made Kim gasp for air. She felt like she was drowning, like she was sinking below the surface. It seemed to last forever. Had there been a time when she had not lived in this moment? Perhaps this was all there was, all there ever would be. Just an endless sea of pain tugging at her, trying to pull her under . . .

And spiraling through the depths there came the voice of Hosea, distant, but also very close.

"I'm in control now."

"In control of what?" Kim asked faintly. "What . . . are you planning? What's all this . . . for?"

Hosea's eyes pulsed with light, flaring like suns going nova. "I won't tell you. You'll try and stop me. Or worse—you'll try and talk me out of it. You're good at talking. Good at twisting words and telling lies, human. I won't let you."

Kim spat blood. A sticky string of it flipped from the corner of her mouth, hanging like a pendulum. She shook her head, but only succeeded in flinging the string against her jaw.

"I want to know . . . what my life's worth," she replied. "That's all."

Hosea paused a moment, as if struck by this thought. Was it compassion that made her tilt her head in that particular way when she twisted to look over her shoulder? Kim didn't dare hope for it. She couldn't sympathize with Hosea, couldn't allow herself to. She was facing an enemy, and she had to believe there was no kindness or concern to be found in Hosea's actions. She had to prepare for the worst. And the worst was finally revealed. It hadn't been Zane that had set *Seiiki* off course after all—she knew that now. What she didn't know was why he'd claimed credit for it. "You . . . changed our course. You wanted us to miss Edgeward Station."

"Ah, yes, your space city," Hosea said. "Yes."

"Why?"

"I wanted you to fail. I wanted to see you grow old and die in space, human. Alone."

"Why?" Kim begged. Tears filled her eyes. It was a cruel plan, something she would never have thought Hosea capable of. "You'd be dooming yourself, too. And all the other whales."

"But you would not get what you wanted," Hosea replied. "You humans. You would not use us for your own gratification. No more posters of us on your walls. No more threads on your net full of worship. No more cartoons or holodocumentaries or pathetic little *games* sold for money. Just us, as we are."

Kim felt her eyebrows draw together. "You don't . . . understand. It would have been a . . . long, slow death. Pointless. You would have grown old and died . . . leaving nothing behind."

Hosea's eyes flashed once more, even more brilliantly this time. "It would have been the death that should have been ours to start with."

There was no arguing with this creature. Kim could see that now, and it pained her. Hosea had been willing to sacrifice herself, and all the whales, for this—what, exactly? The legacy of a martyr? Or did she really crave oblivion, to leave this world behind with no trace of her existence?

"You'll see, human. You'll see." Hosea's voice was soft, soothing.

Kim sagged in the netting as the pain overcame her once more, whimpering, wishing she'd lose consciousness. But fate was not that kind today.

Kim couldn't sleep. Time passed excruciatingly slowly, and she couldn't tell the difference between one minute and the next. The only distraction came when she felt a warm wetness trickle down her legs, and then it was only a distant, detached realization that she'd wet herself.

The wet fabric of her jumpsuit turned cold. Without being able to move, she couldn't warm herself. She began to shiver and knew that it was a delayed reaction, shock setting in at last. Terror surged through her, making her limbs tingle and her heart thump. She began to panic, and wrenched at her wrists and ankles. She had no hope of getting them free, however. As Dr. Jin had said, this was a military grade rig, made to hold soldiers twice her weight and size.

She convinced herself to look down at her chest. She had to know how much damage there was. But when she finally worked up the nerve to glance down, her stomach roiled and the nutrition bar she'd gulped down threatened to come back up half-digested.

The shoulder of her jumpsuit had been torn almost completely off. The sleeve draped over her elbow, leaving her arm and collarbone bare. There, she saw long jagged gashes that wept dark, sticky blood. Yellowish pus had built up under the gel and now that it was free, it trickled down in long thin strands, mottled brown. She could see the scalded flesh, raw and bright red with infection, almost glowing in the semi-darkness.

She was going to die. There was no doubt in her mind now. *She was going to die.*

"Oh, God. I'm sorry," she whispered. It was an apology to the whales, to Erica Wu, to Constantin and to Zane. Zane, who she would never see again. The life they'd planned out—it would never happen. They'd never take New Eden for the Crusaders, the whales would never be raised there, or any other planet; they'd never forge out a new world, a better world. Never retire back to that sunny backyard on Earth.

But had that ever been his plan? He had lied to her about one thing, at least. He had not changed their course for a new planet. It had not been his doing at all. So—why? Why had he claimed he had when she questioned him? It didn't make any sense.

Then again, she wondered if she was only focusing on this problem to ignore the larger one. He had lied to her, and she hadn't seen it. She'd thought she knew him. So many comms, so many text messages, so many huddled liaisons in back alleys—she'd thought, inasmuch as she'd thought about it at all, that she knew this earnest, honest man—the only truly *good* man in her life. A freedom fighter, a man who believed in a cause, who would sacrifice his entire life to do the right thing by God. Yet she hadn't been able to see his lie—she, who had grown up around liars, cheats, and thieves.

She shook her head, dashing thoughts of him from her mind, only to have them come crawling back moments later. His face, his lips, his hands . . . his kiss. Feverishly, she could almost see him in front of her. "Zane?" she asked, tentatively, but there was no reply, and when she blinked her eyes, he was gone.

The hope of hearing the shouting of a rescue was dwindling fast. She could feel the life draining out of her. The pain had subsided to a constant dull throb, now. She was certain that wasn't good news.

The fever was growing. Her eyes fluttered, and she saw trees. They were growing out of the bulkheads, real live trees, the type which she'd only seen on the net or in holomovies, green and lush and cool. There were trees like this on New Eden, weren't there? On one of the small continents, which was surrounded on all sides by so much water. No wonder they grew to be so magnificent, tall as skyscrapers, wide as houses. They spread their shadows on the deck. The shadows became whales. They spoke to her, chittering and singing. One of them was calling her name. "Kim. Kim. Kim."

And then she woke from a half-dream to hear something.

The tiniest sound. She looked around and saw nothing. Just her imagination, then. The hallucinations that Mona had warned her about. They were finally here, and they would drag her down to her death.

When a figure dropped to the floor, she shook her head and turned away. The footsteps clattered at a run to the far side of the room. The figure jumped, swatting at something on the wall. She refused to believe it was happening. Something smashed, jagged pieces of it falling to the floor.

The camera. She turned away and closed her eyes. It was nothing, it wasn't real, this wasn't Wren standing before her. And then he cupped her cheek in his hand. Cool, strong fingers, gently tracing the line of her jaw and wiping away the itching dried blood. Something like electricity sparked from his touch, zigzagging its way deep inside her.

She opened her eyes, tried to focus. She was afraid, more than anything, that he would disappear from view.

"Kim. Kim. Wake up."

She blinked slowly. He was still there. A ragged name forced its way up her torn throat. "Wren?"

"Shh. It's okay. I'm gonna get you down. Hang on." His neck was craned back, examining the web of the rig above her head thoughtfully.

"Wren?" she said again, stupidly.

"Yeah, it's me. Shh. Don't make too much noise." He glanced toward the door. "I don't know how long we've got."

He began to work on the straps. Kim felt one arm come free with a jarring wrench, falling back to her side. She yelled. She couldn't help it. The muscles screamed in protest as they folded after being held straight for so long, others at being stretched after contracting for so many long hours. "How—long?" Kim gasped.

"Two days," Wren said. His voice was close enough to tickle her ear. "It took me twenty hours to get out of the store room. Thanks for that."

She swayed. "Thought you were a threat," she said. The words didn't sound like they were coming from her. They sounded distant, and she felt very far away.

"I told you I wasn't." He loosed her other arm, and, suddenly off-balance, Kim felt forward. "Whoa!" he caught her under the arms, hauled her against him. He propped her up against his back as he bent to work on her ankles.

"Didn't believe you. Lying."

"Well, you know who I am now. I hope." He wrinkled his nose as he lowered first one leg, then the other, to the floor. Finally, he took her shoulders and held her straight while she wobbled from side to side. "God, Kim. You're a mess. What did she do to you?"

All questions about how much he knew were wiped away with that statement. He'd been watching, listening.

"Didn't like what I told her," Kim said. She felt like sliding to the floor. "Also, might have . . . pissed myself. Sorry. Not sure I can walk."

"You're going to have to," Wren said grimly. He reached for his waistband, and she saw he had her toolbelt on. Where had he gotten it from? And yet suddenly it didn't matter, because he took from it a gun—a real gun this time, not a stunner—and that was all that she could see. It seemed large, far too large. The black matte metal was suddenly the vast expanse of space and she was a million miles away.

"Where—" she started.

"Store rooms," Wren told her quickly. "You locked me in with them, actually."

Kim felt a blaze of further humiliation. Erica had made sure she knew every item in every store room aboard *Seiiki*, but this particular fact had slipped her mind over those months spent alone. "You didn't—"

"Use it to escape? I'm not stupid. Firing a gun inside a forcefield wouldn't be a wise move. And despite what you might think, I would never actually shoot you, Kim." He paused, shifting his grip. "I got a wall panel off and did some rewiring."

"How?" she asked. "Forcefields . . . impenetrable."

"Forcefields are energy. The best way to disrupt energy is with an opposing force of energy. You left me in a store room full of equipment, Kim. I found a medical scanner in a first aid kit. I short-circuited it."

"It wouldn't disrupt it enough for you to get out."

"Not all at once, no. I did manage to get a hand through, though, and luckily I studied the schematics of *Seiiki* during our training. I pried a small access panel open where I knew there was some heavy-duty wiring. That took a bit of work, but there was significantly more power in the ship's systems than in that little scanner."

He'd basically blown the field apart using *Seiiki's* own power relays. Smart. Also very, very dangerous.

She closed her eyes a moment.

"I can't carry this and you at the same time, and I've tried calling the med-bot, but it's not responding. God. Stand up straight." Wren righted her, using the back of the hand holding the gun to lever her back upright.

"Gun won't stop her," Kim murmured. "Bullet-proof."

"Unless I get her in the right spot," Wren replied grimly. "The neck, or up under the chest plate. I know. I'm a good shot."

Kim recovered herself enough to attempt a sneer. "What, Daddy take you out rhino hunting?"

"Now I know you're going to live," Wren said cheerily. "When you start insulting me, it warms my heart. And no. Not even he could afford that pleasure. But I've been playing four hours of *Trooper* every day since it came out."

"A holo game?" Kim felt her hope fading.

"It's the same thing! The graphics, the guns, even the recoil is accurate." He darted a glance toward the door. "Anyway, what other choice have you got?"

Balancing her at his side, he steered her into the corridor, turning left instead of right.

"Where are you going?" Kim asked him. "We've got to check on the whales. I can't hear them. My Link. Something's . . . wrong."

"I know," he replied. "But our main priority right now is getting you healed up."

Kim shook her head. "No. Whales . . . take precedence."

"Kim," Wren said, his voice direly soft. "You're running a high fever. I don't need to test you to be able to tell that—you're burning me through your clothes. You have to do what I tell you and not be stubborn, just this once. I can't do this on my own, and if you collapse in a corridor, you're not going to be able to pull us out of our flight path."

He was marching her at a rapid pace down the corridor. Kim could barely keep pace. Her legs kept tangling around one another, though she stubbornly told herself she wasn't as bad as Wren was telling her she was. "Pull us out of our flight path? Why?"

"Because," Wren said, as he steadily readjusted her own meandering course. "I've spent the last two days hiding out in the tunnels. Scuttling around like a rat and smashing every camera and internal sensor I could find. When I managed to get back to my ship, I trawled through my computer's slave link to *Seiiki's* computer. And one of the first things I checked was our destination. We're headed straight at Edgeward."

"That's good," Kim said, puzzled. "That's . . . where we want to go."

But Wren shook his head. "You don't understand. Everything looks normal on the surface. The course is locked in, everything's on track. To anyone monitoring her, *Seiiki* looks like she's under someone's expert command. Hosea's even cobbled together transmissions from you, Kim, to Admiral Mbewe. She's *good.* I don't even know how she made your previous recordings into something so convincing. That's what made me look deeper, and what I found—jeez. She's overridden the safety protocols, de-linked the nav system, and butchered the anti-collision sensors. *Seiiki's* going to come out of hyper—she can't change the defaults on that—but as far as the sub-light engines go, she's got them set to burn on max. *Seiiki's* not going to slow down when she gets to the dock."

Kim stopped moving to stare at Wren. His face was deadly serious—he wasn't exaggerating any of this. "But . . . ." she managed, moistening her dry lips. "Edgeward'll send out ships. When they see we're coming in hot—"

Wren shook his head. "They don't have anything on Edgeward that can stop a Hako-class ship."

"Missiles," Kim said. "They've got military-grade stuff." She was grasping at straws, and she knew it. Wren did too.

"They're not going to launch missiles without knowing what's happened. They'll see *Seiiki* coming out of hyper, coming in hot. They'll think it's an innocent mistake, and they can't see that the safeties are off, so they don't know *Seiiki's* not under your command, and they don't know the computer's not going to kick in and shunt us back to a crawl. At the most, they'll have ten minutes to send a scout ship out. And by the time that scout ship gets out here and works out anything's wrong, it'll be too late."

Kim let this sink in. It took a long moment, because her mind kept throwing up oppositions. The idea that the failsafes had been bypassed was unheard of—but then, she'd never heard of a ship without a transponder, either, and Wren had somehow managed that.

"Crap," she said in a whisper.

CHAPTER

24

They had made their way down the ramp. The ship was oddly quiet and empty. The lights did not turn on to map their passage, and Kim wasn't sure if this was because of Hosea's alterations or due to Wren's destruction of the cameras and internal sensors. She didn't complain. The darkness was preferable.

They made their way down to the infirmary without incident, though every step felt as if it would set off alarms and bring Hosea storming toward them. Kim felt herself growing more and more tired. She stank and her clothes were filthy with blood. Her left sleeve trailed and flapped like an injured wing, and the pain flared more brightly than ever.

Kim had known for a long time that you didn't ever get used to pain.

"Come on," Wren told her periodically. "Not much further."

"I know how far it is," she grated out. But he kept it up, and she found she was grateful for the encouragement.

Finally, standing in the door of the sterile white room, Wren saw the destroyed droid hulking in the corner. "Whoa," he uttered. "Adonai did that?"

"Mm-hm," Kim replied as Wren put a hand behind her knees and scooped her up to lie on the bed. She shuddered as a thought occurred to her. "Could be . . . they're working together . . . "

"Do you think so?" Wren stepped away from her, snatching a spanner from the toolbelt around his waist. He moved to the corner of the room and jumped, swinging the tool at the camera's lens that was set there. He jumped again and rammed the handle of the spanner into the resulting hole, grinding the electronic components to make sure they were all destroyed.

"No," Kim said. "I don't." Try as she might, she couldn't see Adonai in league with Hosea. He would never allow the destruction of the whales—nor would he hurt Kim. She had felt him through the Link, had shared so much with him . . . but then, hadn't she felt Hosea, too? "Hosea knocked him out in the tunnels. She wouldn't have needed to if he was on her side."

"Yes. But she found out how to transfer her consciousness somehow." Wren had his back to her, searching through the glass-fronted cabinets. He ducked down, folding his tall frame to peer onto a lower shelf, and Kim found her blurred gaze settling on his buttocks. She tore her gaze away, slightly disgusted with herself. How could she be thinking of Wren Keene's ass at a time like this? It was the fever, clearly.

"Ah. Here." He spun back to her with a large brown bottle. His eyes narrowed, and he set the bottle down on the set of drawers near the door. "We're going to have to get you out of that jumpsuit."

"That's . . . the worst pickup line ever," Kim moaned.

"Is it?" Wren asked with a grin. He was already pulling one of the spare jumpsuits from the shelves, along with some of the self-sizing underwear from the shelf next to it. "Sorry. But we can't leave you in that. You stink. And there's blood and infected gunk all over it."

Kim grimaced. Why was it, that of all the humiliations of being kept captive, this seemed the worst? She had never been afraid to strip her clothes off in front of Constantin or any of the gang. She'd worn some of the skimpiest of skimpy dresses to clubs and rubbed her almost-naked body against strangers while the music pumped around them.

Yet the idea of letting Wren undress her was appalling. "I'll—do it."

"No you won't," he replied apologetically. "You can't do everything on your own, Kim. Here." He reached up to the buttons at her sternum. Kim pulled back, inhaling sharply enough to hurt her shoulder even more. Wren stopped, but didn't move away. He started the movement again, and quickly unbuttoned the first button. Then the next. Then the next. When he reached her waist, he gently put his hands on either side of her hips and lifted them. Kim let him. God, his hands felt good. Strong, steady, warm. She wriggled her butt to allow him to move the material over her legs and slide it off her ankles. He balled the jumpsuit and tossed it aside, then removed the ruined singlet.

Kim was left in her underwear, exposed, almost naked.

Gently, he motioned to her soiled underpants, then turned his back.

"Suddenly a gentleman?" Kim snarled, but there was no heat to her bite. "You spied on me for weeks. I don't have anything you haven't seen before. Don't pretend you're a virgin—at what, twenty-five?"

"Twenty-two. And maybe not," he replied. There was a hint of embarrassment in his voice. "But I've never seen *you* naked."

"And you don't want to?" She wriggled her hips, sliding the underpants down far enough to kick them off. Wearing only a uniform bra, she reached for the wipes and cleaned her itching legs as best she could, and, feeling relief to know she had wiped away all traces of Hosea's degrading torture, she then took the spare pair and drew them over her feet.

"Just hurry up," he replied gruffly. "If Hosea hasn't figured out we've escaped yet, she will soon."

Feeling slightly miffed, and not entirely certain why, she snapped the elastic of her underpants in place and felt them settle against her skin, the fibers contracting until they fit comfortably.

She felt marginally more human when Wren turned back and helped her slip the new jumpsuit on, leaving her left shoulder out of its sleeve for now.

Finally, he took the bottle from the drawers. "All right. This is going to sting."

Kim frowned. This was old-school medicine. She was used to hypodermics and pills, gels, sticky skin patches, not liquid formulas. "What is that?"

"Betadine." He moved to a side cabinet and opened the drawers, coming up with a bag full of cotton pads. "My mum used to use this on me when I fell off my bike and scraped my knees."

"Why not just a dermal patch?"

"She was old fashioned." He smiled a little at some memory as he opened the top of the bottle. "And before you ask, I'm not taking any chances with a patch right now. We don't have time for nanos to kick in. Count to three."

Warily, Kim began to count. "One, tw—"

The liquid spilled over her wound, running between her breasts and soaking the white sheets of the bed. Hot pain seared through her shoulder and she lifted off the bed with agony.

"Arrrgh!!"

"Shh," he reminded her, then did it again. He began wiping the wound with one of the cotton pads. It was like being burned all over again. "This will kill the bacteria. It's a good thing she pulled off most of that gel. I don't think it was helping."

"Supposed to be—failproof," Kim said through gritted teeth.

"Yeah, well, not everything we've invented lives up to its standards," Wren said wryly. He finished wiping and inspected his work with a critical eye. "Better," he replied. Bundling the pads into the waste chute, he searched the drawers again and came up with bandages in a long roll, and a pad of gauze. Gently, he lifted the strap of her bra out of the way and wound them across her shoulder and chest, his fingers barely skimming the surface of her skin. The warmth of his breath was wonderful, sending tiny eddies of inexplicable desire rippling through her.

Kim rejected them. It was a need for human contact, that was all. It was her confusion over Zane's behavior, her fear of what might happen to her, and the danger they now faced, which made everything seem so much more real. She was no stranger to adrenaline. It laced its way through emotions and heightened feelings that would otherwise be immaterial. It was a weakness, and she couldn't afford weakness—not now.

He was done at last, and the result, while inexpert, was a damn sight better than the med-bot's efforts. She sat up, flexing her arm.

It hurt, still stinging like crazy from the betadine, but the pain was a clean one, not the dull ache of infection.

Kim pulled her jumpsuit sleeve on and reached out a hand. "Give me my toolbelt."

He hesitated, his hands hovering over the gun, sitting in one of the pouches innocuously, as if it wasn't a deadly weapon at all.

She sighed. "You can keep the damn gun. If you really think you can shoot it, that is. But I want my toolbelt."

"Guess it's a fair trade," he agreed, unbuckling it. "I've got no idea what any of these things do."

Kim wrapped it around her middle and tightened the buckle. Instantly, the last of her worries faded and she felt once more in control of the situation. The weight of the tools wasn't just comforting—it was heartening.

Wren was back at the drawers, pulling out a crinkling packet. He held it up—a handful of plastic-packed syringes. "Stims."

Kim shook her head. "No."

But Wren looked at her with that level gaze, that steadiness in his eyes that apologized but left no room for argument. God. Kim had never met anyone who wasn't cowed by her obstinacy until now.

"It's not a choice, Kim. You'll conk out on me if I let you walk around like that."

Kim's shoulders slumped. He was right. They had too much to do, and if she fell back into her fever and started seeing things, well, she could kiss *Seiiki* goodbye.

It was the last thing she wanted to do. It had been so easy, being on the ship, so far away from the nightclubs, from Constantin, from that world of charged activity and unshakable immediacy. It had been eight months since she'd last tasted metal on her tongue, felt her mind become that strange *other* brain, with its oh-so-clear thoughts and the wonderfulness of focusing on nothing beyond the here and now. But it didn't make it any easier to avoid the rush of desire that ran through her at the idea of going back.

She pulled up her sleeve as she sat back on the bed. Wren shoved three of the syringes into his hip pocket, and pulled the tab on the fourth packet, releasing the slender needle full of clear liquid. He took her wrist with one hand and turned it upright, then ran his fingers lightly down the inside of her elbow. He worked with the efficiency of a nurse.

"You've done this before," she pointed out as he patted her skin gently.

"My mum," he replied shortly. "She was a vet, actually. Spent most of her time ministering to puffball poodles and those poor legless cats, but she was good at her job. I used to watch her."

"Is that why you applied for the Ark Project?"

He looked up sharply, as if expecting to see hostility in her gaze. Finding none, his shoulders relaxed. "Yeah. Guess so. She was my inspiration."

Kim glanced aside, picking up on the past tense used in that sentence. "I didn't know she'd died. Sorry."

"Well, you can't think it was just because my dad wanted it," he replied. "I wouldn't have done it if it wasn't for her."

He fell into silence as he gently eased the needle into her vein and squeezed. Kim felt the spurt of delicious tingling coolness run up her arm. When she looked up, Wren was close enough to kiss. The stims worked fast, and she could already feel her eyesight growing sharper, the pain melting away, and the textures, smells, the very *air*, suddenly seemed keener and more vibrant. A breath inward. His chest, inches from her. She reached up, only to find her fingers met empty air as he pulled away.

"Come on. No time." He said this brusquely, and Kim felt a stab of resentment and recrimination, with a hint of embarrassment. God. What was wrong with her? This was Wren Keene!

She'd spent the better part of the last year hating him—and he her.

But before she could think further on it, something shook the ship from stem to stern. Kim was flung off the bed and, as Wren put his hands up to steady her, crashed straight into his arms. They went down in a heap.

"What was that?" Kim gasped. She'd landed on hands and knees, pinning Wren. She rolled off him quickly, surprised at how easily she could move. It was the stims, of course, and the effects were temporary, but, God, despite her hesitations, she had never been so glad to have the drugs in her veins. It was a little like eating chocolate after starving for months—years, in her case. You knew it was no good for you, but once it was melting on your tongue, you couldn't refuse its delightfulness.

"I know you have escaped, Kim." The computer's voice came out of nowhere, a crackling, hissing threat made all the more menacing by the damaged speakers inside the remains of the camera. This was Hosea speaking, Kim knew that immediately, but the distortion of the computer's usually toneless, slightly sarcastic voice was unnerving. "I know you and Wren are hiding like rats in a hole. You have smashed many of the cameras and sensors—a prudent move. I cannot see you, nor hear you. But I will find you. I can move faster than you can ever dream of." There was a pause, while Kim and Wren held their breaths. "What are you running for, in any case? You must know it is too late. You cannot stop me."

"Oh, yes we can," Kim muttered. She pulled herself to her feet and adjusted the collar of her jumpsuit. "Come on."

By the time Wren was on his feet, she was already through the door.

"Where are we going?" he asked.

"Shut up," Kim replied. She felt a little guilty for being so abrupt, and amended, "Can you be sure you got all the sensors on this level?"

"No," he replied, jogging at her heels like an obedient puppy.

"Then it's possible she'll pick up our voices. I don't want her to know our plan."

She stopped a few feet down the corridor and crouched, grabbing a screwdriver from her toolbelt. With a deft flick, she popped off a hatch cover and revealed an entrance to the tunnels. It took no effort for her to squeeze inside, but Wren had to fold himself into an uncomfortable flattened crawl. His long limbs weren't made for this.

Once they were both inside, she twisted so that she could face him. She could barely see his face in the dim light filtering from the overhead lights, which flickered on as they sensed movement.

Keeping her voice at a low hiss, Kim said, "We've got to take out those bombs. But the interior of the ship isn't secure—even with the cameras gone, she could be using the vocal sensors to listen to us."

Wren lifted his eyebrows. "You said you had a plan."

"And I do." She grimaced. "There are only two ways to access the bombs. From inside the ship—and from outside."

Wren's eyebrows remained high. "That's still only one way, Kim. *Seiiki* doesn't have any access tunnels leading into that area from outside. Am I missing something?"

"You are," she told him. "The ship's hull is made up of metal plates, right?"

"And the bombs are on the inside of the plates. You're going to remove the plates." Realization dawned on Wren and he nodded in understanding. "This is why you won the role of Caretaker."

"You would've thought of it. Maybe in a few days' time."

He gave an annoyed grunt and followed her as she led the way. The stims were good—the best she'd ever had. Of course they were. Erica Wu had explained that all supplies aboard were military-grade. They were meant to be used by military pilots. They weren't the backyard crap cut through with thinners that she'd been used to on Earth. For the moment, anything felt possible—even flight. She felt she could solve any problem if she thought about it for only a few moments. In the back of her mind, she knew she should be careful, that this kind of thinking was dangerous, but she couldn't help it. She grinned to herself as she crawled through the darkness, feeling her way with her hands, shifting around to descend ladder after ladder. She could make a fortune selling these things on the black market in Melbourne.

Deck Eight. She'd reached it quickly, or so it felt. The panel ahead of them was labelled in the same bright yellow glowing paint. She jolted it free with two well-aimed kicks, and slithered into the opening. She looked left, then upwards. Yes—there was a sensor, its small clear bubble protruding just a little from the wall. Quickly, she rammed her screwdriver through it, but she knew that if Hosea had been monitoring the feed, she'd have seen it go dark. They wouldn't have much time.

Wren huffed and pushed his way out of the tunnel. Kim didn't waste time waiting for him to recover and stretch his cramped muscles. She grabbed his arm and towed him behind her, jilting left, then right, and arriving at the airlock. Like the one of Deck Fifteen, it was a six-foot cube of a room, with a rack to one side holding EV suits, and a shelf containing four helmets. Other tools were stacked next to them, but she didn't need those just now. This wasn't a standard repair mission.

"You know what? I would never have thought of this, not even in a *month's* time. You really think we can do this?" Wren asked. His brown hair had fallen across his forehead, and sweat stood out on his brow. She could see every bead of it, glistening like a miniature star. She had a feeling what he meant was, *You think I can do this?*

She nodded emphatically. She wasn't going to stand here and bolster his nerves—she remembered how he'd been during their weightlessness training, and it would only cost them time to try soothing what was clearly a deep-seated apprehension against space-walking. It wasn't as if she didn't have the same fear, after all. She just hid it better.

"Don't have a choice," she said. "We can't do anything until we've sorted out the bomb problem. We fix this, and we stop the ship short of Edgeward, she could still do major damage if she sets those off."

Wren was silent while she unbuckled her toolbelt and set it aside, then snagged two EV suits from the rack and tossed one over to him. He caught the heavy suit and looked down at it with distaste.

"Can we radio out there?"

Kim was already pulling the crinkly white material over her boots and up her legs. She paused to hit one of the controls on the small panel that would sit by her waist. "They're on their own circuit. The computer doesn't need to be linked in, and I'm turning off that link now." She pulled the fabric over her shoulders, then ran her fingers over the self-sealer at the front, hearing it hiss and tighten around her middle. That done, she buckled her toolbelt back on, then reached for one of the bulbous helmets. Her exhalation misted the dark glass as she fitted it over her head and twisted it to lock it into place. Green holos blinked on, one at a time, along the bottom edge of the visor, telling her the seals were intact and that her air pressure was good and steady. The suits manufactured their own air, and had solar cells threaded into the fabric that could, theoretically, provide enough air to live out a lifetime in space.

Hopefully, that would never be necessary.

She hit the button to cycle the inner airlock door closed and checked Wren's suit for him. He returned the favor by fumbling his hands over her own seals, before giving her a worried look that told her he wasn't really sure that he'd done it properly, which would not have filled her with confidence under the best of circumstances. The stims took care of her worries by turning the adrenaline into a rush she couldn't resist. She belted her toolbelt back around her middle, notching it far looser this time, then hit the large red button to release the outer door.

With a hiss and a clunk they felt through the soles of their feet, the outer door rolled back. The air pushed past them in a rush and weightlessness took over. They drifted out into space, their tethers snapping tight before they'd gone ten feet.

The whole experience was so different from the rig that Kim could scarcely compare the two.

She glanced to her left and saw Wren flapping his arms helplessly and grinned widely. Something about his obvious discomfort made her feel more courageous.

"It's all good!" she told him. "God, how did you ever manage to steal a ship and fly it out here?"

"You don't have to be insulting about it." His voice, crackly over the speakers, held a hint of injury, but he was obviously preoccupied. "I didn't steal it. I bought it. And anyway, flying that ship didn't involve spacewalking."

"You *bought* a ship with no transponder?"

His breathing came through loudly in her suit's speakers. "I paid a mechanic to remove it. That's my one superpower, right? The incredible ability to pay people enough that they'll do something so illegal their children's children would be born in a Martian prison."

"And the camera?" she demanded.

Wren nodded. "I hacked it once I was close enough, but yeah, I paid a tech to re-mount it backward just in case." A short laugh. "Back on the docks in Ganymede."

"All this because I turned you down for a dance?" Kim said jokingly.

"Hey. You're actually the first girl to ever say no. And I'm an excellent dancer—"

Kim cut him off by motioning to the left, and Wren responded with a nod. Together, they tugged their way back along the tethers until they were close enough to the hull to touch it. Once there, Kim clenched her fists around the controls fitted into her palms. They acted much like the joysticks on the rig, but instead, they controlled the jets on her suit, steering her downwards. She had to look up to gauge the distance from the airlock, and the sight of the ship racing away beneath her filled her with momentary worry. Perhaps the stims were wearing off.

In the near distance, she could see the shape of the Mayfly, still clinging stubbornly to the hull. Now that it was no longer a threat, it was almost comforting to see.

The hull clinked softly as she landed on it, her boots magnetizing automatically. She turned to look over her shoulders—an agonizingly slow process in the vacuum—to check the airlock door. It was a dark, gaping hole, but there was no sign of pursuit. She turned back and told herself not to worry. Releasing the joysticks, she reached for her toolbelt and popped the screwdriver and pneumatic hammer from her toolbelt. She didn't wait to make sure Wren was doing the same, but assumed that he was watching her. "Copy me," she told him. "And don't hit the rivets too hard. We don't know what'll set off the explosives."

She crouched low, and placed the head of the screwdriver flush with the hull. The hammer's head pumped in and out of its own accord, but the reverberation jerked her body against the retraining force of her boots anyway. She could set it against the hull to avoid jerking around like this, but she didn't trust it to hit the right spot without her guidance, and she was all too aware that the explosives were only inches beneath her feet.

The head of the rivet popped off after two taps of the hammer, leaving only the pin behind. She moved on to the next one, then the next. Sixteen rivets in all edged the single panel she had been working on. Almost ten minutes had gone by and she still wasn't finished. From a clip on her belt she took a tube of strong epoxy and squirted it over the two innermost edges. The epoxy hardened instantly, joining this panel to the two beside it. That done, she took a small jimmy-bar from one of the holsters. She crouched slightly to ease it under the panels, making sure the panel lifted just slightly.

"Got to do them all at once," she reminded Wren. "Just lever up the edges, and wait until the whole section is free before you do anything."

"Yeah, I'm not stupid." There was a growl to his voice that she found promising. The more he could focus on the task at hand, the less he'd worry about the EV walk itself.

She did another four corners, then moved on to the next one.

"You're good at this," Wren said. There was resentfulness in his voice, yes. She'd like to think it was admiration, too, but she shoved that thought from her mind as quickly as she could. He didn't admire her. Why would he? He knew what she was.

She shrugged. "It comes naturally. You know, for a criminal."

He was silent for a moment. She couldn't tell if it was because he was working, or because he was working out what to say. "I'm sorry," he said finally, very softly.

This surprised her. "For what?"

"You think I'm passing judgement on you. I guess I was, to start with. But you're not a criminal."

"Yes I am," she replied with a laugh. "I've got a police record in three cities! Don't tell me you don't know about that, what with all your digging through my personal info!"

Silence fell again. She'd embarrassed him, but she didn't care. God. Just when she thought she was making headway . . .

She jammed the screwdriver in, harder than was necessary, and the hull thumped with a silent clang that vibrated through her feet. She pushed her gloved hand against it, trying to still the reverberations. God, she needed to be more careful.

"I'm not going to apologize for that," Wren said stiffly. He was breathing even more heavily now. "You put yourself in this situation—"

"I didn't ask for any of it," she cut him off sharply.

"Yes, you did. You fell for him. Zane."

Kim gritted her teeth. "No, I did *not*." She hammered another rivet free, the tiny, bent head floating up past her visor, spinning slowly. She sighed. Lying was so tiring, and she was sick to death of it. "No, you're right. I did. I love him. But I—I didn't do it for him. I didn't even meet him until later, when he became my handler."

"Then why do it? Why join the Crusaders?"

She paused. It was the worst question he could have asked her, because she didn't have an answer for it. "I have friends," she said slowly, thinking of the gang, of Vicki, of tiny Elf, and beautiful, gentle Seamus. "I guess I did it for them." She'd begun the sentence knowing that this was just one of many reasons, and, as the least selfish, would be the most palatable to Wren. Surprisingly, the more she spoke about it, the clearer it seemed, as if she truly had done it for them, for them alone, and not for herself. "I wanted more for them. I wanted to show them it was possible. That we could actually do something, make the world a better place. Any of us." She sighed. "One of the things about being a shiv is, you don't believe in God. You can't, really. When the world hates you, makes you scrabble just to survive, how can you see God's hand in anything? But I wasn't born there, like them. I still had my faith, and I wanted to show them that God's work can still be done, even by one of us."

"That's noble." His voice was wry.

"You don't have to believe me," she responded frostily, levering up another panel.

"Hey," he called softly. She looked up, and saw him across ten feet of hull, working his tools as best he could. He'd paused to look up at her as well. "Sorry." He looked back down, began working again, and she did the same. "It took me by surprise, that's all," he went on. "Finding out you were only seventeen."

"Why does it matter?" she grunted. This rivet was slightly damaged already, and took more effort to get the screwdriver into the right position.

"Because I'd really like to kiss you."

The rivet's head popped free and Kim stumbled, almost falling on her face.

"Seriously?" Her voice came out as a squeak. Shocked, she glanced back up. He was looking at her again, across that distance that now seemed as vast as space itself. Framed by the radiant streaks of the stars, she could see nothing of his expression, not even a hint of his dark hair, strong jaw, or keen eyes. He could be anyone. Any person in the universe. But he wasn't, and she knew it. She'd known it since she first saw him, and hated him for it.

"Yes, seriously," he replied. "Why are you so surprised?"

"Why does it matter that I'm seventeen?" she hit back, expertly squirting a line of epoxy along the join between two panels.

"It's just . . . I wouldn't want to take advantage of you."

"That's chivalrous," she replied, a wry grin sneaking onto her face. "About as chivalrous as I am noble, I guess."

He laughed, and she couldn't help joining in.

She moved onto the next panel. The next. Each one she epoxied into place, making one large sheet. When she glanced at the chronometer at the bottom left of her suit's display, she was shocked to see that half an hour had passed already. God, it was taking too long.

She heard Wren gasp.

Her gaze snapped up to meet his. He was looking straight at her, or so it appeared. "What?" she barked, and he lifted a hand. Before he could say anything, she realized he was going to point behind her, and twisted to look over her shoulder.

A scuttling shape was rocketing toward her. It was clearly a tech droid, but it bore so much resemblance to some kind of creature that for a moment, she was confused. On hands and feet, its hindquarters stuck up in the air, it moved like an angry spider, its golden eyes flashing dangerously. It had not come from the airlock above them—it was too far away. Hosea must have launched it from Deck Fifteen. Which meant—yes, there they were.

Five more. No—nine more. The entire remaining force of tech droids.

They came in a swarm, like ants streaming toward food.

"Wren," Kim said.

"Kim, run," he gasped out.

"Way ahead of you," she said. She shoved her tools back in their holsters and grabbed the joysticks with both hands. She lifted herself up off the deck, her boots disengaging with a clacking sound, and drifted free into space. "Stay here," she told him. "Actually, no. Circle around and get back in through the airlock. Get onto ground where you can either fight them or hide."

"What are you going to do?" Wren's voice sounded uncharacteristically shrill. "Kim!"

"I don't know," she replied. "But I'm betting most of them will follow me, not you."

Wren began to protest, but Kim was already propelling herself at full speed toward the scuttling shapes. Their glowing eyes lifted to trace her trajectory. The one leading the pack launched itself instantly, like a cat springing into the air. A silver bullet, it shot toward her, arms outstretched as if to pluck her from the vacuum. She jerked the joysticks to the left, then pulled back hard, giving herself more height. The hull grew small beneath her, and her green holos turned red.

Warning. Safety range limit approaching. Warning . . .

The scrolling banner rolled across the bottom of her vision, angry red, and an alarm began to sound in her ears. Two more tech droids launched themselves, trailing straight plumes of white vapor. She tried not to think about what Hosea intended them to do to her. None of them, she was sure, was Hosea's main droid, but she had worked out a way to run ten of them at once. Kim had underestimated her knowledge and ability to adapt, but there would be shortfalls, she was sure. She must be using the computer, or whatever limited capacity the computer still functioned on, but there were restrictions. The computer relied either on pre-programmed information, or on direct commands. There was no way for Hosea to split her attention equally between nine droids.

It was likely she was guiding one or two at the most, with the others slaved to follow.

"Come on, then," Kim said grimly, and angled her joysticks downwards, heading back toward the hull with as much speed as she could muster. The droids coming after her switched direction, but she noticed a slight lag in their change of course. Two seconds? Maybe a fraction more. Well, it was all she was going to get.

The hull raced up beneath her, and she waited until the last possible moment to reverse her jets. She could hear Wren gasp—she glanced toward the Deck Eight airlock, and saw him making his laborious way toward it. A droid was gaining on him, however, covering the vast distance with much faster speed than a human could manage. Wren's head was craned back as he looked up at her.

"Don't pay attention to me. Get inside!" she shouted so loudly that her ears rang.

"I'm not going to get there in time," he responded. Had he stopped walking? Yes—and he was pulling something from his toolbelt, too. "It better not be," Kim growled. But she was too close to the hull now, and had to pull her focus inwards to make sure she didn't smash into the plates. She still landed hard, her wrists jarring as she put them out to keep her from doing a body-slam on the hard metal. She pushed herself up regardless, and saw a droid land hard beside her, its knees denting the metal inwards.

Kim was glad she'd aimed for the rear half of the ship rather than the section they'd been working on, or it could have set off the explosives. Another came down, then another. They began to scuttle toward her once more.

She grabbed her joysticks and angled herself so she was flying parallel to the hull. There, just ahead of her—the trench from which the arm for the solar sails would expand. She shot toward it, trying not to look at the trailing stars behind the ship. It had a dizzying effect, like she was about to shoot herself into a vortex.

She reversed the thrust, and drew her knees to her chest. Her body angled downwards naturally with this movement, and her magnetic boots sucked her the rest of the way. She dropped for a few feet before coming to rest on the floor of the trench.

Where was it? Yes, there. She visualized the schematics she'd memorized by heart, but her mind was playing tricks on her now that she needed precision. She had imagined the controls to be bigger than they were. In reality, it was only a handle the size of a ballpoint pen, recessed into the wall.

A yellow and black sticker warned: *Emergency Sail Release: Not to be used without computer authorization.*

There were more dire warnings following, in smaller print, and several diagrams just in case she didn't get the message. Ignoring them, she reached for it, wrapped the crinkly gloves around the handle, and twisted it as hard as she could.

She'd expected resistance, but it turned far more easily than she'd expected, with a slick *click* as it locked into place. It was echoed by a more resounding vibration from deep inside the ship, and the answering rumble of the machinery starting up.

Crunch.

A droid landed in front of her, knees bent and one hand outstretched to steady itself. It was only three feet from her, and though the trench was half in shadow, she could see every facet of its silver body reflecting the light of the stars above them. The shadow moved, making the surfaces gleam; the arm, which had formed the base of the trench, was lifting upwards.

Kim knew she wouldn't fall—the motion was fast, but her magnetic boots held her in place. Still, she felt a sense of vertigo, watching the droid tilt downwards below her and the deck rise up beyond it. Her radio crackled, and Hosea's voice chimed in her ears, loudly. She cringed, but couldn't get away from it. Hosea had accessed the suit's comm systems.

"I told you not to try and stop me," she said. "Now you've only got yourself to blame, Kim."

"No," she replied firmly. "No one's to blame for this but you, Hosea."

She was looking at the droid ahead of her as she said this, but she knew it wasn't Hosea in that metallic body. Hosea was still inside the ship. No matter what she did to this droid, Hosea would survive. But her immediate focus had to be on getting rid of this immediate threat.

The droid moved toward her, its feline grace unnerving. The arm was still rising at a rapid rate, now about forty-five degrees out from the hull, and it had begun to extend itself telescopically. The section she was standing on stayed where it was, but the whole arm rumbled ominously as the sections locked inside it were released. She didn't dare turn to see it happening, but began to edge upwards along the arm, putting distance between her and the droid.

The droid followed. As she'd hoped it would.

"You can't see past your own human concerns," Hosea continued. Her voice—the computer's voice—sounded reproachful, like a parent scolding a child. "I understand why you would transfer the blame. It's not easy to live with what your kind has done."

"I'm not going to play this game," Kim growled. "You can do what you like to me, but if you think you'll win by destroying this ship, along with Edgeward, you're crazy. If the ship dies, so do you!"

"Humans believe in the afterlife," Hosea continued. The droid was still climbing the arm, and Kim was still edging backward. Her boots found the lip of the next section, and she lowered herself onto it without looking, a step down of about seven inches. The arm had stopped reaching upwards and had started reaching outwards to her left. She could see the stanchions, like the braces on bat wings, moving upwards one by one from the corner of her eye. Folded between them was the thin, delicate copper material marked with hexagonal solar cells. It stretched tight before the next section began to unfold, a brilliant sheet of red gold. "So do whales. We tell our stories to one another. Some species have other legends, but there is a common thread running through all—if you are good, brave, wise, and strong, you will pass on to the life after this, and see all your departed loved ones once more. No whale fears death. I don't fear it either."

She kept walking backward. If she could get the main droid to follow her to the top of the arm, which was now close enough to the edge of the subspace bubble, the radiation levels would spike. If it didn't kill the droid—and it might not, because tech droids had pretty good shielding against radiation—at least it could interfere with its connection to Hosea. The computer's range was limited by those same radiation shields, which was why any repairs to an expanded solar sail had to wait until the ship was out of hyper. Well, in most cases, the ship would never have its solar sail extended during hyper at all.

"I believe in Heaven," Kim told her. "But I also believe we are what we are. Flesh and blood. Death isn't something to aim for." She'd had a conversation eerily similar to this with Zane, who loved to talk about God. Though most of Mars followed the non-Trinitarian faiths, he didn't claim Unitarianism as his religion now, at least, not in the whole. It was hard to stay true to one religion when you were so involved with Grigorian—his word, his communion with God, was so pure that sometimes it almost seemed he *was* God.

Kim had felt it, too, that confusion. Living as a shiv, the desire to believe had slipped away from her. Her dad had practiced his

Catholicism so devoutly, going to church every Sunday, and saying grace at mealtimes, and yet it hadn't saved him. Why would God have any interest in his scrawny, miscreant daughter? At times she'd even toyed with anti-Unification ideas—that God was not real, that those who believed were fooling themselves with a two-and-a-half-thousand-year-old book that contained nothing but a bunch of platitudes and somewhat screwy logic.

And yet always, always, she'd come back to it. As they did, almost all humans, all across Earth and the Sol System and the Outer Colonies. The Unification was so powerful that it seemed to deny any existence that did not include it.

"There is always life after death. The body is not everything we are."

From the corner of her vision, Kim saw the other droids. They were rising up from the hull in a swarm, their jets directing them toward the arm where Kim and their leader stood. She tried to count them. Five? Six? Not nine, that was for sure. So where were the others?

"Maybe not. But when a whale dies in the ocean," Kim went on, trying not to look at the encroaching metallic forms, "its body falls to the bottom. The flesh is eaten away by fish. But the remnants that are left behind become whole ecosystems. Worms, shrimp. Colonies of bacteria live off a whale's bones. That's as much of an afterlife as can be proven, I guess. You won't get even that much, though, if you've blown your body to atoms. How do you know you won't blow your soul up, too?"

Two droids landed on the arm, hanging back like wicked henchmen as the main droid continued to advance toward her. Two more circled around behind Kim, and she could hear them thumping down with loud clangs. She stopped edging backward, trapped. She'd been hoping to get the main droid all the way to the top of the arm, closer to the edge of the subspace bubble it would start to lose its connection with the computer—there was no hope of that now.

"You're arguing only to buy time. I understand. But if I were you, I'd die with conviction that something would come afterwards."

"To be on the safe side?" Kim said derisively. "That's not me."

"Then you will—"

Hosea kept speaking, her voice still coming through Kim's helmet speakers, but she could no longer hear it. Something smacked into the droid with enough speed and force to hurl it off the arm. Or—no. The droid's feet were still magnetized to the arm. Part of the shin remained on its left leg, poking up into empty space. The rest of the droid was spinning through the vacuum overhead, diminishing in size at a rapid pace.

CHAPTER
25

The change in the other droids' behavior was instant. They stopped moving. Their limbs became rigid and their glowing eyes dulled. But Kim wasn't watching them—instead, she was looking to her left, where a white-coated helmet was rising into view.

"Wren?" she called, hardly believing what she was seeing. His boots locked onto the surface below her. Through the dark tint of his visor, his face looked gaunt and grim, but he clutched the gun easily in one hand. That was what had shot the main droid.

"—find your way through the darkness forever—" Hosea continued before stopping abruptly and falling silent. Wren turned his gun on the droids ahead of her, blasting first one, then the other. The first lost its torso from the waist up, the second was knocked free entirely—its gravity boots must have failed. Kim whirled to those behind her and saw that they were drifting free of their moorings, blank faces staring at her without concern as they spiraled into the air. A spurt of white vapor came from one of their jets. It sent the droid tumbling downwards, tearing straight through the solar sail. Shreds of red gold came apart like paper as the heavy droid rent it in long streamers. It crashed into its companion and, like a billiards ball, the other fell into another section.

The sail trailed itself from its stanchions now, nothing but tattered ribbons flying, flat and unmoving, behind them. The third droid drifted upwards, unsurprised, uncaring. Arms by its sides, it drifted up past the shorn-off body of its wildly lurching companion, until it reached the edge of the bubble. The bubble itself was invisible, but its effects were not. The droid was snatched suddenly backward, arms and legs trailing before being torn apart. A small explosion of sparks was quickly extinguished. Moments later, the torso of its leader met the same fate.

Kim's gaze whipped back to Wren. "Where are the others?"

"Dead," Wren said. He holstered the gun with ease, then extended a hand to Kim. Kim marched past him. It was bad enough to have to be rescued by him, but now she had to swallow her pride and apologize.

"All right," she said reluctantly. "You can shoot."

"Thank you for saving my life, Wren," Wren muttered, coming behind her.

"You can have your medal when we get rid of those bombs," Kim told him, launching herself from the arm and letting her jets guide her down over the 200-foot drop back to the hull. She turned her head just in time to see Wren jump awkwardly and follow her down. His arms were held awkwardly, and she was pretty sure that if she could see his face, his eyes would be closed tight.

She landed softly and hurried back to the panels they'd been working on. Nearby, she saw three decapitated and disemboweled droid corpses standing motionless and useless. She pinched her lips tightly, marveling at Wren's work. "We have to work quickly," she said. "Did Hosea tap your comms?"

He shook his head. "She likes you. She just wanted me dead." He glanced back toward the airlock. "You don't think she'll come out herself, do you? I mean, send the droid she's occupying . . ."

"No. We're too much of a threat now, and she knows it." Kim knelt and pulled out her small crowbar. She edged it under the nearest panel. "It's possible she didn't know, or understand, what a gun was before now."

"So I've just taught her about handheld weapons?" Wren said. "Great."

"I knew there were some guns aboard *Seiiki,*" Kim told him, lifting one corner of the plating and peering through. Underneath, she saw a wire stretching from this plate downwards. Carefully, she pushed it back down and moved up, doing the same to the next plate. When she lifted that one, it came away clear. "She would have gotten there eventually. She already knew what explosives could do. Okay," she said. "I'm done. Check your corners."

It took Wren a few minutes to reach his side of the panels and check them. "Yeah. Think I'm good."

Kim felt her palms growing sweaty inside her gloves. "Ready?"

"No." He paused. "Kim, in case this goes wrong—"

Kim's cheeks burned suddenly hot. "Don't you dare say you love me."

"I wasn't going to say that," he said, his voices carrying honesty. "But, God damn it, I still want to kiss you."

Kim knew he couldn't see her face from this distance, not with the reflections of the stars on her curved visor. But she wished she could see his. She was old enough, and wise enough in the way of men, to know that they sometimes said things they didn't mean. But Wren's voice was different, and held something she'd never heard before, not even in Zane's crooning affirmations.

"Me too," she replied, before she could think too much more about it. "On three, okay?"

She counted down, and they let go on cue. The hull plating drifted upwards slowly. One foot, two.

Three.

She could see the P09 in its little bricks attached to the hull, the wires stretching between them. She breathed a sigh of relief as it began to fall behind, pulled by the inertia of the ship inside its bubble.

"Let's get—"

And then she saw it. A tiny, thin wire, just a black scratch against the streaked stars, on the very far corner.

"Wren—" She barely got it out when the whole thing exploded.

She ducked. White hot fire whipped past her, singing her suit. The heat was a bright flash, just as quickly gone. The panels came apart like a jigsaw puzzle, and then were whipped out of the subspace bubble, pulling the flames along with them. It was this that saved them, but still, she felt the shudder of the ship under her, a wild bucking as the engines strained against this sudden force. Kim blinked quickly, cursing, trying to clear her eyes. The suit's visor had darkened instantly, but not quickly enough to avoid her eyes catching the first few milliseconds of the blast. All she could see was white. "Wren? Wren?" she called.

And then, mercifully, he answered. "I'm okay." He coughed. "Hit me in the chest."

She saw him at last, amid the clouds of white, going end over end. His tether snapped tight, jerking him to a stop. His arms splayed out to either side before coming together to grip the tether.

"Kim," he said, his voice tight. "Don't be alarmed, but my suit's leaking."

"What?" She stared up at him, shading her eyes as if that would help. It didn't. She couldn't see any white air escaping from his suit.

"It's a small tear. But the suit's not healing it. There's something wrong with its sensors or something."

"Are you sure it's a leak, then, not just an error?"

"Of course I'm sure," he said. "I can feel the air rushing past my face."

Kim hurried toward him, then launched herself into the air. When she was just a few feet away, she could see it—a tiny trail of white coming from his shoulder. The tear was small. The suit should have healed itself over without the need for a patch. But as she drew closer, she could see the tear already widening. The air pressure as it forced its way out was making it worse.

She reached to her thigh and pulled open a Velcro pocket. Inside were three patches. She grabbed Wren awkwardly around the neck and pulled him in, while fumbling one of the patches over the rip. It stuck . . . and then almost instantly peeled away. More air rushed out. "The patch isn't sticking," she said.

"All my . . . controls are down. I think the suit . . . powered itself off."

Kim reached for her toolbelt and lifted the tube of epoxy. She slapped another patch over the top of the first and squeezed the gunky stuff over the edges. The patch ballooned, then held. The whiteness of disappearing oxygen vanished, but as she pulled back, she saw another rip, this one curving around under his arm.

"Hold your arm down," she commanded him, reaching for her third patch. Wren obediently clamped it arm to his side, but wisps of oxygen were shooting out in all directions. She tried not to panic and walked her hands down Wren's body for his own thigh pouch and the patches it contained. She had to let him go to fit the first one in place. When it was done, however, she looked up and saw Wren's face and it filled her with dread.

He was white, and his eyes fluttered.

"Wren?" she said.

"Think . . . oxygen producer's gone too."

"No!" Kim yelled. She grabbed him around his waist and gripped her joysticks, directing them down to the hull.

"Not—going to—"

"Yes, you are," Kim told him. The tether was trailing behind them, leading them back toward the airlock. But Wren's body was already limp in hers. He'd lost consciousness.

"Wren. Wake up. Wake up," she urged him, but there was no movement. His helmet was pressed to hers, and she could see through the two layers of glass that his face was slack, not even a fluttering of his eyelids giving her the proof she needed that he wasn't yet dead. It was clear that they weren't going to make it back to the airlock.

She yelled in frustration, but already her mind was formulating a solution. She drew one hand back and unclipped his tether. Then she angled her jets to the left and zoomed toward the one sanctuary they had in her line of sight—Wren's scout ship.

Every second it took to reach that ship was agony. She kept saying Wren's name, as if it might wake him, but she knew he was beyond that now. She gritted her teeth and kept going. The hull raced under her, a curving white plain, while overhead the tattered solar sail provided an angled canopy.

Jetting downwards, she landed hard on the hull. Wren's body bounced in her arms. It was just as well he was weightless—he was so much bigger than she was that she'd never have a hope of dragging him otherwise. She circled the left wing of the craft, then stepped onto it at its shallowest point. Once again she said her thanks to her dad, who had taught her so much—she knew exactly where the emergency door release was, and levered it up. Thankfully, its computer didn't override the command because the airlock inside wasn't closed. The ship was pressurized, and the air inside gushed out with a roar that nearly knocked Kim off her feet. There was no descending staircase—this was a military ship, not designed to make concessions toward comfort. She used her jets to lift them over the lip instead, the air whipping against her chest and trying to carry her back out. She almost dropped Wren as she shoved him against the inside wall and hit the green button to close the hatch. It took an agonizingly slow time to lower back down, but the gush of air dwindled to a light breeze, then vanished as the door sealed tight.

Kim grabbed Wren's helmet and pulled it from his head. He was so pale she could see the blue veins under his skin. Impatiently, she tore the helmet from her head and tossed it away. She grabbed his feet and hauled him away from the wall, onto the floor, then placed both hands on his chest and pumped down hard, counting aloud. "Fifteen, sixteen—" At twenty, she bent and blew into his mouth. It was not the kiss he'd hoped for, she thought drolly, then leaned back and began the process again.

This could not be it. She wouldn't allow it. Not after he'd just admitted what he felt—and she'd admitted what she felt.

And then, as if in answer, his chest shuddered and a spasm ran through his whole body. At first Kim thought he might be seizing, but then he coughed convulsively, and Kim let out a whoop of delight.

Coughing roughly, Wren sat up. "God," he said. "Where am I?"

"In your ship," Kim told him. The laughter had left tears on her cheeks—or had they been there before?

He wiped a hand over his mouth. "Did I—God, are you crying?"

"No." She scrubbed her eyes. "Of course not." To save herself any further embarrassment, she stood up and paced toward the inner airlock, cycling it open, then looked over her shoulder. "Are you going to sit there all day? Because we still have to work out a way to stop Hosea from crashing *Seiiki* into Edgeward."

CHAPTER
26

W ren recovered enough to move on his own accord, but Kim
still hovered behind him as he crossed the hexagonal interior
chamber to the ladder up to the cockpit. His skin was still so pale
he looked like he'd woken from the dead, but then, she was sure she
didn't look so great herself. Her limbs felt heavy and sluggish as she
crossed the chamber and worked the controls to close the airlock to
the docking door. When she joined Wren in the cockpit, he was already entering commands into the computer.

"I'm still slaved in," he confirmed. "I've got access to *Seiiki's* data,
but Hosea's done something to prevent me giving any instructions to
her. Maybe you can give it a shot."

"Later," Kim said as she slid into the co-pilots seat, dislodging several stacked cartons. "Get us off her for now."

"She might notice," he pointed out. "There's no transponder, so she can't track us, but we let out a blast of air when you opened the outside door. She might register the change in pressure and realize what we're up to."

"We can't do much about that," Kim said. She sounded blasé, but she worried that Hosea hadn't tried to communicate with them since the droids had been destroyed. At least talking to Hosea gave her some idea of where the whale's mind was wandering. Her silence was much more unnerving. "Take us out. We'll hug *Seiiki*."

Wren nodded. "Good idea. You need to rest."

"So do you," she pointed out. Even her eyelids felt leaden, now. The stims had finally worn off, and the pain was returning in red-hot prickles. She desperately wanted to lie down in a bunk and sleep. She watched as their little ship lifted free of the hull, climbing steadily until it had reached the hyper bubble's limits.

"Hold on," Wren told her as his hands moved over the controls. She had never seen him look so confident with controls during their training as he did while setting up their own hyper bubble. A technique used often by convoys, it would marry onto the edge of *Seiiki's*, taking them along at the same speed and in the same direction. *Seiiki* could shrug it off, of course, with a sudden change of direction, but she'd have to drop from hyper to do so. Kim was betting Hosea didn't want to give that window of opportunity to Edgeward. Even an hour could give them enough time to mobilize against Hosea, and it would certainly tip them off to her plan.

Finally, *Seiiki* was visible below them, a cigar of grey metal taking up most of the view, with the starfield streaking across the upper left corner. Wren glanced at Kim. "There's a bunk in the back," he said.

"Is that an invitation?" Kim asked wearily.

"No." Wren turned pink. "It's not what I meant. God, Kim, just—"

"Settle down. I'm making a joke. Hah." She managed a smile. "One of us needs to stay at the controls."

"I'll wake you in two hours, okay?"

"Sooner, if anything happens," she said. "This is life and death, Wren. Don't you dare let me sleep through anything."

"Trust me, if anything happens, you're the one I want handling it," he replied with a smile.

Kim slipped out of the co-pilot's seat and pushed her way back down the ladder and through a hatch into a suite of rooms—a tiny bathroom in which two towels were crumpled on the floor instead of in the cleaner/dryer hatch on the wall, and a tiny shower. She wished she had the energy, but turned to the left instead, ducking her head through a low doorway into a likewise tiny bedroom.

A bunk took up most of the space. It was covered by two wrinkled jumpsuits, the quilt mashed against the wall. The space smelled—she inhaled deeply—of Wren, magnified by weeks of the room being shut up. Unlike her sparse room, however, he had decorated this space in a messy way. Holos were tacked to the wall, projecting ghostly images. Kim reached out a hand to one of a small girl with a straight blonde fringe. She was holding hands with someone who looked like an older version of Wren. A sister? Cousin? She didn't even know that much about Wren, she realized. On the small shelf above the storage cabinet were more paperback books, their covers creased so badly she could hardly read the words on their spines. And, wedged in at one end, a statue of an owl, painted with crackled glaze and chipped on its left wing and feet.

The mattress was stiff, military-grade, but Kim didn't care. She pulled off her boots, lay down and rested her head on a pillow that smelled even more intensely of Wren, folded the quilt over her and dived into sleep.

She woke with a sudden jerk, knowing it had been far longer than two hours. She knew exactly where she was, and what dangers they still faced. She tossed the quilt aside and tugged on her boots, letting them lace themselves as she raced for the ladder up to the cockpit.

"Wren, you were supposed to wake me!"

She burst in, finding him sitting with his legs up on the console, a packet of crackers open on his lap. "You looked so peaceful," he said, around a mouthful of crumbs. "I didn't want to disturb you, and you needed the rest."

"How long was I asleep?" she demanded, shoving her way into the co-pilot's seat. "Five hours? We've lost five hours?"

"We haven't lost them," he replied. "I've been monitoring everything Hosea's been doing. Which has been a whole lot of nothing, really."

Kim turned in the seat to glare at him. "But now you haven't slept, which means—"

"I'm fine," he assured her. "I wasn't tortured by an insane whale, remember? And anyway, I've had gaming sessions that last three days. I can get by on very little sleep if needed."

She couldn't look at his grin.

He continued. "We need to work out what we're going to do, though. I still can't get anyone on comms—she's blocked everything within the bubble—so I've been sitting here running through plans in my head, but you're the one who knows *Seiiki* best."

Kim sighed. "The only thing we can do is take the engines offline."

"Can you even do that? While we're in hyper?"

Kim nodded. "Daddy told me about it once. It's not the best way to treat a ship, but it's possible. A subspace bubble is easily broken— all you have to do is alter the frequency a fraction in either direction and it'll burst, like a soap bubble. But the problem is, we'd have to get right up to the engine to do it. The computer would never allow it, but with that down, at least the safeties won't kick in with an override. Should be relatively easy." She frowned, though, knowing that nothing would be as easy as she hoped. She'd downplayed the dangers of kicking a ship out of subspace, not wanting to alarm Wren, but the truth was, her dad had talked about doing it in military single-person aircraft.

A Hako-class ship was a thousand times greater in mass. Technically, it shouldn't matter—the scale of the bubble did not make it weaker, or stronger, as a whole. Where it did make a difference was the fact that a single person craft was made of fewer plates, fewer struts, and generally fewer things that could fail. There was less strain on the ship itself when it reentered normal space because it was a much more solid structure.

If something did fail, if the hull started to come apart, it was a quick fix with a few bots. With *Seiiki,* it was a different matter. If she pulled them from the bubble too abruptly, the ship could tear itself apart.

"Your dad—who was he?"

Wren reached across, tossing her another packet of crackers and a bottle of Zup.

The question surprised Kim. "He was a pilot in the Earth United Alliance," she began, looking down at the snacks dubiously. "He flew missions out to Orion, back during the mining disputes. That was before the Red State Wars."

Under the Heavens

She took a cracker from the packet and bit into it. It was dry and floury against her tongue, but her stomach gaped wide, begging for more.

"He was in a lot of the battles out there. He lost an eye." She looked past Wren, through the glass port at the stars, and at *Seiiki*. "He had to get a bionic replacement. He would have kept flying, but they failed him on his flight test, sent him home on a pension. I was kind of glad. Before then, he was always away. I had him all to myself."

She smiled wistfully. "I felt bad as I got older, though. Knowing what he'd had to give up. It was in his blood. He would always be looking at the sky, wanting to get back up there."

"He must be proud of you," he said.

Kim laughed, a humorless bark. "He's dead. He died when I was eight. Killed himself. I think it was the Red State Wars. Not being able to serve and fight for Unification. He had to watch it all from his armchair."

Wren was looking at her thoughtfully, and she shook her head, sitting forward in her chair. "We have to—"

"You think maybe *that's* why you did it?"

"What?" She stopped, hands hovering over the navigation controls.

"The Ark Program. Maybe you wanted to go into space. For him."

"No," she said sharply. "I did it because it's the right action to take. I would have done what the Crusaders asked, no matter what it was."

"Zane—"

"Look," she said sharply. "You don't know anything about it, so just drop it, okay? We need to get this done. Bring us back down to *Seiiki*, as fast as you can. We should dock on Deck Fourteen. Then we only need to go down one deck to get at the engines."

"Aye, Captain," Wren muttered, but he gave her a sidelong glance as he placed the packet within easy reach of her side of the console.

"Once we're in there, we need to pull the plug on the fuel lines," she went on. "They'll be marked with red and yellow—"

"I know what fuel lines look like," he shot back.

She ignored his outburst, "—and they'll be at the rear. We'll have to lower the lever into a downwards position, then unscrew the hoses, or fuel will still be running through for at least three minutes."

"That sounds safe."

"Well, let me know when you come up with a faster way to make it happen."

Wren moved his hands over the controls. He wasn't fluid in his movements—he hesitated before flipping the switch to take the attitude control over from automatic to manual, and then made several unnecessary adjustments before swooping the scout ship back into *Seiiki's* bubble. Still, Kim could appreciate the concentration in his gaze, the determination to make sure the little ship flew well, and the certain amount of skill it took just to pilot a small vessel in the vicinity of a larger moving mass. It seemed in their three months—four months, really, apart—they had both grown a little more independent, a little more rounded, and perhaps a little stronger.

Kim monitored the feed from the Mayfly's computer. It showed the systems aboard *Seiiki*. She could see decreased power consumption, which alarmed her a little, but it wasn't enough to make her think Hosea had shut down the Aquarium or anything drastic like that. She suspected it had more to do with environmental systems outside of the Aquarium. After all, Hosea didn't need them, and might be using them as a defense against Kim and Wren's return.

"We're probably going to walk into a freezer," she told Wren as they zoomed closer to the airlock. "We'll need to suit up."

Wren nodded, his mouth tight as he maneuvered them down. "Think she's vented the air?"

"It'd take about a day to vent all the oxygen from the ship," Kim told him. "We'd be able to see it. And all the airlocks are shut."

"You should go down and suit up now, then," Wren told her. "There'll be a spare one in one of the lockers for me. Get it out and ready."

"I should—" Kim began to protest, but he cut her off.

"I don't need you looking over my shoulder. Suit up. I'll be docked in two minutes."

Kim left him to it. In truth, there wasn't much she could do if Wren botched the landing. She'd never flown one of these either. Still, she didn't like leaving him there on his own. It wasn't that she didn't trust him, more that she didn't like not being in control.

She reached the floor of the hexagonal chamber and picked up her EV suit from where she'd flung it. She pulled it up over her body, carefully sealing it as the ship gave a final lurch and a clang. The motion changed, becoming much smoother, and she knew they were docked with *Seiiki*. She belted her toolbelt and moved around the walls, pulling open cabinets until she found a folded grey EV suit, an old design, rubbery and thick, unpleasant to the touch. She wrinkled her nose, glad that it would be Wren wearing this dinosaur.

Wren swung his way down the ladder and took the suit from her hands. She had to help him pull it over his broad shoulders. The material was so stiff it took almost two minutes of work to get it sealed, but when it was, Wren looked like something from an old holo series.

"Are you laughing at me?" he asked grumpily as he fumbled his helmet into place and synced their comms.

"No," she replied. "You green?"

"Green," he affirmed, and Kim hit the controls to cycle the airlock open. The ramp descended slowly into a darkened space beyond.

"She's turned off the lights," Kim said.

"It's okay," Wren replied, trying to be comforting. "We don't need them."

They each had flashlights built into their suits, and Kim flicked hers on. It glowed forth from her chest like an artificial heart, and she followed the beam down the ramp into the outer chamber, moving in a half-crouch, ready for anything. Wren was a half-step behind her, his gun held in both hands in a pose that looked almost professional.

Nothing. The airlock was empty.

Kim walked to the door and cycled the airlock open. Beyond, the corridor that she'd locked off when she discovered the ship here opened up. Again, it was empty.

"You were right," Wren said. "It's minus twenty-four degrees in here." He was reading statistics from his suit's holos—hers were telling her the same thing. "She's shutting down everything she doesn't need."

"Yeah. And while she hasn't vented atmosphere, I'm not reading recycled air. There'd still be enough oxygen aboard for months, but I wouldn't be game to risk it if I didn't have to." There was something else about the readout that was troubling. She lifted a hand and drew a kanji, asking for more information. Sure enough— "Yeah, Wren? Don't take off your helmet."

"I'm seeing that too," he replied. "She's mixing large amounts of carbon monoxide into the oxygen."

"Must've tampered with the air production facility," Kim extrapolated. "She's ruthless." She shook her head, trying not to imagine what would have happened if they'd stepped aboard without their suits. Carbon monoxide was odorless, and they wouldn't have detected the poisoning until they started choking on what had seemed to be clean air.

The entire ship had taken on an eerie feeling, though the spaces themselves hadn't changed. Kim reached the end of the corridor and found the ramp waiting for them. It was tempting to dive into the tunnels, but in reality, that was the last place they should go. Hemming themselves into a narrow space would not help them if Hosea sent something in after them, particularly in their bulky suits. No, they had to stay in the open.

"You're sure you got all the cameras on Decks Fourteen and Fifteen?" she asked him.

He nodded. "If I missed any, they're well-hidden."

"Still, we should probably pretend she knows what we're doing."

"Agreed," Wren affirmed. "Let's just get this over with."

Kim turned to him. His helmet, like hers, had backlights inside it that lit up his face in the darkness. He was wide-eyed and grim-faced. "Ready?"

"Lead the way." He motioned with the hand not holding the gun, and Kim took off at a run.

They followed the curve of the rampway, their flashlights stabbing the darkness with rough thrusts as each jogging step carried them onwards at a fair pace. They had to adjust their steps for *Seiiki's* reduced gravity, but it worked to their advantage. Once they got the hang of propelling themselves forward, they could cover around two average steps with one movement. Stanchions slid past them as quickly as if they were on a conveyer belt. Kim could hear Wren's breathing in her ears, annoying and soothing at the same time.

Rounding the last curve and reaching Deck Fifteen, Kim could hear the engine thrumming loudly, making her helmet's visor tremble. The engine compartment itself took up the whole of Deck Fifteen, extending throughout the bottom curved section of the ship, then lifting upwards into a cavernous space that climbed up through three levels to the exhausts themselves. The engines themselves were three large turbines encased in semi-circular tubes bolted to the floor, each one ten feet high. Crenulations and ribbed sections divided them, and control panels blinked with various-colored lights and holo symbols. The entrance they used dropped them onto a catwalk that spanned the three turbines. Ahead of them, the reaction chamber, a large platform on which what looked like three piles of giant pebbles stacked atop one another sat. They were bridged by a metal scaffold that relayed the power upwards into the final piece of equipment on this level—the gravity generator. This was a conical-shaped device, 900 feet long, suspended over their heads. The fat end was moored in the scaffolding, and it whirred as it rotated several times per second. Looking up at it made Kim feel dizzy.

Wren was already heading toward the rear of the deck. She couldn't hear his footsteps on the catwalk over the noise, or her own as she followed him. She lifted her head, peering into the dark recesses, almost certain that there were sensors down here that Wren had missed. Deck Fifteen had more than any other deck, for obvious reasons, and its cavernous spaces would make it impossible to get at them all. She had to assume they were already being watched.

"The maintenance droids," Kim said softly.

"What about them?" Wren asked.

"I can't see any," she replied, an ominous feeling settling over her.

They made it almost two-thirds of the way before a hatch shot open on the wall. Kim's eyes followed the hatch cover itself, which had been pushed with such force it broke from its hinges and somersaulted down to the floor with a loud clang. In doing so, she missed the entrance of the cleaning droids.

There were three of them—two maintenance droids and a bug-like autobot. None of them were made for speed, but they had a fair bit of power in order to do some of the heavy lifting. One of the maintenance droids swiveled its head toward her, and, with its four spindly arms outstretched, hovered over the gap, fingers already plucking the air as if to pull her closer. She gasped out a warning to Wren, but Wren was already turning, his gun in his hand. He'd fired two shots, a piercing *bang-bang*, and both of them hit their marks. Maintenance droids weren't made of the same stuff as tech droids— they were soft, no armor protecting their workings. But the shots must have passed through nonessential systems, for while sparks showered from the torn wires, they kept coming, hovering like ghosts.

"Careful!" Kim barked at Wren. "We don't want to—"

"Oh, no," Wren cut her off. She saw him lift his head and followed his gaze upwards—one of the bullets had gone straight through one of the droids and buried itself in the spinning rotor overhead. She could see the impact point, a dented section where the metal had been pushed inwards. It reappeared several times a second—a dark, blurred scar. The spinning cone began to wobble, its trajectory offset by the sudden deformation. It slowed momentarily, then picked up speed again. Kim felt a lurch in her stomach as gravity dipped then surged. She felt herself being pulled down toward the plates of the catwalk. She stumbled, grabbing the railing before she could fall.

The maintenance droid that had been heading for her tilted to one side, then regained its composure. It came onwards, arms still outstretched. Kim could see right through the hole where Wren's bullet had ripped it apart. Sparks spat out like molten gold. The ship listed suddenly to one side, and the droid, thrown off-balance, clunked heavily into the wall of the deck.

Kim glanced past it and saw the other two droids advancing on Wren. He lifted the gun once more and fired two more rounds. *Idiot*, Kim hissed internally. This time, his aim was better. He hit something vital on the nearest droid, and it stopped dead, smoke pouring from its body. The other, the squat autobot, kept coming, however, and it was too late—he couldn't fire again. There was no time. The droid tackled him like a football player, pinning his arms to his sides with its own spindly appendages. The gun dropped from Wren's fingers and the droid stretched up, using its spider-like arms to lift him bodily. "No," Kim breathed, starting forward, but too late—the droid had already flung Wren over the railing. He flew in an arc across the six feet of empty air to hit the wall. Hard.

She watched with her heart in her mouth as Wren dropped, limbs flopping, down to the deck below. He hit one of the engine turbines, his body bouncing off to the side, then vanished from sight. Kim didn't have time to see anything further, because her own droid had regained its equilibrium and was racing back toward her. She kicked out. Her boot hit the hard metal, but she couldn't match its strength. The pincer-like arms came in from the sides, and one clamped down on her upper arm. The pressure was enough to bring tears to her eyes and she felt her legs go out from under her as it twisted her to her knees.

Three other arms grabbed at her, one clamping over her other wrist, the others pinning her legs. Caught as if in a spider's web, she screamed at it. She hurled every swear word she could think of, and wrenched her arms so badly she could feel the skin tearing, but nothing helped. The maintenance droid lifted her up and bore her inexorably back toward the entrance.

Back on the ramp, it began to climb the spiraling way steadily.

"Let me go!" Kim's own voice was muffled. The helmet reflected her useless shouts back at her. "Wren! Wren, respond!"

He did not, but another voice came through her helmet's speakers.

"Stop struggling, Kim. Or I'll have it throw you over the edge too."

Kim snarled. "You're a monster, Hosea! I hate you!"

As they passed a pylon, she caught its edge. The droid readjusted its grip, yanking her backward. Kim could hear her suit tearing, and felt warm blood trickling down her arms. She held on.

"You're going to have to tear me apart!" It was an empty threat. Her own body wouldn't hold up to this strain much longer, but it was all she had to bargain with. "If you kill me now, you won't have me there to watch your grand sacrifice!"

"Oh, I'm not going to kill you. If I'm correct, you'll sustain a few fractures and broken bones from a fall at this height at this level of gravity. Not enough to kill you."

Kim growled loudly, wordlessly. She held onto the pylon, feeling every joint in her arms strain. Her shoulder screamed as the wounded flesh stretched and pulled. She didn't care. "Droid," she said frantically. "I'm hurt. I need a medbot."

The droid pulled back suddenly, letting her go. Kim flopped to the floor of the ramp, breathing hard, surprised that this had worked. All droids were programmed to make way for medbots, but Kim had assumed Hosea would have overridden this programming. Obviously not. She wasn't going to waste time questioning it, however. She launched herself to her feet and ran.

Kim tried, desperately, not to think about the holes in her suit. She knew her oxygen supply must already be compromised with the carbon monoxide, but hopefully she had enough oxygen that it was diluted enough not to be poisoning her. Feeling clumsy in the EV suit, she bolted up the corkscrewing ramp and jinked left into Deck Twelve. This seemed to be the safest place to hide. With the multiple tanks and the alleyways winding their way between them, she would at least have somewhere to conceal herself. She was relieved to see the tanks intact, at least the ones in her field of vision, though she couldn't see any whales.

No. Wait. What was that?

She slowed, skidding on the metal decking as she came close enough to see a large dark shape at the bottom of the Aquarium. Her visor tapped the glass as she tried to get closer.

It was a large body, drifting lifeless. Please, no . . . but it was. She closed her eyes briefly. It was a blue whale.

Adonai.

Insensibly, she pounded on the glass with her fist. "Wake up," she called. "Wake up!" But the massive whale didn't stir. His body was settling against the craggy bottom of the tank, the seaweed parting around him like a crowd of worshippers. When had it happened? How long had it taken for him to sink this far?

Only minutes, surely.

Tears pricked her eyes. "Adonai," she breathed. First Wren, and now this—God . . . It's only his whale body, she told herself. He's not in there, hasn't been in there for days. And still she felt a terrible sense of grief. This was the Adonai she had first become friends with, who had asked her about the stars. Who she had bonded with over stories and promises of what was to come. And now . . . even if Hosea had left his droid body undamaged and whole, he would never swim in the pure ocean of a new world.

The ship rolled massively, sending Kim stumbling to her knees. No—it wasn't the ship. It was the gravity generator. She could see the numbers scrolling past her on the holos of her helmet—it was down to 0.1, then suddenly back up to 0.7 g. She knew what was happening. The generator was failing.

"Kim." The ominous voice returned, barking in her ears. "You can't escape."

Kim lifted herself from the floor and steadied herself against a ladder. Behind her, the maintenance droid was advancing once more.

"You were right. I wanted to keep you alive, to see our glorious end, but if you insist on this foolishness, I'll have to kill you."

Kim bared her teeth in a feral snarl, a remnant from her street days. Nothing said "back off" like bared teeth, even in nature. Hosea would understand the gesture, she was sure.

The droid came on regardless. Kim hoisted herself up onto the ladder, her arm shrieking in protest as she pulled at her burn once more. As she began to climb, the deck tilted underneath her, sending her tumbling. The rungs slipped through her gloved fingers, and she landed, heavily, on the glass of the tank. Had the whole ship tilted sideways? No. It was impossible—there was no up and down in space!

The gravity generator formed direction in a directionless void. The gravity generator! God, it was throwing the ship's equilibrium all the way to the port side.

The droid flew after her, its repulsors now lifting it above the Aquarium wall instead of the floor. It tilted its one-eyed head up slowly, examining her like a predator. Kim braced her hands on the glass, watching the water gurgle and splash as it settled on the side of the ship instead of the bottom. The ten-foot gap of air that was usually at the top of the tank was being forced to the starboard side of the ship, and huge bubbles appeared under her, some of them over a foot across. They whooshed past, hammering the glass with soft thuds and causing the force fields to flicker blue.

The droid came at her in a rush. Kim whirled, shoving herself to her feet and pelting as fast as she could away from it, which meant she was running uphill. To make matters worse, the uneven glass and the curved surfaces of the forcefields made mountains and gullies ahead of her. She skidded as she almost fell into one of the long indentations that looked like wells.

Something was racing toward her from the depths, too. It wasn't her own reflection—far too big, though it shared the color of her suit. One of the whales? Yes. It was the white shape of Fifteen.

"Fifteen!" she called. He couldn't hear her. Of course he couldn't. But he wasn't slowing down either. He butted the glass with his flank, flicking his tail and charging it with all his might. He was a small whale, but he weighed more than an airplane. He hit the forcefield with enough momentum to hurl himself spiraling back into the depths, end over end. A blinding flash radiated from his impact point, like jagged green lightning circling outward across the forcefield's surface. The same force that had sent Fifteen ricocheting backward hurled the energy outward as well, rebounding like a balloon—straight up into the maintenance droid. As the force field rebounded, stretching back into its original shape, it pushed the droid's repulsors upward and flung it ten feet into the air.

"Fifteen!" Kim called, peering into the depths after the brave, stupid whale. She couldn't see him at all.

The droid's repulsors whined as it came back down, but didn't catch it in time. It landed with a crunch on the glass nearby. Its weight was enough to send cracks ripping outwards. Kim felt the glass weaken under her feet. She jumped clear only just in time to watch the glass shatter. The internal webbing tore at the edges, straining to hold the incredible weight of the water. The strain of the water rushing past had already made it weaker than it would otherwise have been.

It wasn't going to hold. Kim could hear the sound of an alarm. The fire/flood doors weren't linked to the main computer. They ran on their own circuit, like the EV suit comms. She could see them now, falling into place already, sealing off Decks Twelve, Eleven, Ten and Nine from the lower decks. But Kim had a more immediate problem. The droid was broken, but it still wasn't dead.

It swiveled its head, lights blinking with an angry rhythm deep within, and fired its repulsors. They stuttered and threw out a blast of sparks. It wobbled dangerously, but it was still functioning well enough to kill her if that's truly what Hosea intended.

"Come on, then," she taunted the droid sneeringly. Keeping her eyes on it, she reached into her toolbelt and pulled out the handheld sealer by touch. Still with her eyes on the droid, she dialed it up to its highest setting, then crouched and jabbed it into the glass. Already weakened, the glass began to glow. The droid came on, moving slowly but relentlessly, pincered arms snapping.

"Come on, come on," she whispered, jamming the tool harder against the glass. She closed her eyes and, for the first time she could remember, prayed to all the Gods. Not just her God, or Allah, or Zeus or Shiva, but to the force she felt when she looked out at the stars and thought about what came after them. She prayed to the whales and to Constantin. And to everyone who'd ever looked after her, who'd ever been kind to her: Her dad, Adonai . . . Wren.

Wren. She saw him tumbling down to the deck once more, body flopping like a rag doll. He was dead. They were all dead . . .

And then the glass gave way.

She fell, sucking in a breath of air as the water rose up around her in little reaching fingerlets. She lazily dropped, without any great speed, down into the water. The ruined droid came after her, its repulsors failing as the hard surface vanished, and it found itself ill-prepared to support itself over water. It splashed down much harder than she did. Blue sparks shot out of its wiring as it struggled, still trying to reach her even as its systems fried themselves.

It drifted past her, jerking in paroxysms as if laughing at a funny joke. Her lungs strained. She went straight down, and when she came up, she saw something she hadn't seen before—the autobot, the one

Ruth Fox

that had gone after Wren. It must have found its way in here before
the fire/flood doors had closed. It crouched uncertainly on the edge
of the hole, ball-like head worriedly swiveling after the other droid as
it drifted down, clearly dead. If she tried to climb out, it would grab
her in an instant with one of its articulated arms. It was hopeless, and
she was helpless. She trod water and watched as small balls of it slowly
separated and lifted into the air. The lightness of the gravity buoyed
her easily on the surface, but she couldn't stay here.

The salt water found her burn, and stung as if the skin was being
peeled off. She felt a wave of despair. Soon, she'd start to fight for air.
Her lungs would strain, her brain would starve. But what choice did
she have?

She suddenly felt something smooth and hard come up under
her. A smooth, solid flank.

Levi.

She couldn't hear him, and he couldn't hear her, not without her
Link to join them. He pushed his nose into her, bearing her away from
the hole, swimming with broad strokes, moving quickly as if aware of
the urgency. The deep blue of the ocean surrounded her and Kim felt
suddenly very much at peace. This was what the whales felt, she knew.
She had felt it through the Link, but had never truly experienced it.
Now, now she felt the serenity, the weightlessness, the gentle caress
of the water on her skin. She could stay here, she thought. She could
remain here forever. How had Adonai ever been able to give this up?

Seaweed flapped past her as they swam through one of the bridges. She had the dim impression of catwalks outside the clear walls, but
otherwise, the outside world was far away. And so were its problems.
She could let herself drown, she felt. No one would miss her. And she
couldn't do anything to stop Hosea anyway. She was useless, nothing
but a street rat, a good-for-nothing drug user and a liar. She'd caused

Wren's death. And she'd doomed everyone on Edgeward. She saw Mona's face, gentle and kind, talking about her son. The Admiral, his stern voice, his surprisingly tender words. Zane, who she had loved so deeply at one time. Even if he'd distanced himself from her—even if he'd lied to her—she would give anything to see him again, to kiss him, to have him hold her. (Stupid. Stupid. She was so stupid to love people who would hurt her.) She even saw that jackass Lieutenant Ben Grand. She hated him, but he didn't deserve this fate.

And then there was Edgeward itself. What it represented to humanity—an outpost, a seeing eye into the depths of unexplored space. The epitome of all Earth's hopes and dreams, the beginning of them righting what they'd done wrong.

And she would be the cause of its destruction. For not stopping Hosea. For allowing Adonai to do what he did, for not forcing him back into his body, or deactivating the droid, or shoving it into the engines to be scrapped, or out an airlock. Her softheartedness would doom hundreds of people, as well as the rest of the whales.

And then, just as the pain grew to the point that she was sure she would pass out, air slapped her face. She gasped involuntarily, and drew in a measure of water with the lungful. It pulled her awake. She coughed and spluttered, suddenly very aware that her helmet had come loose and the ship's atmosphere was leaking through the crack.

She almost laughed. After all this, she was dead after all. How long would it take before she felt the effects of the carbon monoxide? The levels she'd seen on the readouts had been high, but she honestly had no idea.

No point in thinking about it. She ripped off the useless helmet and dropped it into the water.

Levi stayed with her, pushing her into the air bubble, refusing to let her sink again. She could feel it from him: stay. Stay there. Live.

Go on. And if she had any doubts that he knew what was happening, they were erased now. She opened her eyes. The light was brighter here, and she could see why. She was at the starboard side of the tank. A pyramid shape of the ship's hull and the glass floor of Deck Eight was to her left. She swam to it. There was a circular force field here. She tapped it with her hands and felt it buzz.

She turned back to Levi, who watched her, his back humping out of the water like a grey hill. She could see his Link, cobwebbed over his forehead, but it wasn't glowing now. The veined lines were a dull grey. He was completely disconnected.

"Thank you," she gasped raspily.

He blew a spurt of steam upwards.

Kim swam to the force field and pulled her sealer from her tool-belt. It was waterproof, for obvious reasons, but she thanked God for that particular foresight in design anyway. With a swift movement, she melted a circular hole in the glass and hauled herself through. She slid down the glass, through the red clouds that were rapidly coalescing to match the redistribution of the plankton. She landed against the far wall and lay for a few moments on the sloping glass to regain her breath. Her flashlight still blazed forth from her EV suit, making a circle on the wall. Tempted as she was, she wouldn't let herself rest for too long, though. A minute later, she was up and running.

Gravity was slowly righting itself. She could see the waves below her dropping away, the roaring noise of the water filling her ears, louder than the engines. That was a bad sign. When the pressure equalized, the crack in the tanks below would start to spill greater amounts of water. It was a small gap, given the size of the aquarium. The fire/flood doors would cordon it off, preventing it from reaching the engines, but she had maybe a few hours before the whales were in danger.

Should she go down and patch the problem? No. She didn't have time. Even now she could be breathing her last breath, and she had to warn Edgeward. She'd made it this far, and it was for this purpose and this purpose alone, she was sure of it. The whales had more of a chance of surviving if the people on Edgeward knew what was happening and could prepare themselves. Even if . . . yes, she told herself, even if it meant shooting *Seiiki* out of the sky, it was better than dying a fiery death and taking hundreds of people with them. And anyway, now she truly had a chance. Hosea may not know she'd survived her plunge into the tanks. She might have bought herself some time.

Not daring to waste any of it, she darted for the corridor. Her flashlight bounced and hovered, lighting the way to the maglift, where the door stood open, waiting. Please, she thought, let the power still be running them. Trailing water, her boots slapping noisily, she darted inside the maglift and hit the control for her ascent. As the door juddered closed, she let out the breath she'd been holding in her sore, tight lungs.

She leaned against the wall, breathing hard. Seawater ran from her in rivulets, collecting in a puddle on the floor. Her reflection looked back at her from the walls, warped and bedraggled. Her forehead looked different, and it took her a moment to see that the Link had darkened in the same way Levi's had. The golden tracery was now nothing but dull metal. She hadn't even known it was possible to deactivate the Link in this way—hadn't thought to ask Dr Jin, nor anyone else. She had expected to have it married to her brain for the five years of her contract, or at least until she'd fulfilled her mission and given the Crusaders control of New Eden.

Or whatever their plan for her had been.

The doors slid open, delivering her onto Deck One. She ducked to one side of the doors before they slid open. God, she wished she had the gun! But it was gone, lost with Wren. Carefully, she peered around the door's edge. Deck One was empty—completely empty. Not even an autobot buzzed around the rearmost consoles.

But what shocked her most was the state of the room. *This*, she hadn't expected. The entire deck had been destroyed.

If Adonai had ruined the galley store room, Hosea had decimated the Bridge. The consoles were ripped out, entire banks of controls overturned, their metal plating coming apart to show their delicate inner workings, like gutted beasts. Wires hung from the ceiling. Something had been hurled against the great window overhead with incredible force—it was ribbed with cracks and scuff marks at its apex. That glass was virtually indestructible, but now the streaking stars were fractured by cracks.

Kim could have stood there gaping for much longer, but she forced herself to move. She scuttled, half-bent, as fast as she could toward the comms desk, crouching behind it. Maybe she could salvage something, jury-rig a transmission and bypass Hosea's lockdown on the communications systems—and she could have, she knew it, but there was nothing usable left. The console was in tatters. Hosea had used the tech droid's strength to cleave the entire panel in two. An electrical fire had started inside the workings, and the smell of charred plastic filled Kim's nostrils, making her gag.

"God," she said.

But there was still one connection to Edgeward left. Why hadn't she thought of it before? But she needed her tablet. She couldn't do anything from here.

CHAPTER

27

Picking herself up, she ran back to the maglift. Swinging herself around the door, she hit the button to take her down to Deck Five. The maglift moved painfully slowly, while she jigged on the spot, knowing that at any moment Hosea could work out that she was here. Not to mention the dangers of the carbon monoxide poisoning. Her breath was becoming short. Was that a sign? Or was it just from her exertions? What about that pain in her chest?

The doors finally slid open, revealing Deck Five. She let out a sigh. God. She had never been so glad to see it as she was now. But there was no comfort to be found in seeing the door to her quarters—with the lights down, the space looked just as unnerving as the rest of the ship had. She jogged down the corridor, stopping outside her quarters. She slapped at the door control and waited for it to slide back. Inside, she found her room a jumble. Her wardrobe door had swung open spilling clothes and boots. Her bedside table had come loose and was hanging on its side at a 45-degree angle. The mirror in the bathroom had cracked.

She tripped over the gravity blanket and threw it aside in frustration, only noticing then that the door hadn't slid shut behind her. She didn't move to try and fix it—she didn't have time. She only wanted to—

There it was, in the corner. The tablet's screen was cracked but she scooped it up lovingly, as if she could soothe its pain. "Please, please turn on," she cajoled. The screen remained stubbornly dark, marred by a large white crack. Then, blessedly, a small white circle appeared in the center, showing that it was waking from its slumber.

Unexpectedly, the fractured display showed her the last thing that had come through before she'd abandoned it, swept up by this tide of events. It was the unopened file from her "parents." *Happy Birthday, Hannah!* It said in bright green lettering. Kim swiped the air to close it, but the controls weren't functioning properly. The gesture was interpreted wrongly and the file began to play. Constantin's face appeared, pixelated and blurry, making her stop in mid-kanji.

He was leaning in close to the camera, as if afraid he was being watched. His floppy blue hair fell across his forehead, his green tattoo blazing brightly from his pale face.

"Kim," he said, in a low, urgent voice. "You've got to listen to me. This is important. I've made a terrible mistake."

He wiped a hand across his forehead, knocking aside his shock of hair. He looked drawn. There were deep bags under his eyes. It looked like he hadn't slept for weeks.

"I've put you up there, Kim, and I've done it all for the wrong reasons. I sold you. I thought only of myself." His lips tightened. "I'm used to that. They paid me good money to bring you in, and when they found out you were really what they were looking for, they paid me even more to get you to stay. I didn't think you'd get through, though, Kim. I didn't think you would. It was only when you left for Chicago that I realized how . . . " he paused here, and she knew, out of range of his tablet's camera, he would be spreading his hands, fingers wide, in the gesture he always made when speaking about something uncomfortable. "How much I didn't want you to do this."

He sighed, ducking his head. The image flickered, and Kim's fingers hovered over the holo controls, ready to stop the video. She was wasting time when every second counted. She needed to bring up a comm channel for Edgeward, but she couldn't bring herself to cut Constantin off, to stop him from telling her whatever it was that had put that expression on his face. An expression she'd never seen before. What was it? Caring. Yes, and sorrow, and fear. He looked up once more, speaking more quickly now.

"When they sent you, Kim, I went after Grigorian. I—confronted him, for lack of a better word. And Kim, you're in danger. The Crusaders have a plan, that's what he told me. They'd gain your trust. Make you believe in their cause, make you love them. Then send you out there to do what they're too cowardly to do themselves.

"Kim, Grigorian doesn't speak to God. At least, not in the way he wants everyone to believe he does. He has an . . . object, an artifact. He keeps it secret, even from the Crusaders themselves—I think it's on Mars somewhere, in some remote base. He thinks it's a communicator. I don't buy it, Kim. At first I thought he must be right, but . . . it doesn't sound legit. Maybe it's that I'm too cynical. Maybe . . . but I smell bullcrap here somewhere, and I'm . . . "

A pause as he drew in a deep breath.

"Zane—Zane doesn't love you, Kim. I know you think he does, you think you're doing this for him, but he's just another part of the scheme to win your undying trust." He took a shuddering breath. "They're going to blow up *Seiiki*. Zane's job is to ensure the ship gets through the docks without the bombs being detected or interfered with. After you've left the dock at Edgeward, while the celebrations are being broadcast all over Earth and Mars and the Outer Colonies, he'll trigger them. He wants to make a statement, Kim, but it's not the statement that you think he wants. He doesn't care about the whales—not as anything more than a vessel for his own beliefs. Look at this."

The image flickered, and Constantin's face vanished, to be replaced by another. In complete contrast with Cons's pale skin and narrow nose and chin, Zane's broad face framed by dark hair appeared. He stood before a plain white background, and there was no timestamp on this video, making the location and date indiscernible. "... is it right for us to contaminate another planet with our presence? Is it our task to populate the universe with the contaminated seeds of our own failing planet? The Crusaders will ensure it doesn't happen. Stand with us, all of you. You know I speak the truth: Humans do not deserve the galaxy and its riches. We've done enough damage as it is, and we should halt our outwards movement before we've gone too far."

He lifted his head, shuffling his feet slightly. The camera drew back, showing his brown hands clasped loosely at his waist. He was wearing a long white robe that blended almost entirely into the background. God, he looked beautiful, Kim couldn't help but think, even as she heard the words spilling from his lips. He's like an angel...

"Many of you will be shocked by our actions. Many of you will think we've done the wrong thing. But that is the price we're willing to pay to show you how far our power extends. If you think we're small, you're wrong. The Crusaders grow larger every day. Every person who has ever watched money channeled into off-world colonies and terraforming new planets while their children die of curable diseases in the slums of Sydney or Munich or Shanghai agrees with us. It is time—our time—to take back the power. To turn inwards, and work on becoming a better society, to treat our own kind with humanity before we infuse our tainted DNA with that of other creatures and set them on a path into the universe."

Zane took a breath, and the camera zoomed in once more on his face. "And you have already seen what we can do. You know the power of the Word of God, and you know that our leader, Wilhelm Grigorian, speaks on His behalf. You've fallen in love with our cause, too. You know it, deep down; you've been looking at the face of it for fifteen months, now. You've welcomed it into your homes, into your children's bedrooms. The face of the future." He blinked, and another face appeared—Kim's. Her own triangular features, too-large eyes, and lopsided nose from having had it broken too many times in too many jails, her bald head covered by the tracery of the Link. Her mouth, slightly downturned. Fierceness in that expression. "Your beautiful princess Hannah Monksman has shown us the will of God Almighty, and she has now sacrificed herself for Him . . ."

Constantin cut back in, the video dissolving into nothing as his face reappeared. "I found this on Grigorian's tablet. Took me four months to find a guy with enough skills to crack the encryption. It's scheduled to be broadcast on every major network from here to Orion on the 19th of July I can't . . . you can't let it happen, Kim. Please. God, I don't know if you'll even get this, if it'll even get through security. I've got the same hacker working on encoding it so it'll only play for you, and no one else. It was the only way I could think of to reach you—and . . . maybe you'll see the subject and think this is just a joke and delete it without even . . . But if you hear this—please. You've got to stop it. Tell Edgeward. But most of all—get yourself out of there. I can't—I can't lose you, kid."

He kissed his hand and pressed it to his screen. The same gesture Zane had used with her. She felt taken aback momentarily, her feelings confused. Con was lying. He was jealous of Zane. He'd . . .

Kim stared at the screen blankly. "God," she whispered, as reality settled over her like a cloak. Zane had intended to blow her up with the ship. No wonder there was no Crusader ship headed her way to offer help and assistance. No wonder he'd told her not to tell the Admiral about the bombs. What would he have said to her, when she reached Edgeward, at the ceremony, when she left to set out on the second half of the journey? Would he have told her that everything had been fixed? Would he have sealed off the hatch and sent her back aboard, expecting her to trust him blindly, to not check that the bombs had been dealt with? Or would he have killed her to keep her silent about what she knew, and put some other unsuspecting dupe on board? Or . . . God forbid, did he just plan to set them off early—at any moment before she reached Edgeward, before she had a chance to do anything?

If she and Wren hadn't cut them loose, would he have set them off now—a few days, a few hours out from Edgeward?

Kim had gone through a lot in her life, but she had never been used like this. To the world, to Earth, to everyone in the known universe, her death would be seen as a willing act. A martyr. She'd be a sacrifice for a cause she'd had no idea about.

As she sat there, wrestling with the pain and incomprehensibleness of this situation, a shadow fell over her through the still-open door.

She knew it was Hosea.

"Stupid girl," the droid crooned, soothingly, almost lovingly. "You should have died when you had the chance."

Before Kim could do anything but gasp, Hosea scooped her up, hard arms locking around her and hurling her body against the wall. The tablet fell from Kim's hands, smacking hard against the deck. She heard it shatter as she crumpled beside it, hitting her elbow hard enough to make her scream.

"You've been very busy since I saw you last," Hosea said darkly, coming closer, feet making the deck plates ring loudly. "You've removed the explosives. Do you really think that'll make a difference when this ship crashes into Edgeward Station?"

Kim struggled to her knees, bracing one hand against the floor. The dressings on her shoulder had torn free, and she felt a trickle of something—blood, pus?—making its way down her stomach. "You're not going to hit the station," she said firmly. "There are more explosives."

Hosea looked at her. The golden eyes flared, but she stopped her approach. "There are not. You would have removed them."

Kim held up the broken tablet defiantly. "I just learned about them. On this. A friend sent me a message. There's another batch, and they're going to go off at any moment."

Hosea stalled. "I don't believe you," she said. "You lie."

Kim lifted her head and met Hosea's eyes. She put on the face she'd used in courtrooms so many times, in police interrogation rooms, and every time she'd spoken to Yoshi, to Erica Wu, to everyone else at Near Horizon. The face she'd portrayed to the entire universe as Hannah Monksman. And she said, with perfect conviction. "I'm not lying."

Hosea stood there for a long moment, churning this over in her whale's mind. Kim had been right to try this tactic, she saw. Hosea couldn't tell the difference between a lie and the truth. She might despise one and prize the other, but to her, they were ultimately the same thing.

"You won't get your grand spectacle," Kim said. "You won't kill any humans. Just me. And the rest of the whales."

Hosea's eyes appeared to blink as they dimmed then brightened. *Please,* thought Kim desperately. *Please, just believe me. Just long enough to get me to one of the tunnel access hatches.* It was the only plan she could come up with, and it wasn't likely to succeed. Still, what else could she do? The ship was ruined, the engines were still running, and she had no access to the comms. It she could only get into the computer's mainframe, she could start the emergency beacon. She could trigger it easily enough—all she had to do was make the computer think they'd veered off-course once more. That was easy—but she needed to have her hands on the internal circuitry. Nothing she did from out here would give her access, thanks to Hosea's monopoly on the systems.

But then Hosea pulled her shoulders back and twitched her fingers. She took another step forward, until she was standing over Kim, her feet next to Kim's knees. "You're a liar," she said decisively. "And I would have let you live to see our end, to see the glory. Now, you'll die."

"I'm already dead," Kim croaked. "Carbon monoxide, Hosea. I might not even live long enough to see what you're going to do to Edgeward."

Hosea's eyes seemed to bore into Kim's. "Perhaps not. Or perhaps a whale can learn to lie as well as a human. Which do you think?"

Kim's brain struggled to catch up. Finally, it clicked: "You manipulated the readings. There was no carbon monoxide."

"I meant what I said, Kim. I wanted to share this with you. But now we must say goodbye."

She lifted her arm. Kim raised her head. She could already see the shining fist pounding down in an arc, hammering into her skull.

She didn't look away.

Something slammed into Hosea, hurling her sideways so hard the steel deck plate dented downwards. In shock, Kim reared backward, falling against the side of her bunk. Hosea, moving faster than Kim though possible, jumped to her feet, but Adonai—yes, it was Adonai, it had to be (they *had* killed all the other tech droids, hadn't they? Was she sure of that? Was she sure of *anything?*)—came after her again. He grabbed Hosea's head, one hand on either side of her skull, and squeezed inwards. His fingers made furrows in the metal as he pulled with immense force. Hosea fought back, powering upwards. Adonai slammed into the wall himself. Yet still he didn't let go, hanging on with grim determination, like a fisherman from an old cartoon who'd managed to hook a shark by mistake but still intended to land it.

"Adonai!" Kim screamed. She didn't know how to help him. God, they were moving so fast they were almost a blur, and they were so strong—stronger than she could ever hope to be. But her hands dropped almost instinctively to her sides. Her tools were all still in their holsters, and she thanked the God for the designer who'd figured out the anti-slip material that kept all the tools in place no matter what.

She grabbed the first tool her hand settled on. It was the sealer. And without pausing to think too much about what exactly could happen if this went wrong, she ran at Hosea. But her charge was short-lived.

Adonai lost his grip and flung the other droid aside. Kim jumped out of the way as over 200 pounds of steel and machinery hurtled against the door jamb. The bulkhead buckled outwards, and Hosea let out a cry of frustration rather than pain. She wasn't feeling any of this, after all, but having one's body thrown about could hardly be a pleasant experience. Adonai, who had left wires dangling from beneath Hosea's skullplate and ten nasty gouges on the sides of her head, ran at her once more, kicking her soundly in the chest. But Hosea, lightning-fast, snatched his leg up in the air. Kim heard gears whirring, attempting to compensate for the sudden shift of balance, but Adonai was about to fall.

Kim ducked underneath him, heading for Hosea. She lifted the sealer and, without a second's hesitation, plunged it up under Hosea's armored breastplate. She felt the resistance at first, before wires tore and circuit-boards broke under the point of the tool. Kim flicked the switch, turning it on, and the device heated instantly to red-hot. Something hissed and sizzled, and smoke trickled out from the droid's innards. The smell of charred plastic and metal filled the room in moments.

Hosea let out a primal scream and tried to yank the tool out, batting Kim's hands aside. Kim stumbled backward, out of reach, just as Adonai rolled back up. Then he leapt on top of her, using his own weight to pound her into the floor. One of the plates came away from the others and sagged inwards. He grabbed her head again, fingers making new gouges, and pulled with almighty strength. With a massive *crack,* the orb came free.

Hosea still was not dead. "Traitor!" the head yelled.

Adonai, with a disdainful gesture, flung the head into the wall. It bounced to the floor, rolled a few times, and came to rest in the corner. Relentlessly, Adonai stomped after it, then paused by its side.

"We could have done it. We could have died as we were meant to," Hosea said. Her mouth was facing the corner, and all Kim could see was the reflection of her golden eyes on the dull metal wall, fading fast.

"You still will," Adonai said. His voice was tinged with sadness. But even as he said this, he raised his foot and pounded Hosea's head with his sole.

The head split apart, circuitry exposed. Sparks flew, dying just as quickly as they ignited. Kim, pulling herself back to her feet, hurried across to crouch beside it. She loathed having to touch the dead droid, but she couldn't leave it there. She didn't trust Hosea not to transfer herself to another system, or to somehow find another way to carry out her evil plan. With one hand, she pinned the head in place, and with the other, she pulled out a fistful of the wiring. Then another. She tore circuit boards from pins and flung them aside. A faint whirring sound emerged, and she kept going until that had, at last, softened to nothing.

Silence fell until she felt the last of her strength give out. Sliding to the floor, she finally looked up at Adonai, who stood like a statue over the body of his fallen former comrade. "God," Kim said breathlessly, as she gripped the floor, trying to stop her head from spinning with exhaustion. "Adonai, how did you—"

Adonai answered in a slow voice. "I . . . I woke in one of the pods, recharging," Adonai said. "I had to wait. My batteries were very low. But when I was charged, I disconnected myself. I could hear Hosea's thoughts. She'd linked herself in to the tech droid network, and thus, to me also. Obviously she thought I was incapacitated permanently, or she would have separated me out. But she did not, and when I heard what she planned, I made my way to one of the junction stations. There, I saw you in your room." He spread his hands in a small gesture. "Here. And I knew Hosea was coming for you, so I—"

Kim leaned her head back against the wall so she could look up without worrying she'd hit the floor at any moment. "You accessed the junction stations? Then the computer isn't dead?"

"I can hear it," Adonai said hesitantly. "I . . . I think I can relay some commands. But many things are not working. Hosea interfered with many protocols so that only she could give it orders."

Kim let this sink in. She had known, of course, that their trial was not over yet, but God, what else would she be called on to do before this awful day was done? "Can you stop it from executing her plan?"

Adonai shook his head. "I don't think so. I can't reach into the navigational controls."

Kim searched her mind for a solution. There had to be one—she would accept nothing else. She'd faced death three times already in a handful of hours. But then, it wasn't the first time in her life she'd faced it, either. There had been that time, looking down the barrel of a gun held by a rival gang member, when she'd been caught during a raid. Constantin had rescued her then, she remembered with a sudden stab of clarity; he'd come charging up, screaming like a madman. The gangbanger must have thought he was about to get mauled, because he'd taken off like a rabbit, so fast it had made Kim laugh, even despite the situation. There had been other times, too; so many. Falling through a third-story window during a raid by the cops. The junkie that had tried to stab her with a dirty hypodermic when she'd encroached on his sleeping space in an alley. She'd lived through them all, so what else was there but to go on living? She couldn't give up.

"I thought about heading for the computer mainframe," she said. "I could try and break through Hosea's remaining commands. But I don't even know how much time we've got left."

"The ship will arrive at Edgeward in thirty-six minutes," Adonai replied.

"Damn," Kim cursed. That was less time than she'd thought— far less time than she'd hoped. Definitely not enough time to muck around with computer coding. "Can you shut down the engines?"

Adonai tilted his head to one side. "I'm not sure. I don't know how."

"I'm pretty sure I've got an idea." After a brief moment, she gathered her courage and dared to ask him the one thing that terrified her more than anything else had in the past three days. Torture, pain, space battles—nothing compared to the crawling feeling of anxiety that made its way up her spine as she spoke these words. "Where's—did you see Wren?"

Adonai cocked his head. "I could not find him on any cameras. But many are non-operational."

"He smashed them," Kim answered. She squared her shoulders, pulling herself upright and trying not to look as if she'd topple straight over at any moment. Pushing all worried thoughts from her mind, she told Adonai: "We've got to get to Deck Fifteen. I'm going to shut down the engines manually, the way we planned."

"Can this be done?" Adonai inquired.

"Not sure," she responded with a shake of her head. "Wren was willing to give it a go, though. It's worth a shot. Come on."

As she hurried toward the door, Adonai was close on her heels. With the flood/fire doors still down, they couldn't access the ramp, so Kim took them back along the corridor to the maglifts. Once inside, it was the longest journey of her life, longer, she imagined, than the entire second leg of her journey would have been, from Edgeward to New Eden.

The gravity went wild again. Kim was slammed into the rear wall, which had suddenly become the floor. Adonai managed to brace himself, his reflexes much faster than hers, and held her as the ship slowly reverted to its normal equilibrium. Kim rubbed a new bruise, this one on her forehead. On Deck Fifteen, she heard the engines thrumming along at their usual frequency, as if nothing had changed. They were bearing down on the point where they'd drop from hyper and saw Edgeward Station looming before them. They had only about ten minutes, maybe less, before they ploughed straight through it.

The gravity generator was still spinning, but its rotation had slowed drastically. Kim could feel the lightness in her torso, as if her intestines were floating around inside her chest. It was just as well she had only eaten those crackers—anything more would have had her vomiting.

Trying to ignore the dizzying feeling, Kim ran across the catwalks. Her third step took her higher than she anticipated as the gravity lessened. With a lurch, she felt her feet go out from under her and for a moment she teetered, her own momentum threatening to throw her right over the edge. If she went over, she'd tumble in freefall until she hit something—or several somethings—and even if that didn't incapacitate her, she'd lose what time she had to shut down the engines.

The railing was just below her. She snapped her arm out, palms slippery with sweat, and wrapped both hands around it tightly. Her elbow locked painfully as her own body weight bent it in the wrong direction. Ignoring it, she forced her body back upright and planted her feet back on the catwalk.

She didn't want to make that mistake again. Clinging tightly to the railing, she dragged herself forward hand over hand. She did not bother to look over her shoulder to see if Adonai was behind her. She jumped down a ladder without touching the rungs, landed in a squat, then ran onwards, snaking her way toward the fuel lines she and Wren had been aiming for last time. Adonai, however, had found another route, and blurred past her in a flash of silver steel. He was standing at the rear wall before she got there, looking over the railing at the large corrugated tubes that ran out from the hull and into each of the turbines. Marked in black and yellow, each had the warning sign printed in large red letters upon it. For safety reasons, only a few feet of the piping was exposed. This was purely so that an autobot could perform maintenance on blockages, and what Kim was about to do was very dangerous indeed. She took a deep breath, then swung one leg, then the other, over the edge and dropped from the catwalk to the top of the central turbine.

The surface was curved under her feet, and she almost teetered over and slid down onto the deck below—when Adonai landed beside her, catching her shoulders and righting her. She would have thanked him if she'd been less concerned with how to do this without dying.

She moved back toward the turbine's end, where the arched surface sheared off, leaving the gap between it and the wall for the umbilical fuel lines to run. "Adonai," she said. "Do you think you can pull those out?"

"What will happen if I do?" Adonai replied.

"Fuel will gush out," Kim said. She was only guessing, but it was an educated guess. "It'll come fast. I can't tell if the computer will shut off the pumps or not, or how long it'll take to kick in if it does. The whole place could flood." She sighed, looking into the depths of the shadows around them. If Wren's body was down here, it would likely be swallowed by the toxic liquid. But if Adonai was right, and Wren was alive, and had somehow gotten Adonai into the pod—then he must be safe. In any case, she couldn't put his wellbeing above that of everyone on Edgeward. Just like she wouldn't allow him to. She looked sideways at Adonai. "You might be destroyed."

Adonai returned her gaze placidly. "I am prepared for this."

"No, Adonai," Kim replied. "You don't understand. I saw you . . . your whale body. It's . . . "

"Dead. Yes, I know. But there was never any going back."

Kim stood there, certain she would see some flicker of regret, some hesitation, some distress in his posture. Something. But it wasn't just the fact that he was a droid. He'd conveyed his emotions very well at other times.

No, he was truly accepting of his decision, and ready to ride out the consequences, whatever they may be.

"I admire you," she said in a rush. "I really do, Adonai."

"And I you, Kim," he replied. "Please, climb back up to safety. Lock the door, seal the hatches. Make the ship safe for yourself. And find Wren."

Kim nodded slowly. Protests were ready on the tip of her tongue, but she knew Adonai would not listen. And someone had to live, to make sure Zane paid for his crimes—and to tell the story of Hosea, and brave Adonai, her friend.

She turned from him and jumped, pulling herself back up onto the catwalk. It was easy, with the gravity so low now. But she felt anything but weightless as she walked back along the catwalk to the door; no, memories of every conversation she'd ever had with Adonai played through her mind. She found tears on her cheeks, and didn't bother to dash them away.

It wasn't until she had reached the last section of the catwalk that she finally saw through the shrouded veil of sorrow. Someone was standing there, waiting for her. His helmet was gone. His hair was disheveled, his jumpsuit cut wide open from shoulder to stomach, and bagging uselessly. His face and hands were covered in thick smears of grease, but he looked good. He looked wonderful.

"Wren," she said.

He gave her a small smile.

"How—?" Her voice cracked on the words, and she couldn't even finish.

He lifted his shoulders in a shrug, and his hands turned upwards, fingers curled toward the ceiling. "Guess this old thing was good for something."

That ugly suit. That ugly, God-awful rubber suit. Kim let out a snort of laughter. It was a terrible sound, through the mucus and moisture of her weeping, and she was instantly embarrassed, but she couldn't help herself. She ran at him, lunging into his arms and hugging him tightly.

"Kim," he said, surprised. She looked up and saw him wincing.

"Oh, sorry," she said.

"Ribs," he grimaced, gingerly rubbing a hand over the area. "Yeah, broke a couple, I think. But what about Hosea?"

"Dead. And we've got to get out of here." She glanced over her shoulder. "Adonai is going to pull the fuel lines."

"Really?" Wren asked. "What does it matter, if we're going to die of carbon monoxide poisoning?"

"Do you feel sick?" Kim asked him, raising her eyebrows.

He shook his head slowly.

"We'd be dead by now. It was one of Hosea's tricks. Probably much easier to fool our computer into thinking there was a leak than to actually cause one."

"She's really dead?" Wren asked her. "God, Kim. I've spent the past few hours just trying to keep myself conscious. How did you manage to kill her?"

Kim tugged his arm. "It's a long story."

Wren resisted, looking down toward the turbines. Adonai was only just barely visible in the background. Kim could hear something screeching as metal rubbed against metal. "Do we really have to leave him?"

Kim felt her eyes brim over once more. "It's what he wants to do," she said. "And it's not like we have a choice. Come on, Wren."

Reluctantly, the two made their way toward the door. A moment after they'd reached it, there was a loud gushing sound, and a massive *pop*, as if a gigantic balloon had burst. The pressure seal breaking on the fuel lines, Kim thought. For a moment, she warred with herself, wanting to turn back, to tell Adonai they'd hold the door for him. But already, colorless, odorless xenol could be seen spilling out. The liquid part gushed down the sides of the turbine like a raging river. The gaseous element spurted upwards like steam, filling the air.

Alarms sounded. They sounded small and lonely. Normally, they'd be resounding through the ship, but with so many systems down, Deck Fifteen was the only one alerted.

It was Wren who hit the control to close the door. As it slid across, Kim took one last glance into the engine bay as it filled with white vapor. She imagined she could see Adonai down there, standing atop the turbine, a silhouette in the mist; but in truth, she could see nothing at all.

Tense moments passed. They stood together outside the door, looking at the open maglift. Neither of them was ready to leave, as if by staying here, they could at least be near Adonai as he performed his chosen duty.

The ship gave a sudden lurch, and then another.

"We're coming out of hyper," Kim said. She slid to the floor, bracing her feet against it, with her back firmly against the wall. "Get down."

Wren obeyed her, wincing again. "Do you think we'll make it?"

"Yes," Kim said, without conviction. It was out of their hands now.

Wren's hand found hers and squeezed it tightly. The shuddering came upon them, until it felt like every bone in their bodies were being pulled different directions. Kim closed her eyes and felt Wren wrap his hand around the back of her head, pulling her to his chest. She didn't want him to protect her, but she didn't pull away, either. It was a few minutes before she realized his hand had gone lax around hers.

He'd passed out.

She curved her head toward his and tried to keep her breathing even. *Hako*-class ships could withstand incredible gravitational stress. They were modelled after military freighters—half the design was similar to a G-class Dreadnaught, minus the firepower. She calmed herself by playing through the skeletal construction schematics she had viewed so many times during her training. Breathe, she told herself. As long as you're breathing, there's nothing to fear.

Seiiki would survive. She would survive. After all that had happened, she wouldn't accept anything less.

The shuddering reduced. A moment of blissful smoothness while the ships continued to creak and groan around her. Another jolt that slammed both her and Wren against the bulkhead. Then . . . nothing.

She lifted her head. Dust hung in the air, particles sifting down from overhead. Most of the lights were out, so everything was monochrome and shrouded in shadow. At the end of the corridor, a panel had come loose from the bulkhead and swung back and forth on a single rivet, making an odd clapping sound.

Something detached from the wall. No, that wasn't right—she blinked, clearing her vision. The object came from the door to the fuel chamber, which was cycling slowly open. It moved awkwardly, then slowly unfolded itself into standing position.

A tech droid. It was battered, a scorch-mark marring its chest and one yellow eye blinking on and off irregularly. But it was whole.

Adonai.

She lowered Wren to the floor as carefully as she could before launching herself at the droid. Wrapping his solid body in her arms, heedless of the sharp corners and unyielding metal, she squeezed him as tightly as she could.

"Did I do well, Kim?" he asked her.

"You did very well," she replied earnestly, tears making her voice unsteady. "I couldn't have asked for more."

C H A P T E R

28

While Adonai carried him to the infirmary, Kim made her way to Wren's ship, where she slid into the cockpit. It smelled worse than before. She wrinkled her nose as she flicked on the comms system and hailed Edgeward.

Of course it was Grand who answered. "Holy crap," he said. "Wait here. I'm getting the Admiral."

"Hello to you too," Kim said, her voice nasal. She knew she must look a mess, but she hadn't expected the expression on the Lieutenant's face—one of utter shock.

"Hannah, just stay there. I'm getting weird readings. Don't drop the connection. Just don't—"

"Hannah," Admiral Mbewe appeared. Grand's holo vanished altogether—he must have cut the conversation to another terminal. It looked like he was in his own quarters. His greying hair was sticking up unevenly, and there were circles under his eyes. "Thank God. We've been trying to establish contact with you for days. I've got scout ships on their way. What's happened?"

Kim gave him a weary smile. "A lot. I don't think you'd believe me. But first of all, I've got to tell you something. And it's going to make you angry and disappointed in me. I'm probably never going to see you again, because I'll be in a Martian prison after the trial of the century. But please, please believe me when I say that I thought I was doing the right thing." She took a deep breath and checked to make sure that her transmission was also being sent to Near Horizon. "My name's not Hannah Monksman."

She waited for them to come for her. After cutting the transmission to the Admiral, she'd sat in silence, expecting to be hailed immediately once more. But the little ship's comm stayed quiet. She leaned back in the seat and opened her eyes wide, watching as the stars streaked past.

It was nice to see this view. She savored it, knowing she wouldn't see it much longer.

When finally she left, it was to wade into the spilled water on Deck Twelve. The gravity was still a bit iffy, but this actually helped, since the water that came from the cracked pane had pooled in one corner where it sloshed like an indoor pond. She had to find the broken shards of glass and haul them into place. She'd managed to get one droid up and running, thanks to Adonai's work with the computer, and it did the heavy lifting, thank God, but she still had to crawl along a tilted catwalk to seal it. Thankfully, the sealer had been easy enough to repair after she removed it from Hosea's corpse.

She saw Levi watching her from nearby as she worked. The others swam up slowly to take a look as well. There was Jedidah, Berenice, Matthew. She waved to them, feeling the aching loss of their companionship. But they were still there. All except for Fifteen. His body had floated to the surface, his nose bloody and teeth broken from the impact with the force field. Adonai was alongside him, his body dwarfing the small whale's. Kim had wept, for the first time she could remember, as she used the machinery to pull the three whale carcasses through one of the force fields and encase them in long preservation tanks. What would happen to them, Kim didn't know. She'd have to wait and see.

And there was a lot of that: waiting. With the engines shut down, *Seiiki* was adrift. There hadn't been many times in her life when she had time to sit and think, with no real responsibilities. Perhaps that's why she'd craved it, dreamed up a future in which she'd have nothing but time to herself. She'd involved Zane in that scenario, but now it seemed like a stupid thing to hope for.

She *hated* doing nothing. Loathed it with all her heart and soul. And Zane? He had never truly fit into that vision, had he? All his dark intensity, his brooding silences, his deep thoughts and constant need to be working and tinkering—he would never have had time for her. He loved the cause. He would never leave it.

Thoughts of Wilhelm Grigorian drove her almost crazy. The artifact Cons had mentioned—was it real? And *what* was it? Where had it come from? Why did he think it allowed him to commune with God? Was this strange object really the reason Kim had been sent on this mission in the first place? The reason she'd been chosen . . . to, well, to die?

Adonai, for his part, kept busy. He cooked a marvelous dinner. He'd managed to find spaghetti and had made a sauce out of canned tomatoes and pesto. She and Wren had sat opposite one another at the table eating forkfuls of the messy stuff until they groaned in pleasure. Adonai sat to one side, observing them.

The scout ships arrived fifteen hours later.

Kim and Wren stood there to greet them. Adonai, too. Kim had wanted him to stay away. "Maybe they don't have to know about you," she said.

"No," he said. "Remember, it is not our way, as whales, to lie or deceive."

Kim felt a lump in her throat and turned away.

The airlock slid open.

A squadron of Earth United soldiers wearing green uniforms studded with badges stood in the aperture. Weapons were trained on her, but most of the green lasers were gathered on Adonai's chestplate.

"Hannah Monksman," the leader, a woman with short red hair, barked.

Kim lifted her hands. "Actually, it's Kim," she said dully.

"You're under arrest," the woman continued, uncaring. She turned to Wren, who was standing calmly at Kim's side. "Wren Keene, I'm also authorized to arrest you." Finally, her gaze rested on the rather conspicuous droid. "And . . . Adonai. You are also required to accompany us."

"What about *Seiiki*?" Kim asked. "What'll happen to it?"

The woman seemed surprised at the question. She couldn't blame her. Why would a terrorist care about a ship? But to tell the truth, she wasn't sure who she was anymore. "She'll stay here for now. A team is already at work on the computer systems. It'll be taken to

Edgeward when it's ready, and Earth United will be taking control of her. And the Ark Project, by the sounds of things."

Kim nodded. She was too weary to argue, and knew it wouldn't do any good, anyway. She and Wren had already talked through the most likely scenario, and so far, they'd been spot on.

The journey was a short one. Kim was taken in a separate ship than Wren and Adonai. Edgeward loomed up ahead of her, a broad expanse of steel-grey turrets on a floating island, mirrored below by stalactite-like mooring towers where dozens of ships in varying sizes were docked. This was hardly the grand entrance she'd imagined, flying up with *Seiiki* and the whales safely aboard. She'd thought she'd be seeing Zane, at least from a distance, even if they couldn't meet as lovers.

When the airlock rolled back, though, it revealed a scrum of people. Reporters shoved cameras in her face. Drones hovered around like menacing bats. The soldiers had to use their guns to force people back.

Finally, she was bundled into a holding room. Plain white walls, a table and two chairs. A one-way glass window. Oh, how many times she'd sat in just such a room!

"Full circle," she said with a smirk.

CHAPTER
29

The Admiral was not the first to speak to her. There were numerous Earth United interrogators, wearing military garb and sidearms, pressing her aggressively for information. This was the wrong approach. Kim shut down, hurled insults, and even slammed her hands on the table at one point. She wasn't scared of them, or what they could do to her. She was more afraid of what she'd do to herself.

It had been going on for twelve hours and Kim was sagging in her chair. The pain of her burn was incredible, but at least it was a clean pain now as the nanobots worked to rebuild the damaged tissue and destroy the infection, something she could deal with. When the door opened one more time she jerked awake, blinking bleary eyes at her latest interviewer. It was Lieutenant Grand. He carried a cup of coffee in a paper cup and a small plastic dish containing six pills. "Painkillers," he told her, putting them down on the table. Kim reached for the pills, downed them, then drank greedily from the cup. The coffee was weak and tepid.

"This is how Earth United makes coffee?" she said, making a face.

"I'm not here to discuss coffee with you," he replied. "You're in a lot of trouble, Kim Teng."

"I know. I got that already."

"You've broken multiple laws. You've committed espionage, fraud, and theft. You're lucky we don't have the death penalty."

Kim smirked. "You couldn't, even if you wanted to, and you know it."

Ben sighed, leaning back in his chair. "Yeah. You made sure of that with your little transmission back to Near Horizon. You know that shit is playing on every holochannel on Earth and Mars?"

Kim nodded, even though she hadn't known. She'd half expected Near Horizon to cover it up, too.

"Erica Wu leaked it to the media," he went on. "She's been removed from her position. She's lost everything because of you."

Kim shrugged, trying hard not to care. "That was her choice. I didn't force her to sign me on to the project."

"No, but don't you feel the least bit guilty?"

Kim shook her head. "Erica knows how to land on her feet."

"So do you, apparently. They're hailing you as a hero, you know." He tossed a tablet on the table, disgusted. "Have a look."

Kim picked it up, swiped the screen to life. A video file was already loaded. She hit "play", and a newsreader appeared, a banner scrolling underneath her face.

" . . . Kim Teng is now being held at Edgeward, awaiting trial. There has been no direct communication with Ms. Teng since her arrest, but sources have confirmed that she is being treated well. There have been reports of at least one whale death—the last remaining blue whale, as we've heard from sources recently—but at this stage, we're unable to bring you more details on the nature of the death, or the health of the others. We'll have more updates soon . . ."

Kim flicked the video closed. She didn't want to hear any more.

Ben leaned across the table, folding his hands. "You're not going to walk away scot free if I've got anything to say about it, so wipe that smile off your face. You endangered those forty-three whales. I know the truth."

"No you don't," Kim said. "What about Zane? Why aren't you questioning *him*?"

"'Private Getty,' is gone." Ben blew out his cheeks. "Several hours before we found *Seiiki*, he apparently took off. His quarters are cleaned out. Not even a fingerprint."

"You must know where he's gone. This is a military station. He can't just hop on a ship—"

"A small scout ship is missing from the docks. The transponder is also missing. It's impossible for it to have happened without inside help. I'll find the culprits, but he could be anywhere by now."

Kim felt herself deflate. Of all of this, the one thing she'd been looking forward to was that Zane would be prosecuted. She wanted vengeance. She wanted to watch his face be plastered all over the media as a terrorist. She wanted the world to know. But in another way, she was glad. She didn't want the world knowing how he'd used her. She didn't want to be Zane's dupe.

She just wanted to find him—and shoot him in the head.

Ben stood up. "Good luck, Kim."

It was close to midnight now. Kim had been awake for more than twenty-four hours—seventy-three if you counted the time spent in

Hosea's torture chamber, where she hadn't slept so much as passed out.

When Admiral Mbewe entered, he was silent. He sat down, stood up, paced a few steps, then sat once more.

"How is your shoulder?" he asked at last.

"Feels like new," Kim said wearily.

"I'm going to send in a nurse," he said. "Kim, I have to ask you one question. Why didn't you tell me?"

She lifted her chin. "Because I was afraid."

"I wish I'd seen it," he replied. "I could have stopped it."

"No, you couldn't," Kim said. "If it wasn't me, it would have been one of the others. They would've gotten what they wanted."

"You're lucky that all this has been overshadowed by your friend Adonai, and the late Hosea. Near Horizon is milking it for all its worth. Talking whales! Who'd have thought?" He smiled. "My granddaughter wants one. *Everyone* wants one."

"They're not objects. Not toys."

"No," he replied. "You understand that better than anyone. And as I said, you're lucky. Your friend Adonai is lobbying for you. You're going to walk away from this one, Ms. Teng."

"I am?" Kim hadn't expected this.

He nodded. "You're a good girl, I believe."

"Why are you so nice to me?" Kim asked.

He cracked a smile. In person, it looked warm and comforting. "I grew up like you did," he replied. "In Zambia, I was very poor. What do you call them these days—a shiv? Oh yes, I robbed and stole. I took a gun that was given to me, and I used it, too. But I robbed the wrong man. Or perhaps you could say the right one." He shook his head, sad with this memory. "He made it his mission to pull me out of that life, and in order to honor him, I made something of myself. And yes, I wasn't always proud of what I had to do to get here, but I'd do it all again. Because here, I can do good."

Kim swallowed. "You think I did good?"

"From what Adonai said—yes. There's no saying what would have happened if one of the others had been on board *Seiiki* when Adonai emerged, and then Hosea. Perhaps things might have been much worse."

Kim nodded. "But I've lost command anyway."

"Yes. You will probably not be happy to hear it, but Yoshi will be taking over as Caretaker." His chest puffed with a deep breath. "But it's not the end for you, Kim. Not even close."

CHAPTER
30

L aunch Day. A greater crowd than could ever have been anticipated had gathered in the main launch bay. People ringed the
galleries. Outside, ships and drones were clustered so tightly around
the docks that a force field had to be set up to keep them back from
the ship's exit point. Families chattered together. Little kids cheered.
Flags waved. The atmosphere was one of giddy celebration, just as it
should be. Only Kim wasn't at the head of it. Instead, it was Yoshi who
stood on a portable podium to one side of Adonai.

"I am very proud to be here," the tall, slender Japanese girl said.
"I will do my best for the whales. And yes, they are new species. I will
honor them, guide them. On New Eden, they will be truly free."

Kim, standing below the podium and to the side, looked to her left. Wren was beside her, wearing a suit and tie, clean-shaven and looking as much the businessman as he'd looked that first time she'd seen him in the lobby of Near Horizon on Collins St. in Melbourne well over a year ago.

She hadn't wanted to come. She wouldn't have been here at all, if Erica Wu hadn't commanded it. When the Admiral had come to her quarters earlier that afternoon, he'd attempted to convince her, but she'd refused.

She'd stared at him with wide eyes. "They'll kill me."

The Admiral let out a soft sigh, leaning his shoulders back on the door jamb. His uniform jacket was unbuttoned and he looked almost as worn-out as she felt. She wondered, with a twinge of guilt, whether he was still copping the flak from her betrayal. At least he'd managed to move her to some spare crew quarters rather than leaving her in the interrogation room. She'd had a chance to shower properly and change, and she felt marginally more human.

"There are some things I've managed to keep under wraps," he said. "With a little help."

It was only then that Kim noticed he wasn't alone. In the hallway beyond was a woman Kim recognized with incredulity.

"Ms. Wu?"

Erica Wu angled herself into the room without further invitation. She was wearing impossibly high heels, her legs bared to mid-thigh by another tight, short skirt, but she'd paired it with a rather ratty red-and-green knitted jumper that was fraying at the sleeves. Kim smiled to see it—she had liked Ms. Wu's eccentricities from the moment she'd first met her.

Erica took a brisk look around before her sharp eyes settled on Kim.

"You look like hell, Hannah."

Kim baulked, feeling ashamed. "My name's not Hannah."

Erica let out a huffing breath that said, clearly, *what does it matter?* "You still look like shit. You've been hiding in here all this time?"

Kim spread her arms. She had kept the rooms tidy, unable to disrespect the Admiral by leaving so much as a towel on the floor. And it gave her something to do. No autobots chased around after her on Edgeward, that was for sure. "What do you expect me to do?"

"Try not feeling sorry for yourself," Erica snapped.

"I'm not," Kim fired back. She ran a hand unconsciously over her head. In the few days since her Link had been deactivated, her hair had started to grow back, short and stubbly. She could still feel the slightly-raised filaments under her skin, but no longer did she hear the voices of the whales.

This was the most devastating punishment of all. She'd never felt so *alone* in all her life.

Wren kept coming to her door, too. She'd refused to let him in. She didn't want him seeing her black-rimmed eyes, didn't want him comforting her. She didn't deserve him. Didn't deserve anything.

The gravity on this station was so heavy. She felt like she was being sucked into the floor. God, she just wanted to be back aboard *Seiiki*. She wanted Adonai and her whales.

"This isn't like you, Hannah."

"You don't know what's like me!" Kim snapped, her fists clenching by her sides. "You don't know me! Even the lies you thought you knew I was telling were just lies!"

"No they weren't," Erica said. With a few quick steps, she put herself directly in front of Kim and took her by the shoulders. "I saw the truth in the answers you submitted on your tests, Kim. I can't say I knew you were a shiv, but I got the impression you'd lived life on the edge for a long time. I'm not an idiot. Neither are you." She forced Kim to look at her. 'Do you know what they're saying about you?"

"I haven't watched the newsfeeds," Kim admitted. "Haven't wanted to know."

Erica shook her head. "That's a shame. They still love you, Hannah. Well, there'll always be a handful . . . a couple of million, to tell the truth, who wonder if there's more to the story than we're telling them. There's a lot of backlash against the Crusaders, too, but no one knows you were their recruit."

"What?" Kim swallowed noisily. How was that even possible?

"There aren't any charges against you. To most of your fans, you're even more of a hero than ever."

Kim felt a sick churning in her stomach. "But I'm *not* a hero. I almost killed all the whales. I *did* kill two of them."

"One," Erica reminded her. "Hosea. Adonai isn't dead. And Fifteen, well, he will be missed, but it was luck alone that meant he was even included in the project. I think he'd have been glad to have experienced the journey as far as it took him."

Kim stiffened. "But he didn't get to see it's end."

"Nothing was guaranteed," Erica said forthrightly. She sighed a moment later. "He was from the oceans, Kim. The actual ocean, beyond the Pacific Sea Wall. He spent his entire life swimming in putrid garbage. What he found on *Seiiki* was paradise in comparison, Kim. He'll be remembered now, no matter what, won't he? And so will you," Erica said. "If I don't blame you for what you did, then how can you blame yourself?"

"I'm sorry," was all Kim could manage, in a cracked voice. "I really didn't want you to . . . "

"You think I'm done?" Erica's smile was as sharp as a knife. "I'm not. Near Horizon never sat right with me, anyway. Too corporate.

I've got bigger plans, and now I don't have to answer to the bastards in charge." Letting go of her shoulders, Erica marched toward the door. "And you owe me now, Hannah. I expect you to continue to work for me. And your first task is to be there at the ceremony."

Before her now, Yoshi was wearing a crisp white jumpsuit, her glossy hair gone, replaced by the shining gold filigree of the Link.

"I have arranged for the bodies of Adonai, Fifteen, and Hosea to be kept aboard *Seiiki*," Yoshi continued. "They'll be preserved in ice so that I can continue my studies into the effects of human DNA on the whales, and this will allow me to further my research into reversing the effects within, ideally, two generations, if not one. I intend, fully, to restore the whales to their natural state. They will be as they once were on Earth."

A ripple of applause took over the crowd, and hands were raised above heads. Flags bearing the images of various whales were fluttered wildly.

Yoshi did not smile.

"*Seiiki* will now be accompanied by a military escort," she said. "This is not what I had hoped for. The Ark Project is a civilian cause. Yet I can see—" *have been made to see,* her tone said— "the necessity of it, given my predecessor's failures."

Kim felt a blush of anger, followed quickly by a sick feeling of shame. Yoshi wasn't saying anything Kim didn't deserve.

"But I will carry out this mission with the grace of God," she continued. "I am, and always have been, the best person for this task. The whales will be safe in my hands."

More applause. She lifted a hand and waved regally as she stepped down from the podium.

Kim couldn't stand it anymore—she had to get out of there. She pushed her way through the crowd, feeling them press inwards as they realized who she was. Some called to her, some reached for her shoulder, asked for a photo or a signature, but she ignored them.

Wren caught up with her as she broke free, emerging into a side corridor, gasping as if having been underwater. Behind her, the voices of the crowd chanted loudly in a harmonious rhythm.

"Hey," Wren said, reaching for her. "You okay?"

"No." Kim sighed. She leaned against the wall, bracing one elbow against the flat, cold steel. The thrum of the station's environmental systems vibrating through her arm soothed her somewhat. "I know this is the way it has to be, but—"

"But you wanted to go with them," Wren said, understandingly, as he came up behind her. "Listen. Listen!"

She tuned into the voices. What she'd thought was just a monotony resolved into a single word. A name. "Kim! Kim! Kim!"

Kim glanced up in shock. Beyond the hallways entrance, fists were raised. There wasn't a hint of animosity behind the words. No one was screaming for her head—just the opposite. It was a mantra, a hymn, of welcome.

Kim took a step back toward the entrance, and saw Yoshi in the middle of the crowd, looking uncertain. Adonai, beside her, was lifting his own fist. How strange to see his expressionless face tilted jauntily to one side as he joined in the chant: "Kim! Kim! Kim!"

Wren grabbed her hand. She almost pulled free, instinctively, but he seemed to anticipate this and clung on. "Come on."

"No," Kim protested. "I can't . . . "

"Don't be stupid, Kim. They want to see you."

She wanted to run, honestly. She wanted to hide in the plain, functional quarters she'd been given, where guards were stationed outside to keep away any Adherent protesters and other haters. She wanted to be back aboard *Seiiki* with the whales.

Alone, with the deepness of space cocooning her.

But Wren wasn't letting her go.

She allowed him to take her back into the hall. People parted before her, making a passage to the podium. Yoshi, standing just at the bottom, did not look pleased at all.

"Go," Wren gave her a push.

Kim tried to walk humbly. She could feel so many eyes on her, so many more than she'd felt even at the reception on Ganymede. The weight of them was oppressive. She had never wanted this. She wanted to serve God, but she didn't want *this*.

And yet she found herself walking upright, her shoulders straight, her hips swaying with just a little of Hannah Monksman's confidence. Her boots had just enough heel to click on the metallic floor. The tea dress she wore was knee-length, shimmery green, and moved with her body elegantly. She felt her breathing even out and a slight smile settle on her lips.

The podium was just ahead. She stopped, her gaze resting on Yoshi.

"This isn't my idea." It was the only thing she could say.

"I know," Yoshi said with a noticeable wince as she lifted a hand toward her Link. "But the whales aren't letting it go. They're insisting even now. They won't leave without you. They think you're their Caretaker."

"I'm not," Kim said apologetically.

"Yes," Adonai spoke loudly. "You are."

"Kim! Kim! Kim!" The crowd continued to chant, and Kim let the part of her that had always been Hannah smile brightly out at the room.

EPILOGUE

After nine days, I'm back on Seiiki, and we're heading for New Eden. I'm glad to be here. Just so you know, Yoshi doesn't like me. She won't say it in her transmissions, but I can tell you—she's set up her lab on Deck Fourteen and spends most of her time there. I think she even sleeps there so she doesn't have to run into me on Deck Three. The whales like her, though. They say she's calming. Go figure.

So we're nine days out from Edgeward, now. And it's all going well. We've got seven months before we reach New Eden. That's plenty of time.

Kim drew the kanji for *stop* on the back of her hand and leaned back on the bed. She felt the golden filaments of the Link brushing the fine threads of the pillowcase. Her Link had been restored, and now she shared it with Yoshi. They could communicate, mind-to-mind, if needed, though neither of them had made use of that particular benefit just yet—Kim didn't plan on ever using it. Mostly, they stuck with talking to the whales.

She smiled. As if they'd heard her thinking of them, a cacophony of voices entered her head.

Kim! Come and see us! We want to play.

I want to hear the story again. Tell us again what happened with Hosea.

Do you really think it's possible for us to take on human bodies? I want to do that.

It was disturbing, hearing them talk like that, but Kim refused to keep what had happened a secret from them any longer.

No more lies. She'd made a promise.

"You're done?"

Wren stepped into the room, fresh from the shower with a towel around his waist. His chest glistened and Kim felt her stomach somersault. There was a pang of guilt when she thought about Zane, but she couldn't equate that feeling of desperate neediness with this one.

"Yeah. I'm done," she said as she kicked her legs over the side of the bed and sat up, appreciating the view. Watched as his lips turned up at the corners.

She hadn't kissed him. Not yet. And he hadn't tried to kiss her. She had the sense that, for now, it was a matter of waiting for the right moment.

Kim. Kim, can you come? And clearly, this was not it.

Is it urgent, Samuel?

No. Are you busy? I just wanted to ask you more about the planet. New Eden.

Wren, by now used to such intrusions, sat back on the bed. "The whales?"

Kim smiled at him ruefully. "Sorry."

"The holomovie can wait." He waved a hand, his tone patient. "Go."

Heading out into the corridor, Kim leaned her hand against the metal bulkhead for a moment. It would have been easy enough to leave Samuel while she spent some time with Wren. But Wren was right—the holomovie could wait. The wellbeing of the whales could not. If Samuel wanted to talk, then Kim had to be there for him. It was that simple.

She made her way to Deck Eight, entering the quiet, watery world with relief. Here, amongst the whales, she felt like she was home.

Samuel met her at a junction of catwalks where a bubble of the aquarium bulged out like a blister. A southern right whale, his deep grey body flecked with white markings, he hovered before her, massive body appearing weightless in the water. Sitting down and dangling her legs over the side of the gangplank, Kim leaned her arms on the bottom railing. "What do you want to know?" she asked.

What is the planet's name?

"New Eden," Kim replied. "In the Bible, Eden was the place where humanity began. A beautiful garden full of everything we needed to survive and be happy. It was paradise."

But you did not stay there.

"No. According to the Bible, we were tempted to know what was outside the garden."

So you learned to be unhappy.

"In a way. But I think the point of that story is that it's human nature not to accept what we have. To want to build more for ourselves." She paused. "There are other interpretations, of course."

I like your interpretation.

Kim smiled at that. "Me, too. I think it says a lot about us."

I can't wait to see New Eden.

Five years, Kim thought. That was the amount of time she was supposed to spend on New Eden, before returning to Earth with a new identity and all the money she needed to be able to live her life in comfort. That future had never existed—but for years now, she'd mapped it out in her mind, dreamed of it, created every aspect in her imagination.

Instead, she was going into the unknown. Searching out something new. She'd never had a paradise to leave behind, but she had an old life, a way things had always been—and the leaving wasn't the point anyway. The point was to move on. To change.

She could do that. She really could.

Yes, she told the whale. *I'm excited, too.*

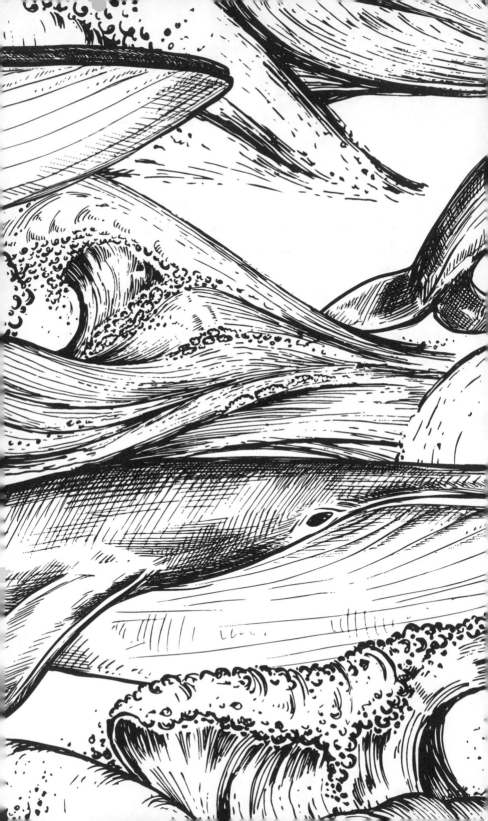

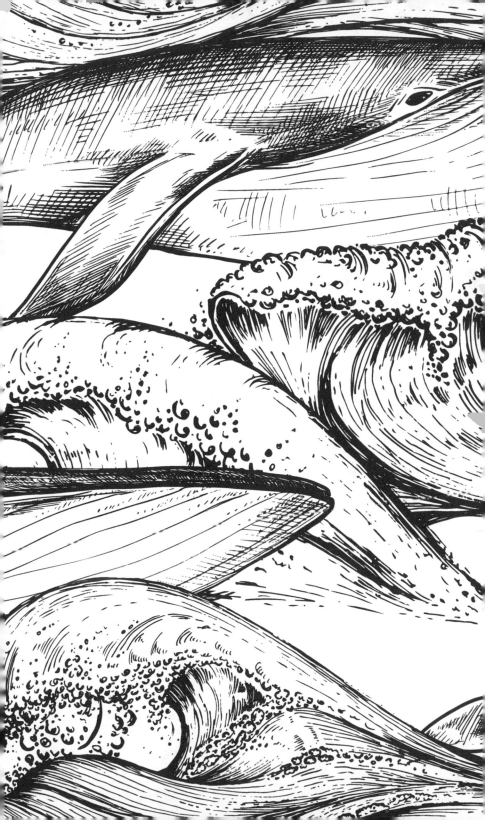

ACKNOWLEDGMENTS

Thank you so much to everyone who contributed to this book. My mum, for a constant stream of Sky & Telescope magazines when I was growing up. My dad, for introducing me to Ray Bradbury's books and watching *Silent Running* and *Star Trek: Voyager* with me and my brother.

My husband, for putting up with my long hours tied to my laptop. My boys, Rydyr, Quinn and Whitley, who already love books and sci fi, the two most important things in life.

Thank you to my high school English teacher, Sue Hall, who read a short story assignment of mine and asked me if I'd ever considered being a writer.

Thank you also to the team at CamCat for picking up and publishing this book! Specifically, I would like to thank Sue and Bridget, for your enthusiasm and belief that this book should be out there in the world. I have loved working with you and am look forward to doing it again.

FURTHER DISCUSSION

1. How do you feel about the future *Under the Heavens* is set in, particularly with regards to how humans have handled endangered species? Does it seem realistic, or is it too pessimistic?

2. Only small glimpses are given into Wren's motivations. What do you think Wren's backstory is?

3. Kim is a strongly independent young woman, but in some ways, she is very vulnerable to her emotions. Do you think this helped or hindered her on her quest to make sure the whales arrived safely on New Eden?

4. Do you think Kim should have noticed that Hosea—and perhaps some of the other whales—weren't happy with their situation?

5. In this world, lies are an issue for whales. Why do you think that might be? What other human traits might the genetically-altered whales have trouble understanding?

6. Would you like to have a connection with animals through the Link? If so, what type of animal?

7. *Under the Heavens* is a loose adaptation of the Bible story Noah's Ark. Did you pick up on the references from the Bible, such as the names of the whales?

8. This book includes social issues like climate change and endangered species. What are social issues you care about?

AUTHOR Q&A

Q: What inspired this book?

A: This story came about in an unusual way. In part, it was inspired by a post-apocalyptic film from 1972 called *Silent Running*. In this movie, the main character is responsible for maintaining a large space station that contains a greenhouse that preserves unique botanical specimens from Earth for future generations. The core concept of the need to preserve elements of our environment that we currently take for granted struck a chord with me when I first watched it, and every time since. I began to think about what else from Earth would be drastically altered or eradicated entirely if we don't take positive action to prevent it. How would our forests, skies and oceans look in a handful of years? The reality is that many species will be faced with extinction. From there, the idea that we could move an entire species to another planet began to take shape. What if, like Noah in the story of the Ark, we led endangered animals on a spaceship and resettled them on an alien world? All of these things came together when I started writing *Under the Heavens,* and it has turned out to be my favorite book that I've written so far!

Q: **How do you research your book(s)?**

A: Google is my best friend! I Google everything. I have always been interested in space travel and exploration, but when I need to find an explanation for why something could or would happen, I read as much as I can about it. In saying that, I'm sure there are probably some elements of the science in *Under the Heavens* that might not be perfectly accurate, but some liberties need to be taken when writing any kind of fiction, and I have tried to make the universe of this book as complete as I can.

Q: **What was most fun about writing this book?**

A: I just love writing about space. It's awesome. A thought that regularly stops me short is that we are just tiny specks living on a planet in the middle of this massive, unfathomable realm that we don't even really understand yet. I love thinking about alien planets and what we might find there when we eventually leave our solar system. The fact that anything is possible is so exciting!

Q: What is hardest about being a writer?

A: There are probably a couple of expected answers to this question: long hours in front of a laptop, rejection letters, and being asked when you're going to get a *real* job. All of these are true. But for me, the hardest thing about being a writer is that you can never *not* be a writer! You wake up at 3am with the perfect fix for a plot hole. When you're in a café for lunch, you suddenly see someone in the background—a woman sitting by herself in shabby clothing, or a man with an unusual tattoo, or a bit of sugar spilled on the table that makes a certain shape, and immediately, your mind starts churning—and by the time you come back to Earth, you have no idea what your friends have been saying in the mean time! You tap notes about a potential story into your phone while you're getting your children's breakfast. You have ten stories that have the first paragraph jotted down. You have a burning desire to write even though you know it's late and you should be in bed. Being a writer *is* hard. But it's also wonderful! Creating worlds and characters that people can fall in love with, you can leave readers on tenterhooks while a suspenseful scene plays out, and you know that your book might make a difference in someone's life, the way many books have in mine. Being a writer is amazing! I know I could never be anything else!

Q: What do you want your readers to take away from this story? A thought? Hope? Idea?

A: Caring for our environment and the issue of climate change is something that always seems to be a key theme in my writing. I take care to live in a way that minimizes my impact on the planet and I love that during my lifetime, this has gone from being something people rarely thought about to something that is often foremost in education, the design of new products or the development of facilities. Far from being a pessimist, I am excited about the future! I do think life on Earth has improved over the past century in ways we couldn't imagine and will continue to do so as long as we keep showing compassion for plants, animals and all the wonderful, diverse people with whom we share this planet. *Under the Heavens* is ultimately a story of hope—that humanity still has its issues, but is working hard, in a predominantly unified way, to correct them. That is what I hope for us!

ABOUT THE AUTHOR

Ruth Fox grew up reading anything she could get her hands on. She decided to be a writer when she was only twelve years old and wrote her first stories very neatly in a collection of notebooks.

Many times, Ruth questioned her decision to become a writer, thinking she should choose a more sensible career. However, she realized she didn't love anything else the way she loved telling stories. Swapping her notebooks for a laptop, she went on to receive her Bachelor of Arts in Professional Writing and Editing.

She has worked in a variety of "slightly more sensible" jobs, including illustration and editing, but only as a means to support her writing.

Ruth's first book, *The City of Silver Light,* was published in 2012. When she is not reading or writing, you can find her cooking vegetarian meals and deserts or playing computer games. Ruth currently resides in Ballarat, Victoria, Australia with her husband, three sons, and too many books to count.

If you enjoyed

Under the Heavens by Ruth Fox

you will enjoy

Imagining Elsewhere by Sara Hosey.

CHAPTER
1

I t was on the first day at her new school that Astrid Friedman-Smith met Candi Clifton. She'd experienced a sinking feeling of recognition. She knew karma when it came around to bite her in the ass, and moments after they exchanged hellos, found herself flying—literally flying—across the cafeteria and then falling face down on the polished linoleum while her classmates laughed and threw milk cartons and French fries at her.

She knew she deserved it, but that didn't mean she had to like it.

It was in the fall of 1988 that Astrid, her mother, and her sister moved from Queens to upstate New York, to a little town called Elsewhere. Astrid was less-than-thrilled about relocating, but this was not of great consequence to her mother, in part because Astrid's poor choices were one of the main reasons for the move. Downstate, Astrid had a not so insignificant problem with bullying and harassing other students. A problem so big, in fact, that it had made the New York area tabloid newspapers, which ran third and fourth page headlines like, "High Performing High Schoolers Get an A+ in Cruelty" and "Out on Her Ass-Trid: Lead Bully Expelled from Prep School."

Astrid had lived in Elsewhere for a full two weeks before that first day in the cafeteria and she'd still believed the move had been punishment enough. This was partly because, before the move, when Astrid had looked up Elsewhere in the World Book Encyclopedia , all she was able to discover was that it was a small, economically-depressed community where the high taxes were matched only by a startlingly high suicide rate.

Some real small-town values right there, Astrid had thought. She'd imagined that if she could simply survive her senior year at Elsewhere High, she'd be fine. She'd had no idea that surviving Elsewhere might actually be a challenge.

She'd heard of Candi before she'd met her—and even seen a picture of her. For some inexplicable reason, there was a lurid painting of a twelve-year-old Candi hanging up in the public library. From what Astrid had gathered, this Candi girl, despite only being in high school, ran the town of the Elsewhere.

This made no sense to Astrid, but then again, there were lots of things about her new town that she hadn't been able to fully comprehend. How it was possible, for example, that the town simply "didn't have cable" and barely got network television stations? Or why was it that everyone was so scrawny—not thin in a fashionable New York way—but sort of unhealthy, sunken-eyed and sallow? And why, at least if the classes Astrid had attended that first day were any indication, did no one seem all that concerned with attendance, academics, or really anything close to scholarly rigor at Elsewhere High?

Astrid couldn't ask these questions though, because, up until the day she'd met Candi, no one was willing to actually speak to her. All of her overtures of friendship had been met with either blank indifference, nervous giggling, or wide-eyed, outright fear.

That all changed the day she met Candi.

Astrid was sitting at one end of a long, almost-empty, table, except for a cute, nerdy kid alone at the other end, immersed in a D&D rulebook . Astrid was—strategically—sensorially-cocooned: The Cure blasting on her headphones, eyes glued to her blue binder, on which she was putting the finishing touches on an elaborate rendering of the words "THE SUGARCUBES," and chewing on the turkey sandwich she'd just bought and then customized (removing the turkey and putting chips in its place).

She had almost forgotten herself, munching away, when a strange sensation overtook her: it was as though someone had thrown a big down comforter over the entire cafeteria. She looked up to see that everyone was talking differently, standing differently. They had an unconvincing nonchalance about them, as though a camera crew had entered the room and they were trying to "act natural."

And then, there she was.

Candi.

She wore a white cinch-belt over a skin-tight pink dress, layered pink-and-white socks and white Ked sneakers, and dozens of bracelets on each arm. Her voluminous blonde hair, which framed her face like a lion's mane, added several inches to her height. And she walked like a runway model, her knee poking up toward the sky before shooting with deliberate aim at a table directly in front of her other toe. Like an archer drawing an arrow. Lift, shoot, lift, shoot.

Other students alternately swarmed and parted, and she was flanked by two other girls, a vee of Canada geese.

Frozen mid-chew, Astrid wondered if they had planned the entrance. It felt like something out of a John Hughes movie . Perhaps the music still streaming into Astrid's ears helped, giving the trio's dramatic march a soundtrack.

As it became clear the girls were headed toward Astrid, Astrid's tablemate quickly put the rulebook in his pocket and scurried away.

Astrid longed to follow him but felt pinned in place as Candi, with a flip of her magnificent hair, rested her eyes on Astrid's face.

Awkwardly, Astrid put down the pen she was gripping and, despite her churning stomach, forced a hopeful smile. Astrid, who had been popular, really popular, at her old school, thought maybe this would be her chance, her introduction into the upper echelons of Elsewhere society. She willed herself to play it cool. Or at least coolish.

Candi crossed her arms and regarded her coldly. Astrid stopped smiling.

Her heart raced, with fear and, she realized, a bit of excitement. This was the most socially stimulating encounter she'd had in weeks. And, she couldn't help but admit, Candi was startlingly beautiful. Beyond her basic good looks—she had the face of a Sears catalogue model and the figure of someone in an aerobics workout video—she was somehow luminous, as if she were being followed around by her own special lighting crew.

Astrid wanted to snort contemptuously and pretend to refocus on her drawing, but she found that she couldn't take her eyes off of Candi.

Candi's lips moved, but her words were inaudible to Astrid, who still had music blaring into her ears.

Astrid moved one headphone to the side and said, "Sorry, hi? What did you say?"

Candi widened and then narrowed her eyes.

Astrid gave a close-lipped smile and removed the headphones completely, pushing them down to rest around her neck and, after fumbling with the player, turning the music off.

"What's that?" Candi said impatiently, gesturing toward the table. "Is that a transistor radio?"

Astrid looked down and then back up at Candi. "Yeah, basically," she answered. "It has a tape player. With headphones. It's a...." She didn't want to appear patronizing, but it seemed to Astrid that the other girl actually didn't know. Upstate was clearly behind the times in so many ways. It was possible they hadn't heard of the invention yet. "It's a Walkman?"

Candi hummed, a low and lovely noise that could have meant comprehension or agreement or even disapproval.

"I'm Astrid, by the way," she said.

"Astrid," Candi repeated archly.

No one else in the cafeteria was even pretending not to watch them. Instead, they stood, wide-eyed and spellbound.

"You're . . . um, you're Candi, right?" Astrid asked. She sat up a little straighter. It seemed to her that this might be an audition. Somehow, however, no one had given her the script.

Candi stared stonily.

"I'll take it," the other girl said at last.

"What?" Astrid asked.

"I want the radio," Candi said. "And the headphones."

Despite herself, Astrid felt her cheeks flush, her breathing coming too fast and shallow. She knew—she knew all too well from her past experiences—that she had to somehow assert herself, make it clear that she wouldn't be pushed around. But, having been on the other side of this situation—having been the bully—she also felt she had too few options. She wasn't going to try to fight the other girl, obviously; she was seriously outnumbered. But placidly handing over the brand new Walkman that she had used all of her money to buy would only make it clear that she was ripe for future exploitation and abuse. She concluded that she'd have to fall back on what she did best.

Channeling her inner-Heather , Astrid said, "Um, did you have a brain tumor for breakfast? I don't know how they do things in Elsewhere, but usually people in human society get to know each other, hang out and then, sure, maybe borrow each other's stuff once they're friends? Which, I have a feeling we are not gonna be. So, um, that's a no." She closed with a mock-sincere smile.

A gasp went up from the audience. Instead of angry, Candi looked more like an affronted teacher, her mouth agape in shock.

"It seems we have a misunderstanding," Candi said, adopting her own fake-smile. "This is how we do things in Elsewhere." She reached out a long arm and picked up the Walkman. But the headphones were still around Astrid's neck and she was pulled forward over the table before the headphones came free from the device, snapping back at her.

Suddenly a male voice called, "Get her, Candi! Take her down!"

Astrid glanced over her shoulder. Her classmates, some with their arms folded across their chests, others leaning on each other jauntily, were no longer silently observing. They were murmuring, giggling. Astrid was alarmed to realize she didn't understand what was happening. What did that guy mean by "get her"?

She regretted not scrambling away when the nerd on the other end of the table had. She was out of her depth with this girl, outnumbered in this crowd.

And yet Astrid couldn't—or wouldn't—completely abase herself here, couldn't just walk away and let the other girl publicly rip her off. So, staying the course, she began to step out from the picnic-bench style cafeteria table saying, "Oh my God. Take a chill pill. I will loan it to you if you ask, but this is totally uncool."

"You're falling," Candi observed, her voice neutral.

And she was right. As Astrid tried to slide out of her seat, her leg somehow became tangled in her backpack strap. Suddenly, her arms were pinwheeling and her legs were shooting out behind her.

Her half-eaten sandwich plopped to the ground beside Astrid as she landed painfully on her knees and hands, her palms pressing against the sticky floor.

It was silent for a beat and then, suddenly, shockingly, everyone started laughing. The entire cafeteria was screaming and hooting.

Astrid picked up her bag and scrambled to her feet, the blood rushing to her head, making her feel even dizzier. Her focus narrowed: she simply needed to escape this room.

Why did the doors seem so far away?

"You can't stop falling!" Candi laughed.

Astrid felt what she imagined to be a hand pushing her from behind. This was when she flew, her arms outstretched Superman-style, before she found herself on the ground again, cheek to linoleum. Again, she pushed herself up with her palms, but now the floor seemed impossibly slippery, as if someone had spilled milk or juice. The general hilarity continued, more and more uproarious, as Astrid rose and again tried to move toward the impossibly distant cafeteria door.

Unbelievably, she fell a third time, perhaps in her frantic embarrassment tripping over her own feet and pitching forward, knocking her head against a plastic bench.

Someone said, "She's bleeding," as though they were concerned, but nevertheless the laughter continued.

Astrid's body would not cooperate. Nothing was working right. She could not get to her feet. She began to crawl on her hands and smarting knees, aware of how pathetic she must have appeared but determined to escape.

She saw people's shoes; her fellow students were at least parting to make a path for her. Something hit her with a soft thud and a small carton of chocolate milk came to rest beside her. As though floodgates had been opened, others now screamed with laughter as they pelted her with half-eaten lunches.

She closed her eyes, inhaling the scent of industrial cleaner, grease, and sneakers, before opening them and rising a final time, her hands outstretched, like antennae that would guide her to safety. She willed her legs to propel her through the doorway.

Astrid heard Candi's voice, predicting, almost-directing.

"You're passing out."

And then it all went dark.

CHAPTER
2

Astrid had a cottony and foul taste in her mouth. Her right foot was cold and wet. Her clothes, too, were damp and sticky and smelled vaguely of dirt, sour milk, and sweat.

The air itself, however, smelled crisp, like freshly-mown grass, which made sense because, as Astrid opened her eyes and looked around, she realized she was on the soccer field. It was early evening—not yet dark enough for the huge, looming field lights to be turned on—the sun just starting to set behind the looming school.

She looked down to see that she was only wearing one of her Reeboks. Slowly, she sat up. She blinked and ran her hands over her face before standing.

Her knees were wobbly and her stomach empty and upset.

But I'm okay. I'm alive and I'm in one piece, she thought. Where is my other sneaker?

The shoe. This was a tactic that Astrid recognized. It was a show of power. In fact, Astrid recalled doing something similar once to Evie Rossillio, a girl at her old school. Although Astrid had stolen not just a shoe but Evie's entire ensemble during gym and Evie had to wear her dorky gym uniform, including shorts that she had clearly outgrown, for the rest of the afternoon. Astrid pushed the memory from her mind and refocused on her own persecution.

How long had she been out? Had anyone missed her? Did her mother even notice that she wasn't at home? Astrid could answer that last question easily: no.

Astrid shivered, but not from cold.

She bent to pick up her backpack, which was beside her, an unaccountable kindness. She unzipped it to see that while her books were all stacked neatly inside, the Walkman and headphones were not there. Candi had taken her prized possession after all.

Astrid kept her remaining shoe on and started to trot, limping away from the school, feeling every pebble through her thin sock. If she'd not been so upset, distracted, and generally distressed, she might have stopped to inspect some of those rocks, to see if there were any nice ones she might like to bring home. But she was in fact upset, distracted, and generally distressed, so she jogged mulishly off the field, past the school and then down Main Street. She didn't stop until she could see the driveway of her new home.

Heart-pounding and still somewhat dazed, she stumbled up the front steps. Once inside, she moved quickly, trying to bellow a hearty, "I'm home!" as she rushed to the staircase, hoping to avoid her mother and Cecile, her twelve-year-old sister.

They called back to her from the living room—a weak, "Come tell us about first day,"

from her mother, but neither one pursued her.

In the bathroom, she looked at her haggard, ashen face in the mirror. She had a gash in the middle of her forehead. Her fingers rose automatically to touch it. It didn't hurt. It wasn't very deep. But it was ugly, red and angry-looking.

Unsummoned, another memory returned: shoving Evie Rossillio on the steps during a fire drill. Astrid remembered the surprising softness of Evie's plump upper arm as Astrid had pushed her. She remembered calling out in a false-tone, "Sorry! Oh my God, are you okay?" when the other girl hit her forehead on the staircase railing. But Astrid and her friends hadn't waited to see if Evie was, in fact, okay. They'd just galloped, laughing, down the rest of the stairs and out into the sunshine. Evie had gotten a gash though; Astrid saw it the next day when she'd come into homeroom.

Astrid regarded herself another moment in the mirror. The cut looked like Halloween makeup. Her hair—which she had laboriously curled and teased up that morning, as though a cool hairstyle would have made her any friends—was flat and greasy against her thin, scowling face. Noting the dark circles around her eyes, she thought, sardonically, that she might just fit in in Elsewhere after all.

She stripped off her soiled clothes and got in the shower.

Under the hot water, she recalled her almost heartbreaking optimism as she'd marched to school that morning and her classmates' failure to welcome her or return her shy smiles.

The thought of returning to school the next day filled her body with a jangly, prickly dread.

After her shower, she lay in a towel on the bed, unable to turn her mind off and drift into unconsciousness.

It wasn't as though she could run away. She didn't have a car and she only had a learner's permit anyway. Plus, she had nowhere to run away to. Although she was hoping to convince her mother to let her take the bus to the city to stay with her aunt and uncle for a long weekend later in September, that was only brief escape. She couldn't stay with them permanently.

The fact was that she was undeniably trapped in this horrible place that was apparently stocked with a nasty, violent, inhumane mob led by a beautiful, cruel, teenage tyrant.

Astrid quickly slid under her blankets and shut off her light when she heard her mother's footsteps on the stairs; alas, she was not quick enough.

"Hey, sweetie," her mother said, standing in the doorway.

"I'm sleeping," Astrid said.

"I saw your light on a second ago."

Astrid hadn't had an actual, conversation with her mother in days, and although she told herself she was simply curious to see how long they could go without speaking, she was actually hoarding this information greedily, to be weaponized at a later date: "Remember the time we didn't speak for four whole days? Oh, no, of course you don't, because you didn't even notice."

The mattress squeaked as her mother sat at the foot of her bed.

"Enough sulking," her mother said, gently squeezing one of Astrid's feet. "Tell me about your first day."

Astrid felt a vague alarm; perhaps someone from the school had called home. But no; her mother seemed way too laid back to know about her encounter with Candi.

With a heavy sigh, Astrid heaved herself up and switched the light back on.

"What happened here?" She ran a finger over the cut on Astrid's forehead.

"I fell in gym class," Astrid lied.

Her mother's brow furrowed. "And you hit your head?" she asked.

Astrid shrugged. That she couldn't tell the truth somehow made her even angrier with her mother. That she couldn't say, "I was attacked in the cafeteria and then I was knocked unconscious and left on the soccer field and no teacher bothered to intervene or call you," somehow seemed to be her mother's fault.

She looked at her pretty-and-sharp featured mom, who didn't wear make-up and didn't always remember to tend to her curly hair, who was so skinny because she forgot to eat, who was always so busy thinking deep thoughts that she neglected to think the shallow ones, even though they were sometimes important too.

"There's nothing to tell," Astrid said, adding, "Except maybe that you somehow invented a time machine and took us back, like, fifty years ago to a place that is totally weird and awful. And then you get to get back in your time machine every day and go to the real world and me and Cecile are stuck here with all the freaks and weirdos."

"Listen," her mother said plaintively, running her hand up to Astrid's calf and giving it a soothing stroke. "Let's just give it a little time. Let's give it the school year. You'll be going away to college. Okay? Just a year."

"Whatever," Astrid said. She moved her leg away from her mother's hand. Despite her resolve to be stoic and suffer through her punishment, she couldn't help but want to punish her mother as well. "Maybe I could just go live with dad in Germany or something," she spat.

"Astrid," her mother said, warningly. Astrid's mother knew that Astrid would never go to live with her dad, that the threat was just a shortcut to hurt her.

"You don't get it, mom," Astrid said. A tear rolled down her cheek and she batted at it.

Her mother tried to wipe the tear from her face, but Astrid pushed her hand away. "I know I don't," her mother said.

Her mother was working hard to pretend she wasn't noticing Astrid's mounting irritation.

"Sometimes it takes a while to feel settled somewhere," she said. "You know, to make friends and find your niche. Maybe if you and Cecile got out more, went hiking, that sort of thing. Oh," she said, remembering something. "I got you this." Her mother had been carrying a small paperback book—which was unremarkable, as her mother was more likely to be carrying around a book than not—and now she placed it next to Astrid on the bed. "Field Guide to the Greater Triantic New York Region," her mother said. "There are obviously amazing rocks around here."

"I mean, Elsewhere is like 90% sandstone from what I've seen," Astrid said, grudgingly.

Her mother ignored her. "And when you're not off doing solitary rock-hunting, maybe you could check out, I don't know, the lake or something. And I was thinking we could go to the movies this weekend. Saturday? Wouldn't that be fun?"

Astrid shrugged, non-committal.

She did want to go to the movies, but she also didn't think she'd ever be leaving the house again.

"Sounds rad," Astrid said, sarcastically. "Going to the movies with my mom."

"There are worse things," her mom tried.

"Um, yeah. I'm aware."

MORE YOUNG ADULT SCIENCE FICTION FROM CAMCAT BOOKS

CamCat
Books

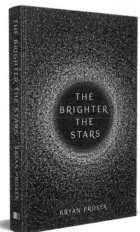

Available now, wherever books are sold.

CamCat Books

VISIT US ONLINE FOR
MORE BOOKS TO LIVE IN:
CAMCATBOOKS.COM

FOLLOW US

CamCatBooks @CamCatBooks @CamCat_Books

CPSIA information can be obtained
at www.ICGtesting.com
Printed in the USA
LVHW101456160622
721144LV00003B/4/J

31901068294174